Apparition

TRISH J. MACGREGOR

Apparition

Book Three of The Hungry Ghosts

A Tom Doherty Associates Book
New York

APPARITION

Copyright © 2013 by Trish J. MacGregor

All rights reserved.

A Tor Book
Published by Tom Doherty Associates, LLC
175 Fifth Avenue
New York, NY 10010

www.tor-forge.com

Tor® is a registered trademark of Tom Doherty Associates, LLC.

The Library of Congress Cataloging-in-Publication Data is available upon request.

ISBN 978-0-7653-2604-1 (hardcover)
ISBN 978-1-4299-4406-9 (e-book)

Tor books may be purchased for educational, business, or promotional use.
For information on bulk purchases, please contact Macmillan Corporate
and Premium Sales Department at 1-800-221-7945, extension 5442,
or write specialmarkets@macmillan.com.

First Edition: November 2013

Printed in the United States of America

0 9 8 7 6 5 4 3 2 1

For Rob and Megan
con mucho cariño, siempre

And thank you to Beth Meacham,
for all her suggestions

Shadows

· · · · · · ·

As the afternoon progresses, our shadows grow longer.
At night, in the dark, we *become* our shadows.

—Tom Robbins, *Jitterbug Perfume*

All things must pass away.

—George Harrison

One
Tess and Ricardo

1.

As Tess drove into the setting sun, Esperanza Spalding sang from the CD player. The orange light burned across the face of the distant Taquina volcano and transformed the thin band of clouds that hugged the top of it into a necklace of fire. The light glinted off the old railroad track that paralleled the *autopista,* causing it to glisten and gleam as though it were brand-new.

The track had been laid in the late 1920s and for nearly two decades Esperanza 14 had hauled locals from downtown Esperanza into the smaller communities scattered through the hills. In 1939, an 8.0 quake had ruptured many of the tracks, hurled fourteen cars over the side of a cliff, and killed more than three hundred adults and children in the village below. Supposedly, every year around the anniversary of the disaster, the ghost train appeared somewhere on those tracks, chugging along, spewing smoke, its windows flung open to the cool mountain air. Some years, so the story went, you could see passengers inside the doomed train, children waving from the windows, the conductor a dark reflection in the glass. Tess had never seen it, but didn't doubt the stories. In Esperanza, anything was possible.

As the sun slipped a little lower, Tess flipped down the visor so she could see where she was going. Traffic along the *autopista* that ran east to west across the city moved at a swift clip, cars whizzed past her in the other three lanes. Her Mini Cooper chugged along. The car would never win a race, but it was her dependable buddy whom she could call upon any time of the day or night to get her from point A to point Z. She had bought it the day that Charles Schulz had died, so in his honor she had named the black-and-white car Snoopy. It still smelled new, the leather seats and floor mats were pristine.

Up until she'd bought Snoopy, she and Ian had been sharing an aging VW Bug. He finally traded it in and bought a Jetta with a souped-up engine. In the end, it didn't matter what you drove in this city as long as it was small and fast enough. Snoopy was fast enough to keep pace with the flow of traffic on the *autopista* and small enough to slip into parking spaces on the narrow neighborhood streets that were best suited for bicycles, scooters, and smart cars.

Ten minutes into her current love fest with Snoopy, traffic slowed, then stalled altogether. Dozens of cars snaked up and down the highway. Shadows now clung like cookie crumbs to the inside of her car. She suddenly felt that something or someone had hitched a ride with her.

The skin across the back of her neck prickled, her throat felt as if she'd swallowed shards of glass.

"Dad?" she whispered, glancing in the rearview mirror.

Her dad, dead twelve years, stayed wherever he was. He hadn't appeared to her in months. And no disembodied spirits or hungry ghosts appeared. Paranoia, she thought.

Tess nervously flexed her fingers against the steering wheel and pressed back against the seat, willing the traffic to move. Darkness now spread across the city like India ink seeping through pale fabric. It spilled down the surrounding mountains as if it hoped to swallow them in a single, heaving gulp. Up and down the long line of stalled cars, headlights winked on, the widely spaced street lamps flared. And still the traffic didn't move and the sensation persisted that she wasn't alone.

Brujos hadn't been sighted in Esperanza since the battle in June 2008 that had annihilated Dominica's tribe of sixty thousand. Tess had no reason to suspect the hungry ghosts had returned, but she couldn't deny her body's sensations.

Sips from a bottle of water helped to ease the dryness in her throat. When she had lived in Florida, she'd carried bottled water with her because of the heat. In Esperanza, she carried it because the altitude, about thirteen thousand feet, sucked away her body's moisture.

So, okay, now she had an alternate explanation for the dry throat—not spooks, not *brujos,* just the altitude. What about the tightness across the back of her neck, the goose bumps on her arms? Those sensations weren't due to altitude.

Recently, the city grapevine had hummed with rumors about *brujo* attacks in other countries. Speculation ran rampant on the Internet that Esperanza's mythology and folklore were factual, that the city actually was a bridge between the living and the dead. As far as Tess knew, though, *brujos* had stayed out of Ecuador since the destruction of Dominica's tribe. And Esperanza had flourished. But the paranoia and terror that had prevailed during the dark years when the hungry ghosts had preyed on the living, seizing their bodies, possessing them, using them to experience physical pleasures, still rippled beneath the surface of daily life. Yet, the sirens that had once alerted the populace to seek shelter from *brujos* hadn't shrieked since that battle in 2008, and every day, she felt the undercurrent of fear losing its hold on the people of Esperanza.

The most likely explanation for her unease was that her dead father actually was in the car and simply chose not to show himself. Charlie Livingston, trickster. "Dad?" she said again.

She thought she caught a whiff of his trademark cigar smoke and heard the incessant snapping of his Zippo lighter. Then her iPhone belted out Janis Joplin's "Piece of My Heart," Ian's ring tone. Tess smiled and took the call. "Hey, Clooney, where are you?"

"Got held up. I'm just leaving now, Slim. Your mom called to report the numbers of births in OB and I wanted to get it into tomorrow's edition. You at the restaurant yet?"

"Stuck in traffic on the *autopista.* How many births?"

"Twelve. The most for a single day since Dominica's tribe was decimated."

She heard a trace of excitement in his voice that had nothing to do with the birth rate in Esperanza. "You've got a guess-what."

He laughed. "You read me too well, Slim. The *Expat News* got picked up for distribution in Guayaquil and the Galápagos. The newspaper will be carried on all the ships that trek through the islands. It means we can now publish daily, hire some new employees, expand our website . . . our newspaper is finally going to turn a profit we can live on."

"*Fantastic.* How'd this happen?"

"The distributor for the islands saw our online edition and liked it."

They had started the newspaper on July 4, 2008, but it had always been Ian's baby, and had become hers by default. Until she'd met Ian, she'd never thought she would be anything but a burned-out FBI agent. "Now what? When do we start advertising for new reporters?"

Ian's laughter swelled with joy. She could see him in her mind, his head thrown back, the crinkles at the corners of his dark, George Clooney eyes. He looked so much like Clooney that when they'd first met, she'd actually thought he was the actor traveling incognito.

"I figured we can discuss it over dinner and a bottle of Chilean wine," he said.

"It'll be waiting for you when you arrive."

"Are Maddie and Sanchez meeting us there?" he asked.

"I texted her, but haven't heard anything. They may have left for Quito."

"Okay. Love you, Slim."

"Ditto, bigger than Google. We have plenty to celebrate."

Two years ago, as the expatriate community in Esperanza had expanded, they had started publishing the *Expat News* as a biweekly newspaper in both English and Spanish, tripled their staff, and kept it in the family. Tess's niece, Maddie, built and maintained their website. Her fiancé, Nick Sanchez, and his father did the Spanish translations and sold advertising. Tess's mother, Lauren, worked at the paper on her days off from the Esperanza Hospital OB ward, doing whatever was needed. Occasionally, Leo, Lauren's lover and an obstetrician, wrote a health column for expectant mothers.

Ian's news meant they would be hiring outside their immediate circle. She could think of a dozen people who would be terrific additions to the staff.

Tess followed a line of cars onto the shoulder of the road and slipped around the fender bender that had caused the traffic jam. As Snoopy picked up speed, the sensation that she wasn't alone swept over her again.

"Okay, Dad. I know you're here."

Something took shape in the passenger seat—but it wasn't the ghost of her father. The ghost who materialized, becoming more solid and real by the second, was a short, thin man, a Quechua with large dark eyes and a thick black braid that fell across his right shoulder. He wore faded jeans and a pale blue shirt with a colorful wool blanket draped around his shoulders.

"Not dad." Slight accent. Amusement in his voice. "Name's Ricardo."

She could barely swallow around the sudden pounding in her throat. The mark on the inside of her right wrist itched terribly. Four years of inactivity and now her *hungry ghost* detector kicked in too late. Despite the chill in the air, sweat seeped from the pores of her skin and she knew he could smell it, smell her fear. Even when he was in a virtual form, a *brujo*'s sense of smell was acute.

Ricardo lifted his chin and made a point of sniffing loudly at the air, mocking her. "Relax, if I intended to seize you, it would be over already."

Tess eased into the right lane, then onto the shoulder and sped forward until she could turn off somewhere, anywhere. She tore across a swale of grass and pebbles, swung into a parking lot, slammed on the brake. Snoopy shuddered, gasped, and died. "You haven't seized me because you can't." Tess held out her arm and the flickering light from the lot fell across the inside of her forearm, so that the mark was easy to see. "Do you know what this is?"

He glanced at her wrist, reached out to touch it, and she jerked her arm back. "You aren't touching that unless I invite you to touch it."

"Oh, please," he murmured, and grabbed her wrist and stroked the mark with his thumb, a cool, creepy touch.

Tess wrenched her arm away and Ricardo just laughed. "You really are quite lovely, Tess Livingston. I love your blond hair, those gorgeous blue eyes, and your elegant height. I would like nothing more than to taste you, seize you, use you. You're the crème de la crème, the prize every *brujo* hungers for. What wonders we could learn from you."

His soft voice moved through her, around her, strangely seductive and utterly terrifying. She kept her eyes on the now moving lights on the *autopista,* on the rising moon, on the neon signs that flashed and flickered up and down the highway. Beyond it all rose the majestic Taquina volcano, moonlight flowing like lava down its sides. The power of *brujos* was like that volcano, an unpredictable force of nature.

"Of course I know what that mark is," he said. "Every *brujo* knows the story. It's part of our collective knowledge, our lore. The big difference between the living and the dead, Tess, is that we know our lore is factual."

"This sounds like typical *brujo* bullshit, Ricardo."

"Four years ago, you were an FBI agent who suffered a fatal gunshot wound, flatlined, and your soul made its way to Esperanza. You met Ian, who'd had a massive heart attack and was also a transitional soul. The two of you fell in love." He grinned and played an imaginary violin. "You were the first transitionals to be admitted to the city in five hundred years, since the chasers brought Esperanza into the physical world. While you were in your transitional state, waiting at a depot for Bus 13 to Esperanza, a Quechua man who had been seized by a *brujo* grabbed your arm, marking it forever. It became your *brujo* detector and a sign to us that you were a special transitional and couldn't be seized."

The old bruise now burned and throbbed like a heart. Tess rubbed at it. "So why're you here?"

"So why're you afraid of me?" he shot back.

She laughed. "Who says I'm afraid of *you*?"

"I smell your fear."

"What you smell is my fear of what your presence here means. The only thing *brujos* have ever meant for Esperanza is death and destruction."

Ricardo slapped his thighs and exploded with laughter. "You've lived here four and a half years and think that qualifies you to speak about the role that *brujos* have played in the long history of Esperanza? Please. You Americans are so insufferably arrogant."

"Why have you appeared now?"

"Ah. Now you're asking the right question. Did it ever occur to you that we've been here all along, but have simply chosen not to reveal our presence? No, probably not. That arrogance again."

Tess caught the odd, knowing smile that turned his mouth into some horrifying parody of a mouth. It was like some sort of Pac-Man icon that chewed its way across the bottom of a computer screen.

"And you read signs," he continued, and reached out and drew his fingers through her thick, long hair.

Tess pulled her head away. "I recognize patterns. And this one is ugly. Stop touching me."

Ricardo grabbed a handful of her hair, jerked her head back, and leaned in so close to her she could smell death in his breath, the stink of rotting eggs and decaying flesh. His dark eyes impaled hers. "Let me enlighten you, Tess. You don't have a clue what's going on. I read that in your hair, your eyes, your very being. I smell it on you."

His tongue, the color of ash, darted from his mouth. It was strangely long, like the tongue of a frog or a lizard, and touched her neck. Licked. Traveled up toward her ear and down again, but slowly. The tongue tasted her and enabled his essence to sample her memories, needs, desires, terrors. Tess fought him, struggled, slammed her fists against his temples and back, punched him in the ribs. He pulled harder on her hair and tightened his hands around her throat.

She screamed, but the sound never reached the air. Ricardo pressed his mouth to hers and sucked the scream into himself, drawing the texture and truth of her terror into his essence, where he would study it, pick it apart, and somehow weaponize it to use against her later. Then he drew back slightly, one hand still gripping her hair, the other holding tightly to her shoulder. He smiled, licked his lips, smacked them like a kid with an ice-cream cone. "I can taste your ignorance. You don't know what's happening inside your own body, don't understand shit. You aren't worth my *time*."

He shoved her away from him and Tess fell against the driver's door, her heart pounding, her breath quick and shallow. Then something huge and monstrous—a crazed, panicked grizzly bear—reared up inside her and she slammed her arm, hand fisted, across his face.

He gasped, his hand flew to his nose, a liquid streamed through his fingers. It didn't look like blood. Thick, viscous, white like pus, it ran down his arms and onto his jeans. As it hit the seat, it burst briefly into flame, emitted puffs of smoke and vanished.

Tess grabbed her bag and threw open the door, lurched out of the car and ran through the parking lot, weaving in between cars, scooters, motorcycles, bikes. It didn't matter *where* she ran as long as she quickly put distance between herself and Ricardo. The mark on her arm now ached and throbbed furiously and never mind that the warning had come too late. How was she supposed to defend herself? Another punch to the *brujo*'s virtual body? What good would that do? Ricardo was already dead. He could bleed and feel pain in his virtual body, the form that Esperanza enabled him to create so that he appeared to be physical. But none of it was *real*.

She reached the front of the shopping center, a bookstore and café to her right, a Tibetan restaurant on her left, people seated at tables along the sidewalk. Safety in crowds, she thought, and ran onto one of the balconies, gulping at the air like a dying fish. She dropped forward, hands pressed to her thighs, and struggled to breathe.

You're safe, he can't hurt you, can't seize you.

"Señora, are you all right?"

Tess rose. A waiter, a young Ecuadorian man, stood in front of her, a tray of food balanced in one hand, a tray of drinks in the other. He was frowning, fretting that a *gringa* who might be deranged had lumbered into the area where his customers were sitting.

"Yes," she managed to say. "Fine. Sorry to intrude like this."

Then the waiter began to twitch—the muscles in his face and mouth and just beneath his eyes throbbed spasmodically. The twitching expanded into his shoulders and arms, but not violently enough to cause him to lose his grip on the tray. Not violently enough to draw attention from anyone else.

His eyes went completely dark, an oily dark that poured across even the whites of his eyes. She knew he'd been seized and was now possessed by a *brujo*, that the ghost's essence had entered him and was fully in control of the waiter's body. Then Ricardo spoke in the waiter's voice.

"Tess, Tess," Ricardo murmured. "You can't escape me so easily. Please tell your father that we all want the same thing, to live peacefully in Esperanza. If the chaser council and the people of this city can't accept that, then my tribe of three million will attack Esperanza so savagely that not a single person in this city will be spared. We'll make the dark years of Dominica's tribe look like kindergarten. And do give Wayra my regards."

With that, a bit of mist, Ricardo's essence, drifted out of the top of the waiter's skull and the young man blinked hard, nearly lost his grip on the tray, glanced around uneasily, then looked at Tess. "How many . . . in your group, señora?"

"None," she whispered hoarsely, and spun around and raced away from the waiter, out toward her car.

2.

With traffic now moving again on the *autopista,* Tess drove like a maniac, whipping from one lane to another, her heart still hammering. She exited near the airport and took a shortcut through El Bosque—the Woods—a sprawling residential neighborhood. Tall, thick trees blanketed the area, many of them grown first in greenhouses in Esperanza, then transplanted here. Trees, at an altitude where trees weren't supposed to grow.

She felt safe in this neighborhood, it smacked of normalcy. Familiar streets. Homes decorated with Christmas lights. Small yards where children played. Schools and sidewalks where teens on bikes sped through the puddles of light the color of melted butter.

She approached Mercado del León, a bodega where she and Ian shopped when they were in the mood for exotic foods imported from all over South America. She pulled into one of the parking spaces between the market and a small church and waited, watching cars that passed. It unsettled her that Ricardo might have seized any of those drivers, that he might be following her even now.

She pressed her fists against her eyes. She could still taste and smell the *brujo's* breath, his presence, could still feel his essence moving around inside of her, reading her like a comic book. Three million in his tribe? *Three fucking million of these suckers?*

The defeat of Dominica's tribe, supposedly the largest tribe of *brujos* at the time, had required help from churches, light chasers like her father, and from twenty thousand individuals from all over South America who had lost loved ones to the *brujos.* Defeating her had demanded a revolution against tyranny. But what defense would Esperanza's thirty thousand inhabitants have against three million hungry ghosts that were invisible to most people and could seize the living, possess them, and use their bodies as their own?

We'll lose. Even chasers, evolved souls who had overseen the evolution of Esperanza since they had brought it into the physical world, couldn't take on three million *brujos.* Tess wasn't exactly sure how many chasers there were worldwide, but suspected their numbers were in the low five digits. Hardly a large enough army to defeat three million *brujos.*

Her arms dropped to her sides, she glanced around again. None of the cars stopped, no pedestrian suddenly started jerking like that waiter had. Still, she had to know for sure.

She drove over to the church, Iglesia del Bosque, and parked in the shade of a tree. As far as she knew, *brujos* generally didn't enter churches and were terrified of cemeteries. She supposed they had individual fears, too, just like the living did. Dominica had been afraid of water because she had never learned to swim. What fears did this Ricardo have?

The church, like every other building in this neighborhood, was decorated for Christmas. Blue, green, and red lights festooned the windows and strings of blinking gold lights spiraled up a tremendous pine tree out front. As Tess stepped into the church, she removed the top of her lipstick tube and dipped it into the bowl of holy water. Just in case. She had no idea if holy water had any effect on *brujos.* But if it did and if Ricardo had followed her in here, she would be ready.

Then again, maybe she had seen too many bad horror movies as a kid. She cupped the lipstick cap in her hand, thumb pressed over the top of it.

Except for an elderly couple lighting candles near the altar, the church was empty. She slipped into a pew and felt strangely comforted by the quiet. A young man emerged from a confessional, then the door opened and a priest walked out, his shoulders so hunched he could barely raise his head. He looked deliberately at Tess and moved toward her. "Are you waiting to confess?" he asked.

"No. I'm . . ."

The oily dark poured across his eyes and he grinned and aimed his finger at her as though it were a gun. "You can't escape so easily, Tess," he said softly. "We are everywhere. Be sure to give your father my message."

Tess hurled the holy water and it struck the priest in the face. But his skin didn't burst into flame, he didn't dissolve or turn to dust. Ricardo just laughed, the sound of it echoing strangely through the church, surrounding her as though it were amplified somehow. "You're kidding, right? *You*, the legendary Tess Livingston, really believed holy water would turn me to dust or something?"

Tess fled the church, leaped into her car, and sped out of El Bosque.

Two blocks from the Café Taquina, where she was supposed to meet Ian, she nosed Snoopy into the first parking spot she saw and sank back against the seat, into the silence. She slipped her iPhone out of her jacket pocket and texted Wayra. *Who's Ricardo?* She had no idea whether he and his wife, Illary, were even in the city this weekend, but eventually he would pick up his voice mail, e-mail, text messages. Even a shape shifter understood the value of technology and rapid communication.

She got out of the car, zipped up her leather jacket, slung her bag over her shoulder and hurried up the street, anxious to be around people, in a crowd. Before she reached the café, Wayra replied to her text message:

Can u b more specific?

Brujo. Ricardo. He sends u his regards. Says his tribe numbers three million.

What else did he say?

2 much 2 text.

Where r u?

@ Café Taquina. Meeting Ian 4 dinner.

Will b there shortly. Time 2 talk.

Tess slid her iPhone back into her jacket pocket, speculations churning through her. A *brujo* who supposedly commanded a tribe of three million ghosts had tapped her to deliver messages to her father and to Wayra, a shape shifter who knew more about hungry ghosts than anyone. But first he had tasted her, plundered her memories, moved around inside of her like a lover. Yet he hadn't tried to seize her and hadn't bled out the waiter and the priest he'd seized. Ricardo had used both men as messengers.

Since *brujos* rarely told the truth about anything, she wanted to believe that Ricardo's tribe was vastly smaller than what he'd claimed, *thirty* or *three hundred* tired old ghosts instead of *three million* chafing at the bit to seize the living. In this way, *brujos* were similar to politicians, bovine blowhards who sought to intimidate in any way available to them. It bothered her, though, that when she mentioned Ricardo's name to Wayra, he replied that they needed to talk.

When she was confronted with a potential horror show, her former FBI training always kicked in. *Pick it apart. Detail by detail. Piece by piece.* First detail: the shifter wasn't a talker. When he shared information and insights, it was only because he felt you absolutely needed to know or because he'd been backed into a corner and had no other choice.

More than three years ago, when Dominica had seized Tess's niece, Maddie, as her human host and fled Esperanza, Wayra had pursued her without telling Tess, her mother, or Ian. He had cut them out of the search as cleanly as a surgeon excised a tumor. Tess now understood he'd done it for fear they would screw things up because of their emotional connection to Maddie. But when it had been happening, she had grown to resent Wayra for excluding them. Tess's mother had refused to speak to him for months. Only Ian had maintained contact, doing what he did best, building bridges in spite of differences.

Esperanza versus the *brujos*. The battle in 2008 hadn't ended anything. It had only delayed what suddenly seemed inevitable.

The thought was so depressing, she paused on a corner near the café and shouted, "Hey, Dad, you there? I could use some help."

A breeze carried her voice through the street and out across the lake to the volcano. Charlie never answered.

Two
Dark Matter

1.

Until tonight, Ian had been to the Café Taquina only once, an embarrassing admission for someone who had lived in Esperanza for more than four years. Known for its cuisine, music, and magnificent view, it was the most famous restaurant in the city. It seemed like a fitting place for him and Tess to celebrate the news that would turn things around for them and the newspaper.

The café, perched at the edge of a hill, overlooked Lago Taquina and the volcano of the same name that rose beyond it. Moonlight turned the volcanic lake into a lustrous mirror that reflected the star-studded sky. From where Ian stood, waiting to enter the back deck, the Milky Way looked close enough to taste. Lean forward slightly, extend tongue, and lick. No wonder people flocked here. When you drank in the view, it was as if you peered back in time more than five hundred years, to the first few moments after the chasers had brought Esperanza into the physical world. Until that moment, the city had been nonphysical, a place where transitional souls came to decide whether they would return to their bodies or move on into the afterlife. For centuries, *brujos* had preyed on those souls. The chasers had brought the city into the physical world and closed it to transitional souls to end the *brujo* feasting. The *brujos* simply evolved to the point where they learned to seize the living.

He spotted Tess at a table at the rear of the wide back deck, loose dollar bills tucked under a candle. Steeped in shadows that the soft, delicate lighting along the floor didn't penetrate, the table was private. The small heaters mounted above the tables kept the air comfortable. She sat alone, a tall, lovely blonde fiddling with her phone.

From the moment he'd first seen her in that bus depot outside Esperanza, when they were both transitional souls, their physical bodies in comas, near death, and separated by forty years in time, she had reminded him of Lauren Bacall in *Dark Passage*. Bacall's nickname in the movie was Slim, and it was what he'd called Tess since the beginning, only to later discover it had been her father's nickname for her, too.

"Can I buy you a drink, Slim?" he asked in his best Bogie voice.

She laughed, glanced up from her phone, crossed her legs at the knees, and in her best Bacall voice, said, "You bet, handsome. Have a seat. Snacks and munchies are on the way." She nudged a glass of wine toward him and raised her own glass. "*Salud,* Clooney. To the *Expat News.*" They clicked glasses. "I heard from Maddie. She and Sanchez are going to meet us for coffee in town when we finish dinner. They were planning on leaving for Quito today, but have postponed the trip for a few days."

Ian was relieved to hear they would be in town a while longer. It meant they could probably get the next edition of the *Expat* out on time and Sanchez could help with the Spanish translation for the paper's website. Ian disliked leaning too heavily on Sanchez. He and his partner owned a remote-viewing consulting firm, and with his partner out of town, everything would fall on Sanchez. In a pinch, he could hire Wayra or Illary to do the translations. They had helped out in the past and were always delighted to be involved. But again, he hated to ask.

He noticed that Tess seemed distracted, not quite present. "You okay?"

"Something happened on my way over here." She dropped her voice. "A *brujo* materialized in my car and tried to choke me."

Ian nearly gagged on his sip of wine. For the first time in more than four years, a *brujo* had shown itself in Esperanza. In Tess's car. "Does this *brujo* have a name?"

"Ricardo." The rest of it spilled out, Ricardo's message, his threats. "My sense is that he's one of the ancient *ghosts,* Ian. It means they're here, that the city has been invaded and none of us knew it." She knocked her knuckles against the table. "Not you, me, not even Wayra or Illary. And my dad apparently didn't know, either."

The waiter came over just then with a platter of tapas—baked plantains, avocado salad, and two bowls of fresh fish soup. As soon as the waiter left, Ian leaned toward her, his voice quiet. "It doesn't make sense. If they've invaded, why haven't they seized anyone?"

Tess tucked her hair behind her ears, fidgeted in her chair. "When . . . he licked my neck . . ."

Christ.

". . . and sucked my scream into himself, he . . . read me inside out. And when that happened, I realized I could read him, too. Not like he read me, just bits and pieces. I don't think he's lying about the size of his tribe. He knew my dad's a chaser. He mentioned Wayra. And Wayra is on his way over here." She passed Ian her iPhone, so he could read the text exchange between her and Wayra.

When Wayra had rescued Maddie three years ago and taken Dominica back to the edge of time, Ian had hoped there would never be a threat from *brujos* in Esperanza again. Now here it was.

The band started playing, four Quechuan men and a woman, all on string instruments and flutes. Andean music. The beauty of it wrapped around them, but the music was too loud for him and Tess to speak without shouting, so they got up to dance.

He pressed in close to her, his mouth at her ear. "What were you thinking about before he appeared?"

"I was thinking about doing a column on the NDE that brought me—us—to Esperanza."

He tightened his arm around her and breathed in the scent of her skin, her hair, read the nobs of bones in her shoulders and along her spine, and shut his eyes. What he really wanted to do just then was drive home, start a fire, and make love.

When his eyes opened again, he saw something odd over Tess's shoulder, something that didn't look right, a thick, expanding shadow the moonlight didn't penetrate. He whispered: "Don't whip around or anything, but there's something strange happening to the air just past the railing, where the hill's slope begins. It could just be a trick of the light, but given what you just told me, maybe it's something else. Let's head back to the table and you take a look."

Tess drew back. "Shit, Clooney, you're freaking me out."

He gripped her hand and they made their way through the crowd, back toward their table. "See it?" He gestured beyond the railing and Tess leaned against it.

"I see light and shadows, Ian. That's physics, not *brujos*." Then the massive blanket of shadows against the slope of the hill darkened and moved, undulating like a giant wave, and crept steadily uphill, toward the café's deck. She hissed, "What *is* it?"

"Nothing good. Move back, Slim."

But even as he said it, the monstrous shadow swallowed everything it touched, like some special effect in a movie, digital magic. The closer it got to the deck, the colder and stranger he felt. A kind of primal terror scrambled around inside of him, as though he were locked in an empty room with a deadly gas pouring through the air vents.

"We need to warn people and get the hell outta here," he said.

"Without creating panic." She stepped away from the railing, plucked her bag from the back of the chair.

Ian spun around and hurried over to where the band was playing. He whispered to the guy on the flute, who immediately glanced over his shoulder, passed the mike to Ian, and whispered something to the female in the band. The musicians fell silent and Ian's voice boomed across the deck in Spanish, then English: "This is not a drill. Please proceed in an orderly fashion off the deck. Take your personal belongings with you."

Murmurs rippled through the crowd, people looked around uneasily and started getting up from their tables. Then a woman somewhere on the deck shrieked, "*Brujos, son los brujos* . . . In the darkness, see? See the blackness moving toward us?"

Brujos. For the locals who had lived through the dark years and lost loved ones, no word was more powerful. They shot to their feet and frantically grabbed their stuff. Tourists who probably didn't have a clue what was going on were nonetheless swept up in the bedlam. Chairs crashed to the floor, panicked diners tore toward the stairs, shrieks and screams ripped through the air. The chaos seemed to cause the blanket of shadows to widen, deepen, and move lightning quick, as though the collective panic of the crowd fueled it. It swallowed up earth, brush, trees, then the corner of the deck.

Ian glanced around wildly for Tess, but didn't see her. He watched in horror as a man he recognized—Javier, who owned the bakery in town where he and Tess went most mornings for coffee—tripped and sprawled on the floor. The blackness, now thick as syrup, consumed him to the waist and he clawed frantically at the floor, shrieking, *"Help, someone help me, oh God, please . . ."*

Ian shoved his way through the panicked crowd, dived for the floor, hooked his feet around the legs of the closest table, and grabbed Javier's forearms. "Hold on, Javier," he shouted. "Hold on, c'mon, good, that's right, hold on tight."

Javier's handsome face contorted in agony. He kept sobbing, struggling. Some people behind Ian held the table in place, and men on either side of Ian grabbed Javier's shoulders and attempted to pull him out of the maw of the abyss. But the force that held Javier's legs was so powerful the table tipped forward and one of the men catapulted headfirst into the darkness, his screams echoing.

Ian's hands, slippery with sweat, began to lose their grip on Javier's forearms, and he yelled, "Hold on, Javier, c'mon, I can get you out, please, hold on . . ."

Javier sobbed, "No, let me go, my legs are gone, shit, gone." Then his eyes rolled back in their sockets, his hands slipped away from Ian's, and he vanished into the darkness.

For a horrifying instant, Ian stared down into the dark matter, a blackness that swirled clockwise, faster and faster, as if it were drilling its way to the center of the earth. It looked slick, almost shiny, like wet asphalt, and the funnel created by the swirling seemed bottomless. Then the swirling stopped and the darkness surged forward again and Ian flung himself back and bolted to his feet.

Around him, pandemonium. A tidal wave of humanity surged forward to escape the deck and everyone inside the restaurant tried to flee as well. Tables and chairs and bar stools overturned, shattered glass blanketed the floor, screams riddled the air. Squeezed from every side, Ian vaulted over the railing and dropped to the narrow rug of earth on the other side. Less than a foot in front of him, the ground dropped off several hundred feet. He turned carefully until he faced the chaos on the deck, and moved quickly sideways along the railing, gripping the wood tightly.

He glanced back once and saw the blanket of shadows flowing behind him, as if following him, and he moved faster, faster, hand over hand, sidling like a crab. When the railing ended, he swung around it and ran into the parking lot, looking anxiously around for Tess, for her blond head bobbing in the panicked crowd.

He didn't see her. The crowd thrust him forward and he made his way left, away from the café and the black wave, toward a nearby field. Sirens screeched, drowning out the shouts and the pounding of feet. Ian stumbled into the field, ran farther, and finally dropped to his knees on a patch of grass and vomited.

His body had reacted the same way when, more than four years ago, Wayra had brought him forward in time from 1968. It told him that whatever was happening here was triggered by something beyond human control—*brujos,* light chasers, or something else.

He didn't have any idea what *something else* might be.

When he rocked back on his heels, a black Lab raced toward him and a sparrow hawk circled overhead. The shifters. Ian leaped up, loped toward the dog, and together they ran across the street and down the block, into a deserted cobblestone alley. The dog instantly shifted into his human form, that of a tall, dark-haired man in jeans, a jacket, running shoes.

"Is Tess with you, Wayra?"

"No. Illary's looking for her."

"I need to go back and find her."

"Illary will find her, amigo. C'mon." Wayra touched his arm. "My truck is a couple blocks from here. We don't want to be here when the police arrive. They're probably going to cordon off the entire area and may try to detain people to question them."

As Ian ran alongside Wayra, he tried to ignore the endless visual loop that played through his head, of Javier slipping away from him, screaming in agony.

2.

Swept up by the crowd, Tess managed to remain upright so she wouldn't be trampled. Then she was outside, running, dashing away, and couldn't remember where she'd left her car. She reached a front yard and her knees buckled and she went down in cool, damp grass.

Sound was sucked out of her world; it was if she had gone deaf. But she felt and saw the raw power of paranoia and terror, those old undercurrents, bursting from the collective psyche of everyone who had been on that deck. Then sound penetrated again, screams and the shrieks of sirens, panic, utter terror.

As Tess stumbled to her feet, a sparrow hawk swept in low overhead, crying out. Illary. Tess hurried after her, shoes slapping the pavement, and followed her into an alley between two apartment buildings. Her cries echoed, Tess could hear the flap of her wings. The alley twisted and curved for half a mile south and emptied into a small neighborhood park with a playground and fountain surrounded by monkey puzzle trees and pines. Illary touched down next to one of the trees and began to shift.

Even though Tess had seen Illary and Wayra shift dozens of times, the transformation always struck her as beautiful, miraculous. Illary's feathers went first, replaced by skin the color of coffee and milk and long hair like burnished copper. Her wings and legs and claws transformed quickly into human arms and legs, hands and feet. Before that process was complete, her human head and face took shape. Within moments, a tall, lovely woman in jeans, a sweater, and boots stood before Tess.

"Ian's in the truck with Wayra, Tess. Let's hurry. Most of the Esperanza police force is out there and they're closing off the neighborhood."

"Did you see it?" Tess asked as they loped through the playground, past swings that swayed slightly in the breeze. "The hideous, moving blackness?"

"Yeah. It seems to be receding now. Or maybe it's just waiting. But the hillside and at least half the deck are just *gone,* Tess. It's as if someone took a gigantic eraser and rubbed it all out."

"Is it the work of *brujos*?"

"I don't know."

If she and Wayra didn't know, then who would?

The sirens shrieked more loudly and several choppers now circled overhead, their bright spotlights cutting through the darkness. "Through here," Illary said, and they dashed back into the trees. "Let's stay out of sight."

"Shouldn't we stick around and talk to the police?"

"We'll talk to Diego directly."

Diego, Wayra's adopted son, was the chief of police.

"We can go to our place," Illary said. "It's close. And we'll get you home in the morning."

Tess's phone belted out Esperanza Spalding's "I Know You Know," Maddie's ring tone. "Maddie . . ."

"Tesso? Jesus, we just heard that something went down at the café. Are you and Ian all right? Where should we meet you?"

"We're okay. If you're close enough, meet us at Wayra and Illary's."

"We're on the way."

A yellow pickup truck roared into view, screeched to a stop. Wayra and Ian were hanging out the windows, motioning for them to hurry up. Tess climbed into the backseat with Ian. He immediately squeezed her hand. "I thought you were . . ."

"I know. I thought it had gotten you, too." She squeezed her eyes shut, blinking back the hot sting of tears that suddenly threatened to fall.

"I tried to pull . . . Javier . . . out of the blackness."

"Javier the baker?" Tess asked.

"Yeah. And another guy who was helping me . . . got sucked in. It's like . . . a swirling vortex of blackness."

"And not a human construct," Wayra said. "Of that much we can be certain."

The truck slammed across potholes and picked up speed. Tess was dimly aware of the ping of stones against the underside of the truck, of dust flying through the open windows. She leaned forward between Wayra and Illary.

"Wayra, who's Ricardo?"

"Long story."

Illary looked sharply at Wayra, one of those looks that passes between couples who don't have secrets from each other. "Well, shit, Wayra," Illary snapped. "That's hardly fair."

"Who is he?" Tess repeated.

Illary, still glaring at Wayra, said, "If you won't tell her, I will."

Wayra looked at Tess in the rearview mirror, his eyes now dark pools of misery. "Ricardo is Dominica's brother."

Police cars suddenly appeared from the side streets, sirens at full tilt, the reflection of their spinning blue lights dancing against buildings, cars, sidewalks. Wayra swerved to avoid being hit by another car, Tess was thrown back against the seat, into Ian.

What did Wayra mean that Dominica had a *brother*? Was Ricardo Dominica's brother during her last physical life in the 1400s? Or did Wayra mean that Ricardo was her *brujo* brother? Was there even such a relationship among ghosts?

But before she could sit forward again to demand answers, Ian slipped his arm around her shoulder, holding her in place. "Let him drive, Slim. He'll explain it later."

The truck sprang free of the cop cars, and sped into the dark hills.

3.

Wayra drove the back roads through the hills, past small villages, greenhouses, pastures, and barns. Fifty years ago, this area had been so dirt poor that electricity was nonexistent and clean water was scarce, except for what was drawn from the surrounding lakes. But then some local politician had realized that such poverty only fostered resentment and rebellion and had convinced the largest and most prosperous churches in Quito to reach out to the rural communities in Ecuador by launching an ambitious improvement project.

Today, every one of these villages not only had electricity and clean water, but most of the roads were paved, and the schools had free Internet and the computers to access it. The buildings had shutters that had protected them against the dense fog in which *brujos* had traveled in their natural forms and cellars where they had hidden during *brujo* attacks. In the years since the annihilation of Dominica's tribe, these villages had prospered by creating a food cooperative that now had the largest outdoor market in Esperanza. It shut down at dusk, and as Wayra drove past it, the truck's headlights briefly illuminated the empty wooden tables and crates that would begin to fill by dawn.

Just past the market, he turned right and followed a narrow road that twisted down through the hills to yet another village. Mariposa—Butterfly—sat on a plateau that overlooked Esperanza. The town itself was built around two village plazas, with many of the homes near or on one of two small lakes. Wayra and Illary lived in a place on the eastern shore of Lago Mariposa, the smallest lake, shaped like the butterfly for which the town was named.

The house, surrounded by trees that had been grown in greenhouses and then transplanted here, was visible for a moment in the glare of the headlights, then blended into the landscape, becoming invisible. Four bedrooms, two baths, large enough to accommodate guests. Usually, their guests consisted of Wayra's family of shape shifters, the three humans he had turned when he had rescued Maddie, or Diego Garcia's two kids whom he and Illary took care of on occasion.

Diego was the head of the Guardia—the Esperanza police department—and was like a son to Wayra, who had adopted him when Diego was orphaned at thirteen, after his parents were killed during a *brujo* attack. He hoped Diego would be able to get away from the Café Taquina at some point, meet them here at the house, and explain things from the official perspective. But the only car in the driveway at the moment was a silver Honda that belonged to Maddie and Sanchez.

The two of them and their golden retriever, Jessie, were sitting on the front steps. As Wayra pulled into the driveway, Maddie shot to her feet, her long, wildly curly red hair bouncing against her shoulders. "Shit, shit, after we heard what had happened at the café, you guys had us really worried." She hurried over to the truck, peered inside the windows, front and back. "Okay, everyone accounted for. What the hell *really* happened at the café?"

"Let's talk inside," Wayra replied, getting out with the others.

Maddie moved and spoke at the speed of light; Sanchez was more deliberate, measured, and less apt to hug everyone hello until he had flipped his psychic switch to Off. He was a former remote viewer for the U.S. government, and his ability was both a gift and a curse. He had been forced to learn to power down before he touched anyone. When he finally greeted the others, Wayra knew he was in his Off mode.

They all went inside, Jessie bringing up the rear, her tail wagging, her nose to the floor as she pursued the many shifter scents that permeated the house. Sometimes when Maddie and Sanchez visited, Wayra ran around the lake in his canine form with Jessie and they communicated through images and symbols that convinced him that Jessie was the most joyful creature he'd ever had the pleasure of knowing.

Her unconditional love for Sanchez—and now for Maddie—spoke tomes about the purity of her heart. He often felt that Jessie's soul was actually human and she had chosen to incarnate in the body of this beautiful dog specifically to explore unconditional love—and to be involved in the evolution of Esperanza. He'd actually asked her this once, a difficult thing to ask in just images and symbols. She had howled with amusement, then had shown him the symbol for infinite, with the word *me* in the center of it. He still didn't know if that meant yes or no.

Wayra directed everyone out onto the enclosed back deck and he and Illary went into the kitchen to get drinks and food. She sliced up vegetables and fruits while Wayra prepared drinks. His wife looked especially beautiful at the moment and he ran his hand slowly down her spine.

Illary glanced at him, her smile quick, elusive. The hawk tattoo on the side of her neck seemed to move. "And so?" she asked.

"There's too much we don't know."

"Do you still have that stone we found?"

Wayra nodded and slipped it out of his pocket. Smooth and dark, it was about three inches long and half as wide. He had picked it up at the edge of the area where he and Illary believed the blackness had begun. "I'm going to ask Sanchez to read it."

"That'd be a good place to start. Tess is going to grill you about Ricardo. I think it's important to tell her everything you know."

"She just caught me off guard. I haven't thought of him in centuries."

Illary rolled onto the balls of her feet, kissed Wayra, and handed him the platter of goodies. "I'll get the drinks. We'll figure this out."

Wayra returned the stone to his pocket and made his way back through the house. Local art covered the walls, pieces he and Illary had collected in their years here together. His favorite artist, Oswaldo Guayasamín, had his own wall. Guayasamín, born in Quito in 1919, was famous for his paintings depicting Andean people. He had exposed racism, poverty, political oppression, and class division in his work, and it reflected that misery and pain.

The painting Wayra loved the most hung in the middle of Guayasamín's wall: that of an alienlike face that portrayed such profound isolation it spoke to the deepest parts of Wayra's being, and to the life he had known when he had thought he was the last shape shifter in existence, before he'd met Illary.

"*Salud, amigo,*" he whispered to the alien as he passed.

Once they were all settled on the back deck, the lights of Esperanza spread out below them, Tess and Ian related what had happened.

"Wow," Maddie said softly, her green eyes widening. "It sounds like *brujo* trickery, especially coming on the heels of Tesso's confrontation with this Ricardo dude."

"That's the most obvious explanation," Wayra said, and glanced at Tess. "To answer your question about Ricardo, he and Dominica were the only children of a Spanish nobleman in the late 1400s, her last physical life. The family was arrogant and broke, so they planned to marry Dominica off to a wealthy nobleman. And I, a sheepherder's son, was in the way of their plans. Her father grew to hate me because she and I loved each other. He ordered Ricardo to track me down and kill me. Ricardo stabbed me in a bar, nearly killed me. Fortunately, I'd been turned by then. My shifter blood saved my life."

"But what's he doing here now?" Tess asked.

"I have no idea."

"What happened at the café may not have anything to do with Ricardo or *brujos*," Ian said. "Look at it from a journalistic perspective. Here in the city of hope, we talk to the dead, break bread with them, negotiate and commune with them. The sick who come here are healed and everyone lives a ridiculously long time. We have shape shifters and chasers, and once upon a time we also had *brujos*, who seized the living and possessed their bodies so they could enjoy the banquet of physical pleasures. But we've been free of them since Dominica's tribe was annihilated. The last two ancient shape shifters in the world live here. One of them is at least six hundred years old and the other is . . ." Ian looked over at Illary. "I don't even know."

"Two thousand," Illary said quietly.

Ian opened his hands. "I rest my case. The dark matter may be just another phenomenon."

"*Supernatural* phenomenon," Sanchez said. "And if it's supernatural, then it has to be the work of *brujos,* chasers, or the city herself. After all, it's the city that keeps us from aging like other people, that keeps us healthy."

"But if Esperanza is responsible for that dark matter, why would she consume her own people?" Wayra asked. "Javier and others were sucked into that blackness tonight."

"It could be a combination of things," Illary said. "Perhaps Esperanza is finally shaking herself awake again, taking control of her own destiny. Shifter legend tells of how Esperanza awakened into physical reality with earthquakes, eruptions, chaos."

"But I thought the city had always been sentient," Tess said.

"There're different degrees of sentience." Illary raised her hands, palms held out in front of her like a blind woman making her way through darkness. "I know there's starlight against my hands, but I don't feel heat or cold emanating from that light. But in a different state of consciousness, I can *become* that starlight. During the decades of *brujo* assaults, I think Esperanza's immune system was so beaten down that her spirit pretty much took flight. She left the chasers in charge. But the years since Dominica's defeat have given her time to heal. She's awakening to her own power."

"Regardless of who or what is behind it, is it going to happen again?" Maddie asked.

"Probably." Illary's fingers steepled together. "Something has been set in motion."

Wayra brought the stone out of his pocket, set it on the table. "Nick, can you RV this?"

Sanchez stared at it, his handsome Latino face tight, closed. "No. I don't work like that, Wayra. I'm not a psychometrist."

"You're able to read people when you touch them. You're able to dowse maps. This is no different."

"But it *is* different, Wayra," said Maddie. "Sanchez works best with random numbers that Delaney or I give him, which represent a target. Sanchez never knows what the target is beforehand."

It made sense, Wayra thought. Numbers vibrated at certain frequencies, which acted as a beacon for someone with Sanchez's psychic ability.

"Okay. I'll assign a number to the place where we found it." Wayra vividly imagined the target—the genesis of the blanket of shadows, its source, who or what had created it. And for that, there was only one set of numbers. "Eleven-eleven, Nick." A portal to higher consciousness.

"I'll need paper and a pencil to sketch with," Sanchez said.

"I've got a sketchpad in the kitchen," Illary said.

Sanchez's head bobbed. "Perfect."

Illary hurried inside and returned moments later with a sketchpad and several pencils, which she set on the table in front of him. He sat back, shut his eyes, and began alternate-nostril breathing, a meditation breathing exercise that brought both hemispheres of the brain into synch. Sanchez's relaxation became so absolute he looked as if he had melted into the chair, becoming one with it.

Maddie moved the paper and one of the pencils to the edge of the table in front of him. After a few moments, he began sketching quickly, madly. He didn't speak, didn't utter a sound, but suddenly pushed his sketches to the side. His eyes snapped open, and he reached for the stone.

He pressed it between his palms and held his hands close to his chest.

"Shit," he breathed. "This is a kind of oracle, the stone of possibilities. I see . . . several paths, each one equally probable. There's wind . . . sand, a kind of tornado that . . . It's a sipapu."

Sanchez's shoulders jerked, he started shaking, and Jessie leaped up, barking, howling, dancing around Sanchez's chair. At first, Wayra thought he'd been seized. But then Sanchez snapped back against his chair, spit ran from the corners of his mouth, his lids fluttered open, and his eyeballs rolled back in their sockets. Wayra understood that what was happening to him had nothing to do with *brujos* and everything to do with the stone.

Maddie grabbed Sanchez by the shoulders and shook him hard. "Sanchez, snap out of it. C'mon, you're here now."

He started convulsing, his entire body shaking violently, only the whites of his eyes showing. Maddie shrieked, *"It's killing him, the stone is killing him!"*

She frantically tried to pry the stone from his grasp, but his fingers had closed over it so tightly that when Wayra grabbed his hand, Sanchez's fingers and knuckles turned bone white. Wayra sank his thumbs into the underside of his wrist, forcing his fingers to open. The stone fell to the floor.

Sanchez's arms dropped over the sides of the chair, his head flopped to one side, his body went still.

Three
Lauren

1.

Lauren Livingston wandered through the OB nursery on the third floor of the Esperanza Hospital, pleased that she had been present for six of the twelve births today. Leo had delivered them, she had assisted, and with every new wail, every small, perfect face, she recalled her own joy when each of her daughters had been born.

Even though the delivery of her first daughter had been difficult and the labor long, she clearly remembered the moment when her OB had placed Ria on her stomach. The utter warmth and dampness and weight of her had seemed miraculous. Charlie, who had remained with her during the labor, proudly announced that Ria Livingston had ten perfect fingers and ten perfect toes and her mother's mouth and her father's eyes.

Tess's birth several years later had been a breeze in comparison. Lauren had gone into labor a month early, in a grocery store, someone had called 911, and she'd delivered her youngest daughter in the ambulance on the way to the hospital, at precisely 5:55 P.M.

They were living in Miami then, where Charlie was a partner in a large law firm, working sixteen-hour days as a defense attorney. By the time he rushed into the maternity ward, mom and daughter were resting comfortably. He lamented the fact that he hadn't been present, but nonetheless went through his spiel about ten perfect fingers and toes and how Tess had her mother's eyes and her father's mouth.

Lauren's relationship with Ria had never been good. They had been estranged for years as Ria struggled with substance abuse and went through several marriages and divorces until religion became her addiction. Lauren had taken in Maddie, Ria's oldest daughter, when Maddie was eighteen, a decade after Charlie's death, and their relationship had always been tight. Lauren often wondered if the difficulty of her labor with Ria had portended their strained relationship.

Tess, born early and fast, had been the light of Lauren's life since she rushed into the world. Eager and impatient to be born, she had followed her own agenda from day one. Charlie wanted her to go to law school, Lauren hoped she would become a doctor. Instead, she had graduated from college with honors and joined the FBI. Easy birth, easy daughter. Maybe that explanation was too facile, but there you had it.

Lauren stopped next to a double bassinet that held identical twin girls, Quechuas, robust beauties at just under eight pounds. The mother had had a C-section and they were due for feedings shortly. As Lauren adjusted the wool cap on twin A, the PA speaker in the hall crackled with the voice of the woman who headed the hospital nursing staff. Her message was in Spanish, Quechua, then English. "All available personnel please report immediately to ER."

In a city where people enjoyed vigorous health and unprecedented longevity, a summons for all personnel to the emergency room generally meant a car wreck, fire, or domestic fight that had turned violent. She was the only nurse on duty in the nursery and debated whether she should head down to ER. Her cell suddenly jingled, a text message from Leo: *That means you, lovely prankster. EMTs say something weird happened at Café Taquina. We've got broken bones, a woman who went into early labor, trample victims.*

On my way, she texted back.

Trample victims meant ruptured organs, multiple bone fractures, the kinds of injuries that would require a team of trauma surgeons. Leo was undoubtedly summoning every physician in the city, but Lauren stopped by the nursing station to find out what Elsa, the OB nurse, knew about the specifics.

Elsa was on the phone, scribbling madly on a legal pad. She glanced at Lauren and mouthed, *Hold on, just hold on.* Then she rushed on in Quechua and Spanish, her voice growing more anxious by the second.

Lauren had never seen Elsa so rattled. The woman had lived through the dark years of *brujo* attacks, lost loved ones to them, and didn't spook easily. Lauren guessed she was embroiled in personal bad news, and rapped her knuckles against the counter. "I'll be in ER. The twins are due for feedings now."

Lauren hurried off toward the elevator but before she reached it Elsa shouted, *"Espérame."*

Lauren turned and Elsa hurried over, one hand clutched dramatically to her chest. "Loreen."

Low-reen. She trilled the *r,* like some sixties stoner whose tongue didn't work right. Elsa looked about fifty, but Lauren's rule of thumb was to add at least twenty years to a local's apparent age. That meant Elsa was probably seventy, not much older than Lauren herself.

"Bad news, Low-reen. That was my husband, he works with the chief of police. Something *muy mal* happened at Café Taquina. They're saying the *brujos* are back, that the creeping blackness that killed and injured dozens is the work of *brujos.*"

"Slow down, Elsa. What creeping blackness?"

"I don't know, like . . . a thick black tide, that's how my husband described it." From the pocket of her uniform, she brought out a rosary and slipped it around Lauren's neck. "You wear this in ER. It will protect you as the patients from the café arrive. It carries a special blessing from the pope."

The *pope*? Had *he* ever been to Esperanza, where the battle between good and evil had gone on for millennia? Did the pope know about chasers? Was he aware of the *brujo* tribe Dominica had led here? Did the pope know about *brujos,* about any of this? And even if he did, would it matter?

Lauren thanked Elsa for the rosary and touched the stones as she rushed to the elevator. *Rosary blessed by the pope:* did that fall into the same category in this culture as the Merry Pranksters and Owsley acid had in the sixties culture in the U.S.? Probably not. But it suddenly felt like one and the same thing, as if she were twenty again, on break from college and on the road with Ken Kesey and Jerry Garcia and, later, with Terence McKenna, bouncing along in the Merry Pranksters bus, certain she was invincible as she tripped on acid that had melted on her tongue like a communion wafer.

It meant that whatever had happened at the Café Taquina was beyond weird, beyond *brujos* and chasers, something altogether different.

When she entered the ER, the mayhem instantly sucked her in. The place was mobbed. Every examining room was taken, patients on gurneys and in wheelchairs waited in hallways, children cried, a woman screamed, nurses, physician assistants, doctors, anesthesiologists, and aides hustled from one room and patient to another.

Lauren made her way toward the screaming woman in examining room 11. According to the patient info on Lauren's iPad, the woman's name was Amy Fuentes, twenty-four, and she had been dilated four centimeters when she was brought in. An aide, Serita, was with her and was visibly relieved when she saw Lauren.

"Her contractions are coming hard and fast now, Lauren. I keep telling her to push, but she's in a lot of pain."

"Any allergies?"

"None."

"Get me a syringe of Demerol, Serita." Lauren grasped Amy's hand and she gripped it with surprising strength, her eyes wide, panicked. She panted, "Help me . . . the pain . . ."

"I'm going to give you a shot of Demerol for the pain, Amy. When the contractions start, push hard, okay?"

"My . . . son . . . he's early . . ."

"He's just impatient," Lauren assured her, and Serita handed her the syringe.

Thirty seconds later, Amy's body sank back against the mattress. Beads of sweat dotted her face, neck, arms, but for the moment her pain was a distant memory. Lauren examined her and found she was now dilated nearly ten centimeters. As the next contraction began, she gripped Amy's hand. "Push hard, Amy. Your son is on his way into the world, but needs some help from you."

Amy pushed and shrieked and Serita gripped Amy's hand and Lauren moved to the foot of the bed. "He's crowning, Amy," she shouted. "Two more good pushes and he'll be out."

Minutes later, the boy was born. Lauren snipped the umbilical cord, and Serita quickly picked up the boy and carried him to a nearby table to weigh him, clean him up. Amy collapsed against the mattress. "Is he . . . okay? Is he breathing? Does he have all his fingers and toes?"

"He's fine," Serita said. "Big beautiful eyes. No jaundice."

The boy let out a monstrous roar.

"Fantastic lungs." Serita laughed. "And he weighs three point one kilos. That's what in pounds, Lauren?"

"Seven pounds." Exactly what Tess had weighed.

The delivery had left Amy badly torn. Lauren stripped off her gloves and moved around the examining room, gathering up the things she would need to stitch her up. Leo hurried into the room just then, a tall man with a square jaw and thick, white hair. Not quite as down-home as Marcus Welby, Lauren thought, and way better looking. He winked at Lauren, then turned his full attention on Amy. "Congratulations, Amy. Your son is just beautiful. I can take over from here, Lauren. You and Serita did a splendid job."

Leo pulled over a stool, Lauren set the tray to his right, then she brought Amy a glass of water with a straw in it, and helped her lift her head to sip. She whispered, "People must be told about this blackness . . ."

Elsa had called it a thick black tide. "What did this blackness do?" Lauren asked.

"Swallowed . . . earth, trees, part of the back deck. People . . . panicked. Everyone thinks it's the *brujos,* that they're back."

Lauren and Leo exchanged a glance. "Try not to worry about that now," Leo told her.

"Where's your son's father?"

"In . . . Guayaquil. I wasn't due for another month."

"You want to give him a call?" Lauren asked.

"Yes, oh yes. My phone. It's in my purse."

Lauren handed her the phone, gave Leo's shoulder a quick, reassuring squeeze, then leaned close to him and whispered, "Let's go home and do it in front of a nice big fire."

His neck turned the color of radishes, but he managed to sound professional when he replied: "Great suggestion, Lauren. I'll keep that in mind."

Lauren moved on to the next patient and then the next. And from each patient, she heard snippets of personal stories about what had happened at the café, what people had seen. One patient, Raúl Griego, was a reporter for *Esperanza Mundo,* the daily city paper that had been in existence, in some form, for about two hundred years. When the bone doc finished setting Raúl's broken wrist, Raúl asked Lauren to turn on his video camera, so she could see it for herself, the awful darkness that had invaded part of the café and swallowed people.

She turned on the camera, and she, the bone doc, and Raúl watched the erratic ten-minute video. It began with Raúl's camera focused on his companion, a pretty woman in her late twenties, who kept giggling like a schoolgirl and murmuring, "*No más,* Raúl. Cut it out."

His voice: "But you're so incredibly lovely."

She stuck her tongue out at him and made a face at the camera. "*Eres un bobo con . . .* What is *that*?" She stabbed a finger at something over Raúl's shoulder.

The image danced and jumped as Raúl got to his feet and leaned over the balcony railing, his voice audible in the background. "*Dios mío,* look at that . . . that blackness."

The girlfriend hissed, "*Carajo, son los brujos.* Has to be . . . C'mon, Raúl, we should leave."

"Wait, wait. Look at it. Look at how fast it's moving, how . . ."

The blackness sped toward them, spreading across the hillside like the shadow of some mammoth aircraft, closer and closer to the deck. Lauren heard panicked shouts and screams, the crash of chairs, the stampede of feet as people around Raúl fled the deck.

Raúl panned the deck once, a blurred image that revealed what looked like a man caught in the blackness, his legs mired in it, his arms and upper torso squirming, clinging to the deck as he shrieked. Several men tried to pull him free and Lauren paused the image there, certain one of the men was Ian.

"That man." Lauren tapped the screen. "Do you know who he is?"

Raúl shook his head, took the camera and advanced the video slowly forward until she saw the man's face.

It was Ian.

And if Ian had been there, Tess had, too.

Anxiety clawed across the pit of Lauren's stomach. She quickly excused herself, hastened into the hall, and up the back stairs to the employee lounge. Privacy. She punched out Tess's number and her daughter finally answered, her voice hushed, tight. "We're okay, Mom."

No words were sweeter to a mother's ears. "Where are you?"

"At Wayra's place. Maddie and Sanchez are here, too. But Sanchez . . . something happened to him."

The story tumbled out and as soon as Lauren heard the word *convulsions,* every internal alarm in her body went off. "Is he conscious now?"

"He came to briefly, then fell asleep. Maddie and Illary are with him."

"Leo and I will get out there as soon as we can. He should be checked out, Tess."

"Mom, this blackness may be spreading, we're not sure. But even without that, it's too easy to get lost out here at night."

Spreading? After what she'd heard and seen on the video, just the possibility disturbed her. "How long did his seizure last?"

"Just a few minutes."

"Was he confused when he came to?"

"Maddie said he talked to her about what had happened, so no, I don't think he was confused."

"Did he have trouble breathing?"

"Illary reported that his breathing was normal. She's got quite a bit of medical experience, Mom. She knows what to look for."

Maybe, maybe not. Lauren hadn't experienced Illary's medical knowledge firsthand and didn't have any idea what this knowledge might be. Herbs? Vitamins? Some sort of shifter concoction that might send Sanchez into arrhythmia? "We'll be out there first thing in the morning to see how he is. But call me if his condition changes, if he has any more seizures."

"I will. I promise."

"Mariposa has an excellent hospital where you can take him if—"

"I know. Don't worry."

"And Tess . . . what the hell was this stone that Wayra handed Sanchez?"

"Wayra found it where this blackness originated."

Tess explained Sanchez's description when he was holding the stone. The words that struck Lauren as most peculiar were *sipapu* and *oracle.*

Had this blackness touched the stone? Imbued it with something? "Did Wayra react to the stone when he took it out of his pocket?"

"No. I don't think it was the act of holding it that sent Sanchez into convulsions. It was his *reading* of it that affected him."

Lauren didn't have a clue how Sanchez did what he did. In his consulting business, Sanchez, together with Delaney, one of the men Wayra had turned during Maddie's rescue, used their remote-viewing experience to solve crimes, find missing people, predict the stock market, diagnose illness. It didn't matter that she didn't understand how he did this; she had experienced the results.

She and Leo had invested money in a stock that Sanchez had recommended, and within four days, they had walked away with half a million dollars. They had given a lot of it to various charities, bought a condo in the oldest section of town, and helped out Tess and Maddie. When a patient of Leo's had had multiple miscarriages, he had consulted Sanchez, who recommended a particular diet and nutritional program that eventually enabled the woman to carry a baby to term. So yes, she was a believer in Sanchez's talent.

"Honey, I saw video of this blackness. It looked like an oil spill." Lauren told her about the reporter's video.

"Would the reporter share his video with the *Expat*? We need to alert people to this, what it looks like, what it does. We didn't get any pictures or videos. We'd just gone there for dinner."

"I'll ask. Tess, is it *brujos*?"

"I don't know. If you see Dad, ask him, okay?"

"Hey, he drops by to see you more often than he does me."

"Not recently," Tess said, and told Lauren the rest of it. Ricardo. A message for Charlie. "Tell Dad all that."

"I will." The damn ghost tried to choke her daughter? "I definitely will. I'll call you later."

Everything her daughter had just said was precisely why people in Esperanza often ended up with partners who were also from the city. You simply couldn't explain any of this to an outsider, couldn't explain that Esperanza was somehow sentient, that she retained a residual power from when she had been nonphysical that conferred health, longevity, youth. You couldn't explain that to someone who hadn't experienced it. It was why all of them, locals and expats alike, stayed.

Lauren could just imagine trying to explain any of this on an Internet dating site, on Facebook, Twitter, Blogger, Wordpress. Put the truth out there and up there and you would be forced to start your own social network just to make a few friends.

Lauren struggled to understand the implications. *If* the *brujos* were back, *if* the assaults began again, would she stay here? Esperanza was her home now, she had burned all her bridges to the U.S. But she knew her decision would depend on what her family did.

Tess and Ian, she suspected, wouldn't leave. They had a life here, the newspaper, and Ian would be afraid that if he left, the heart condition that had killed him would return. She didn't know for sure whether Maddie and Sanchez and his dad would leave. Probably not. They were happy in Esperanza, and Maddie and Sanchez were getting married next month. Sanchez's father wouldn't return to South Florida without them and, besides, his health problems had cleared up within a month of his arrival in Esperanza.

Then there was Leo. He had arrived in Esperanza from Argentina twenty-two years ago on the heels of an ugly divorce, a terrible custody battle that he'd lost, and a diagnosis of leukemia that had given him several months to live. Within six weeks of his arrival, his leukemia had gone into remission and had never returned.

Leo was so certain the city had cured him, that he hadn't left the region since. He had never returned to his native Argentina, but had gotten his Ecuadorian medical license and gone to work at the hospital as the resident OB. His children, now adults, often visited him here.

So if they stayed, she would stay.

Lauren stepped out onto the balcony, the door whispered shut behind her, and she breathed in the chilly night air. Stars littered the black dome of the sky, many of them so bright that if she raised her arms, she might be able to scoop them out of the heavens. Among the Quechua, there was a saying that the altitude of Esperanza made it easier for its people to mingle with the gods.

She hadn't seen any gods yet, but she had seen and conversed with her dead husband from time to time, had had brunch with shape shifters, and felt and looked better and younger than she had in years.

Even though Charlie's proximity comforted her, she often wondered if he watched her and Leo, shadowed them without her knowledge, kept tabs on them, observed them as they made love in front of that wonderful fireplace in their condo. Charlie, voyeur. Yes, she could see him doing that.

After he had passed away, she'd spent a lot of years living by herself in the home they'd bought in Key Largo. They hadn't lived there long when Charlie had died, not even six months, and that had made her transition easier. There was less of him in that house, less energy, fewer reminders. Yet, every time she'd climbed into her king-sized bed, the bed she had shared with Charlie, he had been there, in her head, holding her, making love to her, the two of them laughing.

When she'd started dating an ER doc during her last year in Key Largo, when he'd occupied that king-sized bed, her memories of Charlie and the bed had begun to fade. That bed, she thought, had burned with the rest of the house when Dominica had seized Tess's former lover and partner in the bureau, and forced him to torch the place.

Just as well, she thought. Once the house was gone, she had known her time in Key Largo was done. Her travels with the Merry Pranksters in the sixties had taught her the importance of signs, and that fire had been a biggie. She had fled Key Largo with Tess and Maddie and come here.

Esperanza was close enough to the equator so that the seasons here didn't change much. But because it sat on a plateau at thirteen thousand feet, the air turned cold as soon as the sun set. She smelled smoke from fireplaces all over the city. In the light of the moon, she could see tufts of smoke that burst erratically from the top of the Taquina volcano. In the past several months, she had noticed that the volcano emitted smoke more frequently. Could that somehow be connected to the creeping blackness?

In her four and a half years in this city, Lauren had seen her share of weirdness, the kind of stuff that challenged anyone's worldview. She could accept avaricious ghosts, light chasers, shape shifters. She could accept that in Esperanza, the veil between the living and the dead was almost nonexistent. She could *not* accept a creeping blackness of unknown origin that devoured solid objects and people, that approached, as it did in the video, like some conscious extension of the darkness itself. She could not accept that a *brujo* had tried to choke her daughter.

"Hey, Prankster? You hungry?"

Leo slipped out onto the balcony with her, his voice hoarse with fatigue. He had stripped off his surgery greens and stood there in jeans and a T-shirt with the symbol for pi on it. Lauren touched her finger to the symbol. "Dr. Ordeño. Why that? Why pi?"

"Because it looks like a door. Because it's infinite." He touched her chin, lifting it, and kissed her.

He was only a bit taller than Lauren, maybe five ten, and didn't really need to lift her chin to kiss her. But she liked it, the gentle sensation of his fingertips at her chin, the cool touch of his mouth, liked that he courted her, counted her in, was there for her—and yet gave her the space she needed.

"Are we done here?" she asked.

"Relieved by backup staff." He fingered the rosary around her neck. "What's with this?"

She told him what Elsa had said about Raúl's video. He nodded. "Everyone in ER has now seen the video."

"What do you think about it?"

Leo drew his fingers through his white hair and stood back against the wall. "It's spooky and alarming."

"I need to ask Raúl if he would send the video to—"

"I asked, he said of course, and has already e-mailed it to Ian."

Leo, her personal genie. This tall, beautiful man anticipated her needs and desires, sought to make them happen, and she knew he would move mountains for her. She gave him the condensed version of her conversation with Tess and he frowned and asked her a bunch of questions about Sanchez, most of which she had asked Tess.

"Do you think we should drive out there?" she asked.

"It sounds like he's fine for the night. We can drop by in the morning. If necessary, they can take him to the hospital in Mariposa."

"Yeah, that's what I told Tess."

"Right now, I think dinner is a priority. It's just past eleven."

Eleven? No wonder she was starving. "I need to change. Meet you downstairs in ten minutes?"

"Perfect."

Minutes later, Lauren hurried into the women's locker room in the hospital basement, stripped off her hospital clothes, wrapped a towel around her short salt-and-pepper hair, and took a quick shower. Then she put on clean jeans, a red print shirt, and traded her surgery shoes—Adidas—for comfortable Aerosole flats, slipped on a denim jacket, and slung her purse over her shoulder. Shit, she had it down to a science.

As she moved through the nearly empty basement corridor, Charlie materialized beside her. "Uh, can we slow the pace a little, Lore?"

The first time her dead husband had appeared to her, shock had rendered her mute. She couldn't really say she was accustomed to it yet, but at least she didn't freak out now when it happened. As usual, Charlie wore his customary white trousers, shirt, hat, and shoes, had a cigar tucked behind his right ear, and flicked his silver Zippo lighter constantly, nervously, just as he had when he was alive.

Lauren stopped. "I have a message for you. A ghost named Ricardo tried to choke Tess. He claims he's Dominica's brother and he said to please tell you that everyone wants the same thing, to live peacefully in Esperanza. If the chaser council and the people of Esperanza can't accept that, then he'll unleash his tribe of three million *brujos*—"

"Jesus," Charlie breathed. "Nice to see you, too, Lore. How about starting at the beginning?"

"The creeping black crud at the Café Taquina? Tess and Ian were there. But before that happened, a *brujo* materialized in her car."

Lauren told him the rest of it and, to Charlie's credit, he didn't interrupt.

"Are Tess and Ian okay?"

"Shaken, but they're fine. They're with Wayra and Illary. Maddie and Sanchez are, too."

"Why is Tess always where she shouldn't be?"

"Because she's your kid."

Charlie gave her the *you're being bitchy* look, his dark eyes narrowed, eyebrows forming sharp little peaks. "Oh, so she doesn't have any of your DNA? Hey, I didn't wander around with Kesey and his Pranksters."

"Have you met Kesey yet? Or Garcia? And what about McKenna? I'd love to know what they're doing these days. You told me you'd check on them, remember that, Charlie? I'm the Prankster Forrest Gump. Still here, saw it all, but they're gone."

"You're changing the subject."

"Damn right. Who's behind what happened at the Taquina?"

He kicked at a dust bunny, plunged his hands in the pockets of his trousers. "An emergency chaser council meeting has been called; I hope I'll find out more then. I just wanted you to know that I'm on it. Tess will probably think that's bullshit, but it isn't. As soon as I have some answers, I'll be in touch."

"But—"

"But nothing, Lore. It is what it is, okay?"

"No, Charlie. It's not *fucking okay*." She felt like punching him. "You jerk us around without intending to do so. I get that. But you can't jerk us around for your own pleasure or illumination or whatever."

Charlie looked hurt. "You think that's what I'm doing?"

"I don't have any idea what you're doing. I don't know how you can appear to be so real and solid and then fade away like last summer's tan, Charlie. I don't know *shit*, okay? It's not like you've ever explained a whole lot. I couldn't read your mind when you were alive and I definitely can't read it now. Just *talk* to me, *explain*."

He flipped his hat off his head and slapped it against the side of his leg, like a cowboy getting rid of prairie dust. "Christ, Lore. You never said any of this before. You never told me how you felt."

"You never *asked*, Charlie, and you never stuck around long enough for me to get a word in edgewise."

"Really?" He looked horrified, his bushy brows pushing together just as they had when he was alive, his mouth twitching, his thumb working that Zippo lighter. "Shit. Okay. Okay, let's see. Where to start? I'm the youngest member of the chaser council and the only one of us who still has loved ones who are physical, alive. That makes me the oddball. I have allies on the council—several men, a couple of women, but the two most powerful members of the council can easily sway the others."

"You make the chaser council sound like the board members of some corporation."

"You think politics disappears when you die?"

He lit his cigar and blew a cloud of smoke into the air above them. The smoke, like everything else about Charlie, seemed real. She could smell it. "I always hoped that in death there would be *some* wisdom."

"Well, okay, after I died I knew more than I did when I was alive, but hey, not by much. And it's all politics. Everything is politics. Especially in Esperanza. The council is about spiritual politics—*my beliefs are truer than your beliefs.* Like that."

It was the most Charlie had ever said to her about his situation. Lauren didn't know what to make of it, couldn't connect a whole bunch of dots, like, well, how a hillside and part of a restaurant could just *disappear.*

"So what happened at the café is about spiritual beliefs? Spiritual politics? And why would a stone cause Sanchez to go into convulsions? Is that about spiritual politics, too?"

"Stone? What stone?"

She explained what she knew.

"Is he . . . all right?"

"Apparently."

"I'd like to see this stone."

"Talk to Wayra."

"I intend to. As soon as I find out anything, I'll let you know." Charlie squeezed her hand, a touch that felt real, solid, warm. "How does Tess know this Ricardo is Dominica's brother?"

"I don't know, she didn't say."

"She's with Wayra, so he must've told her."

"Is it true?"

"It's the first I've ever heard of it. But Wayra is the expert on *brujos* and on Dominica, so if he said it's true, then it probably is."

"Then why haven't they seized anyone? How could they be here without any of the chasers knowing about it? Without Wayra and Illary knowing it?"

"Maybe because we've all gotten lax."

"We don't stand a chance against three million *brujos,* Charlie."

"I'll find out what I can, Lore. Just keep in mind that *brujos* lie."

And he faded away. The clicking of his Zippo echoed in the basement. Lauren stood there, anxiety eating a hole through her stomach.

These days, Lauren thought, Esperanza was a city that rocked from dusk to dawn. As she and Leo walked through old town, everything lit up and decorated for the Christmas holidays, pedestrians crowded the sidewalks, couples zipped around on scooters, laughter and music drifted from open doorways, the bars and cafés were jammed with people.

"I guess no one is worried about what happened at Café Taquina," she remarked.

Leo took her hand. "Maybe they don't know about it."

"C'mon. The Internet is free here and everyone older than six has a cell phone."

He flashed a quick smile. "Yeah, I know. I'm just trying to provide a measure of comfort. For you, for myself." He paused and she felt him mulling, turning something over and over again in his head.

"What?" she asked.

"Tell me again what Charlie said."

She'd already related the conversation, but did so again, certain that Leo was now picking apart the details, just as he did when he was with a patient. His diagnostic skills were impeccable.

"The only way no one would realize *brujos* are here is if they've been seizing hosts elsewhere," he said. "There are stories all over the Internet about possessions—but in other countries, not in Ecuador. So if Esperanza is their home base, then their leader isn't going to screw that up by seizing locals. This Ricardo isn't going to repeat Dominica's mistakes. The ancient *brujos* have a strong grasp of history." He glanced at her. "So what else did Charlie have to say?"

More than he has ever said, she thought, but not stuff that Leo needed to hear. "Not much. I hadn't seen him for a while."

"Do you ever wonder what chasers do? I mean, in their daily existence? Do they have routines? Do they have basketball teams? Schools? Libraries? I asked Charlie that once and he said he belonged to a chess club, had joined an acting group, worked in a bookstore, went skiing, coached other attorneys, had fifteen girlfriends . . ."

Lauren started laughing. "Yeah. And he spends his free time watching us."

"I hope you're joking."

"Yeah, me, too."

"Suppose the *brujos* are back, Lauren? Would you leave?"

"You forget, I arrived with the solstice battle. My existence here has been *brujo*-free. But yours hasn't. Would *you* leave?"

He didn't reply immediately. She already knew what his answer would be; they had talked about this when they'd first started seeing each other. "I've loved this city since I first arrived. My life here, even during the dark years of the *brujos,* surpassed anything I thought was possible when I left Argentina. I've been cancer-free for twenty-two years. This city cured me. But if you left, I would have to leave. I can't imagine living here without you."

A lump of emotion lodged in her throat and she raised his hand to her mouth and kissed each of the knuckles. "I'm not going anywhere. If I weren't starving, I'd say let's go home, build a fire, and get naked."

She knew his neck wouldn't turn red now. They were alone, just the two of them out here on the sidewalk. His low, husky laugh told her he'd been thinking the same thing. As he slipped his arm around her shoulders, pulling her close, their stomachs growled simultaneously. "Okay, food first," he said, and steered her into Los Gatos, a vegetarian restaurant named after the two orange-striped cats, Simba and Cobre, who strolled about freely.

The cats were identical, except that Simba had celery-green eyes, rather like Maddie's, and Cobre had eyes the color of the metal after which he'd been named—Copper. Lauren always wondered if they were spirit cats. And that was the thing, really, about Esperanza. You never knew for sure if what you were seeing was alive and real—or an apparition.

Both cats came up to them as they waited for the hostess to seat them and threaded through their legs, purring. Lauren leaned over and stroked her fingers across Cobre's back. His fur was deliciously soft and felt ever so real. Then again, the smell of Charlie's cigar had been real, too.

Los Gatos was crowded and the only free seats were near the bar. She had a full view of the TV from here and wished she were sitting with her back to it. But she faced the damn television, where Raúl's video was now streaming across the screen. She forced herself to look away, to look at Leo, who held out a glass of wine.

"*Salud,* Prankster."

"Where'd this come from? We haven't ordered yet."

"Special order."

"Really." She clicked her glass against his. "*Salud,* Leo." She sipped and the wine tasted divine. "What's the occasion?"

He reached into his jacket pocket, withdrew a small square box, and opened it. Inside was a gold ring shaped like a peace symbol, with a star sapphire gleaming in the center of it. Beautiful didn't quite cover it. The ring was the most spectacular piece of jewelry she'd ever seen. "We just traded in the rest of our stock for precious stones?"

"For this precious stone," he said. "I'm old-fashioned, what can I say? Let's make it legal." He removed the ring from the box, held it out. His brows lifted, forming peaks above his beautiful eyes.

Lauren didn't hesitate. She held up her left hand and Leo slipped the beautiful ring on her fourth finger. It fit perfectly. "Okay, I'm speechless."

"Never. Just say yes."

As she turned the ring, she caught a whiff of Charlie's cigar, heard the *click, click* of his Zippo lighter, and knew he was here, watching.

Go away, Charlie. Please. This is private.

After a moment, the scent of cigar smoke dissipated and she no longer heard the click of the lighter. Had Leo smelled the smoke, heard the clicking? She didn't know, had never asked. And she didn't ask now. She felt that Charlie had left, departed, gone on to his chess club, his acting group, his fifteen girlfriends. She brought her focus back to the ring.

Peace symbol. My God. Leo understood that, understood her stance against Vietnam, Iraq, Afghanistan, all wars, anywhere, for any reason. And for the sapphire to be in the juncture where the lower part of the symbol, the *V,* melded into the *Y* (why??) spoke tomes about how closely Leo had listened when she talked about her experiences of the sixties, about the Pranksters and that very special and psychedelic summer in Northern California.

The sapphire fractured the overhead light, and Lauren suddenly felt like crying. She knew if she gave in, the crying would collapse into sobs, then hysteria. So she leaned across the table and cupped Leo's face in her hands and kissed him. "Yes," she whispered. "Of course. Yes, yes."

Four
Charlie

1.

Charlie moved swiftly across the city, putting distance between himself and Lauren. And Leo and that ring. *They're going to get married.* He didn't want to dwell on that, his Lore married to another man. Even though Lauren and Leo had been living together for three years, it wasn't the same thing as marriage.

So he thought himself along the old railroad tracks that ran through the city and wished he could see the legendary ghost train chugging along these tracks. Supposedly the train appeared once a year, the ghost of Esperanza 14. But he, a ghost himself, had never seen it.

Charlie thought himself forward faster and faster, traveling in the same way that *brujos* did when they were in their natural forms. Since both chasers and *brujos* were physically dead and existed as consciousness in a place that enabled them to interact with the living, they shared more than just the way they moved from one place to another. The similarities had always troubled Charlie. It was as if chasers and *brujos* were simply different sides of the same coin.

In Esperanza, *brujos* and chasers could assume virtual forms that looked as real and solid as the living. They could fade in and out of view as he had just done with Lauren and as this Ricardo had done with Tess. They could both draw on the power of the dead—and on the residual power of Esperanza from when it had been a nonphysical place.

Tried to choke her . . . Could a *brujo* in a virtual form kill the living? He didn't know. He'd never heard of such a thing happening but that didn't mean it was impossible. With a little practice and effort, *brujos* and chasers could create anything from thought—the clothes they wore, their homes, backyards, a courtroom, booze, food, animals. So he supposed a *brujo* could create the sensations of choking and maybe the person would simply die from fear.

The animal that followed him now, an Amazonian parrot, wasn't a mental construct. It kept circling just above him, squawking, *"Hola, amigo, hola. ¿Cómo andas?"*

Literally, *andas*, from the verb *andar*, to walk, meant *How're you walking?* But in the vernacular, it meant, *How's it going?* So Charlie answered in the literal sense, that he was walking with both feet. The parrot made a noise that sounded so much like laughter it prompted Charlie to stop and peer upward at it.

"You a shifter?" he called. "Is that what this is about?"

The parrot circled down toward him and landed on his nonexistent shoulder, cooing softly. No shifter, he thought. He realized this bird was Kali, the parrot that had lived so many years in the lobby of the Posada de Esperanza, the inn where Tess and Ian first stayed as transitional souls. Back then, Kali occupied a perch in the large front bay window in the lobby and he always had thought she was a spirit, not an actual living parrot. Now he suspected she was both, one of those birds, like an owl, a raven, or a crow, that traversed dimensions.

As Charlie approached Wayra and Illary's place in Mariposa, Kali flew off and settled on the fence. Charlie thought himself through the front door and into the spacious living room. Tastefully decorated in browns and soft pastels, the room boasted an amazing collection of original art—Picasso, van Gogh, Frida Kahlo, O'Keeffe, and the Ecuadorian artist Oswaldo Guayasamín.

The living room was deserted. Wayra, Tess, and Ian sat at a table on the screened porch, and before Charlie joined them, he assumed his virtual form as Manuel Ortega, a Quechua—short, slender stature, dark hair and eyes, a colorful blanket wrapped around his shoulders, jeans and a sweater and boots. He slid the door open and walked out onto the deck.

"Sorry to intrude," he said. "I'm glad all of you are okay. How's Sanchez doing?"

"The guy with the answers," Wayra said. "Good to see you, Charlie. And Sanchez is sleeping comfortably."

"We were just talking about you," Tess said, and got up and hugged him hello.

In Charlie's virtual form, physical contact felt real and always made him miss his actual former life as Charlie Livingston.

"You haven't been around for months," Ian remarked.

"Months? Really? It's been that long?" Charlie pulled out a chair and sat down. "I apologize. I guess I've been preoccupied. So is it true? Dominica has a brother?"

Wayra nodded and explained the specifics. "I don't have any idea where he has been all these centuries, but he's definitely here now."

"And he had a message for you, Dad" Tess said.

"Yeah, I heard. I talked to Lauren earlier. Wayra, may I see this stone that sent Sanchez into convulsions?"

"Sure." He slipped it from his jacket pocket, set it in the middle of the table, and got up and turned on a floor lamp. "Illary spotted it near a vanished area at the bottom of the hill where the café sits. It was glowing, so I picked it up."

Oracle. Sipapu. A Hopi word, meaning "an opening in the earth," What the hell did that even mean? Charlie wondered, and picked up the stone.

It was smooth and dark, about three inches long and half as wide. As he pressed it between his hands, the smoothness abruptly changed. He could feel grooves, bumps, protrusions, and its texture was like sandpaper. He held it up to the light and was surprised to see that the surface was now inscribed with symbols.

"Do any of you recognize these symbols?" he asked, and held out his hand, the stone in the center of it.

The others leaned forward for a look. "It was smooth before," Tess exclaimed.

"It's as if the heat of your hands released those marks," Ian said.

Wayra nodded. "Interesting. The stone was found by a shape shifter and a chaser's virtual hands released the stone's secrets."

"May I have a look?"

They all glanced back at Sanchez, who stood in the open doorway in a pair of jogging pants and a T-shirt, his feet bare, his dark hair messed up, his jaw unshaven. Illary and Maddie were right behind him and Jessie the retriever hugged his side protectively.

After everyone chorused how good it was to see him up and around, Ian offered Sanchez his chair. But he just laughed. "Hey, people, I'm all right, okay?" He stabbed a thumb at Illary and Maddie. "I had to practically threaten them before they gave me permission to get up." He gestured at the stone. "Those etchings. That's what I saw. That's the oracle part of it."

"But how do we interpret it?" Wayra asked.

Sanchez picked up the stone. His eyes shut, and Charlie knew he went away, he dreamed, he did whatever psychics did when they were tuned in. When he set the stone down, he said, "Can you touch it again, Charlie?"

"Sure."

Charlie pressed the stone between his hands for a few moments, felt the texture changing again, shifting, moving like a living thing. When he set the stone on the table once more, symbols were clearly visible on the surface of the stone, six of them.

"Sanchez's sketches show these symbols," Maddie said.

Wayra quickly snapped a photo of the stone with his cell.

"So what are they?" Charlie addressed his question to Illary, the oldest among them.

"Well, if the stone came from a sipapu, as Sanchez saw, if it popped out of the opening in the earth, then my sense is that the stone comes from the nonphysical world, the place where Esperanza was born thousands of years ago. I've only seen two of these symbols before, in the stone forest where Wayra and I took the other shifters after we rescued Maddie and left Cedar Key."

With her left hand, she touched one of Sanchez's drawings, then picked up a pencil with her right hand and used the tip of it to indicate the same symbol on the stone. It looked, Charlie thought, like a square with the upper left-hand corner open, and within the square was a tree.

"This one, with the tree in it, and this one." She touched another drawing and its corresponding likeness on the stone. "I think the tree is the tree of life, the ceiba tree. The square is symbolic of the foundation of all things. Perhaps the opening of the square represents the sipapu."

"But what do the symbols mean?" Charlie asked.

Illary shook her head. "I don't know."

Charlie was liking this less and less. Chasers—not *brujos*—had always been in charge of the city: its location, its physicality, its present and its future. "But ceiba trees grow in the tropics, so why would such a tree appear in this symbol?"

"When Esperanza was nonphysical," Wayra said, "ceiba trees grew everywhere. Once the city was brought into the physical world, at this altitude, they couldn't survive. Except for that old ceiba in Parque del Cielo."

"And no one can explain why it flourishes," Charlie remarked.

"What's the other symbol mean, Illary?" Sanchez asked. "It looks like a circle with Shiva inside of it."

"That we are many," Illary said. "And that there is momentum and power in the many. We, the people, must have a say in what happens to this city."

Kali's screech announced her arrival at the porch screen. She squawked, *"Hola, amigos. Hola."*

Wayra laughed and opened the door for her and she swept in noisily. Jessie barked and Kali swooped down over the dog's head, plucked a piece of cheese from the platter on the table, then landed on the back of Charlie's chair and transferred the cheese from her beak to the claws of her right foot. She nibbled at it for a moment, then flung it toward Jessie, who gobbled it up.

"Kali?" Tess exclaimed. "From the posada? But how? I thought she was a spirit, like that cat, Whiskers, who followed us everywhere."

"She lives in many worlds," Wayra remarked. "Right, Charlie?"

"Apparently," Charlie replied. "She's there whether I'm in this form or in my natural form as a chaser."

"Awesome," Maddie said softly. "I only saw her once, at the posada, before I heard she'd flown off. Can I pet her?"

"Sure," Charlie said.

"Awesome," Kali repeated as Maddie moved closer to her. *"Hola, Maddie."*

Maddie drew her fingers over Kali's back, and the parrot made soft, trilling sounds of contentment. "You are one cool bird."

"I really need to shove off, folks," said Charlie. "Please keep me in the loop about the symbols. And I'll let you know what I find out from the council."

Hugs all around, then Tess walked outside with Charlie and Kali. They stood for a moment in the magnificent backyard that overlooked Esperanza, lit up now like some magical city in a fairy tale. "You need to find out what the deal is with Ricardo's tribe. And can you meet us tomorrow morning out at the café? Diego is going to get us into the area that disappeared."

"I'll be there," Charlie said.

Tess hugged him for the third time that night. "Love you, Dad," she whispered.

"Do you realize that's the first time you've called me Dad in, oh, more than four years?" He leaned back from her. "Why's that?"

"I guess I've forgiven you."

"For what?"

"Dying."

"Love you, Slim," he said, his voice soft and choked, then he shed his virtual form and he and Kali moved rapidly back across the city.

2.

Once Charlie reached old town Esperanza, he faded into view as Manuel Ortega again. Kali was still with him. "Okay, I get it. You're really a messenger between the living and the dead, right? Well, I don't have any message yet. But stick around, Kali. Come to the meeting with me."

As she touched down on his shoulder, Charlie turned into an alley, passed a bodega, a takeout place, a hole-in-the-wall used bookstore. Then he ducked into La Última, a café created from collective chaser thought. It boasted the best coffee in Ecuador, the fastest Internet connection in South America, and had a spread of delectable goodies in the display case.

Charlie headed toward the counter, Kali riding on his shoulder, and ordered a *cortadito*—espresso with milk; a slice of spinach quiche; and a cheese pastry topped with coconut. He had to admit that one of the most pleasant aspects of the afterlife was that you could eat what you wanted. No worry about cholesterol, fats, high blood pressure, diabetes, or any of the rest of it.

He made his way to the reserved table next to the window, Kali now pecking at the pastry. A parrot with a sweet tooth. "Hey, I can get you one of your own, you know."

She made that sound again, like a laugh. Charlie broke off a piece of the pastry and handed it to her. She wrapped the claws of her right foot around it and nibbled away.

Outside the window, it was twilight. Long, thin shadows fell across the alley and sidewalk and everything had a beautiful patina to it. But the twilight, like everything else around him, was an illusion. He knew it had been around three A.M. mortal time when he'd left Wayra's place. It was often twilight when the council met.

As usual, he was early. When he was alive, he used to be early in court, too. Some habits stayed with you life to life. He slipped out his iPad, checked his e-mail to see if any of the chasers had dropped him a note about being late. The iPad, like everything else in his world, was a mental construct, one more illusion, and hadn't really come into being for him until shortly before Steve Jobs's death, when Maddie had convinced him to conjure one of them.

After Jobs's death, Maddie wanted to know if Jobs was among the chasers and Charlie had actually checked. This was the genius, after all, whose last mortal words were, "Oh wow, oh wow." He reported back that, yes, Jobs was a chaser, working in a province in China and improving the lot of the workers who assembled the Apple products. Charlie suspected that Jobs might be reborn among those very workers at some point quite soon and no telling what might develop from that.

Victor had sent him an e-mail twelve minutes ago. *On the way.*

Sounded good, Charlie thought. But Victor moved according to his own time, at his own pace, and *on the way* could mean that he would might show up four hours, days, or months from now. Charlie wasn't supposed to give a shit about time in his chaser form. It was an artificial construct, after all, something the living used to order their lives.

But more and more frequently, he found that time was all he could think about.

How much time had elapsed, for instance, between the last physical life of the older council members and now? Centuries? Millennia? For the really ancient chasers, it was millennia. He was the oddball on the council, with loved ones still in the physical world. And because of his intimate connections to the living, to this century, he was able to teach other council members about technology: the Internet, Twitter, Facebook, iTunes, iPhone, the iPad, all of Apple's nifty inventions.

Granted, it was rare that he or any of the chasers could impact the physical world in terms of the actual Internet. Now and then, though, their collective desire enabled them to add something to their *physical, three-dimensional* blog and Web site. Most of the time, chasers communicated through their mental constructs—not unlike the *brujo* net through which Dominica and her tribe used to communicate. Another disturbing similarity.

Some of the other chasers trickled in. Karina saw him, waved, and made her way over to his table, a cup of coffee in hand. "Hey, Charlie, may I join you and your parrot?"

He always felt sort of tongue-tied around her. She was the loveliest female council member—alabaster skin that invited a caress, shockingly blue eyes, a thick, dark braid that curved like a question mark over her right shoulder.

"I'd be delighted," he said, and quickly got up and pulled a chair out for her.

"*Hola,* Karina," Kali said, fluttering her wings and tightening her grip on Charlie's shoulder.

Karina laughed. "Kali. I thought you looked familiar. I haven't seen her for a while."

"She just started following me around."

"Any idea what this meeting is about, Charlie?"

"Maybe about what happened at the Taquina. I was hoping you might know."

She shook her head. "I'm out of the loop lately. I've been over in Africa, helping some of these kids with AIDS pass over."

"Any sign of *brujos* over there?"

"In Africa? Ha. *Brujos* have no interest in seizing people who are starving and sick. Seizures in other countries are increasing, though." She stabbed her thumb toward the door. "Here comes Victor."

Charlie glanced around. Victor, nearly bald and wearing a silly white toga, looked like a throwback to ancient Rome. He quickly thought away the toga and replaced it with modern attire—khaki pants, a black shirt, a jacket. He ordered his usual whipped-cream latte sprinkled with cinnamon, with a huge sugar stick inside of it, and headed over to the table.

"Hi, Karina, Charlie. What's with the parrot?"

"No idea. Ask her."

Victor squeezed his corpulent body into a chair, his eyes pinned on Kali, and pointed his index finger at her. "*¿Qué quieres, Kali?*" What do you want?

She squawked at him, lifted from Charlie's shoulder, and fluttered over Victor's head for a moment. A couple of her soft bluish-green feathers drifted down on his head. Charlie snickered. "You're fortunate she didn't shit on you, Vic."

"Wouldn't be the first time. She's never liked me."

"So what's going on? What's this black stuff that devoured part of Taquina Café?"

Victor sipped noisily at his whipped-cream latte. He looked utterly miserable when his dark eyes met Charlie's. "Come with me for a moment, Charlie. I'd like to show you something."

Charlie hesitated, eyeing Victor's outstretched hand as though it might transmute at any second into a nest of vipers. As the most recently deceased member of the chaser council, the one for whom physical life was still an actual memory and not some loop in the collective chaser soup, he vividly remembered snakes and rats and roaches.

"What about me?" Karina asked.

"You're welcome to come, too," Victor said. "But this little trip remains among us."

Charlie grasped Victor's outstretched hand, and held out his own hand to Karina. She laced her fingers through his, a touch that thrilled him. "Okay, Victor, let's see it."

Instantly, they stood in front of La Pincoya, an abandoned hotel in the heart of old town. The name translated as *mermaid,* ironic, Charlie thought, since they were hundreds of miles from any ocean. But legend had it that the lake at the foot of Taquina volcano was home to mermaids.

The hotel driveway was cracked, the property overgrown and neglected, a faded FOR SALE sign was stuck in the ground. Kali circled above them, squawking noisily. Charlie, Karina, and Victor moved back into the trees across the street from the lopsided hotel. As her hand slipped away from his, he felt its absence.

Victor whispered, "Watch, you two."

"I don't see anything," Charlie said.

"Orbs," Karina said softly. "See them?"

The bright orbs of light danced and floated toward the hotel and vanished through the walls. They didn't reappear. "So it's true," Charlie breathed. "They're *back.* One of them tried to strangle my daughter."

Victor and Karina looked horrified. "When did this happen?" Victor asked.

"Before everything went down at the café."

"We'd better keep that to ourselves for now," Karina said.

"Good idea," Victor agreed.

"Why haven't they tried to seize anyone?" Charlie asked.

Victor shrugged. "I don't know. I don't know if any of the other council members even realize the *brujos* are here. The attacks outside of Ecuador have increased so dramatically that there's been talk among some council members about taking Esperanza back into the nonphysical."

"*What?*" Karina gasped. "That's madness, Victor."

"I know. They feel it's the only way to end the *brujo* scourge once and for all."

"You can't just disappear a city of thirty thousand into the ether without killing everyone," Charlie said.

"*We* know that. Shit, even *they* know. Just the same, I think several of them decided to conduct a stupid goddamn experiment and the events at the café were that experiment. A failed experiment."

"You know all this for a fact?" Karina asked.

"It's an educated guess. I figure that whoever is responsible realized they aren't powerful enough to do this on their own, with just a few council members. They need a majority. Getting a consensus from what—eight thousand of us now?—is nearly impossible. So they're fumbling and it caused the deaths of those people at the café and tore apart some space/time shit. So here we are, trying to figure out how to pick up the pieces."

"A few members on the council can't unilaterally decide to do something like this," Karina said. "A resolution has to be passed by the council and then presented to the rest of the chasers for a vote."

As Karina said this, Charlie was struck by yet another parallel between chasers and *brujos*.

On Cedar Key, Dominica had had a council of *brujos* who oversaw things. In the years before that, when her tribe had attacked Esperanza relentlessly, there had also been a council. How had it come down to a council for both the chasers and *brujos*?

"It's a clear violation of how things are supposed to work on the council," Victor said. "But maybe my theory is all wrong. Maybe it's these *brujo* bastards." He gestured toward the orbs of light, hundreds of them now. "It's too coincidental that one of them tries to choke Tess right before the events at the Taquina."

"Suppose you're not wrong?" Charlie asked. "What the hell can we do about it?"

"Not much. There are some obscure rules from when the council had fourteen members, but I'm not even sure if those rules are valid anymore. I've got to do some research on that."

Victor slung his arms around their shoulders and they returned instantly to the café. The other ten council members had arrived and were chatting among themselves. The three of them took seats at the round table. Charlie was secretly thrilled when Karina made a point of squeezing her chair next to his. Greetings were exchanged, then the oldest member of the council, Newton, called the meeting to order.

Newton looked like the man whose name he'd taken, Sir Isaac, the guy who'd discovered gravity and who, by many accounts, was the greatest scientist who had ever lived. Charlie begged to differ. Einstein, David Bohm, and Richard Feynman had his votes.

Shortly after Charlie had transitioned, he had met the real Newton, an anal guy the chasers tried to rescue and recruit from the astral realms, but he wanted none of it. Newton apparently hadn't believed he was really dead, and until he did, the only thing they could do for him was to assign a chaser to him to act as his buddy, his confidant, and ultimately, his mentor. Dead for centuries and he still couldn't accept the fact.

"We've come together to vote on a resolution that must be passed," Newton said. "It has become clear that *brujos* have been using the Pincoya as a portal to other locations within the physical universe, where they have been seizing the living with utter impunity. It's time to take Esperanza back into the nonphysical."

So all along the council members had known about the Pincoya, Charlie thought. And at least some of them had discussed and experimented with removing Esperanza from the physical world, just as Victor had speculated.

Newton flung his right arm upward and an image appeared in the air above them, a world map with pulsating red hearts that indicated where *brujo* seizures had happened. Thousands of red hearts. "These are the seizures in just the last forty-eight hours. The *brujos* have been using the abandoned hotel as a portal to other countries around the globe. Always in the past, they simply thought themselves to other locations. We don't know what has changed."

"Excuse me," Charlie said. "Your little experiment in the disappearance of Esperanza went seriously haywire, Newton. And I'd like to know who granted you and the other members of the council who participated in this experiment the right to kill and injure dozens?"

Newton looked surprised that Charlie had interrupted his spiel. "We, uh, well, weren't certain that it could be done and decided to try it on a hillside. But things . . ."—he ran his fingers through his white hair—"got out of hand."

"Out of hand?" Charlie's voice sounded shrill enough to break glass. "Explain that to the families who lost loved ones, Newton. When the council brought Esperanza into the physical universe five hundred years ago, the world was a different place. This plateau and everything else beyond the Río Palo were empty, just windblown mountains. In the twenty-first century, you can't just disappear a city and expect that no

one will notice. The Internet exists, remember? With YouTube, cell phones, iPads, *there are always witnesses to everything.*" He pushed back his chair and stood. "I can't be a part of anything that is going to annihilate thousands."

Around the table, a few other members of the council nodded in agreement with Charlie. Victor stood up—and so did three other chasers—Liana, Karina, and Franco. All of them had lived physical lives in Ecuador, so their opinions carried weight on the council.

Victor spoke first. "If we're responsible for the deaths of thousands, then we're no better than the goddamn *brujos.* I'm with Charlie on this one."

"This is such utter bullshit," said Karina, flicking her raven-colored braid over her shoulder. "The council has certain rules that must be followed. You broke a bunch of them, Newton. You may be one of the oldest council members, but you're not Mr. Supremo."

"We're supposedly the evolved souls," Liana said. "To even entertain this . . . this lunacy makes us worse than Dominica and her entire tribe." Her pale blue eyes shone like ice in glaring sunlight and impaled every council member who was still seated. "None of you have any reservations about it?"

Maria, with her perfectly straight, long blond hair, reminded Charlie of a pinup girl from the fifties, one of those babes posing with a cigarette tray around her neck. She sat forward, hands resting on the table, fingers laced together. Her bright red fingernails looked like drops of blood against her pale skin. "Sure, I have reservations, Liana. But Esperanza shouldn't have been brought into the physical world to begin with. If we wait another five hundred years to rectify our mistake, it's going to be an even bigger mess."

"It's murder," Charlie shouted.

"But it's for the greater good," Newton burst out.

Stunned, Charlie just stood there, staring at Newton. "Do you hear yourself, Newton? Do you know what the hell you just said? *Murder* is for the *greater good*?"

Guilty looks around the table. Franco, who bore an uncanny resemblance to paintings Charlie had seen of da Vinci, started clapping. "Bravo, Charlie. You nailed it. The chaser council has been reduced to a group of thugs and killers. Sorry, Newton. But you and everyone else still seated should be ashamed of yourselves. You don't just disappear a city without replacing it with something else. And if you can figure out a way to do that, then you need to give people a choice. Do they go with Esperanza into the nonphysical or do they stay behind in whatever takes its place?"

"Franco, Franco," Maria said in her softest and most seductive voice. "Honestly, it's difficult enough to remove Esperanza from the physical world, but now you're asking us to replace it with *something else*?" She laughed and shook her head. "That's preposterous."

"Absolutely," Newton agreed, then snapped his fingers. "José, give them the facts."

Newton glanced at the tallest man on the council, whose wavy dark hair was swept back from his face and fell to his shoulders. He looked like a male model on the cover of a romance novel. Charlie wondered how long it had taken José and Maria to perfect their images.

When José spoke, his quiet voice and presence carried tremendous authority. "Of the ten thousand, two hundred, and twenty-one chasers worldwide, more than half support the resolution. It's enough chaser power to take Esperanza back into the nonphysical."

Charlie rarely kept tabs on the number of chasers worldwide, but this figure was higher than what Victor had mentioned. And depressingly low compared to the number of *brujos* worldwide.

Karina laughed. "Uh, José, it's *not* a resolution yet because the council *hasn't voted on it*. We clear on that? The council needs a majority to *pass* this resolution, and then it goes to the chasers worldwide. I say we put this to a private vote."

"It doesn't have to be private," Maria said quickly. "We're all friends here."

"This is a bloody waste of time," snapped Simon. Anger pinched his dark eyes and threw his forehead into a runic map of wrinkles.

"Now hold on, Simon," said Pilar, throwing her arms dramatically into the air. Her booming voice shut Simon up immediately. She reminded Charlie of a basketball coach Tess had had in middle school, no nonsense, no bullshit, and all she expected of you was to play by the rules. "Since rules have been violated here, I think a private vote is the only way to go."

Charlie felt like hugging her.

"You idiots are too much." Alan laughed, sitting with his chair tilted back, arms crossed against his chest. With his beard and long ponytail, he looked like an aging hippie. "No matter what we do, we're fucked. Our purpose is to safeguard Esperanza. Period. That's always been our purpose. And we've failed. So to correct our failure, one option is to kill thousands? The other option is to do nothing and let the *brujos* do what they're doing now. No one in Esperanza has been seized since the great battle. The city has prospered. What's wrong with that?"

Rita shot Alan a hateful look. "That's not what you told me a few days ago." She stabbed her fingers back through her hair so hard that the bracelets climbing her arms sang and jingled. "You just say whatever you think people want to hear."

"That's a goddamn lie," Alan snapped.

"Enough!" Newton shouted. "You're twisting everything. Esperanza is flourishing, yes. But the *brujos* are still seizing thousands every day in other parts of the world. Evil is winning. Esperanza is their portal. We can't allow it any longer."

Powerful words, Charlie thought, and for long moments, no one spoke. Kali, perched on the back of Charlie's chair, abruptly squawked and lifted into the air. It released the tension and Dan was the first to speak.

"My, my. Such issues here today." He had a Freudian look about him, ponderous and all-knowing. "I heard things went more smoothly when there were fourteen council members."

"That was way before our time," Newton replied.

"Maybe so," Dan said. "But the longer we sit here, the more we sound like *brujos*. Let's just get on with the vote."

"Private vote," Karina said curtly. "Now." She reached into her large shoulder bag, withdrew a pad of paper, ripped off a sheet, and passed the pad on to the next chaser. She set a bunch of pens in the middle of the table. "And yes, we may all be friends, Maria. But there are chasers at the table who hesitate going up against you and Newton."

"Oh, c'mon," Maria said with a soft laugh, her eyes darting around the table, pausing on this chaser, that chaser. "Hesitant to go up against

Newt and me? Really, Karina. You make it all sound so . . . well, conspiratorial."

"All in favor of a private vote," said Franco, "raise your hand."

Ten out of thirteen hands shot up. Newton glanced around nervously, apparently realizing for the first time that he might not have the support of the majority. Maria and Simon, Charlie thought, looked pissed. "A private vote it is," Charlie said. "Write 'yes' if you favor what Newton is proposing and 'no' if you're against it. Then put your vote in the center of the table."

Charlie quickly scribbled "no" on his piece of paper, slid it out into the middle of the table. Within minutes, all votes were cast. Charlie shuffled them, then he and Maria began to turn them over. Yes votes along the top, no votes beneath.

Once the votes were all turned over, he tried not to gloat. "Six yes, seven no." *Too damn close.* Charlie suspected that Pilar and Alan or Dan had voted with his group. He knew that Newton and Maria would be lobbying behind the scenes to get one of them to change a vote. But for now, Esperanza had won a reprieve.

"Keep in mind," Franco said, "that some of us who voted no might change our vote if provisions are included—something replaces Esperanza and people are given a choice."

"Damn unlikely," Maria muttered.

"You'd rather kill thousands?" Franco snapped, staring at her.

"It'd be easier." Maria snatched her bag off the table, got up, and marched out of the café.

3.

Charlie and Victor walked up a narrow, cobbled alley that led to a park. Early morning light swallowed up shadows. Kali flew above them, her occasional screech echoing. "The bitch should be kicked off the council for that last remark," Victor said.

"Fat chance of that. She and Newton are tight." Charlie hesitated. "Listen, we may have a huge problem, Victor." Then he told Victor what Ricardo had said to Tess.

Victor's virtual form turned completely pale, his appearance went berserk. He gained two hundred pounds, all his hair vanished, his cheeks puffed out, and he looked like a squat little Buddha. He swiftly shed the weight and his clothes changed from khaki pants to toga to business suit. Charlie glanced around uneasily, not entirely certain if they were visible to the living. But the alley was deserted. When he turned back to Victor, his appearance had stabilized—middle-aged man in jeans, a sweater, boots, salt-and-pepper hair, a prissy mouth.

"Sweet Christ, Charlie."

"You *knew* Dominica had a brother?"

"There were rumors. There are always rumors. Thing is, Wayra knew her better than any of us and you know how tight-lipped he is. Even after he and Illary disappeared Dominica, he refused to tell the council where he'd taken her. Frankly, we didn't give Dominica's brother much thought. We had bigger problems."

"Well, now it looks like Ricardo may pose a tsunami of problems."

Karina, Liana, and Franco suddenly fell into step alongside them. "Good work, people," Karina said. "But the reprieve may not last long."

Victor cast Charlie a warning look: *say nothing about Ricardo.*

"Whatever happened to following rules?" Franco remarked.

"Probably Maria's doing," Liana said. "She's appallingly naïve. I'm still not sure how she was ever voted onto the council."

"Newton wanted her," Victor said. "After Eva reincarnated, we had to fill her spot on the council and he lobbied hard to get Maria on. She's staunchly loyal."

Karina snickered. "It doesn't have much to do with loyalty. They're sleeping together. I heard they're planning to reincarnate soon to work out some other life issues they had way back."

Franco shook his head. "At the rate they're going, they may end up with lives in Afghanistan or some other hellhole."

Karina twisted her braid around her hand, then flicked it out in front of her. It came loose and a flowing black veil swung across her face. "Afghanistan's too good for Maria. I think the South Pole would suit her."

Charlie was thinking something worse, like the edge of time where Wayra and Illary had taken Dominica. "She can be very persuasive when she wants to be. She's probably figuring all the angles right now and we can be sure she'll be trying to use her powers of persuasion to change votes."

"Right now," Franco said, "our priorities are to make sure this blackness, this void, is completely gone from the hillside and get a better grasp of what's going on in the Pincoya."

They reached the end of the alley and the five of them gazed out into the park. Charlie heard water spilling over the stones in the fountain. The air smelled sweet.

Karina murmured, "It's so beautiful and peaceful. I really do understand why *brujos* crave physical existence."

Charlie and the others nodded. A kind of collective nostalgia for physical life swept over them. "Here's something to consider," Charlie said. "If Esperanza is taken back into the nonphysical and something else replaces it, it won't just be *brujos* who are disempowered. Chasers won't be able to assume virtual forms, the veil between the living and the dead will become a concrete wall . . ."

"You're jumping way ahead, Charlie," said Franco.

"Besides," Karina said, slipping her arm through Charlie's, "if any of that happens, then we'll all be faced with the same choice that the living deserve—go with Esperanza or stay behind."

Charlie barely heard her. He simply liked her nearness to him. She felt strangely familiar, like a favorite texture or color, smell or taste, or piece of music. He liked the way her arm felt against his, how warm and real her skin was.

"Well, there is a third choice," Victor said. "We can reincarnate."

The mood turned somber and they stood there a moment longer, watching Kali as she lifted from the trees, her blue and green wings painted with sunlight.

"Okay, people," Liana said. "We've got work to do. First stop, the hillside."

"Karina and I will go with you," Franco said.

Victor rubbed his chin. "Charlie and I will check out the situation at the Pincoya. I want to know why these *brujos* stopped thinking themselves to where they want to go."

"Maybe it's just laziness," Charlie remarked.

"Or it could be that the *brujos* are changing in some essential way again," Franco speculated. "We'll get together again when we have some answers."

Karina leaned toward Charlie and whispered, "Let's keep each other updated. Deal?"

"Deal," he whispered back, and was surprised when her soft, cool mouth brushed his cheek. He caught her hand before she moved away from him and added: "You're my coconspirator. That's how this feels."

"We'll explore that, Charlie." Then she squeezed his hand quickly and joined Franco and Liana. "You two ready?"

"Good to go," Franco said.

The three hooked arms and faded away. Karina's scent lingered in the air, a soft sweetness, like night-blooming jasmine. He and Victor crossed the street and sat on a bench in the park. The sound of the water in the fountain was louder, lovely, musical, and soothed Charlie's anxiety.

"Do you want to reincarnate?" Victor asked, his forehead creasing with wrinkles.

Charlie shrugged. "I don't know. I haven't had time to give it much thought. I think I'd rather wait for the people I love to cross over so we could plan a life together. What about you?"

"In the twenty-first century?" He shook his head. "No, thanks. Twenty twelve is a major transitional year for the living, Charlie. Life is about to get very difficult, with a wider chasm between the haves and the have nots, more wars, more religious nuts, more natural disasters, and a whole lot of people crossing over because they can't—or won't—embrace the new paradigm. The world is in the midst of a massive shift. I think I'll wait until the beginning of the twenty-second century when things have settled down."

The conversation was beginning to depress Charlie. "C'mon, let's shed these forms and see what's what at the Pincoya."

"It'll be easier if we go in as birds."

They shed their virtual human forms. Charlie thought his consciousness into the shape of an owl and Victor thought himself into the shape of a hawk. They flew into the sunlight together and eventually swooped down toward the Pincoya and sailed through a broken rear window.

They discarded their virtual bird forms and drifted from one neglected room to another, watching the bits of lights that were *brujos,* darting and flitting like fireflies through the darkness of the abandoned hotel. Their presence apparently wasn't detected, which struck Charlie as odd. In the past, in his dealings with Dominica and her tribe, *brujos* usually knew when chasers were around. Did that mean these *brujos* were less developed? Or did they see him and Charlie and just didn't give a shit?

They followed the darting bits of light into what had once been a ballroom and watched as the lights vanished through a wall of mirrors. *You think the portal's in there, Victor?*

Looks that way. You game?

You bet.

But as they shot toward the wall of mirrors, some of the bits of light encircled them and abruptly assumed virtual forms as large, muscular warriors wearing chest armor and carrying long spears. Charlie and Victor immediately assumed virtual forms—Victor as a towering Genghis Khan clone and Charlie in his usual white trousers, shirt, hat, and shoes.

"Well, well, chasers." One of the warriors stepped forward and bowed at the waist. "Ricardo's the name. You can't pass through those mirrors, gentlemen."

"We can pass through anything we damn well please," Victor replied.

"It takes you through hell," Ricardo said. "No chaser steps into hell and returns to talk about it."

Charlie laughed. "Hell? Please. There's no such thing." He snapped the lid of his Zippo lighter open, shut, open and shut, again and again, a quick, staccato sound. *Hell lies inside this Zippo.*

"Charlie Livingston." Ricardo jabbed his spear in Charlie's direction. "Met your lovely daughter. She tastes delicious. I gather she communicated my message?"

Prick. "If you plan on turning your tribe loose on Esperanza, then get on with it. We're ready for you."

Ricardo and his fellow warriors exploded in near hysteria. "Right, sure you are."

"Let's take the city now," shouted one of the warriors. "We can do it immediately."

"I think not," Victor snapped.

Charlie flicked his lighter once more and tremendous flames whooshed out of it, incinerating two of the warriors instantly. The others fled their virtual forms and dived into the mirrors. Charlie aimed the lighter at the glass and the flames grew brighter, hotter, and the mirror began melting. Victor threw his arms up into the air and hundreds of tremendous crows filled the ballroom, all of them cawing, shrieking, their long wings flapping furiously, fanning the flames as they dived for the bits of light that suddenly seemed to be everywhere.

"Charlie," Victor shouted, and assumed the virtual shape of a crow.

Charlie thought himself into the shape of the gigantic white crow he had used several times on Cedar Key, during Maddie's rescue, and he and Victor soared through the broken window, their wings passing unimpeded and uninjured through glass and brick. Outside, they soared into the sunlit sky. Charlie glanced down only once. Thick fog rolled toward La Pincoya, and within it glistened thousands of bits of lights, the *brujos* Ricardo had summoned, some of the ghosts within his tribe. So damn many of them.

We're fucked, Charlie thought, and flew faster, faster.

Five
Café Taquina

1.

Every morning, Tess and Ian raced the first mile of their three-mile run. The loser was supposed to buy coffee and breakfast. But this morning when Ian exploded off the curb in front of their building, she simply didn't have the energy to try to catch up. She jogged a halfhearted mile through light that seemed as sentient as the darkness that had swallowed part of the hill and café deck last night.

Some mornings, Maddie and Sanchez jogged with them. But after they had driven Tess and Ian back into old town this morning, Sanchez said he wasn't feeling up to a run, so Maddie had backed out, too. Life was apparently in flux again and she hoped it wouldn't mean a complete upheaval.

Tess circled back to the plaza where all the food stalls were set up and bought two *cortaditos* and a full Ecuadorian breakfast. Between the plaza and their apartment, she stuffed her face, appalled that she could eat so much and still be hungry. Since Ian wasn't back yet, she headed to the shower, stripping off her sweaty clothes, leaving them where they fell.

When she was in the shower and the steam had thickened to the point that she could hardly see her feet, the door opened and Ian stepped inside.

"Hey, what happened to you, Slim?"

"I was too hungry to give chase."

He squirted shampoo into his hands and began lathering her hair, his fingers massaging her scalp, then he nuzzled her neck. His soapy hands slipped over her breasts and tummy and then lower. She turned and sought his mouth and guided him inside of her.

For long, sensuous moments, they moved to a rhythm only they could hear, the hot water pounding around them, over them, steam rising up around them. The first time they had made love, they were transitional souls, staying in cottage 13 at the Posada de Esperanza. It had felt as real and magnificent then as it did now.

Tess wondered, not for the first time, if they were still transitionals, their bodies long dead, their individual consciousness spinning illusions. Her gasps and soft moans, his rapid breath against her neck, the delicious sensations of his mouth and hands, the electricity that shot through her: how could this *not* be real?

She reached behind her and laced her fingers across the back of his neck, drawing his mouth closer to the curve of her shoulder. He slipped more deeply inside of her and began to move, slowly and deliberately, his hands slipping over her soapy breasts, her soapy stomach, between her thighs. She turned her head and his mouth found hers. Their tongues dueled, the water pounded over them, and it went on so long that the heat inside of her built to almost unbearable levels, until she was a nuclear reactor in meltdown.

Afterward, they clung to each other. She knew he felt as disturbed about recent events as she did. "Clooney, do you ever wonder if we're actually dead?"

Ian drew his fingers through her wet hair and she tilted her head back and looked up at him, into the dark pools of his eyes. "I hope you're kidding, Slim."

"Only half."

He kissed her, then turned off the shower. Beads of water rolled over his eyelids, out onto the tips of his eyelashes and perched there for an instant like high divers, then dropped onto his cheeks. "So we've lived the last four plus years in, what, *The Matrix*?"

Even *The Matrix*, she thought, couldn't accommodate the fact that Ian had actually been born in 1924 and that when he'd had a massive heart attack and died at the age of forty-four, in 1968, his soul had moved forward to 2008 and they had met and fallen for each other. When they began to emerge from their comas, their souls were snapped back into their bodies, in their respective times. Ian had remembered nearly everything; Tess had remembered nothing. But as she had slowly recovered her memories of what had happened while she was dead and comatose, as he had started to heal and put his life there in order, they had both known they needed to return to Esperanza in order to find each other.

If it hadn't been for Wayra, that never would have happened. The shifter, capable of moving through time, had brought Ian forward to 2008.

Now here they were, more than four years later, two people who would never have found each other if they hadn't died and ended up in Esperanza. She understood now that her father's death some years before that had been necessary in the greater scheme of things; he had paved the way. But even before Charlie had passed on, there had been forces at work in the background, connections she still didn't fully understand and probably never would.

"The Esperanza Matrix," she said with a quick laugh, just to show him she had been joking, that she knew the difference between illusion and reality.

The irony was that a man born in 1924 had so fully adapted to life in the twenty-first century that he could reference *The Matrix*. But what shocked her was that Ian understood as well as she did that until they had died, they each had been living in a kind of cultural matrix, blinded by their limited perceptions of what was possible.

"Here's how I figure it." He opened the stall door, grabbed a pair of towels off the rack, tossed one to her. "If we're dead and are having such great sex and are faced with perplexing and strange mysteries, then death isn't a problem for me. The world's norm is not *my* norm."

With that, he snapped his towel at her ankles, a small biting sting, and darted out of the shower and into the bedroom before she could retaliate.

Did other couples in this city have these weird conversations? She toweled herself dry, wrapped a second towel around her wet hair, and glanced at herself in the full-length mirror. "Hey, Ian?"

He popped his head through the doorway. "Yeah?"

"Do I look fat?"

His eyes slipped up and down her reflection, then turned to her actual body, exploring her as intimately as his hands had moments ago. "Oh, sure, horrendously fat."

"Seriously. I bought enough food for both of us, but I was so hungry I ate everything."

"I seem to recall that you've always eaten like that. Your metabolism burns it up. At least you didn't drink my coffee," he teased. "We should grab a cab in about twenty minutes to get to the café on time. Bring your car keys so we can pick up our cars."

Tess stood in front of the mirror a while longer, toweling her hair dry and turning from one side to another, examining herself in the mirror. Okay, so she wasn't fat. But she *felt* fat. Then again, she'd just stuffed her face, so of course she felt fat.

"Forget it, get moving," she muttered.

2.

In the morning light, the grounds around the Café Taquina looked like a war zone, Tess thought. *Stuff* littered the ground—handbags, shoes, cans, bottles, loose change, jackets, sweaters, plates, and glasses. No corpses: the dead had been removed.

Half a dozen cop cars were parked inside the area that had been cordoned off last night. She also saw a van from the science department at the University of Quito and another from the local forensics lab. Journalists, many of them from neighboring towns, and camera crews congregated just beyond the forbidden area. A few stray cats and dogs skulked about.

"Amigos," someone shouted behind them, and Tess and Ian both turned around.

Diego Garcia strode toward them, a handsome, energetic young man with a bounce to his walk, a quick smile, and dark eyes like those of a child, wide, curious, vibrant. He threw his arms around them both, hugging them hello. "They're about to run the plates on cars left here last night. If you give me the keys, I'll have the cars moved out of here before that happens."

Tess and Ian turned their keys over to Diego, he excused himself and went over to one of the other cops, and returned a few minutes later. He handed them each an ID badge. "Clip these to your jackets. You're now experts from the University of Quito."

They put on the badges and followed Diego around the yellow crime tape toward the steps to the café's rear deck. Choppers kept circling, Diego's radio crackled with voices, a crisp wind blew across the empty parking lot.

As they neared the steps, Diego said, "Engineers are conducting tests to find out if the deck is safe to walk on. Until we know for sure, we can't go any farther than the top step. But you'll be able to get plenty of photos from there."

Tess didn't have to climb to the top step to see the ruin—overturned tables and chairs, a blanket of shattered glass, silverware, shoes, jackets, scraps of papers and napkins fluttering across the debris. Midway across the deck, everything simply dropped away into nothingness. Floor gone, railing gone, roof gone, wooden planks gone, heaters, lights, tables, chairs, everything *gone*. It looked just as Illary had described it, as if a mammoth eraser had rubbed it all away. But instead of the blackness, the erased area was now a blinding white that reflected sunlight like a mirror, like smooth glass, like the surface of a still lake. It flowed erratically downhill, as if some weaving drunk had splashed luminous white paint from side to side as he stumbled around. Here and there stood a lonely pine tree or a bush or a flower bed that hadn't been swallowed up.

"Jesus," Ian whispered, and started taking videos of the area.

Tess snapped several dozen photos. "Why hasn't this part of the deck just crumbled away?" she asked. "How can it still be standing? It's not connected to anything."

"That's what the engineers are trying to determine," Diego said. "But they can't get too close to the erased area. Watch."

Diego moved to the outside of the railing, onto a strip of trampled grass, scooped up a handful of pebbles and tossed them out into the glistening whiteness where the hill had once stood. As the pebbles hit the bright surface, it crackled and popped, then the pebbles disappeared. "Where'd those stones go? Huh?" Diego moved quickly back to the steps.

"The same place Javier went," Ian said.

"And where's that, Ian?" Diego asked.

"I don't know. But when the blackness swallowed his legs, he said they were *gone,* that he couldn't feel them."

"But what the *fuck* does that mean?" Diego's voice turned hoarse, scared, and he rocked toward Ian, almost in his face. "Why's this happening? Is it going to happen elsewhere, too?" Then he shook his head and thrust his hands in his jacket pockets. "Sorry. Lots of questions, no answers."

"What's the official explanation for what happened here, Diego?" asked Tess.

Diego's expression tightened. "Mayor Torres instructed the department to say nothing until the science *muchachos* have done their thing. They're getting high electromagnetic readings around that." He gestured toward the disappeared area. "All that whiteness is like an . . . apparition."

"They can't keep this under wraps," Ian said. "There were at least a hundred people here last night, witnesses. And you can multiply that many times with cell photos and videos, Diego. No surprise that the rumor mill about *brujos* has jammed into overdrive."

Diego nodded. "I know, my friend. I know. One of my cousins was here last night. And now my wife is taking our two kids and her parents out of the city for a few days. Down to Quito. I told her she's overreacting, that there's no proof *brujos* are behind what happened here."

Tess moved along the outside of the railing, just as Diego had done moments ago, and got to within a few feet of where the erasure began. She felt strangely disoriented by the spatial void the reflected light created, so she wrapped one arm around a vertical post to anchor herself before she snapped more photos.

An odd, cloying odor seemed to emanate from the erasure, a smell like ripe fruit that had been too long in the sun and heat. And she thought she could feel the post straining, trembling beneath what she sensed was a tremendous stress. She quickly moved back along the strip of grass.

"Are the photos going into tomorrow's edition?" Diego asked.

"That's the plan," Tess replied.

Ian added, "We've got the online edition up already. But we'll update it later today."

"Then the shit's probably hitting the fan right now." Just as Diego said that, his cell rang. He glanced at the number. "What'd I tell you? It's Mayor Torres. I'd better take this."

As he walked away from them, the cell pressed to his ear, Tess whispered, "Ian, take a look at this." She held out the camera and clicked through the photos she'd taken. "You see it?"

"Just sunlight glinting off the erased area, trees on the right . . . holy shit. What *is* that? Shadows?"

"I don't know. It's like a phantom image within the erasure." Tess clicked through the rest of the photos, and the image was present in most of them, but didn't get any clearer. "Let's drive down to the bottom of the hill and get some pictures from there."

"Sounds good," Ian agreed.

But as they approached Diego, his body suddenly lurched, he dropped his cell, his fists flew to his eyes, and a hoarse, terrible sound issued from him. Then he fell to his knees and gripped his thighs and rocked back and forth, back and forth, his shoulders jerking right, left, backward, forward. He looked as if he were having a seizure. Tess and Ian glanced at each other; they both knew what was happening. By the time Diego's head snapped up again, an oily blackness covered even the whites of his eyes.

When Diego stood without twitching, without any facial tics, Tess understood that a *brujo* fully controlled him.

"Ricardo here. Sorry to intrude like this," he said in Diego's voice, then thrust out his hand. "Mr. Ritter, it's a pleasure."

"First Dominica and now her brother? You gotta be kidding me. Why don't you spooks just admit you're dead and move on to hell or wherever."

"We know we're dead, Ian. You don't mind if I call you by your first name, do you?"

"Not at all, Richie. Hey, Slim, that's a pretty close interp of Ricardo, isn't it?"

"Only if you add *asshole* at the end of it," she said.

"She's pissed off at me," Ricardo said. "For scaring her like I did. For licking her neck. She tastes mighty good, Ian."

"Get to your point, Richie," Ian snapped.

"My point is quite simple, actually. We want the same things that you do. An Esperanza just as lovely and whole as it is now. We're on the same side. No one in my tribe has seized any resident or tourist in this city since my sister's defeat."

"Except for right now," Tess said. "And that waiter and the priest."

"That was just to give you a message. We take our physical pleasures from hosts in other cities and countries now."

Ian laughed. "And that's supposed to make it okay?"

Diego's face turned hard, his eyes flashed with anger. "It means that as far as Esperanza is concerned, *brujos* want the same things you do."

"Only because you're empowered by the city," Tess said.

"As are you. And the chasers."

"If we want the same thing," Tess said, "then why did you erase most of the hillside and the deck and injure and kill dozens?" Accuse to clarify: a good FBI tactic.

"We didn't. Talk to your father, Tess."

The cries of a hawk caused him to drop his head back and shade his eyes as he peered upward. An instant later, a dark form shot onto the steps and landed in front of Diego. Teeth bared, the black Lab instantly shifted into its human form and Wayra said something in Quechua. The only word Tess understood was "Ricardo."

Ricardo said, "Let's say what we have to say in English, Wayra, so our gringo friends understand it all."

Wayra sniffed noisily at the air, turning his head right, left, then leaned into Diego's face. "You smell the same, Ricardo. Like roadkill. The centuries haven't changed you."

Tess had her hands in the pockets of her jacket and felt something she was sure hadn't been there last night, when she'd been wearing the jacket, or even earlier this morning when she'd put it on before leaving Wayra's place. She ran her thumb around the edges of it, felt the cool aluminum, and knew that somewhere on the front of it were her dad's initials. Yes, right there, her thumb found the grooves of the initials: C.L. Her dad's Zippo lighter. Or a duplicate of it. *Thanks, Dad, what the hell am I supposed to do with this?* Had he slipped this in her jacket pocket last night at Wayra's? If so, why hadn't she felt it then?

"I strongly urge you to have a heart-to-heart with the chaser council, Wayra," said Ricardo. "You have pull with them. Most of them respect you. And all of them are scared shitless of you and your wife. They think you two are, let's see, what're the words I heard? *'Unpredictable, evil, not like us, selfish . . .'*"

Wayra chuckled. "Sounds like Newton and Maria and maybe Simon. What do you want?"

Ricardo threw his arms out, a gesture that encompassed all the erasure, the strange emptiness. "Isn't it *fucking obvious*? The chasers intend to disappear Esperanza. If you and Charlie Livingston put pressure on them, they may back off. We want the same thing—human, shifter, *brujo*. We want to be left in peace to draw upon the power of this beautiful and magical city."

Wayra rolled his eyes and laughed, a sharp, ugly sound. "You were always a lousy liar, Ricardo."

Tess and Ian exchanged a glance. She mouthed, *Charlie's Zippo in my pocket,* and hoped Ian understood what she'd said—and what it implied. She could see that pulse beating at his throat, could see that his hands were fisted, and knew that in the next few moments, he would hurl himself at Diego in an attempt to drive the *brujo* out.

"If you release Diego's body," Wayra said, "I'll talk to them."

"Aw, please." Ricardo shook his head and clicked his tongue against his teeth. "You disappoint me, Wayra."

Except that it was Diego's head that Tess saw, Diego's voice that she heard, Diego's face that grimaced.

"Wayra, Wayra, always the negotiator. I suspect you'll talk to them regardless and, quite frankly, I'm the one in a position of power here."

"What do you want?" Ian barked. "What the fuck is it that you really want, Ricardo?"

"Besides your lady friend there, Ian? When're you two going to get married, anyway? My tribe has been waiting for that so we could seize your guests. That's how we *brujos* are. Eternally fucked up and beyond repair." His eyes flicked to Wayra. "Your position of power, my shifter friend, is down there with amoebas. Say bye-bye to adopted son."

Diego gasped, his eyes bulged in their sockets, rolled back into his skull, and then a drop of blood spilled from his right eye and slipped down his cheek.

This fucker is going to bleed him out, Tess thought, and brought out her father's Zippo, snapping the lid the way he did, snapping it fast, hard, trusting that her dad had a good reason for causing it to materialize in her jacket pocket. Then she aimed it at Diego and ran her thumb back over the roller and a tremendous flame shot out, a flame so far beyond the ability of this lighter that she knew her dad had arranged it. She kept flicking it, and with every flick, the fire burned hotter, more brightly.

Diego threw his hands to his face and stumbled back, shrieking. Richie Asshole leaped from the top of Diego's skull, a discolored smudge in the sunlight, like a puff of dark smoke. Tess's hand jerked upward, the flame now so hot and large she felt its heat against her face. But the puff of dark smoke had evaporated, and Wayra rushed toward Diego's crumpled body.

3.

Wayra lifted Diego's head into his arms, and struggled to ignore the beads of blood trailing from beneath his eyes, seeping from his ears, the corners of his mouth. He tried not to shriek, scream, rage, attack. Diego wasn't dead. He was only compromised. He kept telling himself this, over and over again.

If I turn him, he'll be healed, freed . . .

"No." His wife spoke before she had shifted fully.

Wayra's head snapped up. "Shifter blood can save him."

"And it will change his life irreparably, forever. Leo can help him." Illary stood before Wayra, fully human now, her smartphone already pressed to her ear. "He has treated others through the years."

When Leo answered, she turned away from Wayra, and he looked down at the young man whose head was cradled in his arms. After his parents were seized and bled out by *brujos* eighteen years ago, Diego had stopped talking. Wayra adopted him, a request Diego's parents had made of him, and even though Diego functioned and went to school and made excellent grades, he didn't speak for three years. His first words after that long silence were, *I'm not like you, why not?*

Diego was the son Wayra never had, couldn't have. As soon as Wayra had been turned centuries ago, he had become sterile. When Illary had been turned two thousand years ago, she could no longer conceive.

Shifter blood and DNA assured the survival of the species by *turning* humans, not through procreation.

When Wayra had returned from Cedar Key with Illary, she and Diego had hit it off immediately. Now they had dinner every Sunday with Diego and his family, and he and Illary had adopted grandchildren.

Wayra ran his thumbs over the drops of blood on Diego's cheek, wiping them away. He kept talking quietly, speaking to the essence of Diego. Diego stirred, was no longer bleeding from his eyes and ears, but didn't regain consciousness. Wayra couldn't stand it anymore and bit into his own wrist, then squeezed drops of his shifter blood into Diego's mouth and hoped it would sustain him until he could give him more.

When Leo arrived, he knelt next to Diego, took his vital signs. He tugged down the lower lids of Diego's eyes, examined his ears, the inside of his mouth. "The external bleeding seems to have stopped, but his blood pressure is low, so he may be bleeding internally. I'm going to get him started on an IV and admit him to intensive care. Has his family been notified?"

"*I'm* his family," Wayra said sharply.

"No siblings? Wife? Kids?"

"He has a wife and kids, but I think they may be on their way to Quito," Wayra said.

"I'll call his wife," Illary said.

Leo started an IV, fitted the bag of fluid on a portable pole, then examined Diego again. "How long did this *brujo* have him?"

"Maybe ten minutes," Wayra replied.

"Ten minutes too long," Leo murmured, and got on his cell phone. "He's probably got the *brujo* bacteria in his blood. We'll treat it with antibiotics. Was it the same *brujo* who terrorized Tess?"

"Yes," Ian replied.

"So now they've started seizing hosts again?" Leo asked.

Not yet, Wayra thought. What Ricardo had done to Diego was for Wayra's benefit, just to remind him that *brujos* could seize the people Wayra loved and bleed them out if they wanted to. "Maybe not," Wayra said. "May I ride in the ambulance with him?"

"Of course," Leo replied. "I'll meet you at the hospital."

Just then, Tess and Lauren led a pair of medics into the thicket. "Speculation out there is running wild," Tess said. "All those journalists are from elsewhere. I told them Diego slipped and hit his head."

"We're ready for him in the ambulance, Leo," Lauren said. "And intensive care has his room ready."

Leo nodded. "Okay, let's move him onto the stretcher. Lauren, can you ride with him and Wayra?"

"You bet."

"Tess, Ian and I will follow in our cars," Illary said.

Diego moaned softly when the medics moved him. The sound tore Wayra apart and he quickly grasped Diego's hand and spoke to him softly in Quechua, assuring him that he would be okay, that he was already healing.

As they emerged from the trees, people outside the cordoned area surged forward, shouting questions. Wayra ignored them and hurried along behind the stretcher. Before they reached the ambulance, a police car sped into the area, lights flashing, and screeched to a stop alongside them. Martin Torres, the mayor, swung his short, plump legs out of the car and hurried over to Wayra. His squirrel cheeks puffed out, he whipped his sunglasses off his face and motioned toward the stretcher. "What the hell happened here, Wayra?"

"Nice to see you, too, Martin. Diego was seized by a *brujo,* is now unconscious, and for a rundown on his physical condition, I suggest you speak to Dr. Ordeño. I'm riding with Diego to the hospital."

"*Brujos?*" Torres took personal umbrage at the mere suggestion that *brujos* had returned to Esperanza. "There aren't any *brujos* in this city."

"Diego was seized and the *brujo* started to bleed him out," Wayra snapped. "So yes, they're here. If you were doing your job, you'd know that. And the public should be told about this electromagnetic fluctuation. It's all going to hit the newspapers, so why not get a jump on it?"

Torres whipped off his sunglasses, jammed them onto the top of his head, and rocked onto the balls of his feet, leaning toward Wayra, who towered over him. "Don't tell me how to do my goddamn job, Wayra."

He poked Wayra in the chest. "You and your shifter wife are meddling in police business. I could lock you up just for that."

Their enmity dated back a decade, to the day Dominica had seized Torres's wife while she and Wayra were in a café. She had demanded that Wayra make love to her then and there. Wayra pushed to his feet and walked away and Dominica had bled out Torres's wife.

"But you won't," Wayra said, and knocked the mayor's hand away.

He loped over to the ambulance, climbed inside, and one of the medics shut the door. Lauren had just finished taking Diego's blood pressure. "His pressure is way too low, Wayra. Would your shifter blood help him?"

"I gave him a few drops orally. But he could use more."

"Do you have to turn him to do that?"

"No. But if I could get some of my blood directly into his body, it would accelerate the healing."

"A transfusion?"

"Yes."

"I'll have to type your blood and his and then . . ."

"I'm O, Lauren. Diego is A positive."

"You're sure?"

"Yes."

She thought a moment, eyeing her supplies, then nodded. "Get on that other cot."

As the ambulance sped through the city, siren wailing, Wayra's blood flowed into Diego's body. He shut his eyes, vaguely aware of Lauren's voice, of her movements.

Just as his shifter blood had enabled him to survive the stab wounds that Ricardo had inflicted all those years ago, he hoped his blood would now save Diego.

As they neared the hospital, Lauren stopped the transfusion and removed the needle from Wayra's arm. "He got about half a pint, Wayra. You think it's enough?"

"I don't know. Let's play it by ear."

Wayra sat up and looked over at Diego. "His color already looks better."

"Yeah, it does." She took Diego's pressure again. "His pressure has risen slightly, too. Good signs. I'll make sure he gets settled in his room. You'll have to fill out some paperwork." She opened a small fridge, brought out a container of orange juice and handed it to him. "Drink that, so you don't feel light-headed."

As he sipped at the juice, Lauren peeled off her gloves and updated Diego's info on her iPad. Wayra noticed her gorgeous sapphire. "Congratulations," he said. "When did *that* happen?"

Lauren glanced up, eyes beaming, and held out her hand, admiring the ring. "Last night."

"Fantastic. Does Tess know yet?"

"Things have been so nuts, I haven't had a chance to tell her." She set the iPad down and sat at the other end of Wayra's cot. "What do you think is going on, Wayra? Last night when I saw Charlie, he said he was on his way to an emergency council meeting."

"From what Ricardo said, it sounds like some of the chasers have joined Darth Vader's dark side. But I don't believe a damn thing a *brujo* says."

"Some of them may have," Diego said hoarsely, and tried to sit up.

Wayra moved quickly toward him. "*Tranquilo, chico.* Don't try to sit up yet. We're nearly at the hospital. Why do you say that about the chasers?"

"When . . . when Ricardo seized me . . . I found information inside him, just as he found information inside of me, Wayra. He . . . Ricardo . . . spies on the chasers, eavesdrops. At least two of them, Newton and . . . Maria, seem to be the . . . force behind whatever they're doing. Ricardo speculates he might even be able to . . . to *recruit* them. He also thinks . . . there's a traitor somewhere among them."

Or that was what Ricardo wanted Diego to believe, Wayra thought. "A traitor to whom?"

"I don't know."

"You rest."

"No time to rest," Diego said, and struggled to sit up again.

"Nope." Lauren gently pushed Diego back again. "Stay put. Do you know why you've improved, Diego?"

Diego's handsome face lit up and he motioned toward Wayra. "Because he . . . shared his shifter blood with me. I think you and Illary . . .

must donate some of your blood. In case . . . the city falls under siege again."

Wayra looked at Lauren, who flashed a thumbs-up. "I'll see what I can arrange. I think we're going to need every advantage we can find."

Wayra hated to admit it, but he suspected she was right.

Six
What Happens at La Pincoya

1.

Outside the *Expat*'s picture window, shadows lengthened and thinned, streetlights winked on in the park across the street, afternoon surrendered to evening. The reflected lights from the small Christmas tree in the office flickered and danced in the glass. Ian tried to ignore the rumbling in his stomach and turned back to the computer and his update on events at the Café Taquina.

The problem was simple: he wasn't sure who or what was behind the events at the Taquina. *Brujo?* Chaser? Something else? He lacked definitive proof for all of the above.

He decided to present all possibilities, but concentrated on the theory the scientists from the university had provided: an anomaly had occurred that might be tied to the wild fluctuations of electromagnetic energy around the café.

The problem with the scientific viewpoint—which explained nothing—was that everything in this city was an anomaly, a blip in the consciousness of Esperanza. But at the moment, he couldn't figure out how else to write the article.

It took him a while. Once he had a version he liked he started uploading the photos he'd taken of those gleaming white surfaces where there had once been hillsides and the café's rear deck. But the Internet was sluggish and it took forever for just a single photo to upload.

Since the defeat of Dominica's tribe, the Internet had been free to everyone who lived within a fifty-mile radius of the city. Mayor Torres and his city council had deemed it to be vital to the security of the city, so a tourist tax and part of the sales tax paid for it. And usually, the connection was fast, flawless. Ian now found himself jumping to the paranoid conclusion that Ricardo—or his tribe, if it existed—was responsible for the sluggishness.

He tried uploading the photo with his browser, but the spinning beach ball on his Mac indicated it was going to take a while. Ian pushed away from his desk and went in search of something to eat. The office consisted of three rooms—the main work area that looked out onto the narrow cobbled street and the park and plaza on the other side; a small room with a table, chairs, and a couch for their infrequent editorial meetings; and the employee kitchen.

Since he and Tess lived in a third-story apartment above the office, he rarely came into the employee kitchen and was shocked at how much food was jammed in the fridge. All sorts of veggies and fruits, two loaves of bread, three types of cheese, two jars of organic peanut butter, three jars of jam, bottled water, all kinds of fresh juices, frozen fish, tofu meatballs, spaghetti sauces. Where had all this stuff come from?

It suddenly reminded him of how the fridge had looked during his ex-wife's pregnancy, but back then, the shelves held sweets—cookies, chocolates, soft drinks, *crap*. Tess, her niece, and her mother ate more healthfully than his ex-wife ever had, but still, the amount of food in the fridge was excessive even for the Livingstons. Maybe this was part of Tess's plan to make employees feel at home. *My house is your house,* mi casa es su casa, *my food is your food.*

Ian made himself a salad, and just as he was about to call Tess, she called him. "Hey, Clooney, I just left the hospital. Leo says Diego is on the mend. I'm on my way to the store. What do you want for dinner?"

"The fridge in the employee kitchen has enough for about eighteen dinners. Who bought all this stuff, Tess?"

"Me."

"Why? Maddie and Sanchez and your mom don't eat here very often and most of the time it's just the two of us."

"I get hungry, okay? And since when do I have to justify what I buy? How about trout?"

Testy, he thought, and decided it wasn't worth arguing about. "Sure. Trout is fine."

"Traffic's heavy. I'll be home in an hour or so."

"I'll cook up some mushrooms and corn. We need some wine."

"Got it on my list."

"Love you, Slim."

But she'd already hung up.

He wolfed down the salad while standing there, took a bottle of water from the fridge, then returned to the main room. Wayra was sitting in front of the computer, a large backpack on the floor behind the chair, his dark hair pulled back in a ponytail, suggesting that he was in work mode.

"Your photos uploaded. The article is powerful, amigo." He swiveled around in the chair, his large, bony hands resting against his thighs. "You say just enough."

"Or not enough. You think it's true the chaser council intends to take Esperanza back into the nonphysical?"

"Yes, if we can believe what a *brujo* says."

"Is it even *possible*?"

"Not without killing everyone."

"Jesus, Wayra."

"Yeah, I know. I've been thinking about it, Ian. We can take care of this problem at the source."

A conundrum. Wayra often spoke like this, as though Ian could divine what he was actually implying. Most of the time, Ian guessed. This time, he couldn't even do that. "I don't even know what you're talking about."

"The Pincoya."

"An abandoned hotel? What's there?"

"The *brujos* in Ricardo's tribe are using the Pincoya as a portal to other parts of the world where they seize hosts and wreak havoc."

"So it's true? He actually has a tribe? Of millions?"

"Yes. But you're missing the point, Ian. Why do *brujos* need a portal at all? They've always thought themselves to locations, just like chasers. What's changed? Is it that Ricardo's tribe doesn't know how to do this? Have they forgotten?"

"You're the expert, you tell me."

Wayra's eyes impaled Ian. "The story is evolving, my friend, and doing so in unprecedented ways." Wayra crouched beside the backpack on the floor, unzipped it, and pulled open the sides so Ian could see the explosives, flares, and a small pack that held grenades, rags, cans of Drano, matches, lighters. "If we set fire to the Pincoya and blow up their portal, then Ricardo's tribe can't get into Esperanza." He picked up a can of Drano. "It's flammable and effective. We used it on Cedar Key. The—"

"Wayra. I'm a journalist, not a terrorist."

The shifter looked annoyed. "These pricks don't give a shit what you are. One of them has already tried to choke Tess, has issued an ultimatum to Charlie, taunted you, seized Diego and put him in the hospital, and thousands of them are using this portal to move into other cities and countries where they seize the living. If we blow up their portal, it seals it off and annihilates a bunch of them."

Annihilate. When a *brujo* essence met fire, its soul was freed to move on in the afterlife. Ian supposed that to a *brujo,* it was the equivalent of annihilation.

"You're getting even, Wayra. Because of what Ricardo did to Diego. That's dangerous."

"Don't try to psychoanalyze me," Wayra snapped.

"I'm just voicing the obvious. Diego's your adopted son. I get it, okay?"

"You with me or not?"

Ian visualized the abandoned hotel. Set back from the road, it occupied nearly an acre of land and was surrounded by fields. If they blew it up, the fields could catch fire, but it seemed unlikely that anything else would be jeopardized. "Where'd you get all this stuff?"

"Diego arranged the weapons."

"He believes you, in other words."

"Yes, Ian. He believes me. He doesn't have any reason not to."

"Okay, so we blow up their portal. Fine. But then the *brujos* in Esperanza turn on *us.*"

Wayra, crouched in front of his arsenal of explosives, just stared at Ian, who finally looked away. When he had chosen to stay here in Esperanza, aware of all it represented, he had known he was entering into a tenuous life plan. He had known it meant he was living on borrowed time unless he played by certain rules.

The heart problem that had killed him and first brought him here as a transitional soul was no longer an issue. The city had cured him, just as it had cured Leo's leukemia. But if he left, if he was gone from the city for several months, what might happen? This was why Leo hadn't left since he'd arrived twenty-plus years ago.

"We annihilate them before they come after us," Wayra said.

"I don't mean they come after just you and me. If this Ricardo really does have a huge tribe, he might turn them loose on the city just for revenge."

Wayra swiveled around in the chair and stared out through the front window, watching the pedestrians hurry through the chilly evening air. Across the street, Ian noticed that the lights in the park created long, narrow shadows that fell across the cobblestones, the fountain, the pedestrians. A low, thin fog drifted across the park. Ordinary fog, not *brujo* fog, he thought.

"Yes? No?" Ian asked. "Maybe?"

Wayra swiveled around again, facing Ian. "He might. But understand this, Ian. Ricardo's tribe isn't like Dominica's. Most of her tribe lived in a virtual city outside of Esperanza. My bet is that most of Ricardo's ghosts are scattered across the globe and they come and go through the portal. Like I said, they either don't know how to will themselves great distances or they've lost the ability to do this. If so, that's a whole other mystery. If we destroy the portal, we're cutting Ricardo off from the majority of his tribe."

"And if it works? And if the chaser council is behind what happened at the café, will they leave Esperanza alone?"

"I don't know. But it's insanity to even consider taking the city back into the nonphysical. Everyone will be killed. Granted, I never supported this city being brought into the physical world. But I didn't have a vote, I'm not a chaser. I live here now, though, and I'm willing to fight for my continued existence here."

"You know where in the Pincoya this portal is located?"

"Yes."

"And you're proposing we just walk into this place? While all these ghosts are darting around inside, moving back and forth through the portal? I don't think so, Wayra. Tess can't be seized, but I can. And so can you."

"Have you forgotten about the network of tunnels all over this city where people used to take refuge during a *brujo* attack? There're tunnels under the Pincoya. That's how we'll set the explosives. And keep several of these on you." He held out three flares. "A *brujo* comes near you, just point, aim, and let her rip."

Ian set the flares next to his computer. "Can't this wait until after Tess gets home and we eat? Join us for trout, Wayra." It sounded lame and cowardly, Ian thought, but he really didn't want any part of this.

The shifter shook his head and tapped the face of his watch. "In about thirty minutes, thousands of *brujos* will convene on the portal. I don't know why they convene at this hour in the evening, but they do."

"I'll take your word for it. But if they convene every night, let's wait until tomorrow night. By then, we'll have more information about what's actually going on."

"By tomorrow night, amigo, half the city may have disappeared."

"You're exaggerating. And if you've known about this all along, why haven't you ever said anything?"

"I just found out a few hours ago. Remember Pedro Jacinto, the priest from Punta?"

Ian would never forget Pedro. "Without his help, we wouldn't have defeated Dominica's tribe."

"Well, he's retired from the church in Punta and is living in the foothills just outside the city, with his brother and his family. He's been observing these *brujos* for weeks. He called earlier to let me know he'd seen this blackness in a field a block from his brother's house. The area is small, but half the field is gone. Here's the video he sent me."

Wayra handed Ian his phone. He clicked on the video, a full three minutes of darkness that moved like a wall of sludge across the field. It was the same phenomenon they'd seen last night at the cafe, the same shit that had pursued Ian as he'd made his way along a spit of earth on the outside of the deck railing.

It swallowed everything—grass, weeds, stones, earth, trees, bits of plastic, bottles, cans, *junk*. The video paused, then skipped ahead seven minutes. The blackness had been replaced by that blinding whiteness.

"What'd Pedro do about it?" Ian asked, passing the phone back to Wayra.

"Nothing. It stopped on its own, no one was hurt or killed. But the point is that someone or something is consuming bits and pieces of Esperanza. Whether it's chasers or *brujos* or something else, we can't allow it to continue."

Ian rubbed his hands over his jeans. He was an expat in this country, this city. Esperanza had welcomed him, cured him, enabled him and Tess to build a life together, to start a newspaper, and he had been happier here in the last four and a half years than he had been at any other period in his life. But the fact remained that he wasn't a native and didn't feel it was right for him to meddle in something like this.

When he said as much to Wayra, the shifter looked at him like he'd lost his mind, then howled with laughter. "You're kidding, right? Of course you are."

"Fuck off, Wayra."

"Wow. You're not kidding." Wayra moved restlessly around the front room, his long legs eating up the square footage in seconds flat. He combed his fingers back through his hair, shook his head, muttered to himself in Quechua, Spanish, French, then something that sounded like Greek or Russian.

In English, he finally said, "I don't even know where to begin. So I'll start with the bottom line. *No one* is native to Esperanza, not even the people who were born here in the last five hundred years. You can't be native to a place that came from elsewhere, okay? We're all expats. That's what makes Esperanza so vibrant and magical. And if it hadn't been for you and Tess, this city would still be terrorized by Dominica and her goddamn minions. That alone makes you as native as any of us, Ian. So if you don't want to do this, fine. But don't give me some idiotic excuse about not wanting to get involved because you're not a native."

Ian tipped the bottle of water to his mouth, then turned and walked back into the kitchen. He put his empty salad bowl in the dishwasher, tossed the empty bottle in the recycling bin, and pressed the heels of his hands against his eyes. He felt like punching something. Everything Wayra had just said was true.

He slipped his iPhone from his pocket and texted Tess: *Eat dinner w/out me. Checking out stuff with Wayra.* Tess would be pissed. She would be arriving home with fresh trout, expecting to walk into an apartment that smelled like dinner. But no corn would be boiling in a pot on the stove, no mushrooms would be sautéed in any frying pan, no basket of warm bread would grace the table in front of the apartment windows that overlooked the city. No wine would be poured. No toasts would be made.

He hit Delete and scribbled an actual note. He folded it, pressed a strip of Scotch tape on the top, then returned to the front room. "Okay, I'm in. Next step." Ian shrugged on his jacket and slipped the flares in his pockets.

"I'll drive," Wayra said.

Once they were outside, Ian taped the note to the front of the *Expat*'s door, positioning it so Tess would see it when she glanced at the office on the way up the stairs to their apartment. He locked up and fell into step alongside Wayra.

"You're one stubborn guy," Wayra remarked. "I suspect that's what makes you a good journalist."

"And a difficult partner," Ian replied.

"She'll get over it, Tess always does."

Not always, Ian thought. Two summers ago, he and an Ecuadorian teacher had struck up a friendship while walking neighboring treadmills at the gym. Innocent enough, until they had found themselves at the same restaurant late one afternoon and had had drinks together. Although he was attracted to her and knew the attraction was mutual, nothing had ever happened. *Nothing.* No hug, no kiss, no sex, not even an exchange of e-mail. But when Tess had gotten wind of it, they'd had the biggest fight of their relationship and had nearly split up.

Ridiculous, but there you had it, one of the many weird permutations of their relationship.

Wayra drove his truck to Parque del Cielo, Park of the Heavens, the oldest park in Esperanza, the first piece of the city that had been brought into the physical world by the chasers. On the northern side was an old, spacious stone house, now a museum. To the west lay a fountain, the entrance to the tunnels lay to the east, and to the south grew a row of monkey puzzle trees. Just beyond it were dozens of cafés and restaurants. In the center of the park rose the famous ceiba tree, the only one in all of Esperanza, and the plaque in front of it identified it as such. One more anomaly. And because a symbol of the ceiba had appeared on that mysterious stone Wayra had shown them, Ian knew this was significant.

A man stood alone by the tree, his body a thin silhouette. "There's Pedro," Wayra said, pulling up to the curb at the south end. "He's gone through the tunnels under the Pincoya, I haven't. He'll take us in."

They grabbed their bags out of the backseat and got out. The priest greeted them both with a Latino *abrazo,* a kind of group hug. Pedro Jacinto was considerably shorter than either Ian or Wayra, and was thinner and grayer than Ian remembered. He wore jeans, a sweater, a leather jacket, and his clerical collar.

"Great to see you again, Pedro," Ian said.

"The pleasure is all mine, my friend. I need to show you both a few things before we head into the tunnels. Let's get to where there's more light."

They moved over to the fountain, where a street lamp illuminated the fountain's ancient stones, the statue of the Virgin Mary at the top of it, her hands outstretched, palms turned upward. Water bubbled up from her hands and cascaded down her body.

Beneath her feet, engraved into the stones, was the date the park had been brought into the physical world: *January 3, 1500.* Under this was a second date, something new: *December 21, 2012, 11:00 UTC.*

"What the hell." Ian pointed. "That's six days from now."

"That was the first thing I wanted to show you," Pedro said. "And it wasn't here yesterday."

Wayra leaned forward and ran his fingers over the engraving, sniffed at the stones, shook his head. "All I smell here is bird shit. But this engraving looks as old as the other one, so it was done by supernatural means. *Brujo,* chaser, other."

"But why a date six days from now?" Ian asked.

Pedro shrugged. "As a warning?"

"Or a promise," Ian murmured.

"We can't worry about it now." Pedro brought a folded sheet of paper from his pack, smoothed it open. "A floor plan of the building. Drawn from memory."

It looked precise and detailed to Ian, the rooms on the first and second floors labeled. "I'm pretty sure the portal is in the ballroom," Pedro said. "Inside a wall of mirrors."

"If your drawing is accurate," Ian said, "then the ballroom shares a wall with a storage closet and a bathroom. That looks like an ideal spot for explosives."

"Might be a bit too close to the portal," Wayra said. "I think it would be safer for us here." He indicated a garage. "We set the explosives, get back behind the steel door and into the tunnel, then detonate them."

Pedro said, "You realize that even if we're successful with the explosives, we don't have any guarantee that it will shut down a supernatural construct like this."

"Nothing is guaranteed," Wayra said. "But since fire will annihilate *brujos,* I suspect it will shut down the portal, too."

"Is this a stairwell?" Ian asked, tapping a tall, rectangular area that Pedro hadn't labeled.

Pedro nodded. "The building actually has two staircases—the main stairs you see as you walk in the front door of the hotel, then an employee staircase in the kitchen. That's my first choice for explosives. We can get into the kitchen easily from the tunnel, then into the stairwell."

"I'll set the explosives," Wayra said. "You two create the distraction by starting a fire in the kitchen, then toss grenades through the windows to keep them away from the building. They won't come anywhere near fire or explosions. While you're doing that, I'll get into the stairwell."

"The police will be all over the place in five minutes," Ian remarked.

"I can do this in under five minutes," Wayra said.

"How many grenades do you have?" Pedro asked.

"Fifteen. And we've got three flares apiece." Wayra unzipped his pack, removed the smaller pack inside that held the grenades, rags, Drano, and matches, and handed it to Ian.

Pedro gave them both LED flashlights. "The green light is best once we're inside the building. In their natural forms, *brujos* can't see color."

Ian didn't want to be here, but he didn't feel like he could turn back now. He slung the bag over his shoulder. "Let's move."

Since the defeat of Dominica's tribe, the tunnels were no longer used as sanctuaries from *brujos*. But when inclement weather clamped down over the city, especially cold, driving rain, people tended to seek shelter and moved from one place to another through the tunnels. Electric carts were available—sometimes for free, sometimes for a nominal fee. Though it was cold tonight, the weather was pristine, the sky burning with stars. Ian figured the tunnels would be deserted.

2.

The air felt ten degrees cooler in the tunnels. Ian zipped up his jacket, turned on his flashlight. Small glowing lights ran down the center of the ceiling and on either side of the concrete walls, offering enough illumination to see the graffiti—a hastily scrawled record of *brujo* attacks, with dates, names of victims, pleas and prayers. Their footsteps punctuated the tight, eerie silence. The beams of their flashlights darted like mice along the earthen floor.

Here and there, Ian saw signs that directed pedestrians to various bus stops, plazas, or streets. Curves and forks in the tunnel were marked by religious statues and most of them held small offerings—bouquets of dried flowers, photographs, trinkets, coins, pieces of paper with names and prayers written on them. They were the only people down here.

The statue of the Virgin Mary they now approached was surrounded by flowers, wreaths, coins. The priest paused in front of her, withdrew a rosary from his pocket, and threaded it around the statue's fingers. Then he genuflected briefly and blessed himself. "She's the guardian of the tunnels. She remembers everything about the dark years."

Every three to five yards, they passed crumbling concrete steps that led up to steel doors. All the doors lacked handles and boasted round, gold-colored locks. "How're we going to get through a locked door?" Ian asked.

Pedro patted his pack. "We have options. You know where we are now?"

"No idea," Ian said.

"Forty feet below Calle de Milagros, the street where the Pincoya is located."

Street of Miracles. How appropriate, Ian thought. They would need a miracle to pull this off.

They turned down another tunnel, stopped in front of one of the steel doors. Like the others, it didn't have a handle, just a lock. Pedro unzipped his pack and brought out a small, thin tool that he handed to Wayra. "Amigo, your fingers are far more nimble than mine."

Ian shone the beam of his flashlight on the lock, Wayra inserted the tip of the tool, and within fifteen seconds, the door swung open. The air smelled *strange*. It vaguely reminded Ian of how old basements in Minnesota smelled in the midst of a humid summer, of mold, fecund earth. But beneath it lay another, thicker odor so foul he nearly gagged.

"The *brujo* stench," Wayra whispered. "It's everywhere. Flares out, ready. Turn off your flashlights, I'll keep mine on green, pointed at the floor."

Wayra went through the door first, moving slowly, cautiously, sniffing the air. Ian moved along behind him, the skin at the back of his neck prickling with apprehension. The priest shut the door, it clicked softly, and darkness closed over them, a coffin. As they climbed the stone steps, twenty-two of them, Ian counted, he kept his eyes on the soft green dot of light from Wayra's flashlight so he wouldn't trip over his own feet.

The stairs ended at a ramp that took them up another twenty feet. They stopped, Ian heard Wayra sniffing the air once more, then they moved forward again, into a narrow, windowless foyer. The green light exposed clumps of dust, dirt, and mold snuggled like mice in the corners of the walls. Wayra turned off the flashlight and they stood for a moment in the darkness, letting their eyes adjust.

Ian could see a soft, dim source of light through the foyer door and guessed it came from the Pincoya's kitchen windows. If he remembered correctly, the building was set back far enough from the road so that the illumination from the streetlights wouldn't be streaming through the glass.

"Give me a sixty-second head start," Wayra whispered. "Then move into the kitchen and start your fires."

He dashed out of the foyer and across the kitchen and vanished through the doorway on the other side, where the stairwell was. Ian and Pedro soaked rags with Drano and tossed them to the left and right of the doorway. Ian checked his watch.

"Okay, amigo," he whispered to Pedro.

The priest peered out, flashed Ian a thumbs-up. More hand gestures followed, then Pedro moved swiftly into the kitchen, lighting the saturated rags, splashing Drano everywhere. Ian peered around the doorjamb—and saw thin cotton curtains drawn across the kitchen windows. They billowed like sails in a breeze and suggested that one or all of the windows were either open or broken. Curtains would burn fast, the breeze would fan the flames. Ian darted forward.

The billowing curtains reminded him of something you might see in some old vampire film in the moments before the vampires appeared, a prop that set the scene, ramped up the fear factor, and had you gnawing on your knuckles before the eerie music kicked in. He'd seen plenty of those movies. In fact, movies were his best friends. Movies helped him, a man from 1968, acclimate to a world forty years in his future. Tess often marveled that he had adapted so quickly to twenty-first-century life, but he never would have been able to do it without movies. That visual input, he thought, was key. Just as it was now.

He set the curtains on fire and the flames consumed the fabric with shocking swiftness. He hurled one of the grenades through the burning curtains, the broken windows, and it exploded out in the driveway and set fire to the overgrown weeds. Ian spun around.

Flames now licked at the walls where Pedro had lit the saturated rags. The priest hurried across the kitchen, squirting Drano everywhere, and Ian raced to the gas stove and turned on all four burners. "Wayra, we're outta here!" he shouted.

Two bright orbs of light emerged from a section of wall that hadn't caught fire yet and dived straight for him. Ian didn't have a chance to pull out a flare, so he threw himself to the floor, a stupid move. But it bought him five or ten seconds—long enough for the priest to fire two flares. They struck the orbs and blew them apart.

More orbs appeared in the kitchen. Two, four, eight, twelve, twenty, a mathematical axiom, a growing army. Ian backpedaled toward the foyer, through the intense heat. "Wayra," Ian shouted again. "This place is going to blow!"

A swarm of orbs dropped out of the ceiling and the familiar *brujo* chant suffused the room. *Find the body, fuel the body, fill the body, be the body . . .* Ian fired two flares that incinerated half of them. The rest vanished through the ceiling again.

He and Pedro tore into the foyer, Ian pushed open the door and they fled down the ramp, then the steps, and burst through the steel door and into the tunnel. Less than a minute later, the percussive roar of an explosion ripped through the air. It sounded as if the tunnel were collapsing, caving in behind them. Ian and the priest sprinted forward, up and down the labyrinth of tunnels, retracing their steps. Dust filled the air.

The lights suddenly winked out, forcing them to stop and dig out their flashlights. Ian's heart pounded furiously, Pedro gasped for breath. "You okay?" Ian whispered.

"Ye . . . yes."

Flashlights on, they moved fast. Now and then, Pedro seemed to be on the verge of dropping from exhaustion and Ian took hold of his arm, supporting him. He knew they neared the park now, he smelled smoke, heard the wail of sirens and panicked shouts. Behind him, the collapsing cascade in the tunnel continued with thunderous roars and gathering dust.

When they stumbled out of the tunnel into the park, coughing, their eyes tearing, total chaos surrounded them, hundreds of people stampeding *toward* the Pincoya, not away from it, shouting that the place was on fire, there had been an explosion. "Shit," Ian said.

A cop moved quickly toward them, waving his arms. *"¡Epa, hombres, vete de allí!"* he shouted. *"El túnel está cerrado."*

The tunnel is closed. "Let's get the hell outta here," Ian whispered.

"Nos vamos." Pedro raised his hands, patting the air.

Ian grasped Pedro's arm and moved from the entrance to the closest bench. The cop tapped his club against his palm, following them, eyeing them for a long moment, then finally turned away. Maybe he had noticed Pedro's clerical collar and wasn't willing to threaten a priest. He called to some other cops, and they proceeded to block off the tunnel with orange cones and yellow crime tape and large red signs with white letters that read, PELIGRO. *Danger.*

"I think we better leave," Ian said quietly. "It won't be long before the police take down license-plate numbers for the cars around the park. And if they stop people and search their possessions . . ." Ian patted the bag over his shoulder. It still held grenades, and no telling what all was in the priest's bag.

"Café across the street," Pedro said, and they slowly made their way along the periphery of the crowd, behind the benches the priest used for support, and gradually made it to the curb.

Traffic on the one-way street had come to a complete standstill. Some drivers had gotten out of their cars to see what was going on, others were honking, and others had abandoned their cars and were moving into the park. Ian and Pedro threaded their way between the cars and took one of the many vacant tables on the deck. From the looks of it, people had abandoned their dinner and drinks and fled inside the building. Dozens of customers stood at the front windows inside the dining room, watching the chaos in the park.

Badly shaken, Ian quickly texted Wayra, but fifteen minutes later, he still hadn't replied, no one had taken their order, traffic hadn't moved, and more and more cops on foot and on horseback poured into the park, along the sidewalks, headed toward the Pincoya. He worried about their bags being searched. "Isn't there a church nearby?"

"South a few blocks."

"Let's head there. You rested enough to move on?"

"Yes. Definitely."

They rose simultaneously from their chairs, left the deck, and walked briskly toward the corner. Traffic on the side street was also stalled, horns blared, drivers shouted, cops on horseback moved among cars and people, trying to maintain some semblance of order. But at least the shadows here were thicker, darker, and no one stopped them, questioned them, or demanded to see what was inside their packs.

Seven
Wayra

The explosion in the kitchen took out half the staircase wall and hurled Wayra back. He slammed into the opposite wall and lost consciousness. When he came to, flames leaped everywhere, rolling clouds of smoke surrounded him, he couldn't see anything, could barely breathe. He grabbed on to the staircase railing, pulled himself upright, and raced up two flights of stairs, his arm pressed over his nose and mouth.

He ran into the first room on the third floor. Through the window, he saw thousands of bright, pulsating orbs darting toward the hotel. A dense bank of *brujo* fog spread out across the front of the property, close enough so that he could hear the *brujo* litany: *Find the body, fuel the body* . . . Wayra tore out of the room and up the hall, his pack slamming against his hip, and dashed into a room at the end of the corridor.

He turned on the flashlight and hurried over to a window that looked out over the adjacent field. The metal pegs in the window jamb prevented him from opening it. Wayra slammed his bag against the glass, shattering it, then climbed out onto a narrow ledge and ticked through his rapidly shrinking options.

He could take a few *brujos* into himself and survive. But any more than that would cause him to choke and probably die before his shifter immune system could kick in. He could slip back in time, but that option held no guarantees, never had, never would, and too much could go wrong. So he tightened the strap of his pack, securing it on his shoulder, and slipped over the lip of the ledge to a wider protrusion several feet below.

The *brujo* litany had grown much louder, they were dangerously close. He shone his flashlight below, back and forth, up and out, exploring.

Panic tightened like massive hands around his throat. The drop, he guessed, was about forty feet. He would prefer to make this jump in his shifter form, where he had more agility, greater accuracy, but there wasn't enough room on the ledge for him to shift. In his human form, he would survive the jump, but might break a few bones.

Then the beam of the flashlight struck a pile of garbage, some of it in plastic bags, some of it just loose. A tall pile.

Find the body, fuel the body . . .

Wayra clasped his fingers around the strap of his bag, sidled to the far right of the ledge, and leaped.

He landed hard on his feet in the pile of garbage, fell forward onto his hands and knees, and sank into the stink. The fetid odor rushed into his nose, an acrid something in the air burned his eyes. But nothing snapped, nothing broke. He hauled himself up, climbed out of the pile, and raced for cover in the adjacent field of tall weeds. As he ran, he pressed the remote-control device for the explosives he had set in the stairwell—and dived for cover.

He struck the ground hard, rolled, curled into a fetal position, arms covering his head. In the instant the explosives blew, he heard the screams of annihilated *brujos,* their torturous shrieks for forgiveness, salvation, redemption, resurrection. Then there was just a weird, blissful silence. Hundreds, maybe thousands, of hungry ghosts had just been freed to move on through the afterlife.

Wayra felt their collective essence drifting in the air around him like bits of dust in sunlight. Some were confused, others were pissed off, and some understood precisely what had happened and moved quickly forward in the afterlife. He supposed there were helpers every step of the way, but who were they? Chasers? Something else?

It was at this point that the big questions usually broke down for him. Despite the centuries he had lived, some questions remained unanswerable. Who or what was above the chasers? Was there an ultimate Source?

He leaped up and ran through a deserted playground. Already, he could see mounted cops and police vehicles headed toward the Pincoya. He circled back toward the park, but there were too many police around here to risk getting to his car. Wayra kept walking away from the park, the cops, the sirens, exposure. He called Illary.

She didn't answer.

He called Ian.

No answer.

He turned his cell phone off.

When he looked up, Ricardo stood there in a virtual form as an innocuous tourist in a floral shirt and jeans, with slicked-back gray hair, and a sleazy smile. Flanking him on either side were half a dozen members of his tribe.

"You want the death toll, Wayra?"

"Not really."

"More than thirteen fucking thousand and still counting. Gone, Wayra. All of them."

"That's barely a fraction of what your tribe and Dominica's seized over the centuries. Now they're free to move on and make their own choices."

"That's such propaganda crap," snapped a woman on Ricardo's left.

Her virtual form struck Wayra as creative—but odd. Her wild blond hair, long and curly, fell halfway down her back. Elaborate tattoos of a naked woman on horseback traveled the length of her bare arms from wrist to shoulder. Her stunning face was so perfect and gorgeous that Wayra guessed she had been unattractive in her last physical life.

"And you are . . . ?"

"Oh, Wayra, Wayra, how truncated your memory is," she said softly.

And she assumed the form she'd had in her last physical life, that of the homely woman he had rescued from a pyre of burning bodies during the plague years in Europe. She and her son had been barely alive and he had turned them in order to save them.

Naomi.

After he had turned them, he, Naomi, and her son had spent a decade together, wandering across Europe. Her son was never right in the head, and when he'd killed himself, not an easy feat for a shifter, Naomi had blamed Wayra. They had split up, and in the centuries since, he'd assumed she had perished. That much, at any rate, was correct. She had died—and subsequently joined the *brujos*.

"You joined *Ricardo*?" Wayra burst out laughing. "Oh, c'mon, you could've done better than this asshole, Naomi."

"Watch your mouth, shifter," Ricardo said, sliding his arm possessively around Naomi's shoulders. "Naomi and I have done well together."

"I have no history with him, no karma, nothing to work out," she said. "I want you to know that my son went mad after you turned us, Wayra. He was never the same. He hated being a shape shifter. And so did I."

"I saved your lives."

"You should have let us die in that fire."

"That's not what you said then."

"For Chrissake, Wayra," Ricardo burst out. "That was centuries ago."

"I was delirious," Naomi said angrily. "And you know what? I've enjoyed being a *bruja* and traveling with Ricardo and his tribe more than I ever liked traveling with you." Her right arm snapped upward, light shot from her fingertips, and pierced his chest.

An electrical shock drove him to his knees, something so horrifying and powerful that he couldn't defend himself. And when it stopped, he was doubled over, gasping for breath, his forehead pressed to the pavement.

"I've learned a few tricks over the centuries," she said with a laugh.

"Here's the deal," Ricardo said. "In retaliation for your taking out more than thirteen thousand of my tribe, we're going to seize an equal number from Esperanza."

"What fun that will be," Naomi said, clapping her hands like a child who has just been told she can have an ice-cream cone.

"And we're going to start with—"

Wayra shifted before she finished her sentence and took off through the field. The light that had pierced his chest seemed to have empowered him, certainly not Naomi's intent. His chest ached, but it was as if the light had triggered the release of adrenaline or hormones and he could run faster than he ever had.

He tore across the field, raced up and down narrow, cobbled roads, deeper into old town. Sirens kept wailing, traffic poured into the side streets as drivers searched for alternate routes to wherever they were headed. Wayra finally stopped outside the Posada de Esperanza, the inn where Tess and Ian had first stayed as transitional souls.

The single-story building, made of bleached stones and wood, curved like a welcoming smile across the grounds. On either side of the doors to the lobby were brightly lit bay windows, shining like eyes. Dozens of people milled around on the sidewalk out front, speculating about the explosions, their voices laced with alarm.

Still in his dog form, Wayra weaved his way through a forest of legs and trotted into the crowded lobby. Inn employees hustled around, tending to guests, steering them toward the dining room, the café, the gym, the rooms or cottages out back. Many of the employees had lived through the dark years of the *brujo* assaults and associated the distant squeal of sirens and the explosions with the chaos and terror of those years. The smell of their collective fear nearly overwhelmed Wayra.

He slipped around the front desk, seeking a particular scent, that of Juanito Cardenas. When he found it, he made his way toward the back deck. One of the newer employees saw him, didn't have any idea who or what he was—other than an annoying dog—and slapped his hands at Wayra. "*Afuera, perro.*" Outside, dog.

Wayra tucked his tail between his legs and bounded off the deck, nose to the sidewalk that twisted through this vast courtyard and its thirteen cottages. He followed the scent to the door of cottage 13, the same one where Tess and Ian had stayed more than four years ago. The synchronicity disturbed him. Even more troubling was that metal shutters covered the windows, the same kind of shutters that were on nearly every building in Esperanza. For years, those shutters had kept out the fog in which *brujos* traveled.

He didn't want to shift out here, too many people were out and about, so he darted around to the back and moved into the thick brush. When he was human again, he stepped out of the bushes, brushed off his clothes, and rubbed at the center of his chest, where Naomi's light had struck him. The area still ached, but he otherwise felt invigorated, and wondered what it was, how she had learned to manipulate energy in this way.

As he started back toward the front door, a hawk's cry stopped him, and a moment later, Illary landed in front of him and shifted. She wore black jeans, boots, a black sweater that set off the copper hue of her hair, and she was pissed. The smell of her anger rolled off her in waves. "Why did you exclude me, Wayra?"

"You weren't home."

"I was at the hospital with Diego. You could've waited. My stake in Esperanza is as big as yours."

Well, yes, it was. Wayra slipped his arms around her, slid his fingers through her thick, luxurious hair. *"Lo siento, mí amor."* He pulled back, lifted her chin, kissed her. Her mouth tasted cool and sweet, and as her body pressed against his, he sensed that she forgave him. "I spent so many centuries alone, Illary, that even now it takes getting used to."

"Worst excuse I've ever heard," she murmured, but her mouth brushed the tip of his nose and she stepped back, eyeing him from head to toe. "Something . . . is different." She touched the center of his chest. "There. I feel . . . heat? Light? Pain? Definitely pain. I don't understand, Wayra."

"Me, either." As he told her what had happened, her fingers swiftly unzipped his jacket, and she pulled up his shirt, examining the place where the light had pierced his chest.

"No visible scar or wound or anything."

She kept rubbing her hands slowly over his chest, then across his belly, and down inside his jeans. Her mouth nuzzled his ear, her breath warmed the side of his face, she unzipped his jeans. His hands slipped under her sweater, across her breasts, down her spine, and over the delicious flare of her hips. Her skin felt like silk against his hands, his mouth.

He was now so aroused that he picked her up and carried her to the posada's small, deserted greenhouse. He set her down against the soft earth, a cushion of darkness surrounding them. Their hunger for each other was so great that they made love there. Never mind that the location couldn't be more inappropriate, that at any moment someone might enter the greenhouse and find them. It didn't matter. This was about sex as an affirmation of life, a celebration that they were stronger together than they had ever been when they were alone.

Afterward, she whispered, "Regardless of what happens to Esperanza, my choice is always to remain with you, Wayra."

He rose up on his elbows, ran his thumb over her lower lip, then cupped the side of her face. "I can't imagine a life without you in it."

She poked him in the chest. "Then we'd better figure out what the hell is going on here." She rolled away from him, scooped up her clothes.

They dressed hastily, slipped out of the greenhouse, and walked back toward the front of the cottage. "How'd you find me?" he asked.

"I hadn't heard from you, so I texted a bunch of people and asked if they'd seen you. Juanito was the only one who responded and he asked me to meet him here. It would be helpful if you kept your cell turned on."

He slipped out his cell, turned it on, and the text message and e-mail icons lit up. Later, he thought. At the door, Wayra rapped sharply—twice, pause, once, then twice again.

Juanito Cardenas opened the door, grinned when he saw Wayra and Illary, and hugged them both hello. "Come in, come in, we didn't know if either of you would make it."

He motioned them inside, moving as quickly as he spoke. Born in Esperanza seventy-odd years ago, he didn't look a day over forty—black hair, vibrant dark eyes, and the high cheekbones of the Quechuas. Wayra had known him since he was just a boy.

"What's with the metal shutters, Juanito?" Illary asked.

"Just playing it safe. What is said here must remain private."

They followed him into the kitchen. Ed Granger, who owned the inn with Juanito, sat at a table filled with platters of food, and Illika Huicho, leader of the Quechuas in Ecuador, stood at the stove, scooping arepas and vegetables from a frying pan to a plate.

"Mates, good to see you both," boomed Ed. "Glad you could make it. Is it pretty chaotic out there, what with the explosions and fire?"

"It's nuts," Illary replied. "Police everywhere."

"We heard the sirens," Illika said, bringing a plate of arepas and a bowl of salad over to the table. Then she held her arms out and hugged Illary and Wayra hello. "Wonderful to see you both."

She felt frail and small in Wayra's arms, and the faintest odor emanated from her, something too subtle for human senses to detect. He knew what it meant. Illika was not just gravely ill, she was dying. But if she called on the powers of Esperanza to cure her, if she immersed herself in the nearby volcanic spring and focused on healing herself, she might live another century. He doubted she would do that. He sensed her profound fatigue.

As they sat down, Illika's eyes, set in a nest of wrinkles, met Wayra's. "Any idea what happened? What caused the explosion?"

Wayra started to say that the Pincoya was old and rundown, that a gas leak had probably caused the explosion and the fire. But if he lied to Illika, whom he had known for nearly a century, then he was no better than Ricardo or Dominica or any other *brujo*. "Ian, Pedro Jacinto, and I set the explosives and torched the inside of the hotel to demolish a portal that *brujos* have been using to move to other parts of the world. The tribe is headed by Dominica's brother, Ricardo."

The stunned silence told him none of them had suspected anything like this.

"Is the portal successfully sealed?" Illika asked.

"I think so. And more than thirteen thousand *brujos* were freed and thousands of other *brujos* won't be able to get into Esperanza if Ricardo summons them."

"Since when do *brujos* need a portal?" asked Illika.

"Something has obviously changed," Wayra replied.

"How do you know you took out that many, mate?" asked Ed.

"Ricardo told me," Wayra replied. "And I figure he was lowballing that figure."

"What the hell does this Ricardo bastard want?"

Wayrs explained what he knew. Suspected. Speculated. They listened without interrupting, then they all spoke simultaneously.

"They can't just disappear Esperanza," Ed burst out. "What about *us*, the people who live here?"

"They think they're gods," Juanito spat.

"This isn't about us," Illika said.

Wayra nodded. "Exactly. It's about Esperanza. What does the city want? What does the city *expect*?"

Granger looked like he'd swallowed a handful of nails. "Not sure I understand what you're getting at, Wayra."

Illika started passing the various platters around the table. "Really,

Ed. How long have you lived here? Thirty years? Forty? You know as well as we do that the city is conscious. Wayra's right. No one has asked the city what *she* wants."

"How the hell do we do that?"

"The city speaks to each of us all the time," Illary said quietly. "We only have to listen."

"So, this is, uh, like the Gaia theory?" Ed looked amused. "Is that it? All this time we've been dealing with the Gaia theory and no one let us in on the secret?"

"It's a bit more complicated than that," Illika replied. "Esperanza has always had the power to defend herself. But during the dark years, Dominica's power became a kind of cancer for Esperanza. Her immune system was so compromised she couldn't adequately defend herself anymore. The chasers knew it and realized that if the city was to survive, a revolution had to occur. So they permitted Tess and Ian to enter the city as transitional souls. The first in five hundred years. And their presence and the events that followed led to the annihilation of Dominica's tribe and gave Esperanza a chance to heal herself."

"And we've had more than four peaceful years," Juanito said.

"Then why are the chasers meddling like this?" Ed asked.

"A few of them may have been corrupted by power," Wayra replied, and explained what Diego had sensed when Ricardo had seized him.

Ed sat back, locking his fingers on top of his bald head. "Okay, so what's the city saying?" He looked at each of them. "Juanito? Wayra? Illary? Illika? Please enlighten me."

Wayra thought about his confrontation in the field with Ricardo and Naomi, about Ricardo seizing Diego, about the blackness that had swallowed half of the café's deck and a big chunk of the field that Pedro had videotaped. He thought about the *brujo* portal, now destroyed. "I think the city is saying the choice is up to each of us. What do *we* want? The people who live here are part of the city's consciousness."

"Well, shit, mate, that's easy," Ed said. "It goes back to what I said earlier. For way too long, either the chasers or the *brujos* have called the shots. What *we* want, us, the mortals, is a voice in all this, a *goddamn choice*." His massive fists slammed against the table. "A *choice*, that's all."

"Exactly," Illika said softly.

Wayra and Illary exchanged a glance. *What do we want?* his eyes asked.

Us, her eyes replied. *I want a chance for us.*

Eight
Locusts, Crows, and Charlie

1.

Diego chewed at his lower lip and stared at the blood pressure cuff on his upper arm. Then he raised his worried eyes to Lauren's face. "What's the verdict?" he asked.

"Fantastic," Lauren replied. "Your pressure is perfect."

"Am I going to be released tonight?"

"Probably in the morning. I'll find out." She updated his chart on her iPad and noted his blood pressure, that his blood work had come back normal, and he was anxious to return to work.

The transfusion of Wayra's blood had done the trick, all right, and she had already spoken to Leo about Wayra and Illary donating blood. Leo didn't need convincing. He knew as well as she did that there should be *brujo* bacteria in Diego's blood, but the transfusion had apparently eradicated it. Leo promised to make the arrangements so the shifters could donate anonymously.

Diego's phone kept jingling—text messages, e-mail, voice messages— and he finally plucked the phone off the bedside table and scrolled through the text messages. "Shit, I need to get out of here right now."

"What's going on?"

"Trouble." He threw off the sheet, swung his legs over the side of the bed. "A fire and an explosion at the Pincoya."

"Let me get a doc up here who will release you, Diego. Sit tight."

Just as Lauren went over to the phone on the wall to call for a doc, Mayor Torres stormed into the room, his plump cheeks bright red from exertion or rage or both. "You need to get your ass on duty, Diego. We've got a major crisis on our hands."

"Keep your voice down," Lauren snapped. "There are patients on this floor who are sleeping."

Torres glared at her, as if seeing her for the first time. "Leave us alone, please."

"Diego isn't supposed to be having visitors. So you need to leave, Mayor Torres."

"I'd like to speak to him privately," Torres said.

Lauren glanced at Diego, whose expression had turned to stone. "It's up to you, Diego."

"It's fine," he said, his voice tight, cold.

Lauren left, shut the door behind her, then stood outside in the hall, listening to the mayor's rant. "You're head of the Guardia and that means you need to get the fuck out of here and tend to business. And I do *not* want to see Wayra and his shifter wife anywhere in the vicinity of police business. If they're seen, they'll be arrested. Right now, you're needed at the Pincoya."

"What happened there?"

To Lauren, Diego's voice sounded shockingly calm.

"A fire and two explosions, that's all we know," Torres replied.

Lauren had heard enough. She hurried up the hall to the nursing station, where Elsa was on the phone, nodding frantically. She was filling in on this floor tonight. "Yes, yes, I understand." Then she slammed down the receiver. *"Dios mío,"* she murmured, and crossed herself quickly. "You heard, Low-reen?"

"Just now. Casualties?"

"We don't think so. But the administrator wants everyone in ER just in case."

"We need a doc to sign off on Diego's release."

"I'll take care of it."

Remembering that Elsa's husband was a cop, she asked, "Did you hear from your husband about what's going on out there?"

Elsa's mouth flattened to a dash. "They already have three suspects. They were seen entering the tunnel off Parque del Cielo and had large backpacks with them. Only two men came out." She handed Lauren her cell phone. "That's the video from a security camera on the roof of a restaurant across the street."

Lauren pressed Play. The three men huddled in the light of a street lamp in the park, studying something. Wayra, at six and a half feet tall, was easily recognizable. She knew the second man, a few inches shorter than the shifter, was Ian. It wasn't until the men headed toward the tunnel that she saw the third man's face: Pedro Jacinto, the priest. The video skipped ahead to the pandemonium in the aftermath of the explosion. Ian and Pedro emerged from the tunnel, were stopped by a couple of cops, then moved on and crossed the street. It looked as if their destination was the very restaurant where the security camera was located. Wayra didn't appear.

The video didn't prove anything. It certainly didn't prove that Wayra, Ian, or the priest had blown up the Pincoya. But proof was apparently trumped by suspicion. She handed the phone back to Elsa.

Elsa frowned. "You *know* those men." It wasn't a question. "Of course." She hit the heel of her hand against her forehead. "Es-tupid me. Ian, one of the transitionals. Wayra, the shifter. And the priest from Punta. All of them were my heroes from the solstice battle against the *brujos*."

"They wouldn't do something like this unless *brujos* were involved, Elsa."

"Of course not. Heroes rarely act stupidly."

Her insight surprised Lauren. "You're a sweetie, Elsa. I'm headed for ER."

"The administrator has called the graveyard shift in early. As soon as they arrive, you can leave."

"After nearly ten hours here today, I'm ready to leave."

As soon as Lauren turned away from the nurse's station, she punched out Tess's number. No answer. Ian's: no answer. She hit the elevator button, then stared at the numbers overhead as it slowly made its way up from the garage level. As the elevator door finally whispered open, Mayor Torres came huffing and puffing up the hall, shouting, "Hold the elevator, hold it."

Lauren stepped onto the elevator, but didn't do anything to keep the doors open for him. Fortunately for Torres, the doors were slow to close and he heaved himself on, still huffing. "Sounds like emphysema to me, Mayor. You should get your lungs checked out." She pressed the button for ER and the elevator started slowly downward.

"I know . . . who you are," Torres wheezed. "The mother of that transitional. Tess. Yes, that's her name. Tess and Ian of the *Expat News*." He leaned into Lauren's face. "Well, I have news for you, mother of the transitional. Ian is one of the suspects in this explosion at the Pincoya." Then he rocked back, folded his arms across his chest and stood there with a gloating smile.

Lauren suddenly jabbed the Stop button and stepped over to Torres, invading his personal space to the point where he stepped back. "Feels uncomfortable, right? Well, *you* have invaded my personal space, you jerk. The name's Lauren, and I've got news for *you,* Torres. The *brujos* are back and hundreds of people witnessed what happened last night at the Café Taquina. In fact, if you check the *Expat's* Web site, you'll see photos and videos. So no matter how you try to spin this, no one's going to believe you. There goes your credibility."

With that, she turned her back on him, punched the button for ER and the elevator continued its descent.

2.

An hour later, Lauren and Leo stepped out of the hospital and the chilly night air wrapped around them. A light wind blew from the east and carried the residue of smoke from the fire and explosion. She zipped up her jacket.

"No word from Tess or Ian yet?" Leo asked.

"Nope. Nothing. Just the text from Juanito, asking us to meet him at the posada, cottage thirteen."

"That's where Tess and Ian stayed."

"I know."

She suddenly wished for a bowl of hot vegetarian chili from that wonderful vegan restaurant a few blocks from her and Leo's apartment. She wished she were sitting on the back deck of their apartment with that chili, a glass of wine, and a soft blanket draped over her shoulders. Or that she was in front of a fireplace, roasting marshmallows on a stick. She wished she and Leo were anywhere other than where they were right now, hurrying through the nicotine-colored light that bathed the hospital parking lot.

She could still hear the sirens. Smoke blanketed the air. She knew Leo was as spooked as she was by what had happened at the Pincoya. But Leo didn't verbalize his fear, and in that way he was quite different from Charlie, who had verbalized nearly everything he had felt. Yet, even Charlie had had secrets.

Foremost among those secrets was that during the last several years of his life, he had begun meditating to reduce his stress and high blood pressure and apparently had tapped into something involving the chasers and Esperanza. After he'd died suddenly of a heart attack, she'd found a handwritten journal he'd kept about his impressions during these meditations. The entries read like the ramblings of a madman.

Eventually, Lauren had moved forward in her life and forgotten about the journal. She had settled into her life in Key Largo, where she was in charge of the nursing staff of a local hospital. She'd started dating. Then her granddaughter, Maddie, had moved in with her and not long afterward, Tess had been injured in a bust that had gone south and remained in a coma for months. During that time, Tess's soul had traveled to Esperanza and met Ian. And when she had returned, she was changed. As Tess had begun to remember what had happened to her while she was in a coma, some of her memories correlated with the entries in Charlie's journal.

Now here Lauren was, more than four years removed from the events in Key Largo, from her flight to Ecuador with Tess and Maddie, from the annihilation of Dominica's tribe. And she was faced with the same questions, the same dilemma: *What's real? What am I doing? Why am I here? WTF is going on?*

Before she and Leo reached the car, Lauren spotted a low fog snaking across the asphalt. She sensed it was ordinary fog, but asked Leo for confirmation. "*Brujo*-induced?"

"Nope. Too thin. Did Tess say she and Ian saw fog at the café before the black stuff started swallowing everything?"

"She didn't mention fog. And there wasn't any indication of fog on Raul's video. Why?"

"If the blackness that encompassed the café was caused by *brujos,* I think there would have been fog. Did Juanito give you any indication about the meeting?"

"None. We don't have to go, you know. We can go home and curl up in front of the fireplace and I can ravage your body."

Leo laughed and slipped an arm around her shoulders. "That's the most tempting invitation I've heard all day. But given everything that's been happening, I think we should go. Juanito has close ties with the Quechua community and their connection to Esperanza has always been powerful. They may have information that we don't. The police are going to be looking for Ian and Wayra and the priest, you know."

"So the mayor implied."

Minutes later, Leo turned the VW Jetta out of the lot and onto the road, and at the first intersection, turned left instead of right. "I'm betting Calle Central is jammed with cars because of the explosions and fire. We're taking side roads."

"Diego's blood work came back clean, Leo. No *brujo* bacteria."

"Yeah, I saw your note. It's damn amazing."

The way Lauren understood it, the bacteria that showed up in the blood of people who had hosted *brujos,* who had been abducted and seized, was a substance that made the physical environment of a body more comfortable for a *brujo* while using a host body. Leo had been studying the substance for fifteen years and believed that it might actually hold the secrets to the accelerated healing that many hosts experienced. Maddie had hosted Dominica for nine months, she would have the substance in her body for the rest of her life, and, as Lauren had learned, her granddaughter healed from any injury with extraordinary swiftness.

Last year, Lauren, Tess, and Maddie had gone to Otavalo for a few days, to chill, shop, explore. One evening, while chopping veggies in the place they'd rented, Maddie had sliced her finger right down to the bone. Lauren could have stitched it up, but urged Maddie to go to the clinic for an X-ray, to find out if she had nicked the bone. But Maddie simply let it bleed for a while, poured Betadine on it, bound it tightly with gauze. Within six hours, her finger had healed so completely there wasn't even a scar. After that, Leo began to study her blood chemistry more closely. Over the years, he had studied blood samples of other hosts who had survived *brujo* possession, but no one they knew of had survived a possession as long as Maddie had.

"Maddie always said that Dominica kept her healthy—thin but healthy. She never got sick during those nine months."

"Even if she left Esperanza forever, the amount of *brujo* stuff in her blood would probably keep her healthy for the rest of her life."

"Then why treat people for it?"

"Because we think it makes these individuals easier for a *brujo* to find again, that it marks them in some way, it enables *brujos* to track them like branded sheep."

"Only if they're lucky enough not to be bled out."

"Well, for the last four and a half years, that hasn't been an issue."

As they climbed deeper into the hills, most of the traffic fell away, she could no longer hear the sirens, and there were fewer street lamps. Just as Leo clicked on the brights, Lauren felt a sudden chill, as though all the windows were open. "Wow, did you feel that, Leo?"

"Feel what?"

"Maddie never appreciated what Dominica did for her," said the man who materialized in the backseat. "She'll probably live to be two hundred. Aren't they silly, Naomi?"

"Silly, but they'll do just fine, Ricardo."

In the moment before Leo slammed on the brakes and the Jetta died with a shudder, Lauren glimpsed them—the handsome Quechua man leaning forward between the seats and his striking female companion. Their virtual forms weren't complete yet, so parts of their bodies were transparent. But their faces looked as solid and real as Leo's.

Lauren hurled open her door and stumbled out into the road, aware that Leo was behind her, shouting something. But she couldn't hear it over the hammering of her heart. She tore uphill, arms tucked in close to her sides, shoes slapping the pavement. Four days a week, she ran for half an hour up and down the city's hills, through its cobbled streets, into old town, and she was hauling ass now. She might not be able to outrun a *brujo,* but running would buy her a little time.

She tripped over something in the road, pitched forward, and her arms shot out in front of her. She landed hard on her hands and knees, her breath rushed out of her, she gasped for air.

Locusts suddenly filled the darkness, thousands of them buzzing around her head, crawling through her hair, covering her face, nearly smothering her. She slapped at herself, felt the locusts crunching beneath her hands, and doubled over, arms thrown over her head and face, struggling to keep them out of her eyes, nose, mouth.

These locusts were created by the goddamn hungry ghosts.

A biting chill drilled through the crown of her head, and she knew what it was, one of the ghosts trying to get inside of her, seize her, use her. Panic exploded through her, but Lauren remembered Tess's advice, to laugh furiously, hysterically. *No brujo, no darkness, no demon can last long within laughter, Mom.* Lauren forced herself to laugh and yelled at Leo to do the same and rolled across the ground, down a slope, crushing the locusts' bodies, her ribs aching.

She felt the *bruja,* Naomi, trying to extract information from her or to stimulate her brain to create the substance that would make her possession of Lauren easier. Her laughter made it impossible for Naomi to seize her.

The air abruptly burst with the caws of hundreds of crows. Their wings beat the darkness like hands against drums, a fast, steady beat, *three-two, three-two-one, three-two,* over and over again.

Lauren stopped rolling and scrambled to her feet, forcing herself to keep laughing, terrified that if she stopped, the *bruja* would dive through her chest and seize her. The massive crows, their wings impossibly long, blocked out the starlit sky, and moved through the swarms of locusts, gobbling them up.

She ran back toward the car and found Leo lying on his side, in the glow from the headlights. She dropped to her knees, slid her hands under his head, raised it. "Leo," she whispered. "My God, please wake up, snap out of it . . ."

He twitched, shuddered, twitched again and went still. Then he bolted upright, his eyes a thick, oily black, and the *brujo* inside him spoke in Leo's voice: "You can't do anything for him. He's mine, Lauren. I can bleed him out, make him dance, vomit, sing, or rip off his clothes."

"Laugh, Leo, laugh," she screamed.

A white crow with a wingspan of fifty feet or more swept down over Leo, hooked its claws into his jacket, and lifted him off the ground.

Lauren rocked back on her heels, staring at this impossible sight, at

Leo's legs pumping impotently at the air as the crow lifted up higher, higher. Then only the white crow was visible, a kind of phantom against the night sky, flying toward a thicket of trees at the bottom of the hill.

3.

Charlie dropped Leo in a bed of pine needles, then quickly shed his virtual crow form and thought himself into his usual attire—white pants, shirt, and hat. He lit a cigar with his Zippo lighter, and lowered himself to the ground, sitting cross-legged, waiting for Leo to come around.

Ricardo was long gone to wherever he and his tribe hung out when they weren't creating chaos, and wouldn't come near Leo or Lauren as long as the crows were around. Even so, it took Leo a few minutes to regain consciousness and then he snapped to his feet with such ease that Charlie envied his dexterity.

Leo looked around frantically, his eyes sort of wild. "What . . . just happened? I . . . it . . . shit . . . Charlie?"

Charlie got up and blew a cloud of smoke in Leo's face. "Sniff it in, Leo. Secondhand smoke and all that. It won't kill you right now."

Leo waved his hand through the smoke. "I'm really delighted you can smoke cigars and eat carbs and sugar twenty-four/seven in the after-life, Charlie. It's great to know we actually get to do that at some point. But what the fuck are you doing here? Where'd these huge crows come from? What's going on?"

Charlie puffed on his cigar again and this time blew the smoke away from Leo. "When Lauren and Maddie and Tess got here, Leo, and I asked you to help Lore get a job at the hospital, I wasn't inviting you to *sleep* with her. It frankly never occurred to me that you two would hit it off. You and I have known each other how long? Eleven of the twelve years I've been here? I mean, c'mon, I ask you to help my wife get a job and you end up *sleeping* with her? *Living* with her? And now you're *engaged* to her? That's soap opera country, Leo, and fucked up big-time."

Leo drew his fingers back through his thick gray hair, thrust his hands in his jacket pockets, and stared at the ground. It was an Eddie Olmos moment from the original *Miami Vice,* detective contemplating shoes, ground, grass, hoping to remember his lines—or trying to get into the *zone.*

When Leo looked up at Charlie, those blue eyes reminded him of when he had been on a hurricane-hunting plane with a potential client and had gazed into the eye of a category 5 storm. He had felt then, as now, that if that untapped power hit land, massive destruction would follow. To his credit, Leo replied in a quiet, measured voice. "You're dead, Charlie. What did you expect her to do? Spend the rest of her life trying to make love with a ghost?"

He didn't know what he had imagined, that was the problem. You lived, you loved, you died. But you eventually realized your consciousness had survived death, that it could draw on certain powers in the afterlife and that those powers, with the proper attention and focus, could create worlds. But remove the high and mighty from the equation and the bottom line remained: Leo, whom Charlie had considered a friend and an ally, had proposed to Charlie's wife and he felt like strangling the bastard.

"Yeah, I get it. But that doesn't mean that what you did was right, Leo."

"You're a goddamn voyeur, you know that? How many times have you checked in on us, Charlie? How many times have you *watched* us?"

Quite a few, actually. One of the greatest temptations that any recently deceased person faced was dropping in on loved ones, spying on them, listening to them, feeling for them. He hated himself for doing it, but didn't stop. Lauren had been the love of his life when he was alive and death hadn't changed that. In the early months after he had passed, he had dropped in on her every day, struggled to communicate with her, to let her know he hadn't been obliterated.

He was no Patrick Swayze in *Ghost,* had never mastered the movement of objects in Lauren's physical universe. But in the years before she had arrived in Esperanza, he had figured out other ways to speak to her. One day when she was headed to Miami for a workshop, he managed to manipulate events so that she saw three license plates of passing cars that bore his initials—CL—and his date of birth, 429. A fourth car had a license plate that read, C429LMIA. MIA: the airport symbol for Miami, where he had been born and raised.

That one had really gotten her attention, and from then on he had understood how to talk to her through signs and symbols. Once she arrived in Esperanza, she had been able to see him, talk to him, and he had been forced to rethink his ideas about what was possible for him now that he was dead.

"Look, you and Lore, Tess and Ian, Maddie, Sanchez, all of you should leave Esperanza, the sooner the better."

Leo ran his fingers back through his white hair. "I'll . . . die if I leave."

"Hey, there are things worse than death. I'm a testament to that."

"But Charlie, if the rumors are true, that the chaser council intends to move Esperanza back into the nonphysical, the living won't survive such a transition. Tens of thousands will be killed."

"And that's why it hasn't happened yet. But if you love her, if you actually love *her* and not just the sex, then the two of you need to leave. It's getting more and more difficult to keep things under control."

"I'm crazy about her," Leo said. "I wish she'd marry me tonight. But a part of her is still in love with *you*."

"I doubt that, Leo."

But Charlie suddenly felt so miserable and confused he didn't know what else to say. In the years since his death, he had realized that his relationships with Lauren and Tess were the most important in his life as Charlie Livingston. And in a number of other lives as well. The three of them had been together during the Incan empire of Atahualpa, during the heyday of the Mayas, and had lived briefly on the Hopi reservation. They had been together during lives in Europe, Asia, and among the Australian Aborigines. He couldn't quite piece together all the emotional details of these lives, but the larger picture was clear: they formed the core of who he was and might become. Perhaps the three of them were different parts of the same soul.

Leo dropped his head back, staring up at the cawing crows, stretched out like a continent against the sky. "What . . . where . . . Crows that huge don't—"

"We conjured them. They're giving us a few minutes. You and Lore better get back in your car. We can hold the crows in place long enough for you to get where you're going. Where *are* you going, anyway?"

"Cottage thirteen, Posada de Esperanza."

Where Tess and Ian had stayed as transitionals. "For what?"

"I don't know. Juanito Cardenas texted us and asked us to stop by. It's probably connected to everything that's happened."

In other words, Charlie thought, it would be a brainstorming session. Juanito and Ed Granger, who now co-owned the posada, had been part of a group that had fought Dominica and the *brujos* since long before Charlie had died and joined the chasers. He doubted that any chasers had been invited to this meeting.

Lauren tore into the woods, shouting Leo's name. Charlie puffed hard on his cigar. "Just get to the inn fast."

He shed his virtual form, fading from Leo's sight, but hung around, watching his wife and her lover embrace, whisper, kiss. Lauren slipped an arm around Leo's waist and they moved clumsily up the hill, back toward the car, whispering incessantly to each other. A sudden memory surfaced, of him and Lauren whispering just like she and Leo were doing now. They were tiptoeing through their home in Miami, past their daughters' bedroom, hoping neither of them would wake up so they could steal some time alone together.

They had done a lot of that when their daughters were young. Charlie had been working insane hours, Lauren was in charge of ER at one of Miami's largest hospitals, the girls had been in day care. And watching Lauren and Leo now, he felt jealous, pissed off, cheated by death.

Regardless of the advantages that chasers had in terms of understanding what life and death actually were, how intricate and complex reality was, the bottom line had never changed. A chaser, like a *brujo,* existed as mere energy. And even though this energy could create illusions that felt and looked like the real thing, could create virtual forms that looked solid, he could not make love, could not procreate, could not interact in a meaningful, physical way in three-dimensional reality.

Except in Esperanza. Here, chaser and *brujo* alike could create facsimiles of physical life, but it didn't change the fact that they were dead.

"Don't think those thoughts, Charlie," Victor said, materializing beside him. "They only cloud your judgment."

"How the hell would you know, Victor? You haven't been alive for centuries."

"Well, *I* know," said Karina, emerging from the shadows with Kali perched on her shoulder. "I had an itty-bitty life in East Germany for a few years after the Berlin Wall came down." She hooked her arm through Charlie's and tossed her black braid over her shoulder. "Never told you about that, did I?"

He instantly forgot about Lauren and Leo. Karina captivated him—her beauty, impulsiveness, her rebellious spirit. But it was only when she had stood up to Newton and Maria that he understood the depth of his attraction to her. She was like the best adversaries he'd faced in court when he was alive. "How itty-bitty?" he asked.

"Hey, Victor," she called, "make sure the crows stick around until Lauren and Leo get to where they're going, okay?" Then she laced her fingers through his and they walked toward the trees. "Five years, five months, five days. I died at five fifty-five in the morning. I was trying to communicate a message, but my parents were too brainwashed to get it."

Charlie thought a moment. Tess had been born at 5:55 P.M. "What was the, uh, message for all those fives?"

"Freedom. That my freedom was bound up with service, specifically helping others to understand. I kinda failed in that life. My parents never got it. They feared the freedom that the fall of the wall represented." She paused, staring at him, her eyes so intense that Charlie couldn't look away, didn't want to look away. "You need to see some stuff, Charlie." Then she leaned forward and her soft, cool mouth touched his. Kali instantly lifted from her shoulder, squawking as she took to the sky.

In the twelve years since Charlie had passed on, he had never felt anything like this. He had been so wrapped up in Tess, Maddie, Lauren, the chasers, and the ultimate fate of Esperanza that he had never pursued any relationship in the afterlife. He'd heard about chasers who found and lived with their true soul families, their soul mates, their other halves, and planned their next lives with them so that they might all achieve their full creative and spiritual potential. But such relationships here had never interested him.

Until now. "This is going to sound totally out to lunch, Karina." He rocked back, away from her, so he could see her face. "But your place or mine?"

She laughed. "Do you have an actual place, Charlie?"

"Nope. Do you?"

She laughed. "Well, sort of. It's a little hooch that fades in and out because I don't pay enough attention to it."

"Then let's create our own place."

"Really?"

"Right here. In this woods. I'd like a lake, though. How's that sound?"

"Perfect. And every lake needs a dock."

The lake and dock appeared, seductive, inviting, and they walked the long, winding path that led to it, beds of flowers on either side of them. Even in the light of the stars, he could see how brilliantly colored everything was. Greens were emerald green, blues looked deep, bold, luminous, reds deepened to scarlet, yellows and golds sparkled like the road to Oz. Vivid, it all struck Charlie as supernaturally vivid.

When they reached the water, they stood there for a while, neither of them speaking. The surface of the lake captured the perfect reflection of the stars, the moon, the silhouettes of the mountains. "What about the house?" he asked. "Brick? Stone? Wood? Big? Little? A hooch? A cabin? A mansion?"

"I love stone, lots of windows, and space," she said. "And a fireplace. There's something magical about fireplaces."

"We need a canoe and some kayaks, too," he added.

Karina linked her arm through his. "Then let's make it so, Charlie. We need to have a clearer sense of our own power."

They turned away from the lake and gradually a large stone house began to take shape in front of them. "Not happening fast enough," she said. "Did you ever see Mickey Mouse in *The Sorcerer's Apprentice*?"

Only a million times, he thought, when both of his daughters were very young. He roared with laughter and glanced at Karina, who was laughing so hard tears rolled down her cheek. "Here we go," he said, and they simultaneously threw up their arms.

Music from *The Sorcerer's Apprentice* filled the air. Wands materialized in their hands. They drew on the power of the afterlife in a way Charlie had never tapped before. Everything snapped into clarity—the stone house, its bay windows overlooking the lake, the path that twisted down to the dock, the trees, the trout swimming beneath the placid waters.

"Wow," she breathed. "I've never been able to create something this magnificent and real by myself. Race ya." She ran up the shallow rise, toward the house.

For an instant, something distracted Charlie. Something about Lauren, Tess, Esperanza. He felt he should turn back toward that yearning, that issue, that challenge, his loved ones. Then he glanced toward Karina, running toward a stone house that suddenly seemed less solid, toward massive bay windows that grew more and more transparent, and he spun around and tore after her, his heart simultaneously singing—and breaking.

Nine
Chaos

Tess, stalled in traffic for what felt like days, had inched forward into a glorious sunset and then into subsequent darkness. She had eaten through half a bag of chips, part of a brick of cheese, and was seriously considering the uncooked trout as her next snack. Her iPhone was dead, the car charger was in her other purse. Her iPad still had power and the radio worked, so she could keep tabs on the local news about the fire and explosion at the Pincoya.

She kept e-mailing Ian, which he could pick up on his phone, but he didn't reply. She e-mailed her mother to find out if she'd heard from Ian, but her mom was more of a texter than an e-mailer, and didn't even get her e-mail on her phone. Frustrated, hungry, her bladder filled to bursting, Tess finally pulled Snoopy out of the snarl of cars, up onto the narrow sidewalk, and drove slowly forward.

Fortunately, there weren't many pedestrians on the sidewalk; the explosion, fire, sirens, and the growing police presence had chased them elsewhere. Within moments, other cars followed her and pretty soon, a caravan of vehicles drove along the sidewalk.

As she approached the intersection where she hoped to turn off, she saw a barricade of orange cones. Why? That side street would take all of them away from Calle Central, away from the area of the Pincoya, and she and the other drivers would be able to get to another thoroughfare that would be less congested. But half a dozen cops on horseback rounded the corner, saw the line of cars on the sidewalk, and stopped, shoulder to shoulder, blocking the cars.

Pissed off now, Tess slammed her fist against the horn and the drivers behind her started honking as well. Two of the cops on horseback trotted over to her car, shouting at her and everyone else to get off the sidewalk. Tess killed her engine, removed the key from the ignition, jerked up on the emergency brake. She grabbed her purse, her bag of groceries, her packet of documents from the glove compartment. Then she threw open her door and stepped out. "Why're you blocking off that street?" she said in Spanish. "Opening it would relieve the congestion."

The horses snorted and pranced around, spooked by the incessant shriek of sirens, the honking, congestion, all of it. The lead cop dismounted, handed his horse's reins to his colleague, then marched over to her. "Señora, I am saying this only once. Please get back in your car and move it into the street." He touched his holstered weapon, and when he leaned toward her, Tess saw that his eyes were an oily black. He had been seized. *"Now,"* he snapped.

Tess held up her hands. "Fine, fine, I'm getting back in the car." As soon as he turned to move away from her, she swung her bag of groceries and it struck him in the back of the head. He pitched forward, into his horse, some of her groceries flew everywhere, and the beautiful creature whinnied wildly and reared up. The second cop's horse freaked and took off, bucking madly until the cop toppled from his saddle.

She leaped back into Snoopy and tore toward the other four horsemen, certain they had been seized also, that the blocked side street was a way for the *brujos* to keep hundreds of potential hosts trapped—and accessible. Granted, her Mini Cooper was hardly an intimidating presence, but the horses were already so spooked that their riders could no longer control them. They raced off in every direction and Tess swerved into the street, slammed through the orange cones, and sped down the side road to the next intersection, a line of cars following her.

To either side of her, orange cones blocked every side road. More cops on horseback converged from either direction and she assumed they, like the first six cops, were hosts to *brujos*. She floored the accelerator, racing up and down hills, charging through stoplights until she reached an intersection that was clear on both sides. She sped left, some cars followed her, others went right, and still others shot straight ahead.

Tess had no idea where she was in relation to her apartment. She slowed down and used her iPad's GPS to pinpoint her exact location, then followed the red curving line on the screen until she was behind her building, in an alley that led into the underground garage. She finally nosed down the steep hill and into a parking space, and turned off the engine. She sat there, clutching the steering wheel, forehead pressed against her knuckles, her stomach somersaulting.

Shit, it's happening again.

Tess raised her head, reached for her stuff, quickly got out. The car's security beeped when she engaged it, and she ran for the interior of the building, her bag of groceries slamming against her hip.

Inside, the foyer was deserted and the elevator wasn't working. She started up the dimly lit stairwell and wished the landlord used brighter bulbs and would fix the elevator. She felt uneasy in the stairwell, confined. The entire building seemed too quiet, a disturbing quiet, as though it held its breath in dreadful anticipation of something.

On the second floor, she heard the comforting drone of a TV and caught the scent of something cooking. So people were home, she thought, and wondered if she should start knocking on doors and warning everyone that *brujos* had seized police. But that might create unnecessary panic. She needed to get in touch with Diego and tell him what had happened so that he could inform the mayor, who would sound the sirens.

Tess unlocked the door, and as it swung open, the dark silence told her Ian wasn't there. She nonetheless called his name and flipped on light switches.

No answer.

Light from the street spilled through the picture window in the living room. The tall cuckoo clock in the corner, a beauty hand-carved by a Swiss expat here in Esperanza, said it was 9:28. It couldn't be that late. She knew that when she'd left the grocery store it was still light outside. Esperanza was so close to the equator that year-round, darkness fell around six P.M., with just minute fluctuations for the seasons. At the most, she had spent two hours in traffic, so it had to be closer to eight P.M.

She walked quickly into the kitchen, set her seriously depleted grocery bag on the table with her purse, kicked off her shoes. A quick look around the kitchen told her that Ian had been about to start dinner—a pot half filled with water on a burner, two ears of corn on the counter, the table set. And then . . . ?

Something urgent had come up.

Tess zipped into the bedroom, stripped off her clothes, dumped them in the washing machine, and changed into clean jeans and a T-shirt. Back in the kitchen, she hurried around—frying pan on burner, olive oil and trout into pan. Plug in iPad, charge up phone. As soon as she did that all the iPhone's icons lit up, text messages from Ian, Wayra, her mother, Diego, Illary, Juanito.

Ian and Pedro Jacinto were holed up in a church not far from the Pincoya, Iglesia Santa Rosa. That was all his text said—not why he was there or why he was with the priest. Illary asked if Tess had seen Wayra, who asked if she had seen Ian. Her mother said to call her ASAP, then later left a message that she and Leo were headed to the posada for a meeting and please, please call.

A meeting at the posada? With whom? Juanito? Was that why he had texted her? Tess suddenly sensed dots she couldn't connect, stuff happening beneath the surface that no one had let her in on. Did anyone else know that some cops had been seized?

She scrolled back through the text messages, noting the times they had been sent. Except for her mother's text message, which had been sent before six P.M., they all read 9:28. How was that possible?

Anything is possible here.

She called Diego. He answered on the fourth ring, his voice tight, urgent. "Tess, I'll have to call you back. The—"

"Diego, they're seizing people already. A bunch of your cops are hosts now, guys on horseback. They've blocked off some side roads around the park near the Pincoya, trapping people so they're accessible as hosts. The sirens need to be sounded, people have to be warned."

"I convinced Mayor Torres to call out the reserves and they're headed into that area right now. How—"

The shrill wail of the sirens cut him short, a sound that hadn't been heard in this city for more than four years. Tess turned toward the large picture window that overlooked the park across the street. In the park, on the sidewalk below, people stopped, and then within moments, pedestrians poured across the plaza, toward the tunnels.

The sirens paused and a man's voice boomed from the closest loud-speaker and issued directions in four languages: Spanish, Quechua,

French, and English. *"Please proceed into the tunnels or into the basements of the nearest building and remain there until you are told it is safe to do otherwise. No fog has been sighted, but* brujo *attacks have been reported in old town, in the area around the Pincoya Hotel and Parque del Cielo."*

"Tess," Diego said. "I need to get off."

He disconnected before she could say anything.

Tess quickly lowered the blinds and went over to the stove to flip the trout. The sirens started up again and the high pitch stabbed at her, dug into her eyes, bored through her skull. She detested the sound and was terrified what it might mean for her and Ian and everyone else she loved.

When the trout was done, she squeezed some lemon juice on it, picked out the bones, dropped some lettuce and tomato on the plate, and gobbled it as she paced back and forth in front of the window, plate in one hand, phone tucked between her cheek and shoulder. She called Ian, but the call went straight to voice mail.

"Clooney, it's me. I'm at the apartment. Call."

She noticed that the time on her iPhone was 9:28. She glanced around at the cuckoo clock, but the hands remained at 9:28. She picked up her iPad, flipped open the cover. It read 9:28. "Shit." Tess headed into the bedroom to check the digital clock on her nightstand: 9:28.

Alarmed, Tess went into the office and woke up her iMac. The screen came into view and there, in the upper right-hand corner, the time read 9:28.

"Okay, this is freaking me out," she whispered.

Was it happening only to her or was it happening everywhere in the city? If it was happening only to her, then maybe she'd finally gone round the bend. Or maybe she was actually dead. But if it was happening all over Esperanza, then something much larger was going on.

Tess turned on the TV, tuned it to the local news. The emergency broadcast was on, directing residents to seek refuge.

Frustrated, she felt she should be doing something other than stuffing her face and waiting for news. But what? The sirens still screeched, people were panicked, pandemonium would ensue just as it had at the café.

To keep herself from going nuts, Tess started putting away what remained of her groceries. When she'd struck the cop with her shopping bag, she'd lost half of what she'd bought. But at the bottom of the bag she found the item she'd purchased after walking up and down the grocery store aisle several times, arguing with herself. She set the box on the table, finished putting her purchases away, then picked up the box and read the directions on the back. *Yes or no?*

"Let's do it." Tess plucked a paper cup from the dispenser next to the counter, and headed for the bathroom.

Pee in cup, hold test strip in urine for at least seven seconds. Done. Now she had to wait five minutes. She set the strip on top of the box, poured the urine into the toilet, flushed it, dropped the cup in the wastebasket. She stared at the strip, willing it to indicate that she wasn't pregnant.

She and Ian used protection, she couldn't be pregnant. Her ridiculous hunger these past few weeks had to be caused by something else. A chemical imbalance, a thyroid problem, diabetes.

Her iPhone sang out "Piece of My Heart," and she rushed back into the living room and snatched the phone off the table. "Clooney, are you okay? What happened? Why're you with Pedro in a church?"

"Long story short, Pedro, Wayra, and I blew up the Pincoya and started the fire. We sealed off a *brujo* portal. Now the cops are apparently looking for us, as suspects. A security camera caught us in the park. Are you all right?"

"You blew up . . . shit, Ian. Are you still in the church?"

"Yeah, in the basement with several hundred other people. I'll be back when the coast is clear. I left you a note on the *Expat* door, didn't you see it?"

"No. I parked in the garage, not on the street."

She told him what had happened on her way back to the apartment. A moment of stunned silence followed, then Ian whispered, "Christ, it's happening again, isn't it. The past is repeating itself."

"I'll drive over to the church and pick you up," she said.

"No way, Slim. Stay put. I'm safe here. And you're safe in the apartment. But if you see fog, lower the damn shutters. Look, my cell is nearly out of power. I'll call you in a bit. Love you."

"Wait, are the church's clocks—"

His cell went dead, the connection was lost. The sirens had paused again, the booming voice returned, and Tess hurried over to the blinds, parted the slats with her fingers, and peered outside. Hundreds of people now swarmed through the street and across the park, waving torches, chanting something. She raised the blinds, opened the window, and heard, "*Nunca más, nunca más.*" Never again, never again.

She was hiding up here, hiding from these *brujo* bastards who couldn't seize her, and hundreds of locals who *could* be seized were risking their lives out there, daring the *brujos* to attack so they could be annihilated by the torches they carried.

"Fuck this shit." Tess grabbed her jacket off the back of the chair, snapped open the electrical box that controlled the metal shutters for the *Expat* office, and hit the switch to lower them. She unplugged her iPhone, slipped on her comfortable running shoes, and went in search of a broom, rags, a lighter. The broom handle was wood, so she grabbed the mop with a metal handle, wrapped rags around it, and soaked them in lighter fluid. She pocketed the can of lighter fluid and a lighter, shoved rags down into her bag, and tore downstairs. She burst into the street and joined the mob.

Within minutes, hundreds more poured in from the park and people spilled out onto the sidewalks. Before she'd gone more than a couple of blocks, she heard a loud, whirring sound that quickly grew so shrill and deafening that it drowned out every other noise. A thick, dark swarm of locusts swept low over the mob, then settled across it like some preposterously huge quilt made of Velcro.

Locusts flitted across her face, got tangled in her hair, and even though she sensed they were supernatural constructs conjured by *brujos,* they felt *real*, the noise their wings made was *real*. And there were so damn many of them, hundreds, thousands. They landed on her legs, arms, neck, fluttered down inside her clothes, covered her face, and dug into the corners of her mouth. They crawled into her nostrils, ears, eyes, and she dropped her torch and clawed at her face, raking enough of them away from her eyes so she could see that the panicked mob had splintered, people racing away in every direction. Tess tore off her jacket, pulled it over her head, and ran into the park, locusts still clinging to her clothing, writhing inside her shirt.

The wave of locusts suddenly lifted, as if on a current of wind, and struck a hovering field of flames fifty feet in the air, a fire as supernatural as the locusts themselves. Had the chasers conjured the field of flames? As with the locusts, the supernatural flames were real enough so that she smelled the locusts as they burned, heard their bodies snap and crackle in the flames like bacon on a grill. Some of the trees in the park caught fire and Tess swept a burning branch off the ground and ran over to people pressed against the ground—two, three, four, she couldn't tell. Locusts covered them so completely they looked like alien creatures.

She swept the burning branch through the air just above them and most of the locusts flitted away, some of them on fire, others untouched. Two men and two women leaped up and raced for the tunnels. Another swarm of locusts turned toward Tess and she thrust the burning branch at them, incinerating some of them, buying herself a few seconds. Then a larger swarm swept into the plaza and she dropped the flaming branch and flew toward the closest tunnel entrance with a panicked crowd of several hundred people.

The mob poured down the steps to the entrance, then squeezed through the tunnel doors and into the maze of interconnected tunnels. Every sound echoed loudly—the pounding of feet, the shouts and sobs. Tess ran with the others, distancing herself from the entrance, and finally ducked into a culvert to get her bearings.

A statue of Santa Rosa, the patron saint of Esperanza, stood next to her. It was laden with flowers, candies, photos, prayers scribbled on pieces of paper. She glanced around for a sign that would tell her where, exactly, she was, but didn't see anything.

She stepped out of the culvert, into the rushing tide of humanity that continued to pour into the tunnels from other entrances. *"Ayuda viene, por allá, mira!"* someone shouted.

Horns beeped and honked and the crowds moved to the sides of the tunnel to allow a long line of electric carts to get through. Tess knew there were storage rooms throughout the tunnels where carts were kept for people to use while they were here. But she had never seen so many of them in one place before. They were large enough to seat ten, with wide running boards on either side and at the rear that could accommodate another ten or fifteen people.

The crowd surged forward, but one of the drivers, wearing a city worker uniform, shouted, "There's room for everyone, take your time, don't push. More carts are on the way."

Tess hesitated. It struck her as too convenient. Yet, in the past, *brujos* always had avoided the underground tunnels just as they had avoided cemeteries. And since the mark on her arm didn't burn or itch, she finally hopped onto a side running board of the nearest cart.

The long line of carts started moving and then gathered speed so quickly that the tunnel walls blurred past, grottoes and culverts melted together, her eyes teared from the wind. She suddenly realized the carts were chaser manifestations.

Tess tightened her grip on the overhead bar and glanced at the faces around her, looking for her dad in one of his virtual forms. She didn't see him. The people in her cart looked startled, murmured among themselves, but no one tried to leap off.

Mile after mile swept past. *"¿A dónde vamos?"* she yelled. Where're we going?

As if in response, the line of carts slowed down and people started getting off. She could see the tunnel signs now and was shocked that they were near the El Bosque neighborhood, fifteen miles from where she had entered the tunnels. How long had it taken? Five minutes? Six?

Tess jumped down from the running board and followed a small group toward the nearest exit. The line of carts continued on through the tunnels, gathering speed.

At least here, Tess thought, she could find out what was happening in old town, whether it was safe to return. And if it wasn't, she would get a hotel room for the night and take a bus or cab back tomorrow morning.

When she pushed through the exit doors, she was relieved to hear only the noises of a busy neighborhood—cars, distant music, laughter. She trotted up the steps and paused in a small plaza where everything looked normal. Across the street stood buildings made of wood, stone, and concrete, family businesses that catered to the residents of El Bosque, as well as cafés, restaurants, and bars. A lot of people were out and about.

Tess slipped her phone from her jacket pocket; the hands were still stuck at 9:28. She checked for text messages, e-mail, calls. No, no, and no. Okay, first she needed information.

As she crossed the street, she felt that same sensation she'd had before Ricardo had materialized in her car. That she wasn't alone. She paused on the curb on the other side and whispered, "Dad? Or is it you again, Ricardo?"

No one materialized. But the sensation persisted as she followed the earthen sidewalk past bars and cafés. Something was shadowing her.

From a jukebox somewhere, Julio Iglesias sang about love won and lost. Couples emerged from bars holding hands, laughing. Families with young kids got into and out of cars. Life in El Bosque apparently hadn't been disrupted by locusts or *brujo* attacks. It was as if the neighborhood existed in another reality altogether. Had they even heard about what was happening in old town?

It occurred to her, not for the first time, that Esperanza was a massive experiment designed by some higher consciousness. If that was true, then the city was a biblical fable that had leaped to life in 3-D, HD Technicolor, and surround sound, and all of them were just actors on this vast stage who lived and learned as events unfolded. Sort of like life.

Tess stopped in front of Mercado del León, and debated about actually going inside to find out the time. Suppose the clocks here were all stopped at 9:28? What then? Did it mean an attack was imminent? She glanced at the church where she had taken refuge just a day ago.

The hands on its clock tower spun wildly.

She stared at it a moment, anxiety crawling through her, then hurried into the market.

Lines at both registers snaked back into the narrow aisles, merchandise occupied every available space, kids fussed and whined, adults looked anxious and tired, the clerks were rushed and irritable. Everyone seemed edgy, uneasy, a distinct contrast to what she'd seen outside.

As Tess moved farther inside the store, she understood why. The small TV mounted on the wall flashed scenes of the bedlam in old town Esperanza, probably recorded by someone in the midst of it all. She saw the mob of protestors, the swarms of locusts, people dashing for the tunnels, and then the thick fog rolling across the plaza and through the street, *brujo* fog that must have arrived after she had run into the tunnel. The people inside the bodega apparently believed they might be next and were stocking up on food and supplies. It wouldn't be long before everyone else in the neighborhood got wind of this.

She looked around for a clock but didn't see one. She made her way to the customer service counter on the far side of the store and got in line. A short line, three people ahead of her. No one in sight wore a watch. But she bet they had cell phones.

"*Permiso,*" she said to the woman in front of her. "*¿Qué hora es?*"

The woman, a pretty Ecuadorian of maybe twenty, slipped her cell from her jacket pocket, glanced at it, and frowned. "How strange," she said in slightly accented English. "My phone says it's eleven-eleven. But it can't be that late."

Shit, what's this mean?

The woman called to the man behind the customer service counter. "*¿Gustavo, qué es la hora?*"

He glanced at the time on the computer screen. "It says one-eleven. That's obviously not right."

"My phone says the same thing," exclaimed the clerk next to him.

The man at the front of the line whipped out his cell. "I've got eleven-eleven."

Nine-twenty-eight in Esperanza and 11:11 or 1:11 here?

But 9 plus 2 plus 8 equals 19 and broken down that's 10, and 1 plus 0 equals 1. So we're talking 1, 1:11, 11:11. "Holy shit."

Alarmed, Tess spun around to race back outside. But a flicker of movement in her peripheral vision prompted her to glance right, toward the aisle closest to her.

In the middle of the aisle, a black wave spread like oil across the concrete floor and moved up the wall, swallowing boxes of cereal, bags of rice, canned goods, whatever stood in its path. A boy of three or four saw it, too, and screamed for his mother and backpedaled away from it. But another wave of black spread out behind him, trapping him on an island of concrete between the two black waves.

As Tess ran toward him, the boy's mother careened around the end of the aisle, shrieking, "*Sáltalo, Hugo, sáltalo!*" Jump it. The dark matter was now at least five feet wide and the kid wasn't big enough to jump over it. But Tess was.

She backed up to the end of the aisle, then raced forward and leaped. She landed hard but didn't go down, and swept Hugo up in her arms. He sobbed and clutched at her, his mother kept shrieking, and Tess eyed the black wave that stood between her and Hugo's mother, widening and spreading even as she stood there.

It's alive.

"Ssshh, Hugo, it's okay, it's okay," she said softly in Spanish. "Be calm, please be calm, and we'll get across this stuff."

But Tess didn't have enough space in which to gather momentum. So, with Hugo clutched to her chest, she dropped to a crouch, then sprang upward and forward. In the strange, slow-motion moments when she sailed over the dark matter, when everything appeared in such perfect, painful clarity, she knew she would not clear the dark wave, that it would swallow her and Hugo with the same indifference that it had gulped down people at the café.

Then she slammed into the concrete floor on the other side, Hugo's mother grabbed her son from Tess's arms, and Tess's left foot slipped off the concrete and sank into the abyss. A crippling cold seized her foot to the ankle, her entire foot went numb, and felt so heavy, so weighted, she couldn't jerk it out.

"Oh Christ," she gasped, and fell forward onto her hands, then her forearms.

She was vaguely aware of screams and shouts around her, of the stampede of terrified customers, of Hugo's mother shouting at Tess to grab on to her hands. Tess did and the woman pulled and Tess started laughing, laughing hard, hoping that laughter would break the hold of whatever this was. Tears rolled down her cheeks, the tendons in her wrists and the muscles in her arms felt as though they might snap.

Her foot suddenly popped free and she collapsed against the floor, her foot numb yet aching, weighted and hard. She somehow scrambled upright and she, Hugo, and his mother hurried to the back of the store, Tess dragging her foot. She felt like Quasimodo, she slowed them down. She kept shouting, "The exit, get out through the rear door."

She glanced back; the blackness sped toward her, closing in on her. She hobbled the last few feet to the door and charged through it, but not quickly enough.

The last thing she saw before the blackness swallowed her was the parking lot behind the store and Hugo and his mother stumbling into it, away from the black wave. Then the darkness swept over her head and the numbing cold claimed her completely.

Twilight

. . . .

The universe can be thought of as an information processor. It takes information regarding how things are now and produces information delineating how things will be at the next now, and the now after that.

—Brian Greene, *The Hidden Reality*

Ten
Discoveries

1.

Ian woke in a top bunk bed, in a dorm of bunk beds, in the basement of Santa Rosa Church. He felt strangely disconnected, as though he'd left part of his body back in the Pincoya. His eyes were dry from lack of sleep and all the smoke he'd inhaled had irritated his throat.

He had stayed up for hours, monitoring the news and talking with Pedro and some of the other church refugees. He had called Tess repeatedly after his phone had charged, called from the landing on the stairs thirty feet up, but she hadn't answered. That worried him. Hell, everything worried him.

Since the dorm lay forty feet underground and there weren't any windows, he didn't know if the sun had risen yet. When he glanced at his watch, it read 9:28, but he quickly realized his watch had stopped. Ian sat up, his long legs hanging over the side of the bunk, and slid his hand under the pillow, patting around for his iPhone. It was fully charged, but didn't have a signal and, oddly, the time on the phone also read 9:28.

Weird. And because this was Esperanza, the weirdness probably was significant.

He climbed down the ladder, into the glow of the night-lights that kept the dorm softly lit. Most of the bunks were occupied. That meant it was probably still early.

He found his shoes lined up with other shoes along the baseboard, and every pair held a toothbrush and a small tube of toothpaste. A cart against the opposite wall held stacks of towels and small bars of soap. The church took care of its refugees, he thought, and wondered what little elf had delivered these essentials.

Ian pocketed the toothbrush and toothpaste, slipped on his shoes, helped himself to a towel, and walked down the narrow corridor to one of the five restrooms. Most of the church sanctuaries in the city and surrounding suburbs were built to accommodate hundreds of refugees and were usually larger than the churches built on top of them. This church was no exception. The sanctuary beneath the church was cavernous.

He smelled coffee and food and suspected that in the common room he would find a full buffet breakfast, computers with Internet access, televisions with the latest news, a list of the injured and the dead. Even though the city hadn't been attacked in more than four years, the emergency procedures apparently had snapped into place when it counted.

In the restroom, thirty sinks lined one wall, thirty stalls lined the opposite wall, and thirty showers lined the third wall. Except for two other men, Ian had the place to himself. As he brushed his teeth, he thought that the face staring back at him from the mirror over the sink looked haggard, older, eyes pinched with anxiety. Or, as Tess might say, *George Clooney with a thick five o'clock shadow and circles under his eyes.*

He dropped his towel in a bin, then returned to the dorm for his pack and hurried off for the common room. The church employees were still bringing food out to the buffet table, a feast that featured eggs cooked every which way, fresh fruits, cereals, black beans, rice, and plantains, both baked and fried. There were juices, bacon, sausages, a variety of breads and jams. As Ian got in line with a handful of other people, he noticed the time on the wall clock: 9:28. He then overhead a man and a woman talking about how the time on their cell phones appeared to be stuck at 9:28.

He sat at a table by himself, where he could watch one of the three TVs in the common room. Tuned to the local station, all three TVs showed scenes from last night's attack—the mobs pouring through the park and into the street in front of his apartment building, the swarms of locusts and the hovering field of flames, the aftermath of ruin and destruction. A ticker tape beneath these scenes kept a running tab on casualties: 103 injuries, 72 dead. Ian was grateful and surprised that the toll wasn't higher.

But why wasn't the news also covering this strange anomaly with the time?

More people arrived in the common room, Pedro among them. The priest came over with a plate of food and a mug of coffee. "I'm so glad you haven't left yet." He set everything down and pulled out the other chair. "Can you believe this?" He gestured toward the television screen. "They attacked in retaliation for what we did at the Pincoya, Ian. I'm sure of it. What a tragic mess."

"Like we talked about last night, Pedro, we did the right thing. We sealed their portal and cut them off from millions of other *brujos*. This battle was going to happen regardless. Have you heard from Wayra?"

The priest shook his head. "No. Not from anyone. You?"

Ian shook his head. "I don't have a signal down here. Is the Internet working?"

"Sporadically. From what we can determine, the fire drove them out and things in the city are now quiet. The sun came up a while ago and we were able to use the webcam to survey the damage. The park across the street from your building is still cordoned off."

"What's with this time anomaly, Pedro?"

"I don't know. There was just a brief mention of it on the news. It's being attributed to electromagnetic fluctuations in and around Esperanza."

"I suppose that theory came from the physics professors who've been studying this whole thing."

"You've got it."

Physics. Electromagnetic fluctuations. He really didn't like the sound of this. Then he snapped his fingers. "Remember how I told you that Sanchez said eleven-eleven is a portal to higher consciousness?"

The priest nodded. "So?"

"Nine twenty-eight adds up to an eleven. Do you think eleven might be some sort of portal, too?"

Pedro looked troubled. "We should ask Sanchez. If it *is* some sort of portal, are these time anomalies a warning or a promise?"

"Maybe both."

For a moment, neither of them spoke. Ian knew they were thinking the same thing, what a warning might mean for the city, what a promise might mean. For him, warning and promise amounted to the same thing: *threat.*

"I can give you a ride back to your brother's place," Ian said. "But first I need to get back to the apartment and check in with Tess, update the website, change clothes."

"I'll meet you at your apartment within the hour."

"Great."

As soon as Ian started up the stairs from the basement to the church foyer, his phone rang and sang. Icons lit up. He scrolled quickly through the text messages and e-mails, saw messages from Wayra, Lauren, Leo, Juanito, Illary, Diego, Maddie, Sanchez, nearly everyone in his universe except Tess. He called her cell, but didn't even reach her voice mail.

She was probably asleep. It sounded reasonable, but his body thought otherwise and he raced up the last flight of stairs, into the foyer, and exploded through the front doors of the church and out into the crisp morning air. The slant of the light, the way the shadows fell, told him it was probably around eight A.M. On a normal day, nothing in Esperanza really got going until nine or ten. No telling what effect last night's attack would have.

He loped the six long blocks to the apartment and the closer he got to his street, the worse the destruction—store windows shattered, trash cans overturned and garbage apparently set on fire, the hulks of two cars that had been torched, the blackened remnants of trees that had caught fire. It was as if he moved through the vestiges of a massive riot, a collective madness that had been hell-bent on annihilation. But who had done this? *Brujo* hosts? The mobs of panicked citizens? Both?

The park came into view and it was cordoned off, just as Pedro had said. Many of the trees had caught fire, beds of flowers had burned, benches had been overturned. Cops moved through the area with a strange stealth, some of them consulting handheld objects that he guessed were EMF detectors, others videotaping or snapping photos. The entire park was surrounded by city vehicles and several cops directed traffic at the two intersections he could see.

In between those two intersections lay his building. As he rounded the corner, he was relieved to see that the shutters on the *Expat*'s front window had been lowered, which had probably saved it from being shattered. He glanced up at the windows of his and Tess's apartment on the third floor; no shutters, but the glass looked to be intact.

Ian raced up the stairs to the third floor. Even before he stepped into the apartment, he knew Tess wasn't here, that she hadn't been for some time. He felt the utter emptiness of the rooms, caught the faint scent of whatever she had cooked, probably the trout, and sensed the silence wrapping around him, mocking him.

He dropped his bag on the couch and sped through the rooms, taking inventory. The bed hadn't been slept in, her clothes were in the washing machine, her dirty dishes were in the kitchen sink, her car keys hung from a hook on the wall, two chargers were still plugged into the kitchen wall. Her iPhone and iPad were gone. She hadn't been here since last night.

Ian called Lauren first, but she hadn't seen Tess since yesterday afternoon when she had visited Diego. "She called my cell a bunch of times, but I . . . Leo and I were attacked by *brujos* last night. Charlie and a bunch of crows intervened. We're okay," she added quickly. "And right now, I need to get into surgery. We've been inundated with casualties from last night, Ian. Keep me posted about Tess."

He had a thousand questions to ask her, but simply replied, "I will. You do the same."

Since Tess's keys were here, she hadn't driven anywhere. His guess was that she had joined the mob at some point before the locusts descended. And then what? Had she fled into the tunnels? Been trampled in the chaos? Or had she been seized? But she couldn't be seized . . . unless all the rules were changing.

Shower, change clothes, then get the hell out of here and start looking for her.

He showered in the bathroom off the master bedroom, realized Tess's shampoo and conditioner weren't in here. He wondered if the spare bathroom might tell him something. He changed into clean clothes and headed toward the spare bathroom at the back of the apartment.

But when he walked into it, everything except the counter went dark. It was as if a spotlight illuminated a box labeled EARLY PREGNANCY TEST and the strip that rested on one end of the box. The strip that read positive.

"My God," he whispered.

Pregnant, Tess was pregnant. The idea of becoming a father filled him with an uncontainable joy, then nearly overwhelmed him. He would be forty-seven on his next birthday, had a grown son from a first marriage who lived in Minneapolis, and hadn't even thought of this possibility. The heart condition that had caused his massive coronary and resulted in the near-death experience that had brought him to Esperanza had been cured by the city. He was equally convinced that if he left Esperanza, if he and Tess were forced out, his heart condition would return and his next heart attack would kill him. And this time, he wouldn't come to in Esperanza. Whether he left the city or disappeared with it, he and Tess would be robbed of a chance to have a family.

For Ian, the stakes suddenly had spiked much higher.

He heard the front door creak open, then the priest called, "Ian?"

He was early. "Back here, Pedro."

The priest appeared in the bathroom doorway wearing clean clothes, his thinning hair still damp from a shower. "The . . ." Pedro's eyes darted to the box and the test strip on the counter, then flickered back to Ian. "Tess?"

"Well, it's not me."

Pedro exploded with laughter and threw his arms around Ian, hugging him. "This is fantastic, amigo. Congratulations. So, where's the expectant mother?" Pedro stepped back, still grinning, marveling at the good news.

"She's not here. And I don't think she knows yet. My guess is that she got distracted by something while she was waiting for the results."

"What could distract her from something like this?"

"Something huge."

"There isn't much bigger than this, Ian."

"Yeah, there is. If the chasers remove Esperanza from the physical world, this baby will never have a chance to be born, much less live."

Pedro's exuberance seeped from him like helium from a balloon. Before he could reply, Ian's phone rang and Wayra's number appeared in the ID window. "Wayra, is Tess with you?"

"No. That's, uh, part of the reason I'm calling. The blackness ate most of the El Bosque neighborhood last night. And Tess was seen out there. She saved a woman and her son."

Ian could barely speak around the hard, throbbing pulse in his throat. "I'm leaving now," he said hoarsely.

2.

Charlie sat at the edge of a hot tub, his legs dangling in the 101-degree water, and watched Karina drifting naked in the long swimming pool they had created. The jungle of trees around the pool, in the backyard, were home to dozens of species of birds, and Kali felt right at home here. She had settled in the upper branches of a mango tree, which didn't grow naturally in the mountains. The mango and papaya trees had been his additions to the creative collage, and Kali happened to love both types of fruit.

The jungle cast thick shadows against the water and Karina swam into and out of them again. He wondered if her agility and grace as a swimmer had been perfected in that life they had shared as dolphins. This memory was recent and invariably snapped his lawyer brain into action. He imagined a celestial prosecutor grilling him about a life as— *snicker, snort, gag*—a dolphin.

So tell us, Charlie, what did you learn in that life as a dolphin?

And he usually saw himself shocking the jury by saying, *I learned that sex is supposed to be fun.*

With that, he stripped off his swimming trunks, slipped into the water, dived deep into the pool, and swam beneath her. Charlie turned onto his back so he faced her and reached up and touched her beautiful breasts. Karina pressed her hands over his and sank into the water, her legs scissoring around his waist, her mouth pressed to his. They made love beneath the water, honoring that weird life they had shared as dolphins, and this extraordinary magnificence they shared now, as chasers. When they surfaced finally for a breath of air, he asked, "What were we to each other in that dolphin life, anyway?"

"Part of the same pod." She held on to his shoulders, her hair drifting on the surface of the water. "We weren't physically related but you were my mentor and became my lover. We were so monogamous we got tossed out of the pod."

Charlie cupped her face in his hands and kissed her, marveling at how real and soft her mouth felt, how real and beautiful their creation was. At no other time in his existence as a chaser had the afterlife been this peaceful, this magnificent.

"So how come I didn't have issues about monogamy in my life as Charlie? I mean, c'mon, if you're tossed outta the pod for monogamy, then isn't monogamy something you would avoid in your next life?"

Karina dropped her head back into the water, shut her eyes. She flung her arms out to her sides and floated like that for what seemed a long time but probably wasn't. He had no idea how long, in real-world time, they had been here. It felt like forever.

"Not necessarily. I don't think there are a lot of hard-and-fast rules, Charlie."

He started to say something, touched her shoulders to pull her toward him again. But a crippling pain exploded in the center of his chest and caused him to wrench away from Karina. The dead weren't supposed to feel pain, not like this. He stumbled clumsily to the steps at the shallow end of the pool and doubled over at the waist, his body burning up one moment then encased in a numbing chill, then burning up again. And he knew, in that place within himself where he always knew what he needed to know, that something had happened to Lauren or Tess or Maddie.

Or to all of them. Charlie squeezed his eyes shut and willed himself into the sensation. "Tess," he whispered. "Something has happened to Tess."

"Bastards. It's the council, Charlie. They're doing their shit again. I think we need to get to El Bosque. I feel that's where something has happened."

Before he even heaved himself from the water, she was out and drying herself off. She snapped her fingers and was instantly clothed in jeans, a pullover sweater and denim jacket, boots and a pack over her shoulder. Charlie did the same and inadvertently duplicated the way she was dressed. "We look like the Bobbsey twins, Charlie. Remember them?"

"Clearly. Tess found a copy of one of the books in her school library, tossed it in the pool, and informed us it was a stupid story, that she wanted something captivating. So Lauren bought her *Catch-22*. She loved it."

"How old was she?"

Charlie thought a moment. "Maybe seven."

"No way."

"She's wired differently, Karina." He paused, focusing on that feeling again. "I think this is bad."

Karina whistled for Kali, who flew over and landed on her shoulder. Then she grasped Charlie's hand and they instantly materialized in El Bosque, a couple of ghosts on an unpaved sidewalk outside the police barricade with hundreds of locals shouting at the police, women sobbing, terrified children clinging to their parents.

Kali now circled high above them.

Charlie and Karina thought themselves forward through the crowd until they could see beyond the barricade. Where the neighborhood had once stood now loomed a big fat zero of nothingness that reflected the light. It looked like a sheet of ice, blindingly white, uniformly smooth, strangely lovely. And yet, like the café, the area wasn't completely gone. Here and there, spots had survived—a patch of flowers, a kitchen table, part of a greenhouse, a wall, half of a barn where goats bleated, hens clucked, cows mooed. A mirror stood in the midst of the nothingness, as if hovering in the reflected light like some sort of alien craft.

WTF. Charlie moved along the lengthy edge of the nothingness. Half a mile, a mile, two miles. Then the nothingness curved sharply west and continued for another few miles before it turned north, cutting an erratic path through the wooded area after which the neighborhood was named. Charlie thought himself into the nothingness—and came up against an impenetrable barrier. Impossible. Chasers could move anywhere. He tried again, but the same thing happened.

Karina appeared beside him. *We can't get through, Charlie. I've tried it at a dozen different spots along the nothingness.*

Charlie thought himself into his virtual form as Manuel Ortega and Karina assumed a virtual form as a Quechua woman. They extended their arms and patted their hands along the barrier. He could feel its solidity, its reality. He and Karina moved quickly back along the south end of the vanished area. Kali squawked and circled above them, higher and higher, several hundred feet up, so that she was well above the blinding whiteness, then began to spiral downward, faster, faster, until she blurred with speed.

"What the hell is she doing?" Karina murmured.

"I don't know."

The parrot suddenly struck the whiteness—and disappeared into it. Moments later, a small section of the barrier began to solidify in three dimensions—visible yet transparent—until it resembled a square opaque window about a foot tall and just as wide. Charlie had no idea what power or force made this possible, but it certainly seemed to be connected to Kali's descent into the blinding whiteness.

"Charlie, is Kali doing this?" Karina asked. "And if so, how?"

"I have no idea." He pressed his palms to the opaque glass or whatever this substance was and it began to clear until he glimpsed one of the neighborhood streets, a commercial area with cars and scooters parked at curbs, a couple of cafés, bars, a clinic, an outdoor market. But he didn't see any people.

"We need to make this window bigger so we can see more," Karina said. "Where are all the people?"

Charlie didn't want to think about that. He ran his hands over the surface, but the window didn't get any larger. He pounded his fists against it, threw his body against it, but nothing changed.

"The rules are in flux," Wayra said, as he and Illary came through the trees. "You're here, Tess is in there somewhere."

"How do you know Tess is in there?" Charlie demanded. "Have you seen her?"

"No. But other people have."

"You go through."

"I can't. We've tried. Both of us have tried."

"How'd Kali get through?" Charlie asked, hating the desperate tone in his voice. "Illary can fly as high as Kali."

"Charlie," Illary said gently. "It's not about altitude. Kali traverses worlds and dimensions. That's her purpose. We can't assume that what worked in the past will work now."

"So what the fuck are we supposed to do?" Charlie snapped.

"There's only *one* thing to do," Karina said. "Meet with the council."

"That's a good place to start," Wayra said. "But Charlie, first, I'd like you to talk to the woman and her son whom Tess rescued. There may be something in what she says that will help. She's an herbalist and healer, quite famous among the Quechuas."

"The only thing I give a shit about is getting in there," Charlie said.

"What she says may help us figure out how to do that," Wayra said.

They followed Wayra away from the barrier, the crowd, down the street to a tiny restaurant so crowded that people spilled out the open doorways, onto a narrow deck and onto a playground with a merry-go-round and a couple of swings. People huddled together on the playground, comforting several women who were sobbing, children who wailed with fear, men who tried to look courageous and failed completely. The air crackled with tension and uncertainty; voices were hushed, tremulous.

To Charlie's astonishment, he spotted Lauren and Leo, rushing through the playground toward them. Behind them were Maddie and Sanchez, Ian and Pedro Jacinto. "You called *all* of them?" Charlie glared at Wayra.

"Bet your ass, Charlie. This isn't just about chasers and *brujos*. It's also about everyone who lives in Esperanza."

"You think I don't *know* that?" Charlie snapped.

"Maybe you and Karina know it, but the rest of the chasers don't seem to get it yet. It's our city, too."

Greetings were subdued, tense. This was the first time Charlie had been with another woman since Lauren had arrived in Esperanza. It didn't matter that both he and Karina were dead; in their virtual forms, they looked as animated and real as everyone else and the situation felt awkward and uncomfortable. He noticed how tired and worn out everyone looked. Circles like soft bruises lay beneath Maddie's eyes. Sanchez didn't speak at all and his gaze shifted around constantly, as if he were trying to identify the people around him. Anxiety pinched Ian's face. The priest looked as if he felt like dropping to his knees and praying. Lauren was on the verge of tears.

"Any more news?" Lauren asked Wayra. "We couldn't get anywhere near the blocked-off area."

"Ed Granger and Illika are in his helicopter now, trying to get some sense of how widespread the disappearance is," Wayra replied. "Juan-ito is taking a small group through the tunnels that lead into El Bosque, to see if they can get in that way. The mayor brought in a land mover. All flights have been turned away because there's so much chaos around the airport. The last flight out left ten minutes ago."

"A land mover?" Charlie exclaimed. "No land mover is going to get through there. It's not constructed of anything a machine can *move*."

"With the airport closed," Lauren said, "we're being effectively iso-lated. This disappearance created exactly the atmosphere the chasers hoped for, right, Charlie?"

It hurt him that she glared at him. "I didn't have any part in that, Lauren."

"Then who did?" Pedro asked.

"There are seven us on the council who are against this," Karina said. "So what happened in El Bosque was done by the minority of the chasers and goes against every edict that chasers have lived by."

"Then hold them accountable," Lauren burst out. "Don't stand there citing statistics. Get Tess and the others out of there, for Chrissake."

"We intend to," Karina said.

"How?" Ian snapped. "Just how the hell will anyone get in to even get them *out*?"

Before anyone could respond, Wayra urged them all to keep mov-ing. They skirted the side of the building and came out behind it, where a small lake spread out before them. A pair of swans—one black, the other white—drifted across the glistening water, scooping up handfuls of bread crumbs that a young boy tossed them. A pretty Ecuadorian woman, probably the boy's mother, sat on the grass nearby, watching him, pointing as the white swan drifted closer to shore.

"Quintana," Illary said when they reached her. "May we join you?"

"Sí, sí, claro," she said, getting to her feet, brushing off her skirt. She hugged Leo, Wayra, and the priest hello, then her gaze went directly to Ian. "Ian Ritter. I recognize you as surely as I did Tess last night. She . . . saved my son." Her eyes darted to Maddie. "The redhead. You're legend-ary among the Quechua. No one alive has endured possession as long as you did with Dominica and lived to talk about it."

"I try not to think about it, much less talk about it," Maddie replied.

Quintana brought her palms together and bowed her head slightly. Then she reached out and touched Sanchez's arm. "The viewer. Wayra told me what happened when you touched the stone. Are you better now?"

"Not really." Sanchez managed a small, nervous laugh. "I'm having trouble flipping my psychic switch to Off."

She gave his arm a quick squeeze. "We will talk about that in a bit." Her gaze went to Lauren now. "You're Tess's mother. She has your eyes. It's a pleasure to meet you. To meet all of you." Now she frowned as she brought her gaze to Charlie and Karina. "I'm sorry, but I don't recognize either of you."

"They're the chasers I told you about," Illary said.

"I have seen chasers before, in my work, but this is the first time I have spoken to any of you. Isn't there anything you can do to stop this . . . this barbarity?"

"We're hoping you can help us understand what happened here last night," Charlie said.

She tucked her long, black hair behind her ears, glanced around to check on her son, then looked back at Charlie.

"I think it was around nine, but I can't be sure because my watch had stopped at one-eleven."

Charlie noticed the glance that Ian and the priest exchanged and figured they were recalling what Sanchez had said about 11:11.

"I had seen the news about the explosion and fire at the Pincoya and was worried that the *brujos* had invaded the city again," Quintana went on. "So Hugo and I went to the market to stock up on food and supplies. I first noticed Tess as Hugo and I were on our way into the Mercado del León. She seemed . . . confused, like maybe she was lost. Then Hugo and I went inside the market and as I got a cart, I glanced out the front window and saw . . . two chasers. They weren't solid like you and Karina. It was like they were trying to assume a greater substance, but couldn't quite do it."

"Did you get a good enough look at them to describe them?" Charlie asked.

She thought a moment, her gaze fixed on something off to her right.

"One of them had long, flowing hair. The other was bald and seemed to be wearing some sort of long . . . gown."

Shit, Charlie thought. "Like a toga?"

"Yes, that's exactly it."

"Victor," Wayra said.

"And Franco," Charlie added.

"What were they doing out here?" Illary asked.

"No telling," Charlie replied. But it explained why he hadn't heard a word from either of them. "What happened in the store?"

"It was incredibly crowded, I guess everyone in the neighborhood had heard about what happened at the Pincoya and were stocking up on food and supplies. Hugo had wandered away from me and suddenly I heard him . . . screaming. I raced around the end of the aisle and . . . and saw this . . . this strange and horrifying blackness seeping like molasses from . . . the shelves, the wall. I don't know where it came from. Then it spread across the floor, in front of Hugo, behind him, trapping him. Tess was at the other end of the aisle, saw him, and ran for him. At one point, her leg got caught in the blackness. I somehow pulled her free, and even though she was laughing hysterically, she could barely walk. We raced for the . . . rear door and the black wave *chased* us. It was *sentient*, I'm sure of that. Tess slammed open the door so Hugo and I escaped the building. When I . . . I looked back, the blackness was . . . swallowing her."

That image, of the darkness *swallowing* Tess, horrified Charlie so deeply he couldn't even speak. Ian just stood there, his expression revealing all the anxiety he felt. The tight silence was broken by a sound that one of the swans made, a trumpeting, honking, then the loud flapping of wings against the water, and the swans flew at each other. It was like a squabble between a long-married couple, lots of noise and no damage. But Charlie took it as a sign that his best recourse now was to create as much chaos as he could among the members of the council who had done this.

"Did the . . . blackness reach the parking lot?" Ian asked.

"No. It just stopped . . . at the door. It was like it had gotten what it wanted. Tess. Then Hugo and I ran on to my car and I left quickly."

"Shit, shit," Sanchez murmured, pressing his fists against his eyes, his breath a rapid wheeze.

Maddie took hold of his arm, steadying him, and urged him to sit on the ground. She crouched beside him and the two spoke quietly for a moment. She dug a bottle of water out of her purse, handed it to Sanchez, and he rolled it across his sweating face, then twisted off the cap and drank.

"Sanchez, you okay?" Charlie asked.

"Wayra might be able to get in." Sanchez's voice churned out of him, hoarse and gravelly. "But only by making a deal with the devil."

"What does *that* mean?" Wayra asked. "Illary and I have both tried to get in. We can't. Neither can Charlie or Karina."

Sanchez pressed the bottle against his cheek and shook his head. "I don't know, man, I don't know what it means. I keep picking up this stuff, keep seeing it, a steady stream of shit, and I . . . I can't turn it off."

Quintana immediately sat beside him and touched her hand to the back of his neck. "Take slow, deep breaths," she told him. "Yes, that's right, like that. Breathing in, you are safe and protected. Breathing out, you release the stone's hold on you."

She kept repeating this until Sanchez's body visibly relaxed. He pulled his legs to his chest, rested his forehead on his knees, and murmured, "Thank you. It's . . . easier now."

"And will get easier," Quintana assured him.

Charlie turned to Wayra. "Do she and her son have a place to stay?"

"With us. She's insisted that she and Hugo will drive to Quito, but I think that's a mistake."

Even though Charlie had told Leo to take Lauren and leave the city ASAP, he now thought it might not be the safest course. If Newton, Maria, and the rest of them were still experimenting with disappearing bits and pieces of Esperanza, they might practice on areas that were even farther from the city than El Bosque, like the roads to other towns. It would be the best way to isolate Esperanza completely before removing it from the physical world.

"I think you and your son should stay with Wayra and Illary," Charlie said to Quintana. "You'll be safer with them than traveling to Quito alone."

Quintana's face surrendered to the emotions she'd been struggling to hold in. She got to her feet, tears rolling down her soft, beautiful cheeks, and grasped Charlie's hand. "Thank you." Then she winced, drew back from him, and pressed her right fist to her heart. "A heart attack killed you. The pain was . . . extreme. But because of the good you have done since your death, I feel you will be reborn with an exceptionally strong heart." She paused, her eyes widened. "You were *Tess's father.*"

It wasn't a question and didn't require an answer or reaction from him. Good thing. Charlie didn't think he could utter a coherent sentence right now.

Quintana hugged him and Karina, then she and Illary walked down to the pond and joined Hugo. Lauren turned to Charlie and sank her finger into his chest. "Make this right, Charlie. I don't give a shit what you have to do, but *make this right.*"

"All of you should stay with Wayra and Illary. You'll be safer there."

"Safer from what? *Brujos* or you chasers?" she spat. "Jesus, you people are like politicians, Charlie. You don't care who's hurt. Your agenda is the only thing that matters."

"There's another way," Maddie said. "Segunda Vista."

"Second Sight?" Lauren exclaimed. "The magical weed?"

"Count me out," Sanchez said. "That's one thing I *don't* need right now."

"I didn't mean you," Maddie said. "Ian, Lauren, Leo, Pedro, and me."

"It's brilliant," Leo said. "The disappearance of El Bosque is supernatural and what better way to penetrate it than with an equal magic?"

"It might work," Pedro said. "The Queros use Segunda Vista in their spiritual rituals."

"I'm desperate enough to try anything," Ian said.

"Hold on, just hold on," Charlie said, patting the air with his hands. "Karina and I, Wayra and Illary couldn't get in there. It's foolish to think Segunda Vista will get you in."

"We don't need to get in, Charlie," said Maddie. "We just need to be able to see inside, and maybe once we're able to do that, we'll be able to find a way for Tess and the others in there to escape."

Legend said that Segunda Vista was brought into the physical world with Esperanza, that it first appeared with the giant ceiba tree in

Parque del Cielo. It was a feathery weed with tiny, lovely buds in luminous rainbow colors. The entire plant—buds, leaves, stems, even the roots—allegedly enabled you to see the truth.

Charlie knew that many people in and around Esperanza—including Maddie—cultivated Segunda Vista, Second Sight, in their greenhouses. But the Queros were the first humans to discover it and they found that each of the different-colored buds blew open a particular chakra and conferred a distinct ability. The way Charlie understood it, the leaves could cure almost anything. The stems took you deep into the collective mind. The roots connected you to the divine. When all of the elements were mixed together, there were no barriers between the living and the dead. Reality shifted immediately, according to your deepest beliefs and desires, and you became the manifestation of who you really were.

For some people, the cultivation was a business; they sold the weed to the company that resold it as a remedy for altitude sickness. But for most people, Segunda Vista was for personal use. The psychic components of the weed were well documented—far-seeing, precognition, telepathy, clairvoyance.

At one time, the council had talked about destroying all the Segunda Vista fields and greenhouses in Esperanza. Some council members—probably the same idiots who were trying to remove Esperanza from the physical world—thought the weed enabled the people to see too much. But in those days, they'd had *brujos* to worry about and the discussion never went anywhere. So Maddie, he thought, might be on to something.

"Can you get the stuff around here?" Charlie asked. "Or do you have to go to your greenhouse, Maddie?"

"It was sold in the Mercado del León," Maddie replied.

"There might be another place around here that sells it," Wayra said.

"Then see if you can find some. Karina and I will do what we can from our end."

Leo nodded. "There're hotels a mile from here. We can get rooms and start looking for some place that sells Segunda Vista."

"I've got to pass," Sanchez said. "I need to get away from here. Too much stuff's hitting me all at once."

"Illary's going to drive Quintana and Hugo to our place," Wayra said. "Go with her."

"Our dog's still at your place," Maddie said. "So we'd have to stop there first, anyway."

Sanchez looked at Maddie, and Charlie sensed the context of the unspoken exchange between them. Maddie, he knew, was conflicted. Go with Sanchez or stay behind and try to search for Tess through the lens of a magical weed? She finally said, "I'll go back to your place, Wayra, with the others." She pointed at Lauren, Ian, Leo. "But if you guys need any info about Segunda Vista, text me. And oh, someone should act as a monitor, to record your perceptions." She gave Charlie a quick hug. "Tell the council to go pound sand, Charlie."

She and Sanchez walked off toward Illary and Quintana, who were still down by the water. Leo, Ian, Lauren, and the priest headed for their car. When Charlie and Karina were alone with Wayra, the shifter looked as miserable as Charlie had ever seen him.

"You and Karina need to know something," Wayra said. "Pedro, Ian, and I blew up the Pincoya. More than thirteen thousand *brujos* were freed, their portal was sealed off. Ricardo and some of his followers surrounded me in a field and he promised to seize an equal number of Esperanza residents. Diego said that some of the men in the police department were seized and they blocked off an entire area around the Pincoya so that hundreds of motorists, including Tess, were trapped. She got out and some of the others did, too."

"Wow," Karina breathed. "You three really threw a wrench into the *brujo* scheme of things, Wayra."

"But until that happened, Ricardo's tribe hadn't seized anyone in Esperanza to use as hosts," Wayra said. "Now that they're seizing people, it may fuel the belief of your opponents on the council that they are right about taking Esperanza back into the nonphysical."

It was the closest thing to an apology that Charlie had ever heard from the shifter. But why apologize? The three of them had done what was necessary, had done what he and Victor had tried to do, cut off a potential *brujo* army of millions. They simply hadn't taken into account the possible repercussions.

"We need to move quickly, Wayra. We're not only up against *brujos*, but the chaser council."

"And we may lose on all fronts, Charlie."

Alone again and determined to find a way into the disappeared area, Wayra hurried into a thicket of trees near the lake and shifted. As a dog, he had greater latitude to move among the police, scientists, and other authorities without being noticed. He made his way along the edge of the diminishing crowd outside the vanished area, sniffing the air to read the general mood of things.

Terror. Frustration. Grief. Uncertainty. Just like the dark years of the *brujo* assaults. Unfortunately, Diego spotted him and hurried alongside Wayra, talking incessantly.

"Wayra, please don't interfere in this. Mayor Torres is on his way over here. If he sees you or Illary, you'll be arrested. You, Ian, and the priest were caught on a security camera, entering the tunnel with packs and duffel bags. You're suspects in the explosion at the Pincoya, okay? And you can't get into El Bosque; it's sealed in some way. We have yet to detect any human life in that area. We've been working with physicists from the university who say the electromagnetic elevation in this area is substantial."

Wayra moved into a cluster of pines and Diego followed him. He appeared to be healed of whatever damage *brujo* possession had inflicted, so why was he talking like this? Since Wayra couldn't ask him in his canine form, he quickly shifted.

"A suspect? Good. I'll be glad to tell him why the explosion and fire were necessary. And don't worry, I won't mention that you supplied most of the explosives."

Diego looked so miserable that Wayra felt like hugging him, reassuring him it would all work out, somehow. "Nothing is the way it's supposed to be, Wayra."

"And how is that different from what Esperanza has always been?"

"We're fully aware of what's happening now. We're no longer functioning on automatic. Maybe this disappearance is supposed to happen. Maybe it's part of some greater plan; that's what I'm hearing from people."

"Really? Which people? Mayor Torres is in denial, so it can't be what you're hearing from him. Maybe you heard from some of the people who will be killed if the city is taken back into the nonphysical? You just told me no one has been able to detect life inside that area." He paused and leaned toward Diego. "Tess was *swallowed* by that blackness, Diego, and so were several hundred others. Maybe they're all dead, but if they aren't, how're they going to get out? Kali got in. If she did, then so can I."

Diego's fingers tightened around Wayra's wrist. "The parrot is different, Wayra."

Wayra pulled his arm free. "We need to know what the hell we're up against. Please keep your team away from me, Diego." With that, he shifted and raced along the edge of the whiteness.

El Bosque—the Woods—lay just a mile south of the airport and covered about five hundred acres. At one time, it had been completely forested with pines, monkey puzzle trees, and a hybrid species of tree grown in greenhouses outside the city and eventually transplanted in El Bosque. In the last four years, the population west of the city had exploded and this neighborhood had become one of Esperanza's emerging middle-class areas, a mixture of Ecuadorian professionals, young families, Quechuan elders, and expats.

The neighborhood still maintained vast areas of woods that had been converted into parks and nature preserves. The majority of residents didn't want concrete sidewalks or paved streets, so many sidewalks and streets were packed earth or cobblestones. Some of those cobblestones, he knew, bore a name and a date, important personages and milestones in Esperanza's history. Even Dominica had a cobblestone, one she had created for herself, as though she had thought it was Esperanza's equivalent of a star on Hollywood's Walk of Fame.

The neighborhood supermarket, Mercado del León, stood smack in the middle of El Bosque. It was long and narrow rather than fat and wide, and its merchandise was jammed from the floor to its twelve-foot ceiling. Even though it was a long drive for him and Illary, they sometimes had shopped at the mercado because it carried merchandise from all over South America that was often difficult to find anywhere else in Ecuador.

Merchandise like Segunda Vista. And like the liqueur from the Chilean island of Chiloé that facilitated insight into the myths and legends of wherever you happened to be. A stone from the famous waterfall in Argentina could cure vertigo and insomnia and induce profound dreams if you slept with it under your pillow. Aisle to aisle, shelf to shelf, it was like this, one treasure after another buried within the usual, mundane merchandise. His vivid remembrance of the market, his personal association with it, his connection with Dominica and the city's history, convinced him he could get through whatever this barrier was and into the disappeared neighborhood.

Arrogant, perhaps, or simply delusional, but he had to try. He refused to surrender to the chasers' manipulation of events. He had lived too long and fought too hard to free Esperanza from despots.

Wayra ran until he reached the western edge of the whiteness, and darted into a thicket of pines. Some of the trees lay inside the whiteness, so there were no cops back here. They undoubtedly feared that a misstep would suck them into the void, the brilliant whiteness, the disappeared area.

According to Quintana, all the clocks, watches, and digital devices in El Bosque had stopped at 1:00, 11:00, 1:11, or 11:11. If he moved back in time to around eight o'clock last night, perhaps he could make sure Tess left before the blackness began and could warn enough people to get out. Movement in time didn't come with guarantees, but twice in the recent past his ability to move through time had made a significant difference—when he brought Ian forward from 1968 and when he had disappeared Dominica to the dawn of the universe.

Wayra drew the air deeply into his shifter lungs and *reached* for last night, for the sidewalk outside the market. He felt himself straining, his head pounded, his heart hammered. Nothing happened.

Nothing.

He tried again, his focus greater, his concentration more profound, but the strain drove him to the ground and, for long, painful moments, he simply lay there, panting hard, struggling to understand why it wasn't working. In all the centuries of his existence, this had never happened before.

Sanchez couldn't turn off his psychic switch; Wayra couldn't move back in time. *The rules are in flux,* he'd told Charlie, but the truth was that the rules by which he'd lived for centuries were no longer valid. It meant he would have to uncover the new rules, that their survival depended on it.

He got up, shifted into his human form, and moved quickly along the wall of whiteness, searching for that transparent patch, Charlie's little window. He nearly missed it; the sun was at a different angle. The patch had also shrunk and wasn't quite as transparent as before.

He tried to widen it with his fingers, as though it were his iPhone screen, but nothing happened. Wayra pressed his palms against it, as he'd seen Charlie do. It was like glass, cool like glass, but it wasn't glass. He rapped his knuckles against it. The surface didn't just resound, it trembled, it sang, like a vibrating drum. He brought out his car keys, flicked open the blade on his pocketknife, and tried to work the tip of the blade through the white surface.

The blade snapped in half.

Wayra leaned forward and breathed on the surface. It fogged over. On impulse, he brought his finger to the surface and drew "11:11." The window suddenly expanded. He leaned closer, hands cupped at the sides of his head as he peered through it and into the disappeared El Bosque.

And suddenly, his face seemed to be caught in the surface of the window, in the whiteness. It felt less solid, less real, less intractable. The surface sank like foam to accommodate the shape and weight of his face. Wayra leaned his entire body into it, his feet left the ground, and his body surrendered to it completely.

But suddenly he couldn't see, his face was stuck to the surface like iron to a magnet. He struggled to hurl himself back, his arms flailed, his feet moved, he sucked and sucked for air, but nothing flowed into his lungs.

Wayra screamed silently for Illary, hoping that her shifter senses would hear him, would be able to follow his shriek for help. Then he sank into blackness.

Twelve
High Strangeness

1.

Lauren stood outside La Mística, a small hotel made of wood and stone located about a mile east of El Bosque. Leo and Ian had gone inside to inquire about vacancies and Pedro had ducked into a café to buy some breakfast for the four of them. She was anxious to find some Segunda Vista and get this hallucinogenic show on the road, so she started walking south.

She worried that there wouldn't be any vacancies at La Mística or anywhere else and they would be forced to retreat to their apartment. With Tess trapped inside that whiteness, she didn't want to leave the area. It wasn't as if she could do anything regardless of where she was, but she felt better being in proximity to El Bosque. If they couldn't find hotel rooms, perhaps Pedro would know of a nearby church where they could stay.

This small commercial district reminded her of Key Largo—close enough to the night life on the keys, but far enough away so you didn't hear music blasting from bars throughout the night. Small shops and boutiques and B and Bs lined the narrow road, and most of the properties backed up to a wooded area or to a long volcanic lake shaped like a finger. The commercial area acted as a buffer between El Bosque and a blue-collar neighborhood several streets over.

Customers jammed the places she passed, but it looked like panic buying, the kind of thing that happened in the keys when a hurricane threatened. It occurred to her that in addition to finding some Segunda Vista, she needed a change of clothes and some basic toiletries. Leo was accustomed to carrying extra clothes and toiletries in his pack because he was so often detained at the hospital or called in at odd hours. But her pack was pitifully lacking in essentials, and as far as she knew, Ian and the priest didn't even have toothbrushes with them.

Her phone jingled, a text from Maddie: *Did you find any yet?*

Looking right now.

She remembered seeing Maddie's Segunda Vista when she first started growing the beautiful, feathery weeds in her greenhouse. The red buds, Lauren recalled, triggered precognitive visions, the yellow buds facilitated telepathy, the blue variety enabled clairvoyance. She couldn't remember what the other colors did, but when the buds were mixed together with the leaves, stems, and roots, you experienced a shamanic journey regardless of whether this was your intention.

Check drugstores.

Am doing. Where're u?

Nearly at Illary's. Sanchez is a wreck.

Stay safe.

Odd and worrisome about Sanchez, she thought. He was one of the most focused young men she'd ever met, and usually controlled his extraordinary talent. Now, that talent apparently controlled *him*. Why?

Three blocks south, Lauren went into a small, crowded everything shop. She selected a couple of T-shirts, a pair of jeans, underwear, razor, several toothbrushes and tubes of toothpaste, mascara, lipstick, bottled water, peanuts and other snacks. She scoured the shelves for Second Sight, but didn't find anything. She glanced around for someone to ask, but the only two clerks were at registers and the lines in front of both were long. Resigned to a lengthy wait, Lauren got in line.

Mostly women filled the shop, all of them visibly upset. From what Lauren could understand of their rapid-fire Spanish, some of them were headed out of the city—to Quito, Guayaquil, Punta, wherever they could get to first. Others refused to leave—either because their loved ones were trapped in El Bosque or because they didn't believe it was the work of *brujos,* and, therefore, the situation was temporary and order would be restored.

The young, blond woman in front of her, a European, Lauren guessed, gestured at the items in Lauren's basket. "Did your house vanish in there?"

"No. My daughter did."

Her eyes widened with horror. "Oh my God, I'm so sorry."

The emotions Lauren had struggled to contain broke loose, tears flooded her eyes. "I'll . . . get to her." She swallowed hard before she continued. "How many people are trapped in there? Have you heard?"

"At least several hundred. Apparently a lot of people left town when the weirdness went down at the Café Taquina, otherwise the number would've been much higher. An information center has been set up on the next block. They can tell you what's going on."

"That's good to know, thanks. Did you lose someone in there?"

"I nearly did." She combed her long fingers back through her honey-colored hair. "My boyfriend used to work at the Mercado del León. He quit the day before yesterday, thank God. We've had it with this city. We're leaving. Things have just gotten too weird and dangerous. I'm getting some stuff for the trip outta here." She picked up one of a dozen blue boxes in her basket. "I'm stocking up on these. The mercado used to stock it and now this shop is the only place around here that sells it."

The label read SEGUNDA VISTA.

Wayra would call this synchronicity, Lauren thought. Ken Kesey used to call it Acid Speaking. For her, it was a *holy shit* moment, right time, right place, right search, in the groove.

"Do you know what it is?" the woman asked.

Lauren feigned ignorance. The words translated as Second Sight, so she said: "An eye solution?"

The young woman laughed. "Not exactly. It's an extract from a hallucinogenic weed grown here in Esperanza. It enables clairvoyance, telepathy, different kinds of abilities. You don't get sick from it."

Forty years ago, hallucinogens had been as familiar to Lauren as her own name. It was the territory she had traveled with Kesey, Garcia, McKenna. Her life was coming full circle. "Psychic abilities, in other words."

"Yup. Three days before that weirdness at the Café Taquina my boyfriend and I took some and . . . and both of us had the same vision. We *saw* the blackness covering that hillside behind the café and seeping from the walls of the market. We didn't have any idea what it meant. But when it actually happened at the café . . . we freaked out. We realized it was a vision of the future and that if parts of the café had vanished, then the market might, too. So he quit his job and that saved his life and now we're not sticking around. You want to find your daughter? Maybe even find a way into that whiteness? This might help you do it. I took the last of it." She dropped three boxes of Segunda Vista into Lauren's cart. "Take these."

"Thank you. Thank you so much."

"A pinch is all you need. Let it melt under your tongue. It takes four or five minutes to come on and lasts a couple of hours."

"How do these shops get away with selling this?"

"It's sold as a remedy for altitude sickness."

"Any side effects I should know about?"

"Yeah, everything I just mentioned." She flashed a quick smile that dimpled the corners of her mouth. "But nothing dire that I know of." She reached the register and, before she set her stuff on the counter, added, "I hope you find her."

Lauren anxiously awaited her turn, marveling at her good fortune. When she reached the register, she set her basket on the counter and the clerk began ringing up her purchases. Lauren slid her debit card through the slot of the machine and was ridiculously grateful when it worked, that whatever was going on here hadn't destroyed the banking system, too.

Once she was outside, she opened one of the boxes and removed a film canister identical to those California now used to dispense legal pot. She popped off the lid, scooped some of the rainbow-hued flakes out with her fingernail, onto her palm. In the sunlight, they looked luminous, alive, lit from within.

She returned the flakes to the canister, capped it, and hurried on up the street. Leo, Ian, and Pedro were standing outside the Mística. "Any rooms?" she asked.

"We've practically got the place to ourselves," Leo replied. "Looks like a lot of people around here bailed."

Lauren held up one of the blue boxes. "We're in luck."

"You and Ian have the closest emotional ties to Tess," Leo said to her. "You two should be the ones to take this stuff and Pedro and I can be the monitors. How's that sound?"

"That's fine." She just wanted to get moving with this.

"Ian?" Leo asked.

"Let's do it."

The small, cozy hotel lobby featured a comfortable area with chairs and a roaring fireplace. A man and a woman were the only people sitting in there, both of them typing away on laptops. Colorful indigenous throw rugs dotted the stone floor, local art hung on the walls. The dining room off to Lauren's right also had a fireplace, and employees were clearing away the remnants of breakfast. She was tempted to make a quick detour for a bite to eat, then remembered that Pedro was carrying a bag of breakfast goodies. Besides, she didn't want to waste time in a dining room. She wasn't even sure she should waste time eating. Tess had been inside that whiteness since last night.

They took the elevator to the third floor and when Leo unlocked the door to room 11, Lauren was pleasantly surprised. The spacious room boasted a small fridge, thick quilts on the king-sized bed, and a wide balcony that offered a view of the blinding whiteness. Lauren tossed her purse and purchases on the bed and made a beeline toward the balcony doors, opened them, and stepped outside.

From here, a mile east of El Bosque, the whiteness looked like a vast, shimmering sheet of ice, a polar ice cap broken up here and there by trees and plants, parts of houses and buildings and cars, sidewalks and roads that hadn't been affected. The extent of the whiteness shocked her. The erratic shape was horrifyingly huge, as flat as the world Columbus had envisioned, and she suddenly comprehended what immensely powerful forces they were up against. Panic gripped her, she clutched her arms to her chest, and struggled against a rising despair that a few flakes of hallucinogenic weed would make any difference at all in her ability to find her daughter.

Leo came up beside her, slipped his arm around her shoulder. "Whoever is responsible for this, chaser or *brujo* or some other intelligence, doesn't understand that love is a force of nature."

"I sometimes think, Leo, that love doesn't have shit to do with any of it. My inner cynic laughs, okay? The odds against success seem . . . staggeringly high."

"We've fought great odds before, Lauren," Ian said as he and Pedro joined them. "All of us have. And we're still here."

"We'll figure this out," the priest said. "You should eat something first. It helps the substance move more quickly into your bloodstream."

They returned to the room, where Pedro had laid out paper plates of warm croissants with melted cheese and veggies inside, and had lined up tiny cups into which he now poured Ecuadorian espresso. "Lauren, where's the canister?"

She fished it out of her purse, passed it to Pedro, and he sprinkled flakes on two of the croissants. He passed these to her and Ian. "You each should take a pinch and put it under your tongue, too. It will hasten the effects."

Lauren suspected that Pedro had presided at some of these Quero spiritual rituals that had involved Segunda Vista, and realized she had never asked him about his beliefs concerning *brujos,* chasers, Esperanza. She sipped from her tiny cup of wickedly powerful coffee, then said, "Pedro, I need to know something. What are the chasers? Are they angels? Delusional souls? Saints? The other face of a *brujo*? The right hand of God? What?"

"Are you asking me as a priest?"

"I'm just asking because you've been involved in this battle for most of your life. I'm asking because I need answers."

He bit into his croissant, dabbed at his mouth with a napkin, sipped from his coffee. Everything about him just then was slow, measured, deliberate. His eyes looked as dark as walnuts. "I believe the chasers, for the most part, are despots in that they think it's their job to determine Esperanza's fate. They're saints in that they have worked tirelessly against the *brujos.* They were once alive, so they're flawed the way all humans are. They aren't God's right hand. As far as the church is concerned, no chaser has ever met with or consulted with God, any God. In all fairness, though, I don't think any chaser has ever claimed to have met God."

"They seem to be able to tap the same power that *brujos* do," Leo remarked, and related what had happened with the supernatural crows that had rescued him and Lauren from Ricardo and Naomi. "And Charlie himself appeared as a tremendous white crow. He picked me up from the road after Ricardo had seized me and . . . and I guess it was such a shock to Ricardo that he fled my body."

Interesting, Lauren thought. Leo hadn't told her that he'd known the white crow was Charlie. She had suspected as much, but hadn't known for sure until just now.

"Charlie, Karina, Victor, and a couple of others are different from the rest of the council members," Pedro said. "They've maintained a moral compass."

Lauren couldn't argue with what the priest said about Charlie's moral compass. When he was alive, that compass had directed everything he had done, every case he had taken, every legal argument he had made. And it had done the same in his personal life. Yes, he had been manipulative since he had died, but manipulative in the way of a trickster, a Loki disguised as some afterlife version of Jimmy Buffett.

She wanted to ask Pedro about this chaser woman Charlie had been with, Karina, but felt it might be a bit tacky, all things considered. She hadn't felt jealous when Karina had shown up with Charlie; after all, Charlie had been dead for years. But she had been intensely curious— and delighted that Charlie had met someone for whom he obviously had great affection.

Yet, in the four and a half years Lauren had lived in Esperanza, with Charlie appearing to her from time to time, he'd never mentioned anything about a chaser woman. Did you date when you were dead? Did you have sex? Fall in love? She'd thought about these questions before, but never had they felt more pertinent or important, more pressing. She felt fairly sure that a Catholic priest was not the person who could answer her questions about love, sex, and rock and roll in the afterlife.

"As a human being," Pedro continued, "I believe that the chasers represent an archetype that is mostly good and the *brujos* represent an archetype that is mostly evil. But I also know that nothing in life is ever that simple."

Lauren polished off her croissant and knocked back the last sip of her coffee. "As the widow of a man who became a member of the chaser council and the mother of one of the first transitionals, I'm beginning to believe that chasers and *brujos* are just different faces of the same energy, Pedro. Contrasts. Yin, yang. Black, white. Male, female. Child, adult. Saint, demon. The living, the dead. The dark, the light. Knowledge, ignorance. But, like you, I don't believe that anything is so simplistic, so I'm left with a lot of questions."

"And that, my lovely friend, is why the people of Esperanza indulge in Segunda Vista," Pedro said. "They need to know. The weeds strip away the untruths, and leave you with the raw material. That's what they've done for centuries."

While Leo and Pedro tested the recorders on their phones and found paper and pens, Lauren sat down on the floor, her spine against the foot of the bed. Kesey had had rituals, stuff to do before you imbibed anything. Garcia never gave a shit, just bring it on. McKenna had been more deliberate, yet also more explorative, daring. No wonder he'd been the one who had talked to mushrooms and discovered an entire universe of wisdom within plant life.

Her rituals were simple: kick off shoes, settle in. Ian sat on the floor to her right, his back against a chair, his shoes off, toes wiggling around inside his dark socks. Simple on rituals, too, she thought, and liked him all the better for it.

"Quechuan shamans say that it helps if you speak to the spirit of Segunda Vista," Pedro said. "Explain your purpose."

"We'd like to find Tess," Ian said. "We would like to know how to enter the whiteness so we can get her and the others out."

"That sums it up perfectly," Lauren added.

"Now say that directly to the spirit of the plant," the priest said. "In your minds."

Just as Pedro spoke, something happened to Lauren's vision. Forty years ago, it had been called a *rush*; now it stunned her. The walls in the room started breathing, the concrete and wood rose and fell like a human chest. She heard its breath, the steady rhythm of its beating heart, saw blood rushing through its veins and arteries, a tsunami of life racing forward to embrace, expand, facilitate. Then the floor and the ceiling swelled, seeming to move toward each other. She heard the floor inhale and the ceiling exhale, and the walls breathing noisily in the space between one heartbeat and the next.

She pushed back hard against the foot of the bed and pressed her palms down against the floor to ground herself. But suddenly, the balcony doors rattled in a gust of wind, she could no longer feel the bed against her spine, the floor opened beneath her. Lauren plunged downward.

2.

Wayra came to on his side, in a bed of the softest substance he'd ever felt. Twilight clung to the air. It was that magical time in the evening when the edges of things possessed greater clarity—shadows, silhouettes, the sloping line of a roof. The gray sky roiled. It hurt his eyes to look at it.

Odors inundated his senses—sweet and sour, plant and animal, fresh and rotting, *brujo* and human. Another scent ran beneath it all, a psychic scent, that of chasers. Their imprint permeated everything.

As he pushed up, he saw a muscular black man sprawled on the ground to his right, legs splayed, arms flung out to the sides, forming perfect ninety-degree angles against the emerald grass. *Where'd he come from?*

Here and there, dead birds lay on the grass around him. Off to his left loomed an empty lot, a playground, and houses on either side. Wayra had no idea where in El Bosque he was.

He didn't trust himself to stand yet and crawled over to the black man. "Hey, you, wake up." He shook the man's shoulder. "C'mon."

Wayra slapped his cheeks lightly and the man groaned, his eyelids fluttered open. In the moment their gazes connected, Wayra suddenly understood. "You fuck," he snapped, and grabbed the front of the man's shirt and jerked him forward. "You hung around to see if I could get in and then followed me."

Ricardo knocked Wayra's arms away and bolted upward, gasping for breath in the same way a host did within moments of being seized. "Members . . . of my tribe . . . got caught in here," he stammered between gasps, then slammed his fists against his chest, as if to dislodge something and doubled forward at the waist and touched his toes. He sank to the ground, laughing hysterically, curled into a fetal position, pressed his hands between his knees and sobbed.

Wayra scrambled to his feet and walked around Ricardo, pissed off, bewildered, and alarmed. "Hey, Ricardo, talk to me."

Ricardo rolled over on his stomach, face pressed into the grass, then sat up, legs crossed Indian style, and knuckled his eyes like a little kid. "I . . . I can't shed this virtual form, Wayra. It's behaving like . . . a host. I'm breathing with this man's lungs, his heart beats for me, I control his brain."

He'd seen *brujos* do strange and horrifying things, but couldn't recall anything quite like this. "Isn't that exactly what *brujos* want?"

"Well, yeah. But not with their *virtual* forms. Not like *this*. I have no choice about a host, Wayra. We *brujos* can always leap out of a host and either bleed them out or leave them intact. I . . . I seem to be . . . shit, I hate this, but I think I'm trapped in this body."

Wayra's alarm deepened. He couldn't move through time, Sanchez couldn't turn off his psychic switch, Ricardo was stuck in his virtual body, Charlie couldn't get to where Wayra now was. So were these side effects something the council had known about or was this the result of something else, some other power? Or was it just collateral damage?

"Don't you get it?" Ricardo burst out. "This is exactly what the chasers want. Once enough *brujos* are trapped in here, they'll take El Bosque back into the nonphysical and we'll be annihilated in the process."

"And so will anyone who is alive."

"Neighborhood by neighborhood. I'm telling you. That's their plan. The dead, the living, everyone and everything."

Wayra brushed off his jeans, slung his pack over his shoulders. "Whatever. Stay away from me, *pendejo*." He started walking, fast, across the field, through the weird twilight.

"Hey, shifter, hold on," Ricardo called.

Wayra kept walking. Ricardo caught up to him, fell into step beside him. "Stay. Away. From. Me."

"Okay, I lied about everything, is that what you want to hear?"

"I don't want to hear anything from you."

"The only reason we haven't been seizing people in Esperanza is because we didn't want to be detected. All along, I planned to take over the city, to just sweep in with my tribe and be done with the lot of you, human, chaser, shifter."

"Then why didn't you?" Wayra stopped, glaring at him.

"Because . . . we couldn't. Every time we tried to do it, we ran up against something so powerful it was like . . . like a force of nature, Wayra. And each time we tried, something was taken from us. Suddenly, we could no longer think ourselves long distances. So we had to find a portal. Then it became impossible to build our virtual towns and cities, our virtual homes, our thought constructs. We tried to build them outside of Ecuador, but that didn't work, either. All we could do was seize the living outside of Ecuador. So we did, and I kept hoping that some path forward would be revealed."

"If you hadn't materialized in Tess's car, your charade could have continued for decades, maybe centuries. Why did you do that?"

He shrugged his massive shoulders, untied the sweatshirt wrapped around his waist, and slipped it on over his head. "Because I knew the goddamn chaser council was planning something, I just didn't know the specifics. And yeah, okay, I was gloating. Maybe deep down I hoped to start something, to bring all this bullshit to a head."

"Well, you did that, all right." Wayra threw out his arms. "Here we are in the fucking Twilight Zone, Ricardo." With that, he moved forward quickly again, hoping Ricardo would just go away.

But he didn't. He hurried alongside Wayra, panting like the family dog that knew it was too old to keep up but nonetheless tried valiantly. Wayra actually felt sorry for him, for this bastard who had stabbed him so many centuries ago, for this pathetic old ghost, barely a shadow of Dominica.

"Christ, Ricardo. What do you want from me?"

"Let me accompany you now, Wayra. I need to find Naomi and my other *brujos* who are trapped here. You need to find Tess and the living. We have a common goal."

"You've already admitted that you're a goddamn liar, Ricardo. Why should I believe you now?"

"Because the salvation of Esperanza, in some form, falls on us, its oldest inhabitants."

"Sorry, that doesn't convince me of shit. But you can walk with me until you piss me off."

"Which will probably be within sixty seconds," Ricardo said with a snicker.

"So talk fast."

A familiar cry rang out and Kali flew in low over the playground, headed toward them. She landed on the grass in front of them, cocked her head from one side to the other. *"Hola, amigos. Bienvenidos."*

"How'd she get in here?" Ricardo asked.

"She apparently has freedoms we don't."

Kali flew up from the ground, landed on Ricardo's shoulder, bit at a shiny button on his sleeve, and fussed at him. Then she flew upward, squawking noisily, and Wayra and Ricardo loped after her, through one empty street after another. Had the blackness that had covered El Bosque killed everyone who had been in the neighborhood at the time? Or had the blinding whiteness done that? Or was everyone in hiding?

On one street, the neighborhood simply ended with a chimney floating in midair, a numbing emptiness surrounding it. Ricardo tossed a handful of stones into the emptiness, just as Diego had done the other day outside the Café Taquina, and the emptiness crackled and popped, then the stones disappeared. "The same, but different," Ricardo said. "From this side, we can't see the whiteness. Everything just looks . . . erased."

As they followed Kali along the erratic border between here and elsewhere, they encountered hundreds of dead birds scattered in the streets, in yards, on sidewalks. It disturbed Wayra. Even Ricardo found it troubling. "The birds, Wayra. This is the result of heightened electromagnetic activity in El Bosque. That's what killed them. That's how the chasers are doing this, by raising the electromagnetism in a particular area. It must make it easier for them to just slice away entire neighborhoods. The condors must have sensed it and fled."

"Do you have any idea where in El Bosque we are?"

"None."

Since the blackness had swallowed Tess at the market, Wayra thought his search for her should begin there. But first, he needed to orient himself so that he could locate the store and so far he hadn't been able to do that.

They began to see other people, cars moving through the streets, kids on bikes, dogs, cats, all the signs of normal life. But it was normal *only if* you ignored the fact that the sky hadn't changed, it was still twilight, and *only if* you could overlook the hundreds of dead birds and were blind to the places where the neighborhood simply ended and the emptiness began.

A church bell rang in the distance, long, plaintive notes that echoed through the streets. It seemed to beckon them. Kali led them directly to the church, where fifty or sixty people lined the sidewalk from the church steps to the hearse parked at the curb. Pallbearers emerged from the church carrying two coffins, one large, one small, and the people in attendance tossed roses on the coffins as they passed. The mourners didn't utter a single sound. There was no noise at all. It unnerved Wayra. But even more troubling was that no one seemed to see the dead birds strewn across the church's property.

How could you *not* see them? Their corpses blanketed the grounds of the church, their wings fully open, heads turned to one side, beaks slightly parted, as if they had taken one last, heaving breath before they died. They lay on their backs, their legs and claws straight up in the air. If Illary, in her hawk form, had been in here when El Bosque disappeared, would he have found her corpse among the thousands that no one seemed to see?

Just the thought of it horrified Wayra.

When the coffins were put inside the hearse, the crowd started to break up, people headed toward their cars, presumably to follow the hearse to the cemetery. Wayra spotted Javier, the baker whom Ian had tried to save that night at the Café Taquina. He loped across the street and came up behind him. "Javier?"

Javier turned around and looked at Wayra without any recognition whatsoever in his dark eyes. "Yes, I'm Javier," he said in Spanish. "Do I know you?"

Uh, yeah, since you were in diapers. "I'm Wayra. I drop by your bakery a couple of times a week for breakfast. My wife and I attended your son's baptism. Your wife makes the best arepas in Ecuador."

Javier smiled politely. "You must have me confused with someone else. I don't have a son. I'm not married. And I don't own a bakery. Excuse me. I need to get to the cemetery for the burial."

Stunned, Wayra watched him hurry off to a scooter, hop on, and chug away. Wayra scanned the faces in the crowd, but didn't see anyone else who looked familiar to him. He wished Pedro were with him. Pedro knew most of the priests in Esperanza and would likely know the priest in charge of this parish, who now stood on the church steps, talking to several mourners who lingered.

Wayra moved closer, noticed Kali circling silently above the church, and waited until he could speak to the priest alone. When the others had left to join the procession to the cemetery, Wayra approached the priest, a small man with gray hair, a dimpled chin, chipmunk cheeks. Wayra addressed him in Spanish.

"Excuse me, may I ask you a question, Father?"

"Of course. You are . . . ?"

Wayra gave a phony name. "Esteban."

"Thank you for attending the service, Esteban. It means a great deal to the families to see all the support they have."

"Such a tragedy about the child," Wayra said, referring to the smaller of the two coffins.

"Indeed. She was found wandering through the commercial district, blood pouring down her face. She didn't know what had happened. She lasted for only three days in intensive care."

Three days? The black crud had swept over El Bosque only last night. Was there a connection between the priest's sense of time and all the odd hours that appeared on every timekeeping device in El Bosque before its disappearance? "Why is the sky a perpetual twilight?" he asked.

The priest frowned and dropped his head back, peering upward, then crossed himself quickly, kissing his thumbnail as he finished. "No one remembers." He spoke softly, with obvious puzzlement and regret. "Most of my parishioners choose to ignore it. The consensus, I think, is that the *brujos* are behind it. But since we seem to be protected from the *brujos* here, no one questions too closely. What do you know about it, Esteban?"

"Nothing definitive. I was hoping you had the answers. And why haven't the dead birds been cleaned up?" He gestured toward the corpses to the right of where they stood.

"Dead birds?" The priest looked in the direction Wayra motioned. "I don't see any dead birds, Esteban."

This pronouncement told Wayra everything he needed to know

about the extent of the perceptual delusion. It shocked him nonetheless. He walked over to the closest bird corpses, picked up a sparrow and an owl, and carried them over to the priest, holding them up by the feet. "Dead birds, Father. Can you see them?"

The priest looked at Wayra, at his upraised hand, blinked rapidly several times, then backed away from him. "I . . . I . . . listen, Esteban, if you aren't feeling well, there's a clinic two blocks over. You should talk to someone. A lot of us here have been talking to these mental health professionals who—"

"Are you telling me you can't *see* them?" Wayra moved toward the priest, the dead birds dangling from his hand. "A sparrow, a barn owl." He practically rubbed the corpses in the priest's face, who only threw up his hands. "Please, Esteban. You should go to the clinic, to the—"

Wayra turned away from him, still holding the bird corpses, and hurried across the street to where Ricardo waited. "They can't see the dead birds, Ricardo. And they can't remember anything."

The shade of the trees ebbed and flowed across Ricardo's face, his virtual face. The *brujo* reached out and stroked the feathers of the dead birds. "We should bury them, Wayra. We should bury the thousands of birds that have died here."

"It would take weeks. We don't have weeks."

"But we have a few minutes," Ricardo said, and plucked the dead sparrow and owl from Wayra's hand and walked quickly, resolutely, to a pile of leaves at the curb.

He dug a hole through the leaves and placed the corpses gently inside, then moved the fallen leaves over the bodies. Wayra felt strangely moved by the *brujo*'s show of compassion. Dominica had never shown compassion toward anything or anyone.

"I'm going to the burial," Wayra said.

Ricardo stood, brushing his hands together. "No fucking way I'm going to a cemetery."

"You're not a *brujo* here, Ricardo, you don't have to be afraid of cemeteries."

He gave a small, nervous laugh and ran his hand over his bald head. "I guess not. That guy, the baker, didn't recognize you, did he."

It wasn't a question. "No. And he doesn't seem to have any memory of his family or of the bakery. And then there's the fact that no one sees the dead birds."

"When El Bosque was disappeared, it wiped out the memories of everyone in here. Several hundred people."

"But they remember *brujos.*"

"Of course. We're as much a part of their collective history as chasers and shifters."

"I think the amnesia is an unexpected side effect of what's happened here."

"Which benefits *the chasers.* What a perfect coincidence."

He had a point.

"And I'll tell you this, Wayra. These supposedly evolved souls have messed up worse than anyone in my tribe ever did."

Wayra's fatigue swept over him suddenly and completely. He stumbled and Ricardo caught his arm, steadying him, and helped him over to a bench under a tree. Wayra sank onto it. "Thanks."

"Self-preservation, amigo. I didn't know how to get in here to find Naomi and the others in my tribe and I don't know how to get out of here, either. So if you die on me, I'm stuck in this twilight zone and trapped in this body. Like you, I deserve a choice."

"You *brujos* never give a prospective host a choice, Ricardo. This is what it feels like."

Ricardo stepped back, anger flashing in his eyes. "So what're you saying exactly? That being in here is, like, what? Some kind of karma, Wayra?"

"Karma," Wayra repeated. "Bad word. It's more like a mirror, Ricardo. You're now experiencing what your hosts experience and I'm beginning to realize just how old and tired I really am. And these people, who endured so much during the years Dominica's tribe terrorized the city, are suffering from a collective amnesia. The story is changing, Ricardo. Shifter, *brujo,* chaser, the living and the dead. We all knew this would happen eventually. But we never knew *when* or *how* it would happen. The interesting part of all this is that you and I, shifter and *brujo,* and the parrot, appear to be the only ones who have gotten into the disappeared area. What does that tell us?"

Ricardo, usually a master of snappy, hostile responses, was strangely silent. He looked down at his shoes, then off to his right where a siren sounded, then ran his right hand across the back of his neck and stared up into the twilight. "The city is letting us work through this without the chaser intervention?"

"But the chasers *caused* this," Wayra said.

"Yes, but they can't get in now. I don't know what to think about the parrot." Ricardo kicked at a stone in front of him. "I feel like I'm being coerced into ending something I'm not ready to end yet, Wayra. I resent that. Once we're out of here, I'll fight for my tribe's right to occupy Esperanza alongside the living. I'm going to look for Naomi and the others. When one of us has succeeded, we should meet in front of the market. If we can find it."

With that, he sauntered off down the road, muscular arms swinging at his sides, an ancient *brujo* trapped in a black man's body. Wayra stayed on the bench a while longer, watching Kali as she spiraled down through the twilight and landed on the bench beside him. "I wish you could talk, Kali," he murmured. "You know, a regular conversation."

She cocked her head to one side, peering at him with those strangely lovely green eyes, then squawked, *"Vamonos, amigo."* Wayra pressed his hands to his thighs and stood. His bones ached. Cemetery first, he thought, and started walking.

The sky remained locked in a forever twilight, without clouds or stars or a rising moon. Even the air temperature stayed the same, a pleasant coolness, probably around sixty degrees. El Bosque's present state struck him as a kind of limbo—parked in some netherworld where everyone suffered from amnesia, selective perception, and the air temperature and light remained static.

He brought out his iPhone and was surprised he had a signal. He texted Illary and received an error message that the network had insufficient coverage to comply with his request. Suppose he texted someone lost in this place? He composed a careful text to Tess, taking into account that she might be afflicted with the same amnesia as the priest and Javier.

He didn't receive an error message this time, and when he checked the Sent box, the message was there. By the time he reached the cemetery ten minutes later, no response had come through. He refused to speculate about what that might mean.

He walked into the cemetery, where a crowd of perhaps fifty had gathered at the gravesites. The priest Wayra had talked to at the church was addressing the mourners. Wayra made his way to the back of the crowd, listening, observing the people nearest to him, wondering how pervasive their amnesia was.

When the priest finished speaking, Wayra stepped forward and asked if he could say a few words. The priest looked uncertain about it, but was too polite to put up a fuss. He handed Wayra the mike.

"These two tragedies were not accidental," Wayra began. "They are the direct result of what happened to El Bosque when the chasers attempted to remove it from the physical world. It's what they intend to do to all of Esperanza. And apparently, in order to do that, they have to make sure none of you remember what happened. A collective amnesia."

The crowd stirred, people looked uneasily at each other, the priest shuffled his feet nervously. Wayra rushed on. "Javier," he said, looking directly at the young man. "You were at the Café Taquina when a moving wave of blackness consumed most of a hillside and part of the rear deck of the restaurant. You got caught in this blackness and Ian Ritter and several other men—including the gentleman on your right—struggled to free you. But the blackness took you both. Now you're here. Why is the sky a perpetual twilight? Why can't any of you see the hundreds of dead birds scattered around? Try to remember. *Try.*"

"I don't know this man," Javier shouted. "He's an intruder, he's—"

The priest grabbed the mike from Wayra. "Señor, please, this is a private funeral. I must ask you to leave. The—"

"He should be arrested," someone yelled.

"Arrest him, arrest him," the crowd chanted, and surged forward.

Wayra shifted by reflex, and was relieved that it worked, that he could still shift. He raced between gravestones, headed for the nearest thicket, Kali flying high above him. The crowd screamed that only devils could shape-shift, and a handful of men tore after him, hurling stones, waving shovels. Within minutes, a truck barreled through the graveyard, with more men in the back of it—*armed men*—and rapidly gained on him.

If they caught him, they would probably stone him to death or simply shoot him. An elemental panic seized Wayra and he plunged into the thicket, shifted into his human form, but the shift was incomplete, his left hand remained a paw, with fur extending up his forearm.

He scaled one of the monkey puzzle trees, Kali touched down in the upper branches. He was midway up when the truck slammed through the woods, and even though he wasn't fully hidden by the branches, no one looked up.

He climbed higher, wedged his body in a V formed by a pair of thick branches, and hooked his arms around them. It wasn't long before the men on foot appeared beneath him, armed vigilantes. Where had they gotten the weapons? Were they also a byproduct of what had happened here? They suffered from such extreme amnesia they didn't question what was happening around them, to them.

The men spread out through the woods, whistling, laughing, calling for the doggy devil. Wayra didn't move, barely breathed. It was as if he were reliving the dark ignorance of medieval times, when shifters and alleged witches were hunted with maniacal obsession.

When he could no longer hear them, he parted the leaves with his hand and scanned the area. No men, no truck. Did he dare climb down? Would they head back this way?

He moved his body slightly, so he would have a better view of where the crowd had been. Only the cemetery employees remained. He glanced up at Kali, who flew down to his shoulder and rubbed her beak across his cheek.

Now, he thought, and carefully climbed down. "Kali, find Tess," he murmured. "Do you understand what I'm saying? Find Tess."

The parrot cocked her head, those strangely human eyes regarding him closely. Then she lifted up from his shoulder and took off.

He shifted and sniffed at the air, following the scents of the men, and ran in the opposite direction. It occurred to him that he might be pushing his luck. When he shifted back into his human form, would he be even more incomplete? Would he be able to do it at all? Or would he, like Ricardo, be stuck? It terrified him.

Thirteen
Amnesiac

For the longest time, she sat on the curb in front of the market, shoveling baked beans from a can into her mouth. At first, she used a plastic spoon she'd found somewhere, but when the spoon broke, she used her fingers.

The beans tasted delicious. They were salty, but most canned goods were either too salty or too sweet. Open any can of fruit in her cart, for example, and it would be floating in a heavy syrup. She actually didn't mind the syrup. It kept her hydrated and energetic and less dependent on bottled water, which was sadly lacking in her supplies.

She had no idea why she was sitting in front of the market or why she had a grocery cart next to her loaded with *stuff*. She didn't know *where* she was, *why* she was, and she didn't know *who* she was. The mystery of the interrogative pronouns floated around her, just daring her to pursue them—all of them, any one of them.

The *who*. Okay, she would start simple, with the basics. *Who am I?* Nothing.

Where am I?

Blank.

Whom do I love? Who loves me?

She felt something, but couldn't grasp or name it. It just rolled around inside of her, one more loose screw, and triggered flutters of panic in her chest. How could she not know who the hell she was?

When she'd eaten through the beans, she stood and set the empty can in the grocery cart until she could find a garbage bin. Why were there so many dead birds on the sidewalk, in the street? They lay in broken glass that she suspected came from the window of the market behind her, where she presumably had gotten the supplies in her cart. Yet, she couldn't recall being inside the market. And who or what had shattered the window? A vague memory flopped around inside her like a fish out of water, something connected to the market, but the harder she struggled to find the memory, the more elusive it became.

She walked over to the broken door and peered inside. A dozen or more abandoned carts loaded with food and supplies stood every which way, blocking the entrance to aisles. Other fully loaded carts had been overturned and the floor around them was littered with merchandise. The air held a peculiar stink that was somehow familiar. She suspected it came from freezer compartments, where food was going bad because there wasn't any electricity. Why not? What had happened to the power? Was there power anywhere on this road?

How long had she been here?

C'mon, think. Remember. She kicked a can out of her way and it rolled down the sidewalk, across shards of glass and dead birds.

Judging by the state of her soiled clothes, the dry, tangled feel of her hair, the way she smelled, she had been here *a while*. But how long was *a while*? Several days? Weeks? Days, she decided. If it were weeks, she would smell a lot worse.

She felt an urge to slip inside, but didn't want to leave her cart out here unattended. She had seen other street people pushing their carts around, sleeping inside them to keep their stuff from being stolen. She didn't understand why any of this was going on, sensed she didn't usually live like this, but that it was the way she must live now to survive.

So how do I usually live?

Another big, fat blank.

"Shit, shit," she muttered, pressing her fists into her eyes. She couldn't answer the most basic questions about herself. Why not? Had she suffered a concussion? Brain damage?

She ran her fingers through her tangled hair, feeling her scalp. No pain, no cuts, her fingers didn't come away bloody. Had she had a stroke? *Am I dead?*

These speculations only increased her anxiety and frustration. Since the market kept beckoning her to enter, she thought it might hold some clue to her identity. She pushed her cart up to the door, which hung by a single hinge and swung like a pendulum. Her cart's wheels clattered as she moved through the doorway, the noise echoing in the strange, tight silence.

First, she looked through the carts loaded with food and supplies, plucked out items she might be able to use, and dropped them in her cart. The fruits looked overly ripe, the veggies were shriveled or turning brown, but she was too hungry to care. She peeled a soft banana and gobbled it down, and added radishes, a couple of apples, several shriveled oranges, and a zucchini squash to her basket. She found a box of large kitchen matches, some bath soap, and a tall unopened bottle of water. She twisted the cap and drank until her thirst was sated, then put everything into her cart.

She moved the abandoned carts out of her way, pushed hers a safe distance from the door, then picked up a hand basket and started down the closest aisle. A pot or pan, cooking utensils, olive oil, shampoo, towels, a razor, a hairbrush, toothbrush and toothpaste: she could use all of it.

Why had so much merchandise fallen from the shelves? Had there been an earthquake? Was that what had happened here? Was this quake or other disaster the reason she'd ended up living on the street, with no memory of who she was?

She quickly combed through piles of strewn merchandise and was delighted to find a razor, a bottle of shampoo, toothbrush, a heavy iron frying pan, a couple of hand towels. Never mind that the hand towels wouldn't dry much more than her face and that she didn't have access to a shower or a pot to pee in. She might be able to use a fountain in one of the parks to clean up.

Fresh clothes were the next item on her agenda.

At the end of the aisle, she looked right, then left, and a profound unease gripped her. A memory shifted around inside of her, something frightening, but she couldn't grasp it. Why should going *left* affect her at all? To the left stood shelves of noodles, pasta, detergents, pet foods, paper towels, and toilet paper. That aisle led to the registers and was farther from the front door. So what? Why should she fear anything there?

She stared at the merchandise a moment longer, grappling for the memory. She seemed to recall a dark liquid spreading across the floor, but nothing else was attached to the memory.

She turned away from what triggered the unease, and was quickly rewarded with an aisle filled with water—Evian, distilled, volcanic, Perrier, some in plastic, most in glass bottles. She took what she could carry, eager now to get out of here and find someplace where she could clean up.

But when she reached the end of the aisle, a man stood beside her cart, examining the contents. Tall. Caucasian. Dark hair. He seemed familiar to her and she didn't know why. "Hey, you," she shouted. "Back off from that cart. It's mine."

The man jerked back. "Take it easy, I'm not stealing anything."

The closer she got to him, the less substantial he looked. She realized she could actually see through him—the shattered window behind him, the carts piled high with goods, the stuff scattered across the floor. "You're not real." She hurled a bottle of Perrier at him and it soared right through him, struck the edge of the window and exploded.

"Hey," he said quickly. "Tess, it's me. Ian."

"My name's not Tess and I don't know anyone named Ian."

He abruptly faded away. Spooked, she quickly pushed her cart out of the market and down the street. *Tess, Ian, Tess, Ian, Tess, Ian.* The names slammed around inside her, screaming, *Remember me, c'mon you can do it, remember me.*

She remembered nothing related to those names or any others.

She went into a deserted clothing store. Merchandise puddled on the floor, hangers had been tossed around, the cash register drawer lolled like a giant tongue, and didn't hold a single dollar bill. The place looked as if it had been ransacked. She moved through the mess, pawing through the clothes until she found a pair of jeans that looked as if they would fit her, a long-sleeved T-shirt, a lightweight jacket that reached to her thighs, a couple pairs of underwear. Forget bras, who needed a bra? Shoes, she definitely needed shoes, and went through a pile of them until she found a pair of workout shoes that fit her. Keens. They had lots of openings in them, were springy, blissfully comfortable. Multidimensional shoes. Wearing these suckers, she thought, she could become a comic book heroine.

She pushed her cart across the cobblestoned street and up two blocks to the park. The place was deserted—no couples sitting on the benches, no one feeding the birds, empty, zilch. In fact, the only birds she saw were dead ones, and they lay everywhere. Sparrows, humming-birds, blackbirds, blue jays, hawks, wrens, ducks, even wading birds. But not a single condor.

What horror had killed them?

She pushed her cart around the dead birds until it was next to the fountain, dug out her soap, shampoo, razor, and set everything on the wall. She glanced around once more, making sure she was alone here, then stripped off her filthy clothes and eased into the water. It chilled her, held her, caressed her, and felt so utterly magnificent against her skin that for long, delicious moments, she floated in the fountain, her mind a perfect blank. She sank beneath the surface and the face of the man who had appeared in the market drifted into her thoughts. Was her name really Tess and, if so, how had this guy known that? If he was Ian, what was he to her? Why had he looked like a ghost?

She soaped up her body, washed and rinsed her hair, shaved her legs and underarms, then got out of the fountain and dried herself with a couple of the hand towels. Laughable. She put on clean clothes and her superhero shoes. She deposited her old clothes in a nearby garbage can, then looked around through the bushes and trees for a place to sleep. Why was it still twilight?

She didn't want to think too closely about that, about the twilight. An inner resistance. Okay, she would honor that feeling for now and not think about it. *Stay fixed in the moment, don't ask questions, don't think:* that seemed to be the best way to fight her anxiety. Keep her head a merciful blank.

She pushed her cart into the monkey puzzle trees and pines, glanced back at the dead birds. *What happened here?* Why hadn't they been cleaned up? Buried? Had whatever killed all these birds also stolen her memory?

"Stop asking," she told herself, then dug through her cart until she found a box of garbage bags. She pulled out several and started collect-ing the corpses.

When both bags were full, she carried them into the thicket and searched for some place to bury them. Since she didn't have a shovel or anything to dig with, she found a large pile of dead leaves, dug through them with her foot, and emptied the first bag. She spread the corpses out, so the leaves wouldn't be piled too high, started covering them, then stopped to study them.

From what she could see in this truncated light, the birds didn't have any obvious injuries. *Had they all died at once? From what? No questions, no questions.* But she couldn't help herself. Nothing made sense.

She picked up a crow, lifted each wing, ran her fingers down its back, but couldn't find an injury. She examined the crow's beak, its feet, didn't see anything unusual. But how would she, who couldn't even recall her own name, know what was usual or unusual for a dead crow?

She set the bird down in the leaves, quickly covered it and the others, and moved deeper into the trees. She found a burial spot for the second bag of corpses. By the time she finished covering them, she was too exhausted to gather up more birds and decided to resume after she'd gotten some sleep.

Her eyes felt so dry that she wondered how long it had been since she'd slept. And *where* had she slept last? She couldn't remember.

"Can't remember" had become her mantra.

She plucked her sleeping bag from the cart, spread it out against the ground. She climbed into it with her wet hair, her clean body covered in clean clothes, her feet encased in the superhero shoes, and lay there, eyes wide open, staring into the twilight that spilled through the branches of the trees.

I am . . . I love . . . I am loved by . . . Nothing, nothing, nothing. Fuck. She covered her eyes with her arm and struggled against a rising despair. Without memories, she was nothing, a vacuum, an empty vessel.

She might have dozed off, she wasn't sure, but when her arm fell away from her eyes, a pale violet orb hovered just above her. She reached up and touched it, and immediately sensed its energy was female. It felt familiar to her.

She pushed up on her elbows and the orb floated toward her, then hovered right in front of her. It looked like a transparent glass bubble, alien but strangely beautiful. The violet grew darker at the edges and paled toward the center, where it pulsed with light. She wondered if it was the soul of someone who had passed on. She remembered reading somewhere that orbs might be the souls of the departed. Why could she remember *that* bit of information, but nothing about herself? Had someone she loved died recently?

The orb brushed her forehead, a soft, cool touch, like a mother's kiss, then it splintered and broke apart and the bits of violet light drifted into the air, blinking off and on like fireflies. Was her mother dead? What did her mother look like? How could she not remember her own mother?

She watched the lights until they reached the edge of the park and winked out for good. For moments afterward she felt such an acute and terrible loneliness that she nearly leaped to her feet and ran after the bits of light. But just then, two men turned into the park, pushing grocery carts loaded with stuff. Their carts crunched over the dead birds, as though the men didn't see them. But they saw her.

One of them said something to the other, laughed, and the taller of the two men strode toward her. Tess slipped out of the sleeping bag and stood, the cart between her and this man. Even beneath his baggy coat, she could tell he was muscular and probably outweighed her by at least a hundred pounds. Although she was tall, six feet without shoes, he was slightly taller. In the twilight, he looked Latino but not Ecuadorian, and young, mid-twenties, she guessed.

"*Chica,*" he said.

Without even thinking about it, she replied, "*Chico. ¿Qué hubo?*"

It shocked her that she not only spoke Spanish, but sounded like a native. It apparently surprised him, too. Because of her blond hair, he had probably pegged her as an American or a European who was unlikely to speak the language. "*Ah, que bueno que hablas español.*"

"I also speak English. What's your point?"

In equally perfect English, he said, "My point, bitch, is that my friend and I need what you've got in this cart."

He grabbed the front of it, she held on tightly, and he pulled even harder. She snatched the frying pan off the top of her stuff, shoved the cart at him, and he stumbled back, tripped, and went down. She whacked the pan against the soles of his sneakers and pushed the cart away from him. "It's mine, asshole, and if you come near me again, I'll bash your face in. Are we clear on that, *amigo*?"

He scooted back on his ass, but the man's companion raced toward them now, his long hair flying out behind him, his shouts echoing in the air. "Serbio, take her from the right."

Serbio, emboldened by his friend's intervention, scrambled up, darted to her right, and his companion shot at her from the left.

Rage burst from her—rage that her memory was gone, she was homeless, that these two men threatened her. She spun, clutching the frying pan with both hands, and swung it like a baseball bat. It struck Serbio first, and he lurched back, shrieking, hands flying to his bloody nose. The other guy reacted quickly, deflecting a blow to his face that glanced off his shoulder. He tackled her and they both crashed to the ground.

She lost her grip on the pan, punched the man in the ribs, beat her fists against his back, fought to kick him off. But he grabbed handfuls of her hair and slammed her head against the ground. Fractals erupted across her vision, millions of pieces of splintered light that swirled into strange, frightening patterns. She tangled her fingers in his long hair and jerked with such force that his head snapped back. She somehow managed to twist her head to the right and chomped down on his wrist. It felt like her teeth struck bone.

He squealed like a wounded pig, she tasted his blood in her mouth, and as he reared up, gripping his bloody fist, she rolled away from him, swept up the frying pan, and slammed it over his head. He slumped to the ground and her eyes darted to Serbio, who abruptly stopped.

"You're one crazy bitch," he yelled.

She scooped up her sleeping bag, tossed it in her cart. "Leave me the fuck alone." She moved away from him, her spine against the cart, pushing it, and swung the frying pan so that with every backward swing it clanged against the cart, metal against metal. The sound echoed menacingly in the strange twilight, and she kept at it until Serbio picked up his unconscious companion and quickly carried him over to their carts.

She moved around to the back of the cart, gripped the handle and pushed it rapidly into the trees. The wheels clattered over stones and roots, drooping branches snagged on her clothes. She glanced back several times, making sure that Serbio wasn't following her, and finally reached a packed-earth sidewalk that ran parallel to the park. She picked up a handful of smooth stones, large enough to do some serious damage.

She tore up the sidewalk, desperately seeking an empty building, some spot like that clothing store she'd gone into, where the windows and doors weren't damaged or ruined, where she might take refuge until she'd figured things out.

But the things she had to figure out staggered her comprehension. She felt like an ant in Manhattan, scrambling away from all the descending shoes. She had no idea who she was, where she'd come from or where she was, why she was here or what had happened that had transformed the sky into a perpetual twilight and killed so many birds and rendered her homeless. It all felt *wrong*.

Even along the road she traveled now, dead birds lay everywhere. She agonized every time she saw one and stopped again and again to pick up the corpses, put them in a garbage bag, and bury them under leaves. Shoddy graves, she thought, and wished she had a shovel. Or even a metal spoon would help.

Her ribs ached from where the man had punched her and her upper lip felt sore, cracked, swollen. She just hoped she hadn't killed him when she'd hit him in the head.

A bird's cry, the first she'd heard, prompted her to peer upward. A parrot swept down through the twilight and landed at the end of her cart. Shades of blue and green threaded through its feathers. An Amazonian parrot, she knew that much, and wondered why it hadn't perished with the other birds. This parrot and the condors: they were the only types of birds she hadn't seen among the dead.

The longer she and the parrot stared at each other, the greater her sense that they were old friends. "I know you," she whispered. "You're . . ."

She struggled to find the parrot's name, but couldn't. The bird suddenly lifted up from the end of her cart and flew across the street to a storefront. It landed on top of the sign, DEPORTES DEL BOSQUE, and another memory stirred. She knew she'd been here, shopped here, but details escaped her. *Bosque* meant woods. So was this the town of Bosque? Or was it a neighborhood? Every time she posed a question like this she ran into a wall she just couldn't penetrate. But she felt the parrot had led her here because she would be safe in this place for a while.

She opened the door, pushed her cart inside, and somehow wasn't surprised when the parrot flew in alongside her and settled on the edge of her cart again. "I'm starving," she said. "I could use a portable propane grill." The parrot stretched out one of its wings and preened itself. "A lotta help *you* are."

Even though this place lacked electricity, too, the skylight in the center of the store was large enough to admit the twilight. In the third aisle she entered, she found a small, portable camping grill with a single burner and a canister of propane attached to it. Since it was a floor display, she didn't even have to remove it from a box.

She hurried through the aisles, scouring the shelves for something she might use as a weapon. She found a hunting knife and two lightweight metal slingshots. She added them to her cart, set the grill up at the back of the store, then removed the items she would need to make a substantial meal. In rearranging everything in the cart, a backpack at the bottom was exposed.

Where had *that* come from?

Curious, she pulled it out, unzipped it. Clean clothes, an iPad, a wad of cash tucked in a compartment, and an iPhone. How could she recognize things like the iPad and iPhone, but not remember her name or anything else about her life?

She held the iPad out in front of her and snapped a photo of herself, then studied it. *This is me?* Her blond hair nearly touched her shoulders, her blue eyes looked pinched with fatigue, her cheekbones were blade sharp. Now that she knew what she looked like, she clicked the photos icon and went through photos of herself with people she didn't recognize, didn't remember.

In one picture, a tall, dark-haired man had his arm around her shoulders and she recognized him as the man she'd seen in the market. Ian. He felt comfortable to her. The pretty redheaded woman who clowned with another dark-haired man also felt right to her.

But *comfortable* and *right* didn't cut it. *She craved details.* Who were they to her? "Ian, Ian," she murmured, and wondered what the redhead's name was.

The next photo captured her. The woman had salt-and-pepper hair, a compact, slender body, and she was holding hands with the handsome gray-haired man standing beside her. They appeared to be in front of an apartment building and looked blissfully happy.

This woman, she suddenly knew, was her mother. She couldn't remember anything about her—no name or personal info, but her face spoke to some part of Tess that remembered.

Since the text message icon on her phone was lit up, she pressed it. The message, sent at an unknown time on December 19, 2012, read:

> Your name is Tess Livingston. You're in El Bosque neighborhood, which the chasers have parked in this twilit place until they have enough *brujos* trapped inside to take it into the nonphysical world. Send me your location. I'll come to you. Wayra

She said that name, Tess Livingston, out loud, hoping it would resonate, that it would trigger a memory, but it didn't affect her at all. And who was this Wayra person? What the hell kind of name was that, anyway?

She pressed the contact icon and scrolled through a list of names. Some of them had accompanying photos, others didn't. She found Ian and Wayra, but she also found other names—Maddie, Nick, Mom, Leo, Illary, Expat—and none of them resonated. She felt gratified that next to MOM was the photo of the woman with the salt-and-pepper hair. And Leo was apparently the gray-haired man she'd seen with her mother in the photo.

The longer she studied Ian's photo, the more frustrated she felt that she couldn't remember anything about him.

The photo of Wayra showed a handsome man with high cheekbones, sensuous mouth, piercing eyes, curly dark hair that fell to his shoulders. It didn't resonate for her at all. In his text message, Wayra mentioned chasers and *brujos. Brujo* meant witch, but why would this Wayra person mention witches? She didn't have any idea what chasers were.

With her anxiety skyrocketing, she pocketed the phone and concentrated on fixing something to eat. She eyed the ingredients she had set on the floor: a small container of olive oil, two cans of tuna, wilted lettuce, some nuts, flat bread that probably had mold on it, a container of live bean sprouts, a bag of browning radishes, carrots that had seen better days.

She turned the frying pan over and used the bottom of it as her cutting board. She tossed pieces of carrots and nuts to the parrot, who ate pristinely, holding this or that in her claws, nibbling and watching her. The repetitive rhythm of the chopping and dicing stirred yet another memory, of herself and a man in a kitchen, where he chopped and diced with utter fury while something pummeled the building over and over again. She could only see the man's hands, but the memory of the pummeling terrified her.

She scooped everything into her hands, dropped it all inside the frying pan, added olive oil, and fired up her little grill. Another vivid memory burst forth, of herself on a back porch somewhere, cooking on a regular propane grill, one that was waist high and had both a grill and a side burner. The grill stood on a porch overlooking a long boardwalk that jutted across a salt marsh and ended at the edge of a beach. The porch's screens were ripped and flapped in a steady, humid breeze. Some of the trees in the salt marsh tilted at extreme angles, others looked ravaged by a savage wind. Pieces of the boardwalk were missing, the end of it had collapsed.

She could suddenly place the memory: the rear deck of her mother's home in Key Largo, Florida, in the aftermath of a hurricane in 2005. The city's power had gone down; that was why she was cooking on a propane grill. A hurricane seven years ago: was she missing seven years of memories? Or was she missing decades more than this? Key Largo was in Florida. Yet, she had no memory of ever being in Florida, much less living there. And she couldn't even envision her mother in this place. And who was her father? Did she have siblings? Pets? What was her work, career? What were her passions? Whom did she love?

Her head ached with questions, so she turned her attention back to her cooking. When she finally bit into her wrap, juice dripped down the inside of her arm and she welcomed it, licked at it, couldn't waste a single drop. Afterward, she sat there for a few minutes, eyes closed, savoring the sensation of fullness. She felt like a sloth.

She finally pushed to her feet, took the dirty frying pan into the back room and washed it in the sink. She also brushed her teeth, which went a long way toward making her feel human again. She packed up her little camping grill and supplies, brought out her sleeping bag and spread it open on the floor. She removed her shoes and socks and padded barefoot through the store, helping herself to a couple of flashlights, a package of batteries, camping pillows. She put the knife, one of the slingshots, and several of the smooth stones inside her sleeping bag. Once she was settled inside of it, she picked up her iPhone again, scrolled through the text messages, reread the one from this guy named Wayra and responded.

OK, no idea WTF u r, but need answers. Am @ deportes del bosque

She waited five minutes for a response and when nothing came through, she dug through the pack for a charger, didn't find one, and turned off the phone to conserve on power. Then she squirmed down into the sleeping bag, her head sinking into the pillow. Her last thought was the parrot's name started with a *k*.

She bolted awake sometime later and called the parrot by name. "Kali."

The bird landed beside her. *"Bienvenida, Tess."*

Tess. That name again. I am Tess, she thought, testing the name, trying it on for size. It didn't feel any more familiar to her now than it had when she'd tested it earlier, but she decided to claim the name. Why not? It was better than no name.

"I am Tess," she said aloud. "But how do you know my name, Kali?"

Kali trilled softly and preened herself. As Tess dropped off to sleep, she wondered again how it knew her name. When she woke the second time, a tall man sat beside her, Kali perched on his shoulder. She reached for her slingshot, but since the parrot apparently didn't feel threatened by the man, she didn't, either. Besides, she recognized him from her iPhone contacts. Wayra.

"Do you remember me?" he asked.

She wanted to, *needed* to, but didn't. "No. But I know your name is Wayra because you're in my contact list."

"Even if you can't remember me, Tess, I hope you can trust me. We should move on. Neither of us is safe here."

"I've been perfectly safe right here for a while now."

"That may be. But if these bozos catch us, we'll probably be stoned to death."

"*Stoned?*" She thought of the two men in the park. "By . . . ?"

"The ones who were in El Bosque when it disappeared. The . . . transition screwed them up. Question: can you see the dead birds everywhere?"

"Yes. But these two guys who tried to steal my stuff . . . I don't think they could see the birds. Why would that be?"

"I don't know," Wayra replied, "Maybe it means your memories will return more quickly. Let's get going."

She and Wayra gathered up her belongings, piled everything into her cart, and the parrot perched at the end of it, squawking noisily. Wayra pushed the cart out of the store, onto the twilit street. She peered up and down the deserted road. Her head hammered, her heart beat way too fast, she felt like throwing her arms around this stranger, Wayra, and begging him to tell her what she needed to know. Instead, she barely managed to ask, "What's going on here, Wayra?"

"A battle."

"Between who and who?"

"Chasers, *brujos,* shifters, the living and the dead. I don't know. None of the boundaries are clear anymore."

"I don't know what chasers or *brujos* are. And what are shifters? My memory is seriously damaged."

Wayra's frown thrust down so deeply between his eyes it threatened to divide his face in half. "Jesus, Tess."

"I know. It's bad. Thanks to my phone and iPad, I have images of people who are apparently close to me, but *I don't remember them.* I don't know much of anything about myself. But what I really want to know is, how do we win this battle?"

"That's what we're trying to figure out."

"Now *that* worries me," she said. "How do we escape this place, this limbo twilight?"

"I'm clueless. What I do know is where we'll be safe from the crazies. And they're numerous."

"So let me get this straight. I supposedly know you well, you're apparently here to get me out of this Bosque place, you managed to get in, but you don't have any idea how we get out. Does that about sum it up?"

"No. But that'll do for now."

"Well, shit, give me a reason to go with you."

Wayra's dark eyes locked on hers, he kept his hands in his jacket pockets. "Proof, in other words."

"Yes, I guess that's what I need. Proof."

He rocked back onto his heels and slipped his left hand from his pocket. But it wasn't a hand. It was a paw, mostly black with streaks of white, the fur reaching nearly to his elbow, where the human joint and skin began. She didn't know what to think of it, so she reached out and touched it, a real dog's paw, the fur soft, the feet webbed, the claws well worn at the ends.

"I'm one of two ancient shape shifters in existence. The other one is my wife, Illary. There are two other shifters that I turned three years ago, when I rescued your niece, Maddie, from Cedar Key and the *bru-jos*."

"But what's with the paw?"

"Whatever is happening here prevents me from shifting fully, has stolen your memory, keeps chasers out, and traps *brujos* in their virtual forms. In other words, everything is fucked up."

A memory stirred way down deep inside Tess and she relaxed into it, *willing* it to surface, *allowing* it to enter her awareness. And when it did, she saw herself waiting outside what appeared to be a bus depot, with a man who looked like a movie star, and a friendly black dog, a Lab, that got onto the bus with them.

"A black Lab," she said. "I remember you as a black Lab, Wayra."

"That's a start."

"And I remember Illary as . . ." Tess felt another memory surfacing and relaxed into it. In her mind, a beautiful sparrow hawk circled above her, against a magnificent blue sky. "A hawk. A sparrow hawk."

Wayra grinned. "Will you come with me?"

"Absolutely."

"Let's get to a safe haven, Kali," said Wayra, and the parrot fluttered upward, into the twilight, and they hurried after her.

Fourteen
Charlie and Karina

1.

Charlie and Karina stood outside the virtual home that Maria had built who knew when. An eye-catcher. Constructed of recycled materials, it was camouflaged by a jungle of trees that grew in the Brazilian Amazon. "I like our place better," Charlie said.

"Yeah, me, too."

"Let's get this over with, Karina."

"It's going to be ugly."

"It's already ugly."

Thick ferns shrouded the long, curving sidewalk, beds of colorful, exotic flowers blanketed the rolling grounds, purple and red orchids grew from the trunks of nearby trees. The attention to detail in this place, Charlie thought, revealed a great deal about Maria herself.

When he rang the doorbell, John Lennon sang "Imagine," and it sounded as if he were standing right next to them. A creative touch, Charlie thought. But the music didn't match Maria's sour expression when she threw open the door. She looked ravaged—emotionally, intellectually, spiritually—and bore little resemblance to that gorgeous, reserved babe from the last council meeting. He could hardly believe she was the same person. Her colorful dress looked as if she'd slept in it for days, a coffee stain shaped like Sicily stained the front of it, she was barefoot and the toenails on her right foot were painted bright red, the toenails on her left foot had no polish on them at all.

"Oh. Charlie, Karina." She stepped out onto the porch and quickly shut the door behind her. She stabbed her fingers through her long, tangled blond hair, flicked it over one shoulder, fussed with it. Her toes curled and uncurled against the wooden landing. She knew she looked like shit. "What's up?"

"We need to talk," Karina said. "May we come in?"

"Now really isn't a good time, Karina. The—"

"Now is the *only* time!" Charlie moved past her and opened the door.

Newton stood just inside, his eyes wide and startled, like those of a teenager who has been caught having sex with his underage girlfriend. His longish gray hair was stringy and greasy, as though he hadn't washed it recently, and his clothing—jeans, a T-shirt—looked soiled, old, faded. "It's, uh, not a good time, Charlie, to talk about anything."

"It's the perfect time." Charlie swept past him, into the spacious front room of Maria's carefully constructed home.

But nothing inside the place looked carefully constructed. The living room, though spacious, faded in and out, a testament to the fact that neither Maria nor Newton had their acts together enough to keep things solid, real, tangible. Magazines and books spilled off a coffee table to the floor. Dirty dishes and glasses and piles of discarded clothing lay everywhere. Animals scampered around—meowing cats, barking dogs, squeaking hamsters racing around in cages, birds that shrieked and cried. Cat poop, dog poop, hamster poop, bird poop dotted the counters and had been ground down into the grout between the floor tiles.

"Chaos," Charlie murmured.

Karina wrinkled her nose. "Stinks, too."

"You can't just barge in like this," Maria snapped, coming up behind them. "Get out, just get out of here."

"Stay," Newton pleaded. "Please stay."

"What gave the minority of the council members the right to disappear El Bosque?" Charlie demanded. "Several hundred people—including my daughter—were in there when you did that."

Newton sank into one of the chairs, his face etched with such abject misery that Charlie almost felt sorry for him. But only *almost*.

"It was *her* idea." He stabbed his thumb toward Maria. "She got Simon and José to help her. I told her it was a mistake, that I didn't want any part of it, that it went against the way we've always done things. I refused to help them."

Maria, apparently locked in a full meltdown, shouted, "That's a goddamn lie," and lunged at Newton.

Karina grabbed the back of Maria's dress before she reached Newton, jerked her back, and shoved her down on to the couch. Maria's face went radish red, her eyes flashed with rage, and she threw up her arms, trying to knock Karina's hands off her shoulders. When she didn't succeed, she demanded, "Take your hands off me, Karina."

"As soon as you're calmer, I will."

Maria raised her hands. "Okay, I'm calm, I'm calm. I won't kill him. I promise."

"He's already dead," Charlie remarked.

"Yeah, exactly," Newton spat. "But Maria's intent on our reincarnating as soon as Esperanza has been removed from the physical world. That's what the rush is about. She forgot to mention *that*."

"Why does Esperanza have to be disappeared before you reincarnate?" Charlie asked.

"Once the city is taken back to where it came from," Newton said, "our obligation to Esperanza is finished."

"Others on the council have reincarnated," Karina said.

Maria rolled her eyes. "Get your facts straight, Karina. Only one member of the council has reincarnated since Esperanza was brought into the physical world."

"So, Maria, have you already chosen your parents?" Karina asked. "The place? The details?"

"No," Newton said.

"That's not true," Maria said quickly. "I've got some possibilities, Newt."

"Yeah, all of them in shitty rural towns in South America. No, thanks. I'm going to be reborn in the U.S. or Europe this time, and not in some backwater town, okay? And I'm not going to be coerced into an arrangement I don't like."

"Uh, excuse me," Charlie said. "You two can argue about your next lives when you're alone. Right now, you need to reverse the travesty you've committed and free El Bosque and everyone who got caught up in its disappearance."

"It can't be reversed," Maria snapped.

Charlie felt such sudden and profound despair that for a moment, he couldn't speak, couldn't think, couldn't even move. Then anger swept through him, freeing him from his paralysis, and he seized on the first idea that leaped into his mind.

"If I'm not mistaken, Newton, there's an obscure rule that allows any council member to request that another member be suspended for making decisions based on self-interest rather than for the common good of Esperanza and her people. Maria has clearly done that. So I'm invoking my right to kick her off the council."

"*What?*" Maria looked horrified. "There's no such rule. Show me where that rule is written down, Charlie. This is such bullshit."

Charlie didn't know whether such a rule existed. Victor had first told him about some obscure rules that had been in force when there were fourteen council members. He'd said he would research it and find out if they could invoke one of these rules to prevent the council from removing Esperanza from the physical world. But Victor had never gotten back to him. Even if such a rule didn't exist, it should, Charlie thought. Judging from Newton's bewildered expression, it was apparent that he was as much in the dark as Charlie.

"Newt, tell him," Maria said, growing agitated again. "There's no rule like that."

"I . . ." Newton stammered. "I, well . . ."

"Actually, there is such a rule," Karina said with a gleeful snicker.

Charlie struggled to hide his surprise.

Maria rolled her eyes again, more dramatically, and flung her arms out at Karina. "You are *so* transparent, Karina. You're just saying that to support Charlie."

"No, that's something *you* would do. During my earliest years as a chaser, I worked as a researcher for the council. The law Charlie is referring to was used only once, thousands of years ago, to remove the fourteenth member of the council."

"These are lies, all lies," Maria burst out. "Newt, why was the four-teenth council member removed?"

Newton shrugged. "How the hell should I know? It was well before my time."

"But you're the oldest member of the council," Maria rushed on. "If you don't know, who does?"

Newton tilted his head toward Karina. "She obviously does. And she has studied our history."

"The fourteenth member was removed from the council because she went against the majority at that time by advocating for council members who represented animals," Karina said.

It was news to Charlie. Was Karina making up this stuff?

"*Animals?*" Maria burst out laughing. "That's ludicrous. Souls aren't confined to any species, certainly the fourteenth member must have known that."

"But just as some souls are predominately male or female," Newton said, "it's also true that some souls prefer reincarnating as animals."

Maria's cheeks flared with color again and she shot to her feet and faced the three of them, hands on her narrow hips. "You can't just kick me off."

"Yeah, we can," Charlie said. "You, Simon, and José. Be sure to let them know."

Newton pushed up from the chair, and he, Karina, and Charlie turned their backs on Maria and clasped each other's hands. It was what a herd of elephants did when one of their own had died.

Without uttering a word to her or to each other, they walked toward the front door. Newton opened it, stepped outside, and Karina followed him. Just before Charlie joined them on the porch, he glanced back. "If the three of you reverse what you did to El Bosque, then we'll reconsider."

"You're trying to blackmail me," she yelled. "Leave! Just get the fuck out!"

Gladly. They headed down the sidewalk, not talking.

Before they reached the dirt road, a bright red Porsche roared toward them, a cloud of dust rising up behind it. The car squealed to a stop and Franco hopped out. Except for his clothing—khaki pants, a pullover sweater, and shiny brown loafers—he looked more like da Vinci than he ever had.

"Karina, Charlie, Newt," he said, striding over to them.

He looked Newton over from head to toe and Charlie suddenly saw Newton through Franco's eyes—a disheveled old man in a soiled shirt and wrinkled pants who looked half mad. "What the hell happened to you, Newt?" Franco blurted out.

Newton looked down at himself, at his soiled, wrinkled clothes, and jerked his thumb toward Maria's place. "*She* happened."

"Maria's signaling so much distress every chaser within miles could hear it," Franco remarked. "What's going on?"

"Why did you and Victor take Tess to El Bosque?" Charlie demanded. "What possessed you to do that?"

Franco threw up his hands. "Hold on, Charlie. Hold on. We didn't take her there; she went on her own, when she sought refuge in the tunnels during the *brujo* attacks in the plaza. We followed her to keep her safe."

"You sure did a lousy job," he spat. "And why didn't either of you contact me about it?"

"Where the hell were you?" Franco fired back. "I tried to get in touch with you. To tell you about El Bosque."

"He was with me," Karina said. "And I don't remember hearing any Franco voice summoning any of us."

"He said, she said." Franco rolled his eyes.

"You need to talk some sense into Maria," Newton told him, gazing off at her rapidly fading house. "She, José, and Simon disappeared El Bosque, with several hundred people inside."

"Including my daughter," Charlie said. "But you already know that, knew it within minutes of it happening since you and Victor were standing outside the market when Tess went in."

Franco frowned, and for a second Charlie thought he was going to say, *How do you know that?* Instead, something came into his eyes that Charlie found deeply disturbing, a spiral of shadows, each one a bit darker than the one before it. Then Franco emitted a small, clipped laugh and the spiral of shadows vanished, and Charlie thought he probably had imagined it.

"Are you accusing me of something, Charlie?"

"Yeah, of poor judgment."

Newton, agitated now, threw up his arms. "Please. No one is making accusations. We're just trying to find out what happened, Franco."

"Tess went into the market to find out if the clocks in El Bosque were all stuck at nine twenty-eight. She was in there so long that Victor and I decided to go inside and look for her, and that's when the screaming and panic ensued. Then . . . we saw the blackness creeping . . . covering the walls, and it started spilling toward us. Once this black shit is set in motion, that's it. The disappearance has to run its course."

Charlie glanced at Maria's house, fading one moment, flaring with color and definition in the next. "Unless the chasers who created it pull it back," he said.

"No chasers can get into the disappeared area," Karina added.

Franco rubbed his beard and nodded. "We're all having trouble maintaining or doing anything we've always taken for granted."

"Franco, if you have any pull at all with Maria, then you need to convince her the situation has to be reversed," Newton said. "Like you said in the meeting, people need a choice."

"What makes you think she'll listen to me?" Franco snapped. "She hasn't spoken to me since I sided with Charlie and Karina and the others. And come to think of it, Newt, *you* were the one who voted with her, so why am I suddenly the scapegoat here?"

"You're not a scapegoat," Newton said quickly. "Maria's crazy. And I regret the day I lobbied to get her on the council. Just talk to her, okay? And if you happen to run into Victor and Liana, let them know what's going on."

Franco looked at the house, still fading in and out of view, and nodded reluctantly. "All right, I'll talk to her. But I'm not expecting much." He turned toward the Porsche, clapped his hands twice, and the car dissolved away. "At least we can still do stuff like that, right?"

Yeah, Charlie thought, but for how long?

He watched Franco trot up the sidewalk and walk through the fading walls.

"Franco will keep her occupied for a while," Newton said. "But just in case she's thinking about following us, let's take a drive to put some distance between her and us." He clapped his hands three times and a sleek, shiny blue Prius appeared. "Let's enjoy it while we can still do this. Hop in, my friends."

Newton slipped behind the wheel, Karina got into the passenger seat, Charlie took the backseat and leaned forward between them as Newton drove. "One of the rules that has been in effect since the beginning is that what one chaser creates can't be undone by any other chaser," Newton said.

"But a chaser can undo what he or she has done," Karina said.

"That's been true in the past," Newton said. "But circumstances are so extraordinary now, who knows if that's even true anymore? Even if it is, Maria did this with the help of her cronies, so they would have to agree to undo it."

"That's not likely to happen," Charlie remarked.

"Exactly. But I thought of a way to bypass that stupid rule."

"Let's hear it," Charlie said.

"The ghost train."

"I didn't even think of that," Karina exclaimed.

"You know the story, Charlie?" Newton asked.

As with most urban legends in the city, everyone knew the basics. The train tracks that crossed the city from north to south and east to west, then branched out into the surrounding hills, had once been home to Esperanza 14. It had actually been two trains—one that ran between Quito and Esperanza and another that had been local.

More than a century ago, in the late 1800s, Roberto Baptista, the Ecuadorian equivalent of Henry Flagler, had built a railroad between Quito and Esperanza. It had taken decades. The altitude had been his primary challenge—from just over nine thousand feet in Quito to thirteen thousand in Esperanza. His employees had been stricken with altitude sickness, the needed supplies arrived late or not at all, and landslides had sometimes halted work for months.

The tracks through the city had actually been completed first, then the route had been expanded into the surrounding areas. By 1929, the track between Quito and Esperanza was laid and the train was operational and available only to the wealthy who could afford it. But the train across the city had already been hauling thousands of locals from Esperanza to the numerous Indian villages and settlements around it.

In 1930, Esperanza 14 crashed en route from Quito to Esperanza. A dozen cars had plunged down the precipice at around eleven thousand feet, crashed into a village, and hundreds were killed. The track was shut down. The local Esperanza 14 train had endured for another nine years, until an earthquake had ruptured many of the tracks, hurled eight cars down a hillside, and killed more than three hundred adults and dozens of children.

Baptista refused to be defeated by a quake, so he and his men spent several years laying new tracks across the city. But Baptista died before a new train could be brought in, and when the company subsequently went bankrupt, the entire project halted.

Year after year, usually around the anniversary of the crash of Esperanza 14 or around the anniversary of the quake, the ghost train appeared somewhere on the tracks and was fully visible to anyone in the area. Charlie had yet to see it.

"We're in the right time frame," Karina said.

Newton nodded. "The train that traveled between Esperanza and Quito crashed on June twenty-first, 1930, and exactly seventy-eight years later, Dominica's tribe was annihilated. Interesting coincidence, isn't it? The quake that hurled eight cars from the local Fourteen down the mountain and into the village below happened on the twentieth of December, 1939. Today is December nineteenth. Another interesting coincidence. In the past, the train has been sighted shortly after midnight on the nineteenth, pulling out of the building where the depot used to be. I think if we're there, we have a good chance of hopping the train and getting into El Bosque that way to bring everyone out."

"It'd be simpler if we could just restore the neighborhood, Newt," said Karina.

"Of course it would." He sounded irritable now. "But that's just not going to happen unless Maria and her gang restore it. So we have to find a way around them and I think the ghost train is our best bet."

"Too bad you didn't vote with us to begin with," Charlie said. "We could have saved ourselves a lot of time and energy."

"I regret that and I apologize. I was . . . well, completely taken in by Maria's arguments. She can be quite—"

"Seductive," Karina said.

Newton looked embarrassed. "Uh yeah. I've known for years that she and I needed to work out some issues from a life way back, and I was willing to explore our options. But she's a manipulative bitch and I'm postponing any lifetime that includes her. I've decided that if I reincarnate, it's going to be into circumstances where I can develop creatively."

"Victor says he's going to wait around until the next century," Charlie remarked. "When the global and political turmoil have evened out."

"See, that's part of the big problem with the chaser council. Except for you and Karina, Charlie, the rest of us have been nonphysical too long. We've distanced ourselves from humanity. We don't have any business making these kinds of life-and-death decisions for the people who live in this city."

"What about the *brujos*?" Charlie asked. "I thought the whole purpose of removing the city from physical reality was to get rid of *brujos* once and for all."

Newton shrugged and pulled up to the curb of a park in the old city. "Maybe we're delusional. Even if Esperanza no longer exists, *brujos* will, somewhere. It's the nature of evil to persist. And there will still be confused souls, lost souls, souls who join tribes like Ricardo's." He turned off the car and sat there with his hands gripping the steering wheel. "Everything is in flux, changing, and I don't know what the answer is to any of it."

Charlie heard the misery in his voice and gave his shoulder an affectionate pat. "Let's focus on the ghost train right now and then worry about the rest of it later. We'll meet you before midnight at the old train depot."

Charlie and Karina got out of the car, and after a moment, Newton joined them on the sidewalk. He looked down at himself, just as he had earlier when Franco had given him the once-over, and thought himself into fresher attire, clean, short hair that was a rich brown instead of a drab gray. "I'm going to find Victor and Liana."

The plaintive cries of a hawk prompted them all to glance upward. Illary flew in wide, sweeping spirals against the blue sky, then touched down on the ground in front of them and shifted. "Do any of you know where Wayra is?"

"We haven't seen him," Charlie said.

The hawk tattoo that climbed from her shoulder and up her neck shimmered in the light, as if it were coming alive. "He isn't answering his phone and I haven't heard anything from him since I left El Bosque last night with Maddie and Sanchez."

"I think it's safe to assume Wayra got into El Bosque," Charlie told her.

"So he's stuck in there with everyone else," Illary said sharply, and looked at Newton. "What's the plan for getting them out, Newt?"

Her glare caused Newton to visibly wither. "The ghost train."

She thought about it and nodded slowly. "It might work. But in the meantime, please explain to me why I can't move back in time, why Sanchez can't flip off his psychic switch, and why none of us can get into El Bosque under our own volition."

"Isn't it obvious?" Newton sounded exasperated. "Nothing works the way it's supposed to anymore."

"And how do we rectify that?" she shot back.

"We don't," Newton replied. "We try to work around it, like with the train."

"Christ," she spat, and instantly shifted and took to the sky, the echo of her lonely cries underscoring their collective hopelessness.

"The ghost train better be the answer, Newt," Charlie said, then he and Karina shed their virtual forms and thought themselves *away*, fast.

2.

They ended up at the edge of El Bosque. The glaring white area was still cordoned off, cops were still present—on foot, horseback, patrolling in cars. But the mob of spectators and mourners had thinned considerably, traffic was moving in one direction only—out of El Bosque—and the commercial area a mile south was jammed with people. Charlie guessed that panic buying would soon wipe out all the food and supplies in this area and shops and markets would close. By tonight, the commercial district and the neighborhoods around it would resemble a ghost town.

He and Karina drifted into an alley in the commercial district to think themselves into their virtual forms. But as Charlie's Quechua form began to appear, it was riddled with tears and holes, like a piece of old fabric that moths had feasted on. His right arm and hand didn't materialize at all. Horrified, Charlie looked helplessly at Karina. Her chin and neck faded in and out of sight, her legs were missing from the knees down, and she fell to the ground. "My God, Charlie." Her voice spilled out of her. "Now it's hitting us big-time."

"Shed your form, Karina. *Fast.*"

Charlie shed his form and tried again, but this time only his left hand materialized, and it hung in midair like some bizarre special effect in a horror movie, fingers moving, curling, as if seeking something substantial to grab on to. Completely freaked out, he thought himself toward Karina, who couldn't shed her legless form and just huddled in a patch of sunlight, sobbing.

Charlie thought himself to the ground next to her and put his nonexistent arms around her and screamed at her in his head: *You can do it, c'mon, shed it. You've been doing it for centuries, you're stronger than whatever this is.*

Charlie, it's . . . it's a force, I . . . I can feel it, clutching at me, holding me back . . .

Desperate, Charlie merged his essence with hers, something he'd never done before, something he didn't realize he could do. He *felt* the force, *felt* it clutching at her, at them, fighting to hold them in a twilight state between their natural chaser forms and their virtual forms. He flung his chaser arms upward, forcing Karina's virtual arms to rise as well, and called upon every resource available to him.

Within moments the alley filled with hundreds of the giant crows, their caws and cries a deafening cacophony. Their wildly flapping wings created a tornadic wind that swirled madly through the alley, whipped upward toward the sky, and broke the grip of whatever force held Karina in her virtual form. With their essences still merged, the wind picked them up and hurled them out of the alley, down the block.

Deeply shaken, they thought themselves to the sidewalk and Charlie separated his essence from Karina's. He felt disoriented, strange, as if he were suffering from vertigo. He recalled this sensation from when he was a young father, riding on one of those Tilt-A-Whirls with Tess in an amusement park. When the ride had ended, he had stumbled off, dropped to his knees and vomited.

But how could he, a dead man, feel such sensations now?

Charlie, what was that? What kind of . . . power?

Maybe it's a preview of what it will be like for chasers if Esperanza is removed from the physical world and something else takes its place.

So we'll be, like, what? In betweeners? Nowhere people?

He didn't know. He didn't seem to know much of anything at the moment. It was almost as if the power that had held Karina in her incomplete form, that had prevented him from assuming a virtual form, had emanated from the city itself. Was Esperanza, after all these centuries, finally seizing her own destiny? Illary had said something to that effect. Was this why Illary—and presumably Wayra—could no longer move back in time? Was this why he hadn't been able to get into the disappeared area? But if the city was reclaiming her power, then why had she allowed Maria and her chaser allies to lock up El Bosque in a twilight zone?

Maybe that had been the turning point, the event that had prompted Esperanza to fight back.

Charlie, can you get a fix on Lauren? Ian? Any of the others?

He focused and felt a slight tug several blocks north. Lauren. It felt like Lauren. He and Karina thought themselves forward, but it seemed as if he were moving through honey or molasses. It alarmed him.

Perhaps this was what had happened to the *brujos,* why they needed a portal in the Pincoya. If chasers lost their ability to think themselves to where they wanted to go, what the hell would happen then? What would happen to *him*? A Dostoevsky moment when he would come to in his coffin twelve years ago? Or would he even be conscious at all?

Terrified that he—like the *brujos*—might face annihilation, he struggled to move forward more quickly and felt Karina doing the same. Shadows that spilled across the road grew longer, wider, thicker, and he understood that in clock time, in real time, it was taking them way too long to move a single short block.

Just ahead, Karina, on the next block, not much farther. I think they're at the Mística.

We're useless. We can't help them when we're like this.

Maybe it's about them helping us.

When they reached the front steps of the hotel, exhaustion spread through Charlie. It wasn't possible that he, a dead man, could feel such

profound fatigue. Yet, he barely made it into the hotel lobby before he
had to stop.

What's happening to us, Charlie? Karina's voice was the barest whisper in his mind.

Nothing good. Let's rest a second. Right here. Next to the fireplace. If
he'd had eyes to shut, he would have shut them. If he'd had a body, he
would have lain on the floor right in front of the fire, curled up in a ball,
and fallen fast asleep. He struggled to think himself to the nearest chair
and drop into it. A cat, curled up next to the fireplace, lifted its head,
stared directly at him, then shut its eyes again. Karina thought herself to
the floor at his feet.

I feel like I've just run a marathon, Charlie.

I feel like I did in the days before I died.

An urgency kept needling him, prodding him to move, to home in
on Lauren.

The door to the hotel opened, and Diego Garcia, chief of police,
hurried into the lobby with three cops and a short, plump, self-important
man whom Charlie recognized as Martin Torres, the mayor of Esperanza. Decked out in fatigues and combat boots, he was dressed like
Fidel Castro during the revolution in the 1950s, a man ready for battle.
He didn't carry a weapon, but Diego and the other cops did. Charlie
suddenly had a bad feeling about this.

The mayor, obviously angry, rattled away in Spanish. "What's wrong
with these goddamn gringos, anyway? They inserted themselves into
the affairs of Esperanza, pissed off the chasers and the *brujos,* and just
how did your father get into that whiteness, Diego?"

"We don't know for sure that Wayra is—"

"Witnesses saw him and a tall black man vanish into the whiteness.
The black man may be a *brujo,*" the mayor snapped. "As chief of the
Guardia, you need to seize control of the situation and arrest these gringos, Wayra, the priest, and anyone else suspected in the explosions at
the Pincoya. I shouldn't have to step in here, Diego."

"We can't just arrest the Americans for—"

"What floor are they on?" Torres interrupted.

Diego shook his head and called out to the clerk, *"¿Señora, en que
piso quedan los americanos?"*

The woman behind the desk held up three fingers. *"Piso tres, habit-ación once."*

Third floor, room 11.

Shit, we need to get up there, warn them, Karina.

We're stronger as one. Karina merged her essence with his.

He disliked merging. It made him feel soiled, corrupted. It was too close to what *brujos* did when they seized human hosts. But Karina was right. Merged, they were so much stronger they propelled themselves quickly through the ceiling, up to the third floor, and through the door of room 11. Then they separated.

Lauren and Ian sat on the floor, helping themselves to flakes of Segunda Vista. Father Jacinto sat nearby, Leo paced back and forth in front of the sliding glass balcony doors. The air felt tight, tense, strange, urgent. "So Tess has amnesia?" the priest asked.

"That's sure how it seemed," Ian replied.

"And she was filthy," Lauren added. "As if she'd been in there for days and had no idea what had happened or where she was. That's not like her. She's always been so fastidious."

Charlie separated from Karina and shouted, *The cops are on their way up here. Get out of here now, all of you.*

Lauren's head snapped up and she glanced quickly around, frowning, her eyes so large and bright that Charlie knew she had taken some of the magic weed already and was now about to depart for the purple haze once again.

"Did you guys hear that?" Lauren asked.

"Hear what?" Leo asked, pausing in his relentless pacing. "Why's it so cold in here?"

"It sounded like . . . Charlie."

Leo looked irritated and rubbed his hands over his arms. "He wouldn't dare come here. Not now. What's wrong with the heat in this room, anyway?"

"I didn't hear anything," Ian said.

"Nor I," the priest said, then added: "But Leo's right. It's freezing in here now." He blew out and his breath formed a visible cloud.

Lauren shrugged on her jacket, got to her feet. "Charlie, you here?"

Show her you're here, Karina said.

How? How the hell do I do that?
Move something.

Now he felt like Patrick Swayze in *Ghost,* struggling to interact with the three-dimensional world. He tried to knock a glass off the table, but his hand passed right through it. He attempted to slap the canister of flakes from the coffee table to the floor, and again his hand sliced right through it.

Karina moved toward him, into him, and once they were merged, they stood at the glass balcony doors. The air in the room was now cold enough so that Lauren and the others were visibly uncomfortable, their breath visible. A light frost formed on the glass. Charlie and Karina focused their collective energy, raised their nonexistent arm, pressed their index finger to the glass and scrawled a message in the frost.

Fifteen
The Pranksters

The room breathed, its heart hammered, and Ian's senses went berserk. He saw shadows coiled within shadows, heard sounds within sounds, smelled odors within odors, everything layered, complex, unbearably beautiful and horribly strange. Alien, all of it.

The temperature in the room kept dropping and it was now so cold his teeth chattered. The others felt it, too, so it wasn't due to the Segunda Vista. The priest moved around the room, blowing into his hands to warm them, and finally stopped in front of the TV, where a broadcaster reported the latest news on El Bosque and the wildly fluctuating electromagnetic readings around the area.

"I think there's something wrong with the thermostat," Leo said, fiddling with it. "It's now reading thirty-eight degrees in here and the temp is still dropping."

"It's Charlie," Lauren said. "Charlie's here."

"Then why the hell doesn't he show himself?" Leo replied. "He's never been shy before."

"Look," Pedro said in a hushed voice, pointing at the balcony doors. "Frost is forming on the glass."

Ian, sitting on the floor, his back against the foot of the bed, zipped up his jacket and tucked his hands in the pockets. He didn't trust himself to stand. His legs felt as if they were made of rubber and his feet were growing like weeds, the toes elongating, the heels now the size of small tree stumps. The sides of his shoes split open, the tops peeled away like sheets of tin in a high wind, and the skin on his feet flaked off in layers, exposing bone. Ian wrenched his gaze away from his feet and rubbed his hands over his face, fast and hard.

Focus, focus.

Great. But what should he focus on?

He had never done more than smoke an occasional joint and hadn't expected what had happened earlier, when his vision had exploded open, his consciousness had separated from his body, and he found himself in front of a grocery cart in Mercado del León. These sensations were much different. Now he felt as though his entire body might separate from *physical existence.*

Everything was visual and disorienting. He felt nauseated. When his arms dropped to his sides, everyone was staring at the balcony doors, at the letters scrawled in the frost that covered the glass: *Cops on way here get out now take everything w/u*

Was it real or was it another visual effect like that of his feet growing? "Is that real?" he managed to say, pointing at the door.

The priest ran his finger through the frost on the door. "Real, it's real. *¡Carajo!*"

"It's Charlie," Lauren breathed. "I knew Charlie was here."

"You two, get out of here now," Leo said urgently. "Pedro and I will deal with the cops."

Lauren stood in front of Leo with her hands on her hips, her face tight with determination. "I'm not leaving you here."

In the moments before Leo spoke, Ian recognized that Livingston iron will—and witnessed the words and gestures that turned it to liquid. Leo slipped his arms around Lauren and said, "Prankster, I can't go where you two are going. But we've got your backs. Just get the hell out now."

Then he cupped her face in his hands and kissed her with such passion that Ian felt a kind of shock that Lauren and Leo weren't quite the old farts he and Tess sometimes kidded about, that their sex life was probably as good as or better than his and Tess's. Maybe when the possibility of pregnancy was no longer a factor, the libido opened up like some greedy beast and sex became a conduit to something else.

He realized the Segunda Vista had him flying, that he could barely stand, that even when he grabbed his pack and Lauren's, his body felt as malleable as hot glass. He moved rapidly to the door. The floor rippled and trembled beneath him, the walls kept moving in and out, he heard water rushing through the pipes in the building. He and Lauren somehow made it out into the hall and headed for the exit sign at the end.

"You okay?" Lauren asked, her voice soft.

"Other than the fact that your face looks like melting wax, yeah, I think so. You?"

"I'll feel better once we're outside."

Just as he opened the door to the stairs, he heard a ding from the elevator and knew the cops had arrived. He had to grip the railing to keep from tripping over his own feet and couldn't look down at the steps; they vibrated, moved, slipped and slid like seaweed on the surface of water.

When they reached the lobby, his head throbbed, the inside of his mouth tasted dry, hot, as though he were burning up with fever. His hearing suddenly magnified again, as if he were inside a tunnel where voices echoed. He heard the whispered conversation between the clerk behind the counter and a man who had emerged from a back office. He told her the latest emergency news bulletin was urging everyone within a three-mile radius of El Bosque to leave. Evacuation orders were going to become mandatory within the next thirty minutes because of the wildly fluctuating electromagnetic levels.

"But what about . . . the guests?" the clerk asked. "The Americans and the Germans on the second floor."

"The police will take care of the Americans. Go notify the Germans. And then get yourself out of here."

Shit. As he and Lauren exited the hotel, Ian told Lauren what he'd heard. "They'll forcibly remove Leo and Pedro, Lauren."

"They can take care of themselves. They both know the mayor. Leo delivered his grandson." She hooked her arm through his. "My sense of smell just went bonkers. That woman . . ." She jerked her thumb toward a woman who hurried past them with bulging bags of food and supplies hanging over her shoulders. She got into a truck that pulled up to the curb. "She uses Dove soap. Her shampoo is made mostly of passion flowers. She's fleeing with her boyfriend. They just had sex and she faked her orgasm."

"What's my odor tell you, Lauren?

"That you could use a hot shower."

Undoubtedly true. "That bad, huh?"

"Just kidding. What you really smell like, is, Jesus, Ian. You smell like a prospective father. Is Tess *pregnant*?"

With everything that had been going on, his discovery of the pregnancy test had gotten pushed to the back of his mind and now seemed like it had happened weeks ago. He worried aloud that the baby might have been harmed. Or that Tess had miscarried. Or that the baby might have been disappeared along with El Bosque.

Lauren squeezed his arm. "Think more positively, Ian. Maybe this baby is marked for something special because of what's happened."

Suddenly overwhelmed by emotion, Ian didn't trust himself to speak without his entire being collapsing like some profoundly stressed ecosystem.

They walked fast, north along the sidewalk, following the flow of traffic headed toward the *autopista*, the fastest route away from El Bosque. Long, narrow shadows fell across the sidewalk, suggesting it was late afternoon. That had to be wrong. It couldn't be late afternoon already. He glanced at his watch, at his phone.

"Shit, the hands on my watch are spinning, and the time on my phone reads one-eleven. What time do you have?"

Lauren plucked her iPad from her bag, flipped open the cover, frowned. "It just stays on eleven-eleven. Quintana said this same thing happened in El Bosque before the blackness invaded the market. You heard her say that, you were there."

Ian felt as if the mother of all ghosts had just strolled over his grave. His heart hammered wildly, he grew short of breath, beads of sweat rolled down the sides of his face. Earlier this year, Tess had written a column on the *Expat*'s website titled "Is 12/21/12 Doomsday?" It had gotten nearly three thousand comments, ten thousand hits, more than any other article they had published since the paper's inception. Ian had read it with great interest, and ever since, he had noticed the proliferation of Web sites and books about the end date. They ranged from the bizarre to the fantastic.

On a mountain in France, for instance, a hundred thousand true believers were gathering and preparing for the end day, when they believed

UFOs would beam them up and fly them away to safety. Other websites, geared to urban survivalists, urged people to hoard food and supplies, build bunkers, arm themselves. With the enormous upheavals occurring on a planetary scale—from natural disasters to uprisings in the Arab countries to destruction of the environment through vast oil spills, rising ocean levels, and political chaos—Ian felt certain an evolution in consciousness was underway. He didn't have any trouble believing that. But the end of the planet? Space brothers sweeping in to save the faithful?

Two days from now. He suddenly felt overwhelmed. He stumbled and Lauren caught his arm before he pitched forward onto the pavement. "Hey, take it easy, Ian. We'll get through this."

He started to say something, but his tongue felt swollen, clumsy, like an intruder in his mouth. Regardless of whether it was early or late afternoon, he figured Tess had been trapped inside the twilight for at least thirteen or fourteen hours, maybe as long as eighteen hours.

He always had believed that he would know, at some deep level, where she was, that love was a kind of GPS system. But at the moment, he felt nothing. Nothing at all. And it terrified him. *If she was dead, then what had the last four years been about?*

As they approached the area cordoned off by the authorities, Illika Huicho, the leader of the Quechua, fell into step with them. To Ian, she looked like an elf with hunched shoulders, her wild gray hair falling to the middle of her back. "Follow me," she said, and led them along the outside of the orange cones and yellow police tape that kept the crowd of the curious well away from the blinding whiteness. She paused and pointed a long, bony finger at a place where the whiteness pulsed and throbbed like a stressed heart. "Here."

"Here, what?" Ian asked sharply.

"Mercado del León lies on the other side of this barrier," she said. "A bus or a train will take you in. Remember what the oracle said. 'We, the people . . .'" Then she faded away.

"Uh-oh," Lauren murmured, her voice tight, hoarse. "She wasn't real."

Or she was vividly real, Ian thought. "A bus or a train? What's that mean?"

"I don't have any idea."

Ian glanced around for landmarks so that he and Lauren would be able to find this spot when the hallucinogenic magic had worn off. Directly across the street, at 137 Valle Boulevard, stood a bookstore where he and Tess browsed whenever they were in the neighborhood. A fire hydrant stood on the curb in front of it.

"We need to remember those landmarks," Ian said, pointing them out.

Lauren nodded, activated the recorder on her phone, and made note of the landmarks. "I'd like to text Leo and let him know where we are."

"Better not do it yet. The police probably took his phone. Wait until he texts you."

Moments later, her phone sang "Me and Bobby McGee." "Text message." She glanced at it. "Bastards."

Lauren passed the phone to him. The text message from Leo was brief: *Being removed from area, mandatory evac under way, they r looking 4 u and Ian. Stay safe. Meet u @home. Luv u, Leo.*

He handed the phone back to Lauren. "So we can't return to the hotel."

"We can't be seen out here, Ian. I'm not going to be hauled into the city in the back of some cop car while I'm this high. Fuck that." She turned rapidly into an alley, Ian at her heels, and for a few minutes, they stood there, peering out at the traffic and the pedestrians who swept past.

The visual effects of Segunda Vista came at him more strongly now, powerful undulations that made him feel as if he were on the deck of a small boat in wind-tossed seas. He felt like puking. He dug a bottle of water out of his pack and sipped at it.

Maddie and her friends took Segunda Vista fairly frequently and, according to Sanchez's father, she had joined a shamanic circle with some Quechuas in old town. Ian had never thought to ask what sorts of experiences she had on this stuff, but he knew that she'd learned to cultivate the weed from one of the locals, and grew it right alongside tomatoes and lettuce and broccoli, in a small greenhouse behind the home where she and Sanchez lived. He also knew, through Tess, that Sanchez didn't partake and that it annoyed the shit out of him that Maddie did.

And because he had thought of her just then, Ian texted Maddie.

She replied within fifteen seconds. *Just heard from Leo. He's asking Diego to bring them here to Wayra and Illary's. Segunda can be a trickster. Ask Lauren why Leo calls her Prankster. B careful. Question everything.*

"I'm supposed to ask you why Leo calls you Prankster," he said.

Lauren rolled her eyes. "I never shoulda told Maddie that story."

"So tell it to me."

She looked over at Ian, her pale blue eyes still ringed by navy, Lauren's trippy eyes. "You know how weird it is that you and I are out here, Ian, high on Esperanza's sacred psychotropic, trying to break through some sort of supernatural barrier?"

Weird? He had better adjectives than that.

"In the sixties, I was a hippie in the truest sense of the word. Tess has always been more traditional than me."

"Straighter," he said.

Lauren gave a small, clipped laugh. "Exactly. I sometimes forget you're actually from the sixties."

"I never did more than smoke a joint now and then. I was a married professor with a kid," he said. "I demonstrated against Vietnam, marched with King and Jesse Jackson, voted for Kennedy, but drugs just weren't my thing."

"Well, you won't find this kind of stuff anywhere else in the world. Even McKenna would tell you that."

"McKenna," he repeated. "As in Terence?"

"Yeah."

Tess had told him about her mother's adventures in the sixties with the Merry Pranksters, the Acid Summer of the late sixties, when Leonard Cohen had sung about San Francisco and Ken Kesey and Jerry Garcia had taken off across the country in their psychedelic bus, *Further*. But from what he knew of that time, neither Garcia nor McKenna had been regular passengers.

"I read McKenna," he said. "Pretty wild stuff."

"While doing psychotropics, McKenna recognized that the sixty-four hexagrams of the *I Ching* are archetypes, patterns of energy, and that they explain certain universal forces. While tripping his brains out, Ken Kesey met his future self, the famous cult hero. While doing mescaline, Jerry Garcia composed some of his best music ever. I tripped with all these guys, loved them, and am diminished in some essential way because all of them are gone. I *outlived* them, for Chrissake, that wasn't supposed to happen."

Ian, momentarily rendered speechless, finally blurted, "Well, ask for their help."

Lauren looked surprised, then delighted, and threw up her arms and yelled, "Ken, hey Ken, I could really use some help here. Get Jerry and Terry to come with you, okay?"

Her voice echoed through the alley, drawing the attention of a man and a boy who hurried by on the sidewalk. *"Locos,"* the man said to the kid, and touched the boy's back, urging him to pick up his pace.

Crazies. Ian exploded with laughter, slapped his hands over his mouth to stifle it, and stood there snorting and snickering. Crazies, yeah. He'd definitely gone round the bend. What sane man would attempt to find the woman he loved by taking hallucinogenic weeds to get into an area that had been supernaturally displaced?

"¿Epa, qué está pasando aquí?"

Ian spun around, Lauren stopped laughing, and the two of them stared at a pair of cops who stood at the mouth of the alley with rifles slung over their shoulders. Behind them was a third cop, on horseback and, in Spanish, he said, "Gringos. This area is under mandatory evacuation. If you do not have transportation, there are vans and buses just up the street that will take you into Esperanza."

Rarely did a cop in Esperanza refer to an American as a *gringo*. Before Ian could say anything, Lauren whispered, "Ian, look at their eyes."

Slick and oily dark. "Do you have the time?" Ian asked in English, tapping the face of his watch. "My watch has stopped."

Brujos tended to be somewhat unimaginative and, as he hoped, the unexpected question threw them. As the cops glanced at each other in confusion, Ian grabbed Lauren's hand and they tore up the alley, knocking over garbage cans that clattered across the cobblestones, bags of trash spilling from them. The *brujo* on horseback galloped after them, the horse's hooves clobbering across the cobblestones. When Ian glanced back, the horse was deftly dodging the bags of trash and the rolling cans. The other two cops raced on foot, slightly behind the horse, shouting and threatening to open fire.

Faster, dodge, faster, zigzag, faster . . .

The end of the alley loomed in front of them, an erratic rectangle of light through which Ian saw pedestrians rushing to evacuate, some with packs and suitcases, others clutching small children. He saw people on bicycles and scooters, and a line of cars stuck in traffic. Ian assumed more *brujos* were out there somewhere, perhaps hosted by other cops or even by some of the fleeing residents.

"Let's split up, Ian."

"No way."

Then the cops started shooting and Ian and Lauren dived behind a huge Dumpster on wheels. Bullets pinged off the front of it, tore through bags of trash. The gunfire echoed loudly, was heard out in the street, and people rushing past on the sidewalks suddenly started running, shouting about gunshots.

Ian and Lauren leaped up and leaned into the Dumpster, struggling to push it out away from the wall and into the middle of the alley. Protection for the people on the street, and for them. It creaked and moaned and finally started to move. The Dumpster swung into place, taking up most of the alley, and Ian and Lauren dashed out into the street and joined the burgeoning mob of people trying to get out, away.

A cop's horse whinnied and snorted, then tore past them, riderless, its hooves thundering over the cobblestones. Men and women and kids abandoned their cars now and took off up the road in droves, hauling their *stuff*—packs, bags, pet carriers—and pulling dogs on leashes. Cops on horseback swarmed into the road—*brujos,* more goddamn *brujos,* a trap. Ian sensed hundreds of *brujos* in their natural forms traveling with the cops, seeking hosts. People started twitching, jerking, stumbling as they were seized.

Someone screamed, *"¡Brujos, los brujos están aquí!"* and the crowd broke apart, people stampeding in every direction, up and down sidewalks, into the side roads, over the abandoned cars. Ian and Lauren dashed through the crowd, around and over cars to the other side of the street, where tables and chairs and potted plants in front of restaurants and cafés had been overturned. They ducked into one of the empty cafés, dozens of people crowding in behind them. Someone slammed the door.

"Tables," Ian yelled. "Push tables up against the door."

He and several other men pushed three tables against the door, piled chairs on top of them, and Lauren herded everyone else toward the exit at the rear of the café. When the door was barricaded, Ian joined Lauren.

She threw her weight against a fire exit door and it swung open. He recalled that when he was attempting to return to Esperanza, he had fled a *brujo* fog in San Francisco in the same way, through the rear exit of a restaurant. But that time, he was able to make it back to his hotel. This time, if he returned to the hotel, he would be arrested.

Sure enough, a thick *brujo* fog rolled into the alley entrance to the right, and the air filled with that familiar chant, *Find the body . . .* He and Lauren abruptly turned and raced left, to the south. Screams tore through the air as people were seized, as others stumbled and fell and were either trampled or killed. The fog moved swiftly, swelling like a giant tick, and closed in on Ian and Lauren.

A cloud of dust suddenly rose at the end of the alley, something you might see in an old John Wayne movie, a swirling maelstrom sweeping across the empty plains. Except they weren't on the plains and this dust glowed from within. Maybe it was what a UFO would look like to the true believers, Ian thought.

Then something exploded out of the dust storm, an old bus painted in psychedelic colors. A large, metallic peace symbol hung from the front grille and the roof rack was loaded with stuff—suitcases, bundles, bags of clothing and fruit. It barreled toward them, horn blaring, two long-haired men hanging out the side windows, waving their arms and shouting, "Lore, we heard you!"

"*Holy shit,*" Ian whispered.

He recognized the Merry Prankster bus, *Further,* with Ken Kesey behind the wheel and Jerry Garcia and Terence McKenna hanging out the windows. Ian and Lauren and the others leaped to the sides of the alley, the old bus kept trundling toward them, that cloud of dust gathering speed and momentum, swallowing *Further,* coughing it out again.

When it screeched to a stop in the middle of the alley, the dust cloud covered it completely.

"My God," Lauren squealed. "It's them, Ian, it's the Pranksters!" And she raced toward the psychedelic bus, her bag banging against her hip.

Kesey himself swung off the bus and threw his arms open. "Lore!" he shouted.

Lauren flew into his arms and he hugged her so tightly that Ian was sure she would disappear into him. McKenna and Garcia got out and greeted her like long-lost lovers. Maybe she was. Maybe she had been a lover to all three of them.

She had traveled on this bus with them when she was twenty years old, had dropped acid with these guys, seen the sixties in a way that he had not because he was too old then to have been a hippie. He just stood there, staring, aware that the dust cloud provided partial cover for a reunion that was clearly impossible. After all, Kesey, Garcia, and McKenna were dead. People around him murmured, whispered, pointed, hung back. Lauren turned toward them and motioned for them to get on the bus.

"C'mon, we'll take you out of here," she said. "Anyone who wants to head into the whiteness to find loved ones is welcome. If you just want out of here, we'll drop you off in a safe area."

For a moment, no one moved. Kesey said, "Hey, did any of you people see the movie *One Flew Over the Cuckoo's Nest*? Jack Nicholson was the main dude. I wrote that book."

This elicited a few nods.

"You people done magic mushrooms?" McKenna called out. "I'm the guy who talked to them. McKenna's the name, Terence McKenna."

A few more nods.

Garcia ducked back into the bus and emerged a moment later with a guitar. And then he started to play "Knockin' on Heaven's Door," a Bob Dylan song that was performed by Dylan and the Grateful Dead on a joint tour in 1987. Mesmerized, Ian knew he had fallen down the rabbit hole and that from this point onward, he couldn't go back. There was nothing to go back *to*. He moved forward—and so did everyone else around him.

While Garcia continued to play, Kesey and McKenna shook hands with everyone who came aboard. As Ian climbed into the bus, Kesey gripped his hand tightly. "Dude, it's a pleasure to finally meet you."

"Likewise. I used to cite your books when I taught journalism. *Tell a story just like Kesey did.* And I'd get these looks and some student would invariably inform me that Kesey wrote fiction. That student usually didn't pass my class."

Kesey's bellowing laugh was as large as he was, like a force of nature. "No shit, man. Doesn't matter what it is, truth or not, if you tell it like a story with heroes and villains and all the soap opera stuff in between, it speaks to the heart every time. Our lives are soap operas—and so are our deaths." He threw out his arms. "We're proof of that."

Then Ian stepped into the bus and was shocked by its spaciousness. It was the interior of a large commercial bus, with seats along either side painted in luminous reds and yellows and blues that sported large, hand-painted silver peace signs. A dozen vertical poles marched down the middle, so that when the seats were taken, the overflow of passengers could be accommodated.

"Ian," Lauren called.

He spotted her at the front of the bus and moved through the crush of other passengers until he reached the seat she'd saved for him, right behind the passenger seat.

"We need to stick together, Ian."

"Was *Further* actually this big?"

"Nope," she said, then swung around in her seat, lifted her legs, and pressed her shoes against the dashboard like a little kid who had just been told that Santa Claus was right outside the front window.

Garcia was the last on board, the door whispered shut, Kesey dropped into the driver's seat, and picked up a mike. "Amigos, we have choices to make." His voice boomed through the bus. "Up ahead, we've got *brujo* fog that hopes to swallow us." He revved the engine. "Inside the whiteness, you have loved ones who need to be taken out." Another rev of the engine. "Around us, we have chaser council members who are disappearing bits and pieces of Esperanza. And then we have the city herself. She's starting to fight back. Otherwise, how could the three of us and our bus even be here?" Kesey laughed. "So what's it going to be, folks? Who wants to be let off? Raise your hands."

Not a single hand went up.

"All right, it's unanimous, then. We're headed for the fog filled with fucker *brujos* and then into the whiteness."

"Adentro, adentro, adentro," everyone chanted. Inside, inside, inside.

Kesey revved the engine once again, then released the hand brake and *Further* leaped forward like a young stallion, charging toward the *brujo* fog, speeding toward what was unknown and hidden. And then the bus tore into the fog.

For seconds, the *brujo* litany echoed in the fog, its collective voice rising and falling and rising again, a kind of national anthem, the one thing to which they clung above all else, that which united them. Then the hungry ghosts hammered the old bus like gigantic hail pellets on a roof. The light outside the windows turned soft, strange, muted, like descending twilight. Moments later, *Further* appeared to be airborne, soaring like a 777 through the upper stratosphere.

Despite the effects of Segunda Vista, Ian knew what he was seeing and where the bus was headed and why. He had an approximate time and date for his experience. But as a journalist, he struggled with the rest of it, all the finer details, like how he could be in a bus that had died with its owners, who were nonetheless alive, well, and apparently flourishing.

He concluded that he just didn't have the answers and probably never would.

They emerged on the other side of the *brujo* fog, the bus slammed over the cobblestones, gathering speed. It headed toward the barricade of orange cones and yellow crime tape and cops on foot, on horseback, in their cars, and Kesey aimed it at the glittering whiteness.

Ian knew the bus was visible to others. Pedestrians outside gawked, pointed, shouted. The police horses reared up, throwing off their riders, and galloped up the sidewalk. The cops on foot opened fire on the bus and bullets pinged off its sides, cracked the windshield, and probably flattened all the tires.

But the bus didn't stop, didn't slow down, and the cops took off, racing for safety. Now the police vehicles peeled away from the barricade so fast that two of them crashed into a third car and then *Further* was beyond them, beyond all of them, beyond everything, and plunged into the whiteness.

Everything went still, soundless.

Sixteen
The Hostiles

1.

Tess and Wayra took refuge in an empty school on the western edge of El Bosque. They had gotten in through an unlocked side door and were now crouched at either side of a dirty window, searching the eerie, twilit street for movement, for the source of the shouts they'd been hearing for the last thirty minutes.

"See anything yet?" he whispered.

"Nothing. But I smell smoke. Why would these people be burning their own neighborhood? What's *wrong* with them?"

"Like you, they can't remember anything. They can't remember who they are, what they're doing here, why they're here. I think they see strangers as a threat, as invaders."

Tess glanced around at the parrot, perched on the back of a chair, barely visible in the twilight that penetrated the window. She could hear Kali's soft trilling, a sound she apparently made when she preened. Now and then, Tess felt the stirring of memories about the parrot and about Wayra, but so far, no specific memories had surfaced. She felt incomplete, like half a person. The contact list on her iPhone and iPad remained mostly a mystery.

"Is Kali your pet?" Tess asked.

"Nope." Wayra sounded amused. "For years, she occupied a window perch at the inn where you and Ian stayed when you first arrived as transitionals. Back then, I thought she was a spirit. For a while, I entertained the possibility that she was a shifter. But she seems to be one of those magical birds, like an owl or quetzal, that traverses dimensions. It's why she could get into El Bosque when none of the rest of us could."

Wayra had told her how they'd met when she and Ian were transitional souls who didn't realize they were in comas in their respective states, separated by forty years in time. At first, she and Ian had known Wayra as a dog, his shifter form. Tess had seen his left paw, so she didn't laugh. In fact, this explanation *felt* right, which she took to be a positive sign. Even if she couldn't consciously remember squat, her intuition seemed to be remembering some things for her.

Wayra had filled her in on *brujos* and chasers and told her how, after the battle that had annihilated Dominica's tribe more than four years ago, Dominica had seized Tess's niece, Maddie, and fled Ecuador. He told her about the *Expat News*, the newspaper she and Ian had started. He had told her enough so that if her memories began to surface, she would be able to connect some of the dots. But every time she looked within, struggling to find something—anything—about her past, it was like tuning into a band of white noise on a radio.

"I need to find something to eat," Tess whispered. "Maybe there's food in the school cafeteria."

"I'm starving, too. I'll go with you."

Wayra whistled softly for Kali and the parrot flew over to him and touched down on his shoulder, her wings fluttering. He turned on a flashlight and they moved through the classroom and out into the hall, past rows of lockers, open doors to other classrooms, and into the cafeteria at the back of the school.

The large cafeteria had a wall of windows on the left that revealed the perpetual twilight. It made her deeply uneasy. Anyone could peer in through those windows and see her, Wayra, and the parrot. Too exposed here, she thought.

They threaded their way between dozens of rectangular and circular tables, toward the back of the cafeteria. Here was the self-serve area, where dishes, bowls, and glasses were stacked ever so neatly to one side of the empty aluminum bins. To the far right of the serving area, the door to the kitchen stood open. Tess headed straight toward it, Kali flying along ahead of her, Wayra behind her.

The kitchen, long and narrow and meticulously tidy, was lined with pots and pans that hung within easy reach from hooks along the ceiling. Stacked neatly in the cabinets were plates and bowls. At the very end of the kitchen stood a fire exit door. In between were stoves, micro-waves, and an industrial-sized fridge. Tess opened it and was relieved to discover that the electricity was still on and that the fridge was crammed with food.

She pulled out a six-pack of bottled water, a loaf of rye bread, a pack-age of Swiss cheese, wilted lettuce, a couple of tomatoes, mustard, part of a turkey, and apples. As she proceeded to make sandwiches, Wayra located paper plates, sliced up the apples, and scooped some slices onto a plate for Kali. The parrot waddled across the counter to the plate, picked up a slice with her beak, then held it between her claws and hap-pily nibbled away as Tess made four sandwiches.

She and Wayra wolfed down the food while standing at the counter, two sandwiches apiece. But even when she finished the last of hers, she was still hungry, so she helped herself to several slices of turkey and gobbled them down, too. Wayra said, "I've never seen you eat so much at one time."

"Really? How do I normally eat?"

"Usually, you're picky. You sort of graze throughout the day." He suddenly rocked forward and *sniffed* at her.

Tess leaned back, away from him. "Jesus, Wayra."

"You're pregnant," he blurted.

"That's crazy. I can't be pregnant."

"My sense of smell is rarely wrong, Tess."

"Well, it's wrong *this* time."

But as soon as she said it, a memory exploded into her conscious-ness, of herself using an early-pregnancy test, setting the test strip aside. But she couldn't recall anything beyond that—such as the results. Or where she'd been when she'd done the test.

Kali suddenly emitted a shriek and soared around the kitchen, squawking, *"Ya vienen, ya vienen."*

They're coming.

Within seconds, glass shattered somewhere nearby, shouts rang out, and the pounding of feet thundered through the air, as though wild horses were loose outside. "Shit," Wayra hissed. "Out the fire exit."

Tess grabbed a couple bottles of water and ran after Wayra, to the back of the kitchen. As they slammed through the fire exit, the alarm went off, a steady, deafening shriek that announced, *We're here, hey, we're here . . .*

They raced after Kali and plunged into a wooded area behind the school. But it turned out to be just a narrow band of trees that grew parallel to the western edge of the disappeared area. Nowhere to run. Wayra stabbed his thumb at Kali, who circled the upper part of a monkey puzzle tree, then vanished into the leaves.

"Can you climb a tree?" he asked.

"Of course I can." She tore off her sneakers, shoved them in her pack, and shrugged the pack onto her back. Then she climbed the tree fast, like a crab, hands here, feet there, up and up and up. It shocked her that she had meant what she said, that she knew how to climb a tree. *But it used to be mango trees.* This thought triggered a cascade of memories of a tremendous mango tree that had grown in her backyard when she was a kid in Miami.

Like a ceiba tree she had seen somewhere, that childhood mango tree had had more branches than Shiva had arms, most of them thick and sturdy enough to hold an eight-year-old kid. She had climbed to the very top of the tree, where the plumpest, ripest mangoes hung, and plucked one. She had peeled it while sunlight streamed over her, and drank in its color and texture, a rich reddish gold, smooth and thick. Then she'd bitten into it and that sweet warmth had rushed into her mouth, squished between her teeth, slipped down her throat, and dribbled out the corners of her mouth and down onto her chin. She had felt deliriously happy.

And now, as she clung to a Y juncture high in the branches, the monkey puzzle tree she had climbed *physically transformed* into that mango tree from her childhood. The branches thickened beneath her hands, the leaves proliferated until the tree was as full and green as the one in her memory. Plump, ripe mangoes hung from the branches.

She didn't know what version of the tree Wayra perceived as he climbed, but he appeared to be climbing the same tree that she saw. As he got closer to her, he said, "Mango trees don't grow in this region, not outside of greenhouses. But this is a mango tree. And now every other tree here is a mango tree, too."

"This tree is in my head, Wayra. A vivid memory that has taken on . . . a physical reality."

Even in the muted twilight among the thick leaves, she could see his eyes widening with sudden comprehension. "The city is our *ally,* Tess. I think Esperanza is evening up the odds. What we imagine is manifesting *fast*. Imagine a fire."

"Fire?"

"A wall of flames between us and the school."

He shimmied out on a thick branch next to hers, shut his eyes. Tess gripped the branches more tightly, pressed her forehead to the bark, tried to imagine a wall of flames. The fire alarm kept shrieking, the stink of smoke grew stronger, and down below she now saw moving torches, flashlights, the mob pouring through the fire exit door. Fear pumped through her hard and fast, fear that the mob would spot them, that they would set the tree on fire, that she and Wayra would die in this horrible place. She couldn't move past her fear to visualize anything.

The mob was closing in, she dug her fingernails into the bark. *Fire, fire, fire, a dancing wall of flames.*

Suddenly, a wall of fire sprang up between the building and the trees where she and Wayra were hidden. Tongues of flames leaped twenty, thirty, forty feet in the air, and licked at the twilight, yet didn't touch the trees. The flames actually leaned outward away from the trees, toward the building, as if blown that way by wind. But there wasn't any wind, the air didn't stir at all, and Tess realized the wall of flames was Wayra's creation and he was pushing it out away from them.

He shimmied toward her and pointed down. "The flames will hold long enough to screen us."

"How do you know that?"

"I feel it." He gestured toward Kali, now circling high above the trees and the flames. "She'll scope things out."

As they scrambled down from the tree, the wall of fire remained intact, the flames leaping, crackling, emitting a tremendous heat that she felt against her face and arms. Shouts and screams from the mob pierced the air. She and Wayra dashed northward through the high weeds, across ground so dry it was as hard as concrete. The barrier of flames moved swiftly parallel to them, keeping them hidden.

Even when the trees gave way to low shrubs and bushes, the flames paced them, protecting them from being seen. It was as if once Wayra had imagined the wall of flames, Esperanza had drawn upon its own power to create and maintain them. She wondered if the mango trees were still intact, real.

Now that nothing lay between them and the curved dome of twilight on their left, she thought she could see shadows and silhouettes on the other side of the twilight, as though it were a kind of translucent screen. Wayra apparently noticed this, too, and moved toward it. Tess followed him closely. Even Kali swept in for a look, and landed on Wayra's shoulder.

They stopped about three feet from the wall of twilight. It shimmered and danced, as if covered with sequins. She noticed how the light vanished into the ground and swept upward as far as she could see. The shadows on the other side were definitely shapes—rectangular, square, circular, and then shapes like swaying trees, maybe pines.

"Those shapes appear to be from outside, Wayra. Is the whiteness becoming transparent?"

"I think the city is trying to break free of whatever the chasers did. When you're outside of El Bosque, it looks like the entire area has been erased. When I first got in here, it was twilight like it is now but the twilight didn't shimmer and you couldn't see anything on the other side of it."

"How can we bolster whatever the city is doing? I held a vision of a mango tree, you held an image of a wall of fire. Both materialized. Maybe we should try holding an image of the neighborhood as it once was."

Wayra thought about it, but not for long. "Can you remember what it was like before, Tess?"

"No. But I can sure as hell hold an image of a blue sky or a sky strewn with stars."

Kali suddenly squawked and flew upward. Then the wall of fire winked out like a match, and when Tess glanced back, she saw they were on the west side of a street filled with houses and apartment buildings. A small group of men and women moved toward them, armed with baseball bats, shovels, pool sticks, stones, and behind them was a much larger crowd carrying torches and weapons. The man leading the small group yelled, "There they are!"

"Shit, Wayra."

But Wayra was already walking toward them, patting the air with his hands, calling, "Javier. I spoke to you earlier at the church."

Tess stood rooted to the ground, her heart somersaulting in her chest. She desperately wished she had an army on horseback at her disposal, an army of mythological Olympians who would gallop into the road from the north and the south, the east and the west, and surround these mobs.

"I remember you," Javier shouted, raising his hand, signaling the group behind him to stop. "From the church. From the funeral. You and the woman don't belong here. You're invaders, you mean us harm, you—"

"This twilight is your enemy." Wayra threw his arms out at his sides. "It has robbed your memories, made you violent and aggressive, messed up your—"

"Liar," Javier shrieked. "Get them, take them!"

As the two groups rushed toward them, hurling rocks, swinging their shovels and bats and pitchforks, an army of giants on horseback poured into the road from every side, the deafening thunder of the horses' hooves magnified by the dome of twilight that still gripped El Bosque. The giants swung long, thick clubs covered in spikes, wore chest armor and metal helmets that gave them a distinctive alien look. Some sort of white substance flew up around them—like snow or powder or pale beach sand—and it thickened and blew around as more and more of these giants on horseback appeared.

That's how I imagined them, Tess thought, then both groups of hostiles tore away from the road, Wayra leaped back, Tess grabbed his hand, and they raced for the nearest building, a humble one-story house sealed up like a tomb. They ran along the right side, following Kali as she swept toward a small greenhouse out back. Padlocked, the doors were padlocked.

"Shit, Wayra . . ."

"This way."

They tore around to the back of the structure, Wayra dropped to the ground, rolled back on his ass, and slammed his feet against the opaque glass.

He broke open a hole close to the ground, wrapped his jacket around Kali. The parrot squawked and tried to bite him as she struggled to free herself. Wayra shoved his jacket through the opening, Tess pushed her pack through, and dropped onto her stomach. She propelled herself forward with the balls of her feet and grabbed on to whatever she could in front of her, pulling herself through the opening, her chin scraping against the ground.

Once she was inside the greenhouse, she quickly freed Kali from Wayra's jacket and the parrot flew high into the greenhouse, squawking, irate. Tess gripped Wayra's forearms and pulled him through the opening. He shot to his feet. "Hurry, we've got to hurry, they're really close." He pushed a potted tree in front of the broken glass and they raced after Kali, through a corridor lined by citrus trees.

"That army," Wayra said softly. "Did you . . . imagine them?"

"More like wishful thinking."

"Nice job."

"It didn't get us far."

"It bought us time, Tess. Mango trees, fire, an army of giants. Now we need to visualize and create something—"

The sound of breaking glass interrupted Wayra and he and Tess quickly ducked into the citrus trees. *Stay here*, he mouthed, and dropped to his hands and knees. Bones and muscles and tendons in his hands and face began to ripple beneath his skin, his arms and hands turned into legs and paws, his legs shortened, his clothing vanished, fur sprang from the pores in his skin. His face and head elongated, his human eyes and mouth and ears transformed into those of a dog. He grew a tail. Tess wondered if he would be fully human when he shifted again, or if his left paw would become even more pronounced. Or if he would even be able to shift into his human form again.

And then he took off into the greenhouse and Tess just stood there in the citrus trees, in the grips of a complete memory of the first time she had seen Wayra shape-shift.

It had happened when she was a transitional soul, in a tunnel beneath a greenhouse similar to this one, where she and Wayra, in his dog form, had been hiding during a *brujo* attack. At the time, she hadn't known he was a shape shifter, she'd thought he was just a smart dog named Nomad. He had left her at one point and she had gone looking for him and seen a man in the greenhouse arguing with someone. That man had been Wayra. With this memory came fragments of another, of herself and a man she knew was Ian pursued by *brujos* as they fled into the countryside around Esperanza. They were transitional souls then and suddenly knew the only way they could be together was to find their way back to Esperanza in their physical bodies.

They stole my memories, these bastards stole my memories.

Which bastards? Chasers? *Brujos?* Both?

A mark on the underside of her wrist now itched and burned like crazy and Tess dropped into a crouch and dug her fingers into moist soil and rubbed it over the mark, soothing it. Wayra had told her about the mark on her wrist, how it burned when *brujos* were nearby. She picked up several large stones, pulled her slingshot from her bag, and slipped away from the protection of the trees. She moved quickly and silently toward the sound of voices, a man and woman arguing.

Then she saw them, a black man and a diminutive Ecuadorian woman, huddling close together, near the window they had broken to get into the greenhouse. The woman was nearly hysterical, frantically stabbing her finger at Wayra, still in his dog form. *"I hate dogs, get that dog away from me. Look, it's baring its teeth, it's going to attack us. Hit it, Ricardo, hit it with your stick!"*

"It's not a goddamn dog, it's Wayra, a shifter, a shape shifter, Naomi, can't you remember anything? Show yourself, Wayra."

Naomi grabbed the stick from his hand, and just as she swung it into the air, Tess shot the largest stone. It struck Naomi in the cheek and she dropped the stick and stumbled back, shrieking in pain, her hands flying to her face, blood streaming through her fingers. Ricardo spun around, saw Tess, and shouted, *"We're trapped in these forms, we can't hurt you."*

"Get away from Wayra or this next stone is going to pierce your fucking eye," Tess snapped, moving toward him, the slingshot armed, ready.

Wayra shifted into his human form, fur now extending past the elbow of his left arm, and leaped between her and Ricardo, waving his arms. "Back off, Tess, back off. They don't mean us any harm. Ricardo and I have a truce."

"You made a truce with a *brujo*?" Tess burst out. "I thought you told me—"

"You made a truce with *him*?" Naomi screamed. "With the shifter who turned me and my son?" She pressed her fists to her mouth. "I remember," she said softly.

Bits and pieces of Tess's disconnected memories abruptly slammed together. Even though she now understood who Ricardo and Naomi were, she couldn't fathom a truce. "*Brujos* lie, Wayra."

Ricardo finally hurried over to Naomi, now sitting on the ground, weeping. He slipped his arm around her, spoke softly to her, pulled a hanky from his pocket and pressed it against the gash on her cheek. His obvious affection for her, his solicitousness, shocked Tess. She tossed her stone into the trees, slipped the slingshot in her back pocket, and joined Wayra, who now was peering out the broken window.

Torchlights flickered in the distance. "Nearly every greenhouse has access to the tunnels," Wayra said. "We need to find the tunnel under this one." He whistled shrilly for Kali, who swept in over their heads. "Find the tunnel, find the opening."

"I'm not following *you* into any tunnel," spat Naomi.

"It's a way out," Wayra shot back. "But suit yourself."

"We're going," Ricardo told her, taking Naomi by the arm.

"So we get out and then what?" Naomi asked. "The dead and the living and shifters all live happily ever after?"

"Of course not," Wayra said.

"I'm not asking you, Wayra," Naomi said irritably.

Wayra stabbed his thumb toward Ricardo. "He said he would fight for his tribe's right to occupy Esperanza alongside the living."

Naomi glanced at Ricardo. "You actually said that?"

"Yeah. Meant it, too."

The mob was nearly on them, their shouts so loud that Tess could distinguish individual words. *Get them, kill them.* She spun around and loped after Kali, now flying fast and low between the lines of citrus trees.

When Lauren came to, it took her a moment to orient herself, to re-member that she was in *Further,* in the old bus that had belonged to the Merry Pranksters. A whiteness surrounded the bus and it was as thick as clam chowder.

Fog? Was it *brujo* fog? She didn't hear the *brujo* litany, but she couldn't dismiss the possibility that it was *brujo* fog. Worse than the whiteness was the stillness, the utter lack of noise. She couldn't hear anything, not even the sound of her own breathing.

Lauren glanced over at Ken Kesey, slumped against the steering wheel, arms resting on top of it, forehead pressed into the crook of his elbow. Alarmed, she looked back and saw that Garcia was flung back against his seat, mouth open, his guitar resting across his thighs, and that McKenna lay on his side on the floor, curled up like an infant. Ian was folded like a rag doll over the back of Garcia's seat. And the dozens of people who had been with them were now gone.

"Shit, shit, what's going on?" She shot to her feet and shook Kesey. "Ken, c'mon, wake up. You're freaking me out."

He didn't wake up. She pulled the upper part of his body away from the steering wheel, pushed him back against the seat, raised his eyelids. His pupils weren't dilated, he was breathing, his color was good, his pulse was strong. Alive, but unconscious. Except that he wasn't alive, he had died on November 1, 2001, she had read about it in the *Miami Herald.*

Lauren hurried over to Garcia, carefully removed his guitar from his thighs and set it upright against the side of the bus, and checked him over just as she had Kesey. Same thing. Alive but unconscious. She knelt on the floor next to McKenna, rolled him onto his back. Eyes, breath-ing, pulse, color. Alive but unconscious.

Terrified now that everything she'd experienced since ingesting Se-gunda Vista was nothing but hallucination, that she was actually still sitting in the hotel room with Leo and Pedro and Ian, Lauren moved quickly to Ian. If she touched him, would her hands slip through him? "Ian," she said loudly. "Wake up."

He didn't stir.

Lauren slipped her arms around Ian's waist, relieved that he was real, that her arms didn't pass through him, and pulled him back against the seat. His head flopped to one side. Beneath his lids, his eyes moved rapidly. REM sleep. Ian was dreaming. Was she dreaming, too? Was her dream lucid? Lauren pinched her forearm so hard the skin briefly turned a bright red. Not a dream. Then again, when Tess and Ian had had their near death experiences that had brought them to Esperanza as transitional souls, everything for them, Tess had told her, had seemed undeniably real.

She checked Ian. His pulse was fast, but he otherwise appeared to be okay. She shook him by the shoulders, and when he didn't respond, she slapped him hard across the face and screamed, "Ian, wake up!"

He suddenly bolted upright, eyes wide open, and grabbed her wrist.

"What the fuck," he sputtered, and released her wrist and looked around slowly, like a man coming out of a dream. "This looks like . . . *brujo* fog."

"I don't think it is. It doesn't drift through the open windows. I . . . don't hear the litany. Whatever it is, it doesn't move. I can't rouse the others. Their vitals are fine, but they're unconscious."

Ian held her gaze for a moment and she sensed he was about to say the obvious, that dead people didn't have vital signs. "What happened to everyone else?"

"No idea."

Ian gave her hand a quick, reassuring squeeze, then pushed unsteadily to his feet and drew her over to the open window. They leaned out into the whiteness.

"It's not cold or warm or damp or anything," Ian said softly.

"It just sits here."

"Does the bus start?"

"I haven't tried it."

"Let's see."

They had to move Kesey from the driver's seat to the floor, not an easy task; he weighed more than two hundred pounds and, at the moment, it was all deadweight. They finally got him on the floor. Ian grasped him by the ankles, Lauren took hold of his arms, and they dragged him back to where McKenna lay. Neither man moved or regained consciousness.

Crouched on either side of the two men, she and Ian stared down at them. Lauren suddenly felt that the whiteness was listening to them, that it was somehow conscious. She whispered, "Maybe the bus won't start for the same reason these three Pranksters are unconscious."

Ian's gaze met hers. "Because they aren't real?"

"Because they're dead."

"And the bus was conjured from their collective memories."

"Exactly. Maybe their purpose was to get us into El Bosque. The rest is up to us."

"We don't even know for sure that we're in El Bosque, Lauren."

"Well, we know the bus plowed into the whiteness, we saw that happen."

They moved quickly to the front of the bus. Ian slipped behind the steering wheel, Lauren dropped into the passenger seat. The key was still in the ignition, Ian turned it. The ignition clicked, the engine refused to turn over, and Ian tried again. And again. "Wait a minute," he said. "*You* traveled on this bus, you still have a memory of it. That may be the only reason the bus is still solid and here. You try it. Let's switch places."

Lauren was shorter than either Kesey or Ian, so she adjusted the seat, then sat there for a moment, hands on the steering wheel, and vividly recalled those months more than forty years ago when she had traveled on *Further* through northern California with Kesey and Garcia. She knew that McKenna and his brother had traveled with them, too, but she couldn't recall whether it was for a couple of days or months. And where had she met McKenna? She couldn't remember.

Her hands tightened on the wheel, a wave of panic washed through her, she squeezed her eyes shut. *I know this, I know this . . .*

Then it came to her. She had met McKenna at a party in San Francisco. They had done peyote and spent hours talking about the nature of reality. She had introduced him to Kesey and Garcia.

"Lauren?" Ian said.

"Yeah. Yeah. I'm just pulling my memories in around me." She patted the steering wheel and lovingly ran her hand over the old radio, the dashboard, the door, the key and ignition. She turned the dial on the radio and music abruptly boomed from it, one of the top hundred

songs from 1968, the Rolling Stones' "Jumpin' Jack Flash." "Yessss."
She pumped her fist into the air, then turned the key and hit the gas
pedal simultaneously.

The engine roared to life, *Further* lurched forward, and the whiteness parted like the Red Sea, creating a narrow corridor through which
she drove. The odometer needle read 110,952 miles. Lauren switched on
the headlights, the Stones kept singing, she picked up speed, and pretty
soon, the speedometer needle swung toward eighty, then ninety.

But why didn't the wind whistle through the open windows? Why
didn't the whiteness on either side of them drift apart as they passed?
Why were the numbers on the odometer spinning? Why did she suddenly feel a tremendous, agonizing pressure in her skull?

Lauren glanced at Ian. His shoes were pressed against the glove
compartment and he rocked backward and forward in the passenger
seat, hands pressed to the sides of his head, his mouth open in a scream
she couldn't hear. Then the pressure in her skull blew out through her
crown and she gasped and her hands flew to the top of her head as if to
hold her brain inside.

The bus swerved crazily through the fog, and even though she
grabbed the wheel and took her foot off the gas pedal, the speedometer
needle leaped past a hundred and ten, *Further*'s top speed. The pressure
that had gripped her head now seized her entire body. Her bones felt as
if they were being crushed, her musculature collapsed, the skin on her
face peeled away. In the ensuing seconds, the odometer stopped spinning, each digit locking into place with a resounding click until it read:
111,111. The mother of all mystical portals.

Then the world turned from white to black and the blackness swallowed her.

Seventeen
Memory

1.

Charlie felt like it took him and Karina hours to think themselves into old town Esperanza. They moved like slugs, every inch a struggle, every mile counted by the miles still to go. Twice, they tried to assume their virtual forms, but simply couldn't do it. When they merged their essences, they gathered a bit more momentum, and were finally able to break free of whatever force gripped El Bosque and the area around it. Once they felt stronger, they separated their essences and moved forward under their own volition.

Suppose we can never assume virtual forms again? Karina asked. *I won't be able to touch you, Charlie. We won't—*

Then we incarnate. The words rushed from his mind so quickly that it shocked him. He didn't want to incarnate just yet, not unless he could remember his twelve years here and his life as Charlie Livingston. But because every soul had to cross the river Styx—the Río Palo was its equivalent here—he knew he wouldn't remember much of anything about his previous lives or his life in the between.

And that infuriated him. What good was any of this if you had no memories?

He and Karina finally reached Parque del Cielo, the city's oldest park. They thought themselves onto a bench in the shade of the giant ceiba tree, the tree of life, the first piece of Esperanza to enter the physical world. Neither of them spoke immediately. They understood the stakes: if they couldn't assume their virtual forms here, where the energy of the city was the strongest, then it wouldn't happen anywhere.

Charlie? She repeated her question.

We go to plan B.

Which is . . . ?

I don't know yet.

Charlie created a mental image of his favorite Quechuan form, but when only his right arm appeared, he quickly shed it and thought himself into his Charlie Livingston form, white trousers, shirt, hat, shoes. Only his head materialized.

It's not working, Karina whispered, just her mouth and her black braid visible.

New forms, we need new forms.

The moment he thought this, his new virtual form emerged, lightning quick, almost as if it had been waiting to be summoned. He went over to the fountain and looked at his reflection in the water. Not bad. Latino dude who looked to be twentysomething, with thick dark hair and the muscular body of a gym rat.

"It worked, Charlie, it worked," Karina said, hurrying over to him. Her new virtual form was that of an Asian woman, a form he had never seen before, and he couldn't stop looking at her. His eyes moved slowly from her face to her toes and back up again. "You're stunning. I feel like I should ask you for a date."

She touched his muscular arms. "Maybe I'd better join a gym. How'd you know it would work?"

"I didn't. The real issue is why these new forms worked and our old ones didn't. C'mon, let's go find the others."

They hurried through the park. Several elderly men and women were feeding the birds, a young mother sat in the shade, chattering away on her cell, absently pushing a stroller with her foot, and several young men shot hoops on a small basketball court. No one paid any attention to them. Were he and Karina even visible to any of them?

Charlie walked over to an old lady tossing handfuls of seed to a pair of doves. He just stood there, waiting for her to glance up. When she didn't, he spoke to her in Spanish. "Where did you buy the birdseed?"

No response.

Karina sat down on the bench next to the woman and also spoke in Spanish. "Excuse me, but can you see us? Hear us?"

No reaction.

"Shit," Charlie murmured.

Karina got up and walked behind the bench and ran her hand over the woman's hair. She flinched, glanced around uneasily, but that was all. *Invisible to the living.* Misery gripped him. His eyes met Karina's and the two of them hurried forward, hands clutched tightly, as if to reassure themselves that they were, at least, visible and real to each other.

They entered the cobblestone alley and both of them broke into a run and headed for La Última, the café where the council usually met. They passed the bodega, the Chinese takeout, the used bookstore, and stopped.

The café, the place created by collective chaser thought, was a boarded-up ruin and had a NO TRESPASSING sign plastered to one of the planks.

Charlie tore off the sign, ripped away the plank across the front door, and kicked it open. The door swung inward, creaking and complaining, the light from the alley barely penetrating the dark interior. He and Karina stepped inside, into air that smelled wet, moldy, old, the way Charlie imagined a leaky coffin might smell. He heard water dripping somewhere, puddles of water glistened on the floor. The emptiness shocked him. All that remained were the counter, two round stools, and the table where the council members had sat during their last meeting.

He walked over to it, drew his fingers through the inch of dust, and turned, staring at the counter where he had placed his order only days ago. How many days? He no longer knew. He could no longer keep track of time in the world of the living.

"Charlie," Karina said softly, and pointed at the clock on the wall behind the counter.

The hands were frozen on 11:11.

Like in El Bosque. Deep inside his chest, something exploded and he lurched toward the stools and sank onto one, wheezing like an old man with emphysema. Panic attack, he thought. He was having a panic attack.

Karina gently rubbed his back. "It's okay, Charlie. Breathe through it."

"Breathe through *what*?" he burst out. "For years, I believed there was nothing worse than death. Now I believe there's nothing worse than being a marginalized ghost."

She sat on the stool next to him. In the dust that covered the counter, she drew a heart with their initials inside it. "That's our power."

Love. Okay. Fine. No argument with that. But his and Karina's love for each other couldn't rebuild a place the council had constructed, couldn't fight against the force that had prevented the two of them from assuming virtual forms earlier. The city, Esperanza herself, had seized control of her own destiny and he was just beginning to understand what that meant for him. For Karina. For the chaser council. For all of them, the living and the dead.

Fissures suddenly exploded through the counter at which they sat and they both wrenched back. Then the café's floor belched, heaved upward, and the counter split in half, and Charlie and Karina leaped up and stumbled back. The floor heaved again, knocking Karina off her feet, and Charlie grabbed her by the arms, jerked her up, and they ran out into the alley.

Seconds later, the roof of the café caved in and the remnants of the building collapsed. A thick cloud of dust billowed up and out and moved through Charlie's new virtual body, the dust of collective thoughts and desires, a chaser dust that spanned centuries, that held the DNA of Esperanza. He slammed to the ground in a recessed doorway on the other side of the alley, and for the longest time, he and Karina lay like spoons in a drawer crowded with silverware, the dust falling over them, around them.

Then it occurred to Charlie that he didn't have any idea why he hid, why he was afraid. He couldn't die again, neither of them could. But self-doubt might annihilate him.

"They've scattered," Victor said, appearing abruptly in front of Charlie. "Most of the chaser council has gone elsewhere." Victor's virtual self sped through period clothing—Renaissance, Dark Ages, ancient civilizations—until he settled on shorts and a T-shirt fit for modern times in the Florida keys. "We're pretty much on our own. You, me, Karina, Liana, Franco, Newton. Pilar is probably on our side, too, but I don't have any idea where she fled. Our task is—"

"To free those in El Bosque who can be freed," Charlie said.

Victor pointed his index finger at Charlie, and suddenly they all stood in front of Maria's home. It looked like an old sepia photo, flat and faded, a bygone memory.

"This is happening all over," Victor said. "Wherever council members have lived, wherever chasers have congregated, the buildings are disintegrating, fading away. Collectively, the council members are withdrawing their energy from Esperanza. Even the three of us are doing it to some degree, Charlie."

"Speak for yourself, Victor."

"Then how do you explain that?" He swept his arm toward Maria's place.

"Esperanza is claiming her own power and we're being rendered irrelevant."

Victor frowned. "That's cynical, Charlie."

"It may be cynical," Karina said. "But it may also be true. If I remember correctly, the fourteenth council member predicted something like this centuries ago, before she was tossed off the council."

"I thought she was tossed off because she advocated for an animal representative on the council," Victor said.

"That was part of it. But the bottom line, Victor, is that the chaser council at that time believed that nothing was more powerful than they were. And here was one of their own telling them that at some point in the future, Esperanza herself would become so powerful that she would determine her own fate."

Victor's expression spoke volumes about the shock he felt just then. "If what you're saying is true, Karina, then we may not be able to free those people from El Bosque unless that's what Esperanza wants. Even the ghost train may not be able to penetrate the whiteness."

"That's the problem," Charlie said quietly. "We don't have any idea what the city wants. So we'd better make an attempt to find out."

"How?" Victor asked.

"Let's go meet the ghost train."

2.

Outside, the angry throng pelted the greenhouse with stones. The sound of breaking glass told Wayra they probably had less than a minute to find the opening to the tunnels.

Kali suddenly dropped down to a bench filled with small plastic containers that held cuttings from other plants. She squawked and fussed and fluttered her wings as if scolding Wayra for not understanding. He dropped to his knees next to the bench and ran his hand and paw over the ground beneath it, searching for a hatch, a loose board, something. But he couldn't find anything.

"There's no door here," Ricardo said. "And we're running out of time."

"Every greenhouse has a hatch that opens to the tunnels." Wayra looked around frantically, certain the opening had to be in this vicinity. Otherwise the bird wouldn't have led them to this spot. "It's here. It has to be here."

"I told you not to trust him," Naomi snapped. "This is a trap. This whole thing is a trap. And why should we be following a stupid bird? Tell me that, Ricardo."

"Shut up, Naomi," Tess said, pushing the bench out of the way.

Kali, still squawking, flew upward, then dived at Naomi, and she stumbled back, waving her arms, shrieking, "Get away from me, you stupid parrot, get away from me!"

She fell back into a second bench, knocking it over, and sprawled in a thicket of tomato plants. Wayra pushed the fallen containers out of the way and dug through dirt and weeds until he felt a cool metal surface. "Here, it's here." He unlatched the hatch, opened it, and peered into a dark hole faintly lit by the glowing lights most of the tunnels had. The drop was maybe six feet. "Get inside, fast."

A great explosion of glass at the other end of the greenhouse announced the mob's arrival. *Smoke them out, smoke them out,* they shouted, and the flickering flames of their torches set trees and plants on fire. Tess dropped through the opening first, then Ricardo. Naomi hung back, arms clutched to her body, and shook her head violently. "No, no, it's a trick. You tricked me once, Wayra, never again."

"They'll kill you."

"I'm already dead."

Wayra threw his arms around her and dropped her down the hatch. Kali swept in after her, and Wayra quickly pulled the bench over the opening, an awkward maneuver with just one hand. He hoped it would buy them a few minutes. Then he crawled under the bench and eased himself over the side of the hatch, his right hand gripping the metal handle. As he dropped, the hatch slammed shut.

This tunnel, like others beneath the city, had small glowing lights that ran along the base of the concrete walls. The lights along the ceiling didn't work, Wayra noticed, but there was still sufficient illumination for him to see the others—Kali, perched on Tess's shoulder, Naomi on the floor, sobbing that she had broken her ankle, Ricardo crouched beside her, moving his hands over her ankle.

"It's not broken," Ricardo told her. "You just sprained it. C'mon, we need to keep moving." He tried to help her up, but she wrenched back from him.

"I can't walk, okay? I . . . I can't walk and . . . and Wayra threw me down here, he—"

"He saved your ass," Tess said. "So stop whining. Right now, the parrot is our best bet out of here." With that, she loped after Kali, who flew straight down the middle of the tunnel.

"I'll carry you, Naomi," Ricardo said.

"Stay with me," she pleaded. "I don't want to travel with them. I don't trust them."

"I'm not dying in here," Ricardo told her.

"We're already dead," she shouted. "Why do you keep talking like we aren't?"

Wayra leaned into her face. "Let me spell it out for you. Your virtual form became a host body, you can't get out of it, and you can die in that body."

Shouts, directly above them. Wayra hesitated a moment longer, wondering why he bothered, then took off after Tess and Kali.

3.

The tunnels spread out beneath El Bosque like splayed fingers on a giant's hand. Tess followed Kali up one finger, down another, up and down. Once, she lost sight of the parrot and Kali flew back to find her. By then, Wayra had caught up to her and Ricardo was directly behind him, with Naomi hobbling along behind him. That was when she heard the echoing shouts of the mob, smelled the smoke, and realized the crazies had found the hatch and at least some of them had entered the tunnels.

Kali vanished into yet another tunnel, Tess ran faster. The shouts sounded closer, closer. Beads of sweat rolled down the sides of her face, fear coiled in the pit of her stomach, a viper ready to spring. Then the tunnel abruptly dead-ended. Kali made a heart-wrenching sound, a cry that sounded almost human to Tess, and quickly flew back the way they had just come.

"A trap," Naomi gasped, panting hard. "Just like I said."

"The parrot has been down here before and we haven't." Wayra's voice sounded tight, tense. "If you've got a better idea, go for it."

"Well, shit, it looks to me like the parrot is lost," Ricardo spat.

Kali swept toward them, past them, her wings flapping hard, and flew back and forth in front of the dead end, left wall to right to left again, a space of perhaps six feet. "What's she doing?" Tess asked.

"It's like she's . . . weaving," Wayra replied.

"We're trying another tunnel." Ricardo sounded terrified. "That mob is just minutes away."

"Look," Tess exclaimed and pointed.

As Kali repeatedly flew back and forth, the wall started to fissure, then crack, and the cracks sped quickly toward a central spot in the wall. An opening appeared in that spot and the faster she flew, the larger it got. It was as if invisible hands were pulling back on the concrete, widening the opening.

"She's no parrot," Ricardo breathed. "She's . . . something else."

Kali circled around them once, squawking, then sailed through the opening. Tess could hear her on the other side of it, fussing, talking. "Vamonos, amigos, rápido."

Wayra climbed through first; his head appeared in the opening moments later. "Quick, I don't think she can hold it like this much longer."

"C'mon, Naomi," Ricardo urged, tugging on her hand.

But she jerked free of his grip and backed away from him, tears rolling down her cheeks. "I'll . . . I'll find my own way out of here."

Tess pushed through the hole, with Ricardo quickly following her.

Naomi didn't appear. Wayra shouted for her to hurry, but Naomi wasn't in that tunnel anymore. Kali flew back and forth across the opening, the tips of her wings brushing against the fissures and cracks in the concrete, until they began to vanish. The hole started shrinking, but not quickly enough. One of the crazies raced into the tunnel, waving his torch, yelling, *"In here, they're in here. Behind the wall."* He dropped his torch and dived for the hole even as the concrete around it continued to repair itself, to weave together.

Tess and Wayra rushed forward to help him, to pull him through, but within seconds, the hole had closed completely, severing his right shoulder, arm, and head, which dropped to the ground.

"Fuck, fuck." Tess lurched back. Her stomach somersaulted, she nearly gagged on her own bile.

Wayra grabbed her arm. "We can't do anything for him, Tess."

He pulled her away from the wall and she whipped around and raced after him and Ricardo and Kali, into a shorter tunnel and up a flight of crumbling stone steps. Wayra and Ricardo threw their bodies against the old wooden door, it swung open, and they stumbled into the altar area of a small church. Tess hurried after them, shut the door, bolted it, and sank down against the wood until she was sitting on the floor.

Kali landed on Tess's forearm, her beak open, her soft green breast throbbing. Tess shrugged off her pack, unzipped it, and pulled out a bottle of water. She poured some into her hand and Kali dipped her beak into it, drank, paused, drank some more, then hopped to the floor. Tess tilted the bottle and slowly poured water over Kali. She unfurled her wings, tilted her head back, preened herself, and made a soft, trilling noise of contentment.

Tess polished off what was left of the water, fished out two more bottles and got up and gave them to Wayra and Ricardo. The *brujo's* eyes darted around as he gulped from the bottle. When he finally had sated his thirst, he wiped his arm across his mouth. "A church. I don't do churches."

"Or cemeteries," Wayra reminded him.

Tess wondered if he would burn up if she poured holy water on him. With that thought, another memory surfaced, of herself hiding in this very church. It had been deserted except for an elderly couple and . . . a priest, yes, a priest. And then another chunk of the memory crashed into place.

"I hid from you in here," Tess burst out, staring accusingly at Ricardo. "You seized a priest and threatened me."

Ricardo looked guilty. "The situation was different then."

"Yeah, you weren't trapped in your virtual body." She noticed that the mark on her wrist didn't burn or itch even though she was only a foot from him. "I like you better like this, Ricardo."

"Only because I'm no threat to you."

"It's more than that. I think you've changed."

He seemed bemused. "Before I was Darth Vader and now I'm Luke Skywalker?"

"Maybe not quite as extreme as that."

She pushed to her feet and went over to one of the stained-glass windows. In the center of a blue pane, part of the Virgin Mary's robe, was a piece of clear glass the size and shape of a dinner plate, a replacement pane. Tess peered out.

Twilight still clung to the air, the road out front looked deserted. Definitely the same church, she thought. Next door was the Mercado del León, the market where the blackness had taken her. She had come full circle in El Bosque.

After a while, Wayra joined her at the window. He gestured at the blankets and pillows piled in one of the pews. "I found those downstairs. You and Ricardo should get some sleep. I'll take the first watch."

"We're still in El Bosque. What're we doing in here?"

"I have no idea. But this is where Kali brought us." He tilted his head toward the pew closest to them, where Kali huddled, trembling. "And until she's rested and can show us the way out or until the city decides what to do with us, we're stuck here."

"What is she, Wayra?"

The shifter shook his head and jammed his hands in the pockets of his jacket. "Whatever she is, she apparently commands the residual magic of the city. She might nibble at any of the food we still have. I'm going to find some reinforcements for the front door, just in case the crazies figure out where we are."

Tess nodded, retrieved her pack, picked up a couple of blankets and a pillow, and went over to the pew where Kali was. She made a bed for herself, gently picked up Kali, set her on the plump pillow, and dug a battered apple from her pack. She bit into it and offered the piece to the parrot. Kali pecked at it a couple of times, then lost interest and waddled to the edge of the top blanket and disappeared beneath it. Tess drew it carefully over the two of them, aware of the parrot nestling down against her leg, her body chilled.

Tess's head sank into the pillow, her eyes screamed to shut. She turned on her side, her spine against the back of the pew, and drew her knees up toward her chest, offering Kali a culvert of denim and body warmth. Maybe she dozed, maybe she only thought she dozed. But when she snapped into full consciousness, Ricardo sat in the pew in front of her, a tall black man, a *brujo* trapped in his virtual form, his chin resting on the backs of his massive hands.

"I can't remember what it was like to die, Tess. That's how long I've been what I am."

"For me, it wasn't much different than being alive," she said. "There were things that didn't make sense, but once I realized I was dead or near death, everything clicked into place."

"So where is Naomi now?"

"Maybe she found another way out of the tunnels."

"And maybe not. Maybe those loons killed her."

Tess didn't say anything.

"You know, it's weird. I want to hate you. But I can't seem to muster it. I want to hate your father, Ian, your mother, Maddie, your whole group of intruders. But it's just not there for me. It was for my sister and I think it's what made her so powerful."

"It's also what destroyed her."

"Probably so." His smile smacked of resignation, sadness, and profound regret.

Another memory clicked into place for Tess. "In the lead-up to the solstice battle against Dominica's tribe, there was a woman who brought together tens of thousands of people whose loved ones had been seized by Dominica's tribe. They were willing to fight against her to avenge the deaths of their loved ones. When Ian and I first wrote about that battle in the *Expat News*, a reader commented that we hadn't given that woman enough credit. He talked about it like the battle was a novel where we'd ignored an important plot point. But he missed the central message. That battle, Ian and I meeting as we did, my dad as a chaser, it was *our* story. Other characters in that battle, in those dark years, have other stories. Do you see what I'm saying?"

"We're the heroes of our own stories."

"Joseph Campbell."

"Dominica hated his work."

Tess laughed. "That figures." She lifted up on her elbows and bit into the apple she'd tried to feed Kali. "But what's *your* story, Ricardo? I think that's what you need to ask yourself."

"Sordid, opportunistic, homicidal, sexually deviant. Not too many heroics there."

"You can turn that around."

"Yeah? How? By dying and starting over again?"

"Maybe. Or maybe you can start doing it just by thinking different thoughts, by being mindful of what you're thinking moment to moment."

"The Zen of *brujo* conversion." He shrugged and a frown carved its way down between his dark eyes. "I sometimes listened in on that *net* that connected Dominica to the rest of her tribe. She really hated you and Ian. She particularly hated the fact that she couldn't seize you. I think that's when I knew her days were numbered. I have to admit that I was surprised when she seized Maddie."

"That was a dark and terrible time for us. But especially for Maddie."

"And when Maddie was able to survive one month after another, I started cheering for her. Dominica never had a host like her."

"If it hadn't been for Dominica, Maddie might never have met Sanchez. *Brujos* changed the course of all our lives and for that I'm grateful, Ricardo."

"The other day when I tasted you? I discovered you're pregnant with twins. And the souls haven't yet entered their bodies." Then he fussed with the bed he'd made on the pew in front of hers and settled into it, vanishing from her view.

Twins?

4.

One moment, *Further* raced forward like a stallion on steroids and Lauren, now driving, pumped her fist in the air. Then they struck something, the impact knocked Ian out, and he came to in a cloud of dust that drifted through the open windows, Lauren slumped over the steering wheel.

Merchandise surrounded him, some of it on floor-to-ceiling shelves, most of it on the floor. Rolls of toilet paper and paper towels tumbled off *Further*'s hood. A can of baked beans rested against the windshield wipers. He was pretty sure he was in the market where he'd seen Tess in the early part of his hallucinogenic fest.

The Segunda Vista had long since worn off, all of this was real, palpable. He tasted the dust on his tongue, felt it at the back of his throat. He heard something rolling across the market floor, felt the solidness of his body as he got up and moved over to Lauren.

"Lauren, hey, c'mon, wake up." He patted her face, but she didn't move. He touched his fingers to her carotid and felt frantically for a pulse. Faint, almost not there. "Shit, you need a doctor."

He quickly squeezed behind the steering wheel, pumped the gas once, turned the key in the ignition. *Further* wheezed, backfired, lurched forward, and promptly died. Ian shot to his feet, slung their packs over either of his shoulders, then picked up Lauren and carried her off the bus. He moved as fast as he could through the disheveled aisles, kicking cans and boxes out of his way, talking to her, begging her to stay with him. Had her head hit the steering wheel? Had she had a heart attack?

She didn't stir. Her head hung limply over the side of his arm, her mouth open slightly. He could hear her quick, shallow breathing. Beads of perspiration dotted her forehead and upper lip like perforated lines. At the front of the store he put her into an empty grocery cart. He glanced back and could see the hole that *Further* had punctured in the whiteness, the edges jagged, the color of metal, white stuff like snow or dust drifting through the air around it.

He heard an explosive crackling sound and suddenly the rest of the whiteness around the hole blew apart, as if detonated, and for seconds, he glimpsed moonlight, stars. Then the market started falling apart, crumbling like a cookie, pieces of it raining down over him, over Lauren. Ian raced for the door, the cart clattering across the floor, then across the earthen sidewalk outside, and he shouted, *She's dying, I need a doctor, hey, is anyone here? Please, shit, c'mon, please, she needs help.*"

Everywhere he looked, he saw dead birds, hundreds of them blanketing the ground, and then he saw mobs armed with torches and Christ knew what else, racing toward him from every direction. Forget a hospital or clinic, he thought. He needed to get somewhere safe.

Behind him, a great, heaving, unnatural screech sundered the air and the market collapsed completely, concrete and wood and dust flying up, forming a cloud as huge and unnatural as the whiteness had been. It obliterated the moonlight and provided a barrier between him and the mobs. Ian tore forward, screaming for help, praying there was someone in the church nearby who could hear him.

"Don't die, please don't die, Lauren. Stay with me, I know you can hear me." The cart's wheels clattered across stones and packed earth. His mind emptied of everything.

The door to the church suddenly flew open, a blue and green parrot fluttered out into the twilight, and Tess and Wayra tore down the steps, toward Ian. Even in this strange light, he could tell Tess had lost weight, her cheekbones as sharp as razors, the flare of her hips chiseled away. Her blond hair hung loosely, a tangle. And she was still the most beautiful woman he'd ever seen.

"*Slim,*" he shouted, and ran toward her, and she barreled into his arms and nearly knocked him over.

They clung to each other, the scent and feel of her as familiar to him as his own skin and bones. "My God, my God, you're here," she whispered over and over again. Then she wrenched back from him, her face ravaged with emotion, and turned to her mother. Tess tried to rouse her, just as Wayra was doing.

"She needs medical help," Ian said, his voice riddled with urgency. Up the street, shouts rang out. Through the unnatural cloud, he saw the flickering lights of the mob's torches.

"The hostiles," Wayra hissed, and scooped Lauren out of the cart and tore toward the church.

Ian and Tess raced after him, their arms around each other, Tess intermittently sobbing and asking what had happened, how had he and Lauren gotten into El Bosque.

They sprinted into the church and Ian slammed the massive wooden doors. Not enough, he thought. They needed more protection. A crowd like the one outside could easily break through these doors. He looked around frantically, spotted an industrial-sized broom nearby, grabbed it, and slid the metal broomstick through the doors' handles. Then he backpedaled, his eyes traveling up to the stained-glass windows, so many of them, but at least they started six feet up from the floor. If the horde broke the windows, they wouldn't be able to climb into the church unless they had ladders. But they could hurl those torches, he thought, and set the interior on fire.

He spun around and hurried over to where Wayra had set Lauren, on a blanket on the floor. A tall black man came over with another blanket and a pillow. "If she's going into shock, you need to keep her warm and elevate her legs."

"Who're you?" Ian asked.

"Ricardo."

"Ricardo," he repeated. The *brujo*? What was he doing here? "I won't even ask. You have medical knowledge?"

"Some. From a host. But there's nothing in the church that will help her and there's no hospital left in El Bosque. The crazies burned it. There's a clinic not far from here, but the staff has probably fled."

Tess suddenly said, "I can't find a pulse, her heart's not beating." Her wild, panicked eyes impaled Wayra. "You have to turn her. Your shifter blood will save her."

Wayra hesitated. "I can't bring the dead back to life, Tess. She doesn't have a pulse."

"You have to try," Tess begged. "She might still have a faint pulse, we don't know. We don't have a stethoscope. Please, Wayra. Just *try*."

Ian tore open Lauren's bag, pulled out her stethoscope, and went over to Lauren. He mimicked what he'd seen her do and detected a faint—almost nonexistent—pulse. "She's still with us, Wayra."

The shouting outside got louder, the mob had moved much closer. Ian made a beeline for the closest window, the only one with a circular pane of clear glass. He could see them now, the burgeoning herd of crazies torching cars, trees, buildings, anything and everything.

Ian spun around. "Get on with it, Wayra. Fast. The crazies are nearly on top of us." Then he ran over to the rear pew and struggled to move it up against the door. Ricardo hastened over to help. The sucker was heavy, but Ricardo's host, or virtual body or whatever the hell he was, proved to be as strong as he looked. They shoved and pulled, shoved and pulled until the pew stood up against the door.

"You think it'll hold?" Ian asked.

"It should. It's heavy enough."

"Look, I don't know what you're doing here, but thanks for helping," Ian said, then returned to the others, Ricardo behind him.

Wayra's hands pressed against Lauren's forehead. Ian knew that as soon as light shot from his palms, Wayra would bite his own tongue hard enough to make it bleed and then sink his teeth into Lauren's carotid, infusing her body with shifter blood. But nothing happened. Wayra rubbed his hands together again, hard and fast, and touched his palms to Lauren's heart.

Nothing.

"Jesus, do something," Tess sobbed.

Wayra tried again, but the outcome was the same. He finally rocked back on his heels, misery etched in his face, and just sat there, staring down at Lauren.

"Sanchez can't flip off his psychic switch," Wayra said quietly. "Ricardo is stuck in his virtual body, the chasers can't get into the disappeared area, the council can't reverse what's happening. And I've lost the ability to turn anyone." He turned his gaze to Tess. "I can't help her."

Ian pressed his fists against his eyes. He blamed himself. If they hadn't taken the Segunda Vista, if he hadn't suggested she ask the Pranksters for help, if they had been escorted out of the area by the cops, as Leo and Pedro were, perhaps she would still be alive. It tore him apart when Tess dropped to the floor next to her mother, shaking her, sobbing, begging. Then she slipped her hands under her mother's back, lifting her off the floor, pulling Lauren's body against her, and rocked and sobbed.

Ian went over to her, touched her shoulder, and started to draw her away from Lauren's body. But a hail of stones crashed through one of the stained-glass windows and something monstrously huge slammed against the door.

Then two things happened simultaneously—the first torch sailed through the broken window, into the church, and a fierce wind rose, whipping through El Bosque with such tornadic frenzy that the windows rattled, the door shook. Ian ran over to the torch and stamped it out. He moved to the window but couldn't see anything except sand swirling through the air.

"Ian," Ricardo shouted.

He raced to the front of the church where sand was blowing under the door and starting to accumulate on the floor in small drifts. He and Ricardo frantically pressed sheets and blankets and pillows against the crack to stop the flow of sand, but the wind blew so hard that their efforts were useless. Sand struck the door, windows, the roof of the church, the sound like that of a thousand rats clawing to get in.

"Where's Kali?" Wayra shouted.

"She flew out when we ran out of the church and didn't return," Ricardo said.

"Behind the altar," Ian yelled. "No windows back there!"

Wayra picked up Lauren and he and Tess tore toward the altar, with Ian and Ricardo right behind them.

Wayra set Lauren on the floor, between the altar and the wall. Ian and Ricardo moved two of the smaller pews onto the elevated area— one on their right, the other on their left—and flipped them on their sides so the four of them were now enclosed in a small square. Ian leaped over the barrier to snatch the last two blankets off a nearby pew, and tossed one to Tess, the other to Wayra, and they covered themselves and Lauren's body the best they could and huddled with their backs to the wall. The blankets might protect them from flying glass, but if the roof collapsed, they would be crushed.

He and Tess pressed up so close to each other he could feel the wild pounding of her heart.

Then the first window exploded and the tempest roared into the church.

What Is Remembered

· · · · · · ·

If time is an illusion, if reality is created by our own consciousness, can this consciousness ever truly be extinguished?

—Robert Lanza, M.D., *Biocentrism*

Eighteen
Ghost Train

1.

The ghost train didn't run on anyone's timetable. Midnight came and went and Charlie, Karina, and Newton still waited in their virtual forms, outside the old depot in downtown Esperanza. They stood in the shadows of the abandoned building, between the road and the tracks, so that both were visible.

The narrow cobblestone road ran through a neighborhood of family-owned shops, cafés, and several bars where music pumped from open doorways. A young, hip crowd spilled onto the sidewalk, their laughter ringing out. Some of them crossed the street and Charlie watched them, decked out in tight-fitting jeans and colorful shirts, sweaters and jackets, the women with their flowing hair, the men with their cocky laughs.

He wondered what it would be like to be their age again, young twenties who didn't seem to have a care in the world. Hadn't they heard about what had happened in El Bosque? Or at Café Taquina? Didn't they have any idea what the hell was happening in the city, how these events threatened its very existence—and theirs?

"They don't want to think about it," Newton said, also watching the crowd outside the bars. "When your personal Armageddon looms, it's sometimes easier to just order another beer."

Irritated that Newton poked around inside his private thoughts, Charlie snapped, "I would appreciate it if you didn't do that, Newt. It's intrusive."

Newton, who now looked like a European tourist in jeans, a pull-over sweater, and a worn leather jacket, just rolled his eyes. "Charlie, you're such an open book that I don't even have to reach into you to read what you're thinking." He gestured dramatically toward the young hipsters. "Their parents and grandparents and great-grandparents lived through the dark years of *brujo* seizures. Most of them probably lost relatives to *brujos*. But it's been more than four years now and memory is short. When they hear about weirdness at the Café Taquina, in El Bosque, when they hear the *brujo* sirens, they tune it out. If the *brujos* are back, if some corrupt chasers are moving portions of the city out of the physical world, they don't want to know about it. That's how it is, Charlie."

"That's not how it is for his granddaughter and Sanchez," Karina said.

"Yeah," Charlie agreed. "Maddie's in her twenties and Sanchez is in his early thirties."

"They're new to the city. And they're exceptions." Newton rocked forward and sank his index finger into Charlie's chest. "Everyone connected to *you* is an exception."

Charlie heard someone shouting his name and looked around. A car had pulled up at the curb and Leo and Pedro, Maddie and Sanchez piled out and hurried toward them. Illary circled above them, watchful, silent, keeping her distance, then flew off. "Here come my exceptions," Charlie said, and Maddie barreled into his open arms. How real and solid she felt, he thought. How warm and alive.

"A chaser dude named Victor told me to come here," Maddie said, her voice soft, almost breathless. "Something about the ghost train. Is it true? Can the ghost train take us into El Bosque?"

"We think so," Newton replied.

"*Think* so?" Sanchez shook his head. "That's not good enough."

"It's a theory," Newton said. "No one has ever tried this before."

"I tried to get into El Bosque," said Maddie. "I'd gotten a text message from Ian after he and Lauren had taken Segunda Vista. They figured it might enable them to find a way into the disappeared area. Anyway, I couldn't get in."

"The mandatory evacuation orders cover everything within five miles of El Bosque," Leo explained. "The science guys have apparently measured vast electromagnetic fluctuations in the area, just like what happened around the Café Taquina and El Bosque before the erasures happened. Or so they said when they picked up Pedro and me. Fortunately, Diego made them drop us at Wayra and Illary's place." Leo's eyes met Charlie's. "That was clever, Charlie, what you and Karina did, making the room so cold that you could write a message in the frost."

"Clever but risky," Pedro added. "The cops could've seen the message. Luckily for us, the message had faded by the time they broke open the door to our hotel room."

"We didn't have a choice," Charlie said. "We couldn't create virtual forms until we got back into downtown Esperanza. All the rules have been turned inside out. Have you heard from Lore, Leo?"

"No. But she's in there, I'm sure of it. With Ian and probably with Wayra, too." Leo jammed his hands in his jacket pockets. "Nothing good is happening there, Newton, so can we get this train here and moving?"

"Hey, Doc, it's not up to me," Newton said.

"So how do we board a ghost train?" Sanchez asked.

"We'll ask the conductor," Newton said. "I'm not sure." He gestured at their packs, and bags. "It'd be better if you left your stuff here. It may slow you down. I'm not sure how this works."

"Oh, great," Charlie said. "And here I thought you knew what you were doing."

"My medical bag stays with me." Leo's fingers tightened over the strap of the bag that hung from his right shoulder. "Right here."

"My stuff stays with me," Maddie said, and fitted the strap of her large black canvas bag over her head and arranged it so it fell along the right side of her body. "And, oh, Jessie's joining us." She slipped two fingers in her mouth and whistled shrilly, sharply.

Shit, no, Charlie thought. But what he thought at that moment about the dog or the ghost train or any of it didn't matter. Maddie's whistle brought the golden retriever racing around the corner of the depot, onto the platform, and Sanchez snapped on her leash and told her to sit and she did. He slipped her a treat.

"I don't know if the conductor will allow dogs," Newton said, eyeing the dog with obvious distaste.

Jessie tugged on her leash and moved closer to Newton, sniffing at his shoes, his jeans, then she sat down right in front of him, barked, and held up her paw.

"What the hell does *that* mean?" Newton asked.

Sanchez rolled his eyes. "It means she'd like to shake your hand."

"I don't do paws," Newton said.

"For Chrissake, Newton," Charlie muttered. "She's a dog." He leaned over and shook Jessie's paw. "See? She isn't going to drool on you or bite you or piss on your shoes."

Newton stepped back, refusing to touch Jessie. "Like I said, we'll have trouble with the conductor letting her aboard."

"He will," Sanchez said.

"You can see that psychically?" Newton asked.

"No." Sanchez ran his hand over the dog's back. "Now and then, Jessie lets me in her head. And she's assuring me she can charm anyone, even a ghost conductor."

A gust of wind suddenly whipped through the trees on either side of the depot. It blew Maddie's red hair across her face, tossed Karina's braid over her shoulder, stole a hat from one of the hipsters across the street, and toppled a trash can.

"That was strange," Karina said. "Where'd that weird gust come from?"

"Holy crap," Leo said. "What is *that*?"

He pointed west, at what looked like a huge swarm of insects or maybe a massive flock of birds in the distance, in the direction of El Bosque. Charlie saw that the formation stretched for miles to the north and south, and then began to turn in on itself, whirling faster and faster until it became a tremendous tornado.

"*Locusts?*" Victor scoffed. "The *brujos* already did their locusts."

"*Sand,*" Sanchez gasped. "It's a tornado of sand. I saw this when I held the stone, Charlie. Wind, sand, a tornado . . ."

Charlie remembered someone telling him how Sanchez had said these very words right before he had gone into convulsions on Wayra's back porch. "*Get inside,*" he hollered. "That sucker is headed toward us."

They dashed for the depot's nearest door, Jessie barking wildly, several young people racing after them. Charlie expected the depot to be locked, but when Sanchez pulled on the handle, the glass door swung open, and they darted inside. Seconds before the door shut, Illary flew into the building and landed on the back of one of the benches.

Except for the benches, the depot was empty and had been for a long time. Anything of value had long since been removed and auctioned off or taken to a museum in the city. The depot's glass door and picture windows were equipped with aluminum shutters and Charlie found the circuit box that controlled them. But since the depot was no longer used, the power had been turned off.

"The benches," he said urgently. "Let's stack them up against the windows and doors."

Two of the young men grabbed either end of a heavy bench and hauled it toward the door. Charlie and the others pitched in, and within minutes, six benches were stacked to the top of the glass door and windows. The only bench they hadn't touched was the one where Illary perched.

"What's with the hawk?" one of the young men asked.

In a flash, Illary shifted and snapped, "The hawk is here to tell you that something very wicked this way comes."

The kid drew back, his expression seized up in shock and horror. "What the . . ."

Fuck, Charlie thought. Illary's shift was incomplete. Hawk feathers grew from her hairline, spread out across the top of her skull, and fell past her shoulders, like an Indian headdress. She ran her hand over the feathers and looked at Charlie, Karina, Maddie, each of them, looked slowly and deliberately, accusingly.

"Yeah, I know. The shift doesn't work right anymore. Nothing works right anymore. I'm going into El Bosque with you. The tornado was born there. It or something else ripped apart the whiteness and several hundred people need a way to get to safety. That's our job."

The kid backpedaled and joined his two friends, who gawked at Illary as she hurried over to one of the peepholes in the barricade of benches. Since the benches weren't all the same size or even the same size as the windows, the barricades had rather large peepholes at either end. Charlie and his group followed Illary to her peephole, Jessie hugging Sanchez's side, and the young people huddled together at the other end.

"So the disappearance of El Bosque didn't kill everyone?" Maddie asked.

"I don't know about everyone," Illary said. "I was about three hundred feet up when that tornado tore open the whiteness and it didn't take long for people to begin fleeing. They're panicked and confused."

"Did you attempt to get in there?" Charlie asked. "To look for Wayra, Tess?"

"I couldn't get anywhere near it. But I think the ghost train can."

"Well, where *is* it?" Leo asked impatiently.

"Maybe it's hiding from whatever wickedness is headed our way," Maddie said.

Charlie heard the tornado before he saw it, a roller coaster roaring out of control, a sound so powerful it rattled the windows and shook the door violently. The stacked benches trembled, threatening to topple. And then, through the peephole, he saw it, a swirling maelstrom, a thing so huge and grotesque he knew it had to be a supernatural construct. A tornado conjured into being by who or what?

Esperanza had never been afflicted by tornados. Never. Not a single tornado in five hundred years. The weather in Esperanza simply wasn't conducive to tornadoes. But this tornado swept over the depot, hurling granules of sand and dirt so sharp, at such high speeds, that they pierced the glass. Sand seeped through the openings and cascaded to the floor. So much sand poured through the spaces between the benches that it piled up a foot high, driving all of them away from the windows and doors, deeper into the empty depot.

"This isn't a normal tornado." Leo had to yell to be heard. "Otherwise the depot roof would be gone."

The roof was still intact, but it throbbed like a drum. The tornadic fury seized the building and shook it like dice in a gambler's fist. Even though it seemed to withstand the assault, sand streamed through a vulnerable spot in a corner of the ceiling where the wind had torn something loose. In minutes, that corner of the depot looked like a beach. Charlie went over to it, drew his fingers through it. White, it was perfectly white, as soft as an infant's skin, and felt like beach sand, something from a north Florida beach, Pensacola, Panama City. Yet, when it had hit the building and the glass, it was razor sharp.

Dichotomies, he thought. Vivid contrasts. The landscape of Esperanza now changed so swiftly, so abruptly, that nothing could be taken for granted. Just look at Illary, with her head of feathers. Or look at himself and Karina, unable to assume their customary virtual forms or to get into El Bosque after it had been disappeared. Look at Sanchez . . . And on it went, a cascade of *you can't, you won't, impossible.*

Charlie suddenly felt so exhausted, so spent, so completely drained of energy and will that he sank onto the bench with the others, and barely stifled an urge to crawl under it and hide.

2.

The storm began to ebb. The wind still blew, but not like before. Charlie shot to his feet and hurried over to the peephole. The others crowded around him. Sand blew through the air, cellophane and other trash tumbled like weeds across the platform. All the garbage cans had been blown over, spilling stuff everywhere, and the wind had whipped it all into a frenzy.

Off to Charlie's right, perhaps a mile down the track, something became visible in the falling sand, and emerged with form, shape, substance. Esperanza 14. The train sped toward them, light and sand flying away from it. Even from his limited viewpoint, Charlie could see the train's illuminated windows, the silhouettes of people inside. Its plaintive whistle rang out, light abruptly exploded from the crevices and cracks in the old depot. The concrete glowed, then appeared to expand from within, like a hot air balloon.

"That's it," Newton shouted. "Our cue!"

Newton lurched toward the front door and wrestled with the benches stacked against it. The entire barricade tumbled to the floor. Newton pulled the door open and the sand that had drifted up against it poured across the depot floor. They trudged through it, bodies slanted into the wind, arms thrown up to protect their faces. By the time they reached the platform, the wind had stopped altogether. The sand continued to fall, as silent as snow.

"From this point on, there's no going back," Karina said, her mouth close to his cheek. "Are we ready for that?"

Charlie kissed her fully. And in that kiss he tasted all the possibilities, the permutations, the promises waiting to be fulfilled. But he had no idea what those possibilities, permutations, or promises might be.

The train clattered and clunked its way up the track, an artifact from the late nineteenth century, a coal-belching machine that didn't look as if it could travel even a few miles without breaking down. Sand peeled away from it and a brilliant light radiated from it. Charlie felt he was seeing the train the way Esperanza wished for him to see it or as the train wished to be seen, a bright, shiny, sleek, and powerful contraption that would get them where they wanted to go.

"It's the ghost train," someone shouted in Spanish, and the hipsters poured into the station, onto the platform. "The falling sand has made it visible."

They giggled and laughed and pointed, the sand falling over them, and snapped photos with their cell phones and tiny digital cameras, their excitement radiating from them like an odor. Charlie ran over to them, waving his arms and herding them away from the edge of the platform. "Get back, get back so you don't fall onto the tracks. The train's wheels will crush you."

Would they? Was that part true?

One of the hipsters, a young man, swaggered through the accumulated sand and waved his bottle of Dos Equis at Charlie. "Who the hell're you, huh? What d'you know?"

"More than you do, asshole." Sanchez stepped forward, his tall, slender form illuminated by the light that radiated from the ghost train, his arms flung out at his sides. "So move the fuck back."

The young man hurled his Dos Equis bottle at Sanchez. He ducked, the bottle whistled over his head and shattered against a pole. The young man stumbled forward, swinging his fist. One of the other men grabbed him by the jacket and jerked him back. *"Hombre, déjalo. Estás borracho."*

Leave him alone. You're drunk.

Charlie grasped Sanchez's arm. "Thanks for intervening, Sanchez. But in this virtual form, I'm not an old man. Besides, I'm already dead."

Sanchez laughed nervously. "Yeah, I forget that sometimes."

Charlie and Sanchez hurried over to the others, and seconds later, the ghost train squealed to a stop. The conductor, a short Ecuadorian man with ebony hair, hopped down. "All aboard," he called, then saw Jessie and shook his head. "No dogs . . ."

Jessie plopped down at his feet, rolled onto her back, and the conductor smiled and stooped over to rub her belly. "Okay, okay, I can see you're well behaved. But you have to stay on your leash. Your group is headed where?"

"To El Bosque," Charlie replied.

Frowning, the conductor looked carefully at Charlie and the rest of them. "You're *that* group?"

"You heard about us?" Newton exclaimed.

"Of course. It's why we're visible. And why the train is empty of passengers."

"But earlier, I saw people," Charlie said. "Saw their silhouettes, saw—"

"Illusions, my friend," the conductor said with a quick smile. "All illusions."

"Who told you about us?" Pedro asked.

"What the city knows, we know. First car. We'll take you directly there." His eyes fixed on something behind them. "*Apúrate,*" he hissed, and Charlie looked back.

The swaggering young man rushed toward them, with several dozen other swaggering young men behind him, all of them now dressed identically, in black jeans and black jackets. *What the hell?*

The young men moved through the sand like dancers in a carefully choreographed musical, with great deliberation and precision, every step in synch, as if they had rehearsed for months. They simultaneously leaned forward, snapping their fingers, clicking their tongues against their teeth, the sounds preternaturally loud, echoing. And at the same instant, switchblades appeared in their right hands, glinting in the strange light.

Charlie felt as if he were watching a scene from *West Side Story,* and these dudes were the bad gang. But what, exactly, *were* they? *Brujos?* Apparitions Maria had tossed at them? Chasers, in their virtual forms, who sided with Maria?

The conductor waved Charlie and the others to move behind him. "Get on the train."

His arm shot into the air, then jerked down, apparently a signal to the engineer to get the train moving. They scrambled into the first car and the train started moving, the conductor running alongside it. Charlie gripped the railing and leaned out, arm thrust toward the conductor. "Grab my hand," Charlie shouted.

The conductor ran faster, grabbed on to Charlie's outstretched hand, and Charlie clung tightly, straining to pull him up. But the man's hand, slippery with sweat, slid away and he was sucked under the wheels. Blood suddenly sprayed across the side of the train, streaked the windows, and splattered Charlie's cheeks and clothing. Shock shuddered through him. The conductor couldn't die; he was already dead. But when Charlie rubbed his hand across his face, he felt the dampness of the conductor's blood on his cheeks. Saw it smeared across the back of his hand, coloring his knuckles, seeping into the lines and crevices in his skin.

He hurried inside the car and nearly collided with Newton. "Jesus, Charlie, you're covered in . . . blood."

"Listen up, people," Charlie shouted. "The conductor is dead, I don't have a clue who's driving this train, but I think we'd better find out."

"*Dead?*" Leo exclaimed. "He was already dead. This is a *ghost train,* Charlie."

"Forget all that. We're not on a ghost train. We're on a real fucking train and the dead can be killed."

Even chasers.

3.

Lauren drifted above her body, shocked at how she looked: ashen face, lips a faint blue, eyelids the color of eggshells. A filament, a thread of some kind, seemed to connect her spirit to her body. It lengthened when she thought herself upward, and shortened when she drifted down toward her body again. It was like an umbilical cord; she had read about it, heard stories about it from patients in ER who had died and returned.

Ian and Tess, Wayra and a black man huddled together around her body. It suddenly freaked her out to see herself like this and she shot up through the blankets of this little shelter and into a raging tempest of sand, glass, and debris that spun through the church. It looked and sounded like a ferocious hurricane. How was any of this even possible?

Then a weird silence clamped around her—no wind, no raging, just quiet. And she heard a female voice say, *You have a choice, Lauren.*

It took a few moments for Lauren to see the woman who spoke, a pretty little thing about five feet tall. She stood against the wall, hands fixed to her hips. Her dark hair tumbled past her shoulders, and she wore jeans with patches on the knees and a soft blue shirt that matched the color of her eyes. She looked to be in her late twenties and radiated such peace that Lauren instantly liked her.

Who're you?

The quintessence of Esperanza.

So you're the, what, consciousness of the city?

Close enough, although it's more complicated than that.

Did you cause that raging storm out there?

I did. Otherwise, the amnesiacs would have burned down the church and all of you in here would have perished.

I perished anyway.

Which is why you have a choice. You can return to your body or you can stay.

What's going to happen to Esperanza?

That depends. It can be removed from the physical world or can be stripped of its magic or both. Or something else altogether. I'm not sure yet. But everyone must have a choice—to stay in whatever takes Esperanza's place or to go wherever it goes. And if there's any amnesia associated with this, it won't be like what afflicted Tess or the others. What are we without memory? It's our sanctuary, our history, our place in time and space. It's how we define ourselves. Memory is the current of consciousness.

Lauren couldn't argue with that.

Many of the amnesiacs weren't just robbed of their deepest memories, but of their very identities, and it drove many of them crazy.

Can't you just take Esperanza somewhere else? Why does it have to return to the nonphysical universe?

It may be a failed experiment.

But even when it was nonphysical, brujos *were seizing souls.*

Back then, their seizures were confined to souls at the edge of death. Once the city was brought into the physical universe, brujos *evolved to the point where they learned how to seize the living and use them as hosts to experience all the physical pleasures of life. Now there are millions of* brujos *worldwide. They personify evil.*

Then take Esperanza, its consciousness—you, that's you—somewhere else, somewhere hidden, where legends flourish, some spot where the dead can't find the city. Learn from the failed experiment and create something better.

Doubt flickered across the woman's features. *I don't think I'm the optimist I once was. The corrupt chasers are still fighting me and some of the* brujos *can still seize the living. Until those things are rectified, you have time to get to safety, if you choose to return to your body.*

That's my choice. To return.

You're sure?

Yes.

She pointed at the blue blankets, now covered with sand and bits of glass. *That black man is my best hope. Do you recognize him?*

The woman moved her hand through the air and the blankets became transparent, so Lauren could see through them. She didn't have any idea who the man was. But the longer she looked at him, the clearer he became to her, and she understood that in this accelerated state of consciousness, she could see things she ordinarily couldn't. *The* brujo. *Ricardo. The head of the current tribe, the one who seized Leo and tasted Tess.*

That's right. And if the consciousness of even a single brujo *can evolve, then there's hope and Esperanza wasn't a failed experiment. Depending on what he ultimately does or does not do, I can adjust what I do.*

Then you're still an optimist.

The woman laughed, softly. *Maybe I am.*

Am I going to be brain damaged when I return?

No. What killed you was breaking through the barrier into El Bosque. Once you and Ian did that, I could capitalize on it. But that first tear had to come from the living. From here on in, all of you live or perish without intervention from me. If you choose to stay in whatever replaces Esperanza, you should get to the El Bosque train depot. A train will take you to safety.

Safety where?

The engineer knows. Wayra will doubt that I am who I say I am. So tell him that many years ago, he left a note for me tucked inside one of the many roots of that ceiba tree in Parque del Cielo. The note was addressed to the spirit of Esperanza. It was one word: "Why?"

What was your answer?

She leaned toward Lauren and whispered something.

I hope I can remember all this. What's going to replace the city?

I don't know yet.

So you're the ultimate decider?

No, all of you are. She threw out her arms, a gesture that encompassed everyone who lived in Esperanza. *More than thirty thousand of you.* Then her arms came around Lauren, the most gentle and loving embrace she had ever felt. She heard a loud snap, as if someone were cracking a whip next to her ear, and her eyes snapped open.

The first thing she heard was the fierce wind. The first thing she tasted was the desert dryness in her mouth. The first thing she saw was her daughter's beautiful face, tears streaming down her cheeks, leaving tracks through the sand stuck to her face. The first thing she touched was Tess's hand.

"Mom, oh my God." Tess slipped her arms under Lauren, helping her sit up. "I thought . . . we thought . . ."

"I was," Lauren said hoarsely.

She saw shards of glass everywhere on the floor around them. The wind whistled through shattered windows, sand blew through the church. But a moment after these details registered for her, the windows started repairing themselves. It was like watching a video in reverse, pieces of glass flying up from the floor to the window frame, each bit, each fragment, fitting together until the windows were whole again.

"Christ," she whispered.

"It's Kali doing that," Tess exclaimed. "She flew out the door when . . . when we all saw you and Ian and ran outside. It's what she did in the tunnel."

Lauren didn't have any idea what Tess was talking about. Wasn't Kali a parrot?

"Lauren, wow, you . . . haven't had a pulse for . . . I don't know how long," Ian burst out, and pressed a bottle of water into her hands. "Sip this. It isn't cold, but it'll do the trick. Jesus, welcome back."

As Lauren sipped, Wayra touched her forehead with the back of his hand. "Do you feel all right?"

"Just . . . thirsty. You were . . . going to turn me. To save me. But . . . you can't do it anymore."

"I'm just grateful you're still with us, Lauren."

She squeezed his hand. "Thank you for trying." She looked at the black man. "Ricardo, you're her best hope."

"You *recognize* me?"

"When I was dead, I did."

"Whose best hope?"

"The woman I met. She said she was the quintessence of Esperanza and that if the consciousness of even a single *brujo* can evolve, then there's hope." Lauren saw the looks that Wayra, Tess, Ian, and Ricardo exchanged—not looks that said she was nuts, but looks that said they understood completely. And why wouldn't they? Tess and Ian had both experienced NDEs, Wayra was a shape shifter, and Ricardo was a ghost stuck in a black man's body. "Each of us needs to decide whether we're going to stay here and take our chances on whatever replaces the magical Esperanza, or whether we're going to accompany the city to wherever it goes if it returns to the nonphysical."

Ricardo ran a hand over his head. "How does that apply to me?"

"I don't know," Lauren admitted.

"I know how it applies to Illary and me," Wayra said. "We live out the natural span of our lives from this point forward. No shape shifting, no turning anyone. And that's fine with me. She and I have lived way too long already."

"You'll be the only man in town with a paw," Ian remarked.

Wayra held his paw up and laughed. "My eternal reminder of what was."

"I'm staying," Tess said.

"Me, too," Ian said.

"Do you know you're going to be a grandmother again?" Ricardo asked Lauren.

"Ian told me."

"Twins," Ricardo said.

"You learned that from a pregnancy test?" Lauren glanced at Tess.

"No. Ricardo discovered it when he tasted me . . ." She frowned. "Well, whenever that was. I've lost track of days."

"So this woman you met," Ian said. "She claimed to be the consciousness of Esperanza. If we've all decided to stay, then we should get to El Bosque's train station. A train will take us to safety."

"Where?" Wayra asked. "Where is safe?"

"I have no idea."

"You sound suspicious, Wayra," said Ricardo. "Do you think it's a trick?"

"I'm not sure what to think."

"It wasn't a trick," Lauren said.

"I would love to have a conversation with the embodiment of Esperanza," Wayra said.

Unmistakable sarcasm, Lauren thought, and suddenly remembered what the woman had said about Wayra. "She said you'd be skeptical. I'm supposed to remind you about a note you wrote to her and tucked in one of the roots of the ceiba tree in Parque del Cielo."

Wayra looked amused. "Really. Did she tell you anything else about it?"

"Yeah. The note was addressed to the spirit of Esperanza and had a single word on it—*why*?"

His smile shrank.

"That's true?" Ian asked.

"Uh, yeah, it was centuries ago. I'd forgotten about it."

"Were you and Dominica together then?" Ricardo asked.

"Barely."

"Is this something a *brujo* could find out from a host?" Ian asked Ricardo.

"Probably not."

Wayra ran his long fingers through his hair. "Did she give you an answer, Lauren?"

Lauren thought a moment, struggling to remember, then snapped her fingers. " 'Because I can, and you always had a choice about whether to participate or not.' That's what she said."

Something ancient and hidden flickered through his dark eyes. Lauren couldn't read it. But incredulity and acceptance brought a smile to his mouth.

"Wow. Okay." He pushed to his feet. "The wind is starting to die down. I say we head for the neighborhood train station. If you're up to it, Lauren."

"Definitely," she said, and Wayra held out his hand and she grasped it and he pulled her to her feet.

Nineteen
The Shift

1.

When Tess emerged from the church with the others, the twilight was fading, giving way to an open sky, a rising moon, stars, and hundreds of birds flying south, silhouetted against the moonlight. Had the dead birds come back to life, like her mother did? Tess wondered. Or were these birds from elsewhere in Esperanza? Their cries and squawks and songs sounded like an orchestra tuning up, sometimes off key, sometimes perfectly in synch. Blankets of sand glistened in the moonlight, and several dozen men and women stumbled through it, shouting, headed for the nearest way out of El Bosque.

Others ran out into the sand that covered the street, waving their arms and pointing skyward. One man stood in the middle of the road and yelled, *"My memories, I have my memories back!"*

And so did she. Before the twilight had started crumbling, she had recovered fragments of her memories, isolated pockets disconnected in time. But now they rushed back to her like homing pigeons who knew where they belonged. They filled her, these memories, each one vivid, perfect, pulsating with life, remarkably clear. The twilight had not only stolen memories, but hoarded them, locked them up. Once a hole had been torn in it—that gaping mouth where Mercado del León had once stood—people's memories began to return.

"Do you feel it?" Ian said softly. "It's not finished. There's more coming."

Tess nodded. She knew what he meant. She smelled it in the air, like ozone before a thunderstorm, something heavy, thick, pervasive. The others seemed to smell it, too, and glanced around for its source, as though it might be emanating from a trash can or from one of the cars half buried in sand or from a burned-out building.

They moved up the street, across the endless sand, she and Ian behind Wayra, her mother, and Ricardo, who walked abreast. In places, the sand had drifted up so high they were forced to find a way around it. In other spots, it simply formed a second skin across the surface of the ground, a thin, shimmering blanket of granules that flew upward with every footstep, like dust from another world.

Tess noticed that her mother had linked arms with Wayra and Ricardo, one of those universal unity gestures that were part of every demonstration against a larger threat—war, segregation, apartheid, social injustices large and small. Ian tightened his grip on her hand. "They feel it, too, Slim. And so did the birds. That's why they're flying at night."

"They're leaving Esperanza," she said softly.

They passed more crowds slogging through the sand, small homes buried to their rooftops, burned-out stores. A pack of barking dogs raced past them. Somewhere not so distant, fighting cats screeched. And always, there were shouts, sobs, cries of relief, fear, and flat-out panic.

A quarter of a mile from the church, a herd of horses and donkeys stampeded toward them, forcing them to seek cover behind a sand-covered fountain. Following the horses and donkeys were flocks of chickens and ducks, another pack of dogs, a tribe of goats. Then giant shadows fell over it all, and when Tess looked up, her breath caught in her throat.

Condors.

Eight, ten, maybe a dozen of them, winged southward in a wide V formation, their wings moving in perfect rhythm, as though they were controlled by a single mind. They didn't make a sound. Behind them was another, larger flock in a wide V formation, and behind them, a third and fourth flock. In all, there must have been more than a hundred of them, their white faces perfectly visible in the moonlight.

Scavenger, vulture, predator: that was how they were usually characterized. But in Esperanza, especially among the Quechuas, condors were revered as powerful magic. But when the magic was headed out of the area, what did that tell her?

Another memory surfaced and with it came a surge of emotion that nearly choked her. "Ian, I remember that when we were in the posada as transitionals, you were fascinated with condors."

"And you were fascinated by the hummingbirds." He touched her chin and drew her face toward his and kissed her.

Such desire rose up inside of her that she flung her arms around him and pressed her body against his.

"Slim, Slim," he whispered. "It's okay. We'll make it through this."

Would they? Could they? And what was *this*? What was it now? This second?

"What will we do with twins, Ian?" Tess stepped back and touched her stomach, which seemed larger than it had been earlier.

"The same thing we'd do with just one kid. Twins explains why you've been so hungry. You've been eating for three. Did Ricardo know if they're identical?"

"He didn't say. Hey, Ricardo," she called out, and he looked back. "Are the twins identical?"

He glanced back, moonlight seeping into the deep frown that thrust down between his eyes. "I don't know. And I don't have any idea about gender, either."

"Wayra, you're perceptive," Lauren said. "What do you pick up?"

"Only that Tess is pregnant. The—"

The rest of what he said was lost in the thunderous arrival of cops on horses galloping through the street, chasing the crowds that raced out of El Bosque. Some people were trampled, others dived out of the way, and still others were seized, their bodies jerking, stumbling. Were these *brujos* using the cops as hosts or were they stuck in virtual bodies, just like Ricardo? Tess couldn't tell.

"All of you, get into those trees," Ricardo shouted. "I'll deal with them."

"Bad idea," Wayra told him. "We're grossly outnumbered."

"They're my tribe, Wayra."

"They *were* your tribe. You're no longer like them."

Ricardo slapped Wayra on the back. "*Go, fast.*" Then he ran toward the cops on horseback, waving his arms and shouting like a madman, all of them showered in moonlight that made the whole scene surreal. He stopped in the middle of the road, a tall, muscular, imposing black man with massive arms and a booming voice. "You can't seize anyone here."

One of the cops on horseback galloped to within a foot of Ricardo, except that it wasn't a cop. It was Naomi, as stuck in her virtual form as Ricardo was. She pulled back sharply on her reins and the horse snorted and danced. "You failed your tribe, Ricardo, just as your sister failed hers. We don't negotiate with the living. We seize them."

"Naomi. This is madness."

"Madness is doing nothing." Then she yelled, "Seize them, those of you who can seize, do so now!"

Her horse reared up, its hooves just inches from Ricardo's head, and he stumbled back as Naomi laughed and laughed.

Shit, Tess thought, and pulled out her slingshot, jerked open her little bag of stones, and ran toward Ricardo. She fitted a stone into her slingshot and aimed it at Naomi. As she breathed in, she focused on her target, pulled back on the slingshot, and let the stone fly. It struck Naomi in the center of her forehead and she fell back in her saddle, dead before her head hit the horse's flanks. She tumbled to the ground and her horse took off.

Another stone, another target. But there were so many targets and the horses were so spooked by the commotion, the strangeness, the odors, their *brujo* riders, that she couldn't shoot fast enough. All the *brujos* on horseback faced her and the mark on her arm burned and itched furiously. Tess pumped her arm in the air. *"Come and get me, assholes!"*

Their horses raced toward her, hooves pounding the ground, *brujo* faces set with grim determination. Ricardo kept waving his arms, shouting at them to back off, and led some of them away from Tess. She shot more stones, hit some *brujos,* missed others, but all of them were suddenly less important than the trees that abruptly appeared around them.

They sprang upward through the sand, giant sequoias and ceibas with branches that burgeoned outward in every direction. Hanging gardens of ferns turned gold in the moonlight. Thickets of huckleberry bushes appeared, stuff burst from massive trunk systems of trees she couldn't identify, had never seen. She and Ricardo raced into this strange jungle, into the thick shadows that provided a measure of concealment.

Tremendous braids of ivy covered the ground, their leaves so massive that Tess and Ricardo hid beneath them, close enough to one of the giant tree trunks that the horses missed them when they raced past. The vibration of their passage reverberated through her body.

The odor that had haunted and unsettled her earlier now invaded her senses. Her hands sank into its wetness, its reality, earth so dark and damp and succulent that her arms vanished to the elbows. "Ricardo?" she whispered.

"Here," he whispered back.

"Thank you."

"She . . . Naomi . . . hoped her horse's hooves would strike me. Apparently we *brujos* can be killed in these bodies. I think she knew that. You freed her, Tess, and saved my ass."

Interesting that he used the word "freed" rather than "killed," Tess thought. "What do you think this jungle means, Ricardo?"

"Another Esperanza memory. Let's go find the others."

They pushed up, the giant leaves slipping away from them, and darted through the deepening shadows. The wild lushness of the canopy prevented most of the moonlight from reaching the jungle floor. More trees sprang up around them, coconut palms, mango trees, shoots of bamboo that rapidly multiplied, as though the earth here were so fecund that years of growth happened within minutes.

Had the sand seeded the jungle in some way? Was the sand seeding whatever would replace Esperanza? Was that what it had been about?

As she and Ricardo darted toward a thicket of ceiba trees, Ian suddenly dropped out of the branches, Lauren dropped from another tree, and Wayra from yet another. "How many of them are left?" Wayra asked Ricardo.

"I'm not sure. A few dozen. They've split up, gone in different directions. Like us, they're more vulnerable when they aren't in a group."

"They can be killed," Tess said.

"Given how quickly the landscape is changing," Ricardo said, "I don't think we can count on anything."

Even as they stood there, whispering and speculating, trees pushed upward from the ground, fully formed, as large as condominiums. With each birth, the air boomed with sound, dirt exploded upward, and they were forced to move, fast, to keep from being buried. Thick vines hung from the branches of these newly born trees and swung back and forth like giant pendulums. Their leaves, the size of cars, shone in the moonlight as if invisible gnomes had been polishing them. The gigantic fruits that hung from some of the trees—bananas and mangoes, coconuts and oranges and grapefruits—could feed the people of Esperanza for months.

The air had turned humid, sultry, and hot. Tess's physical discomfort was now so great she felt like tearing off all her clothes. She shed her dirt-covered jacket and tossed it over a low-hanging branch, then peeled away her pullover sweater and the blouse beneath it until she was wearing just a tank top, jeans, socks, her running shoes. She felt horribly fat, her belly now pressing up against the tank top. At the most, she could only be seven or eight weeks pregnant. But she now looked like she was three months.

Beads of sweat rolled down her face, into her eyes. The muscles in her legs screamed, her stomach churned and growled with hunger. She stumbled once and Ian caught her hand, keeping her upright and moving forward, just as he always had.

Suddenly, dozens of dense, bushy vines pushed up from the jungle floor as if summoned by some hidden snake charmer, and whipped across it like serpents, forcing the five of them apart as they leaped out of the way again and again. They zigzagged their way through the jungle, barely able to stay ahead of the vines that kept popping up from the ground, thrashing around like living things.

Tess scooped up a stick and whacked the vines as they shot toward her. Then one of them whipped up behind her and wrapped around her ankles, jerking her legs out from under her. She knew that she screamed, but didn't know if the others could hear her above the shrieks and cries of monkeys that now swung through the jungle with wild abandon. She landed hard on her hands and knees, twisted around, and grabbed at the vine, trying to rip it away from her legs. But it was too thick, too strong, and its grip so tight she felt her feet going numb.

Near panic, she tore off her pack and slammed it against the vine. It simply tightened its grip on her legs and climbed higher, to her knees. As she swung the pack again, Ian barreled toward her and drove a knife into a section of the vine just beyond her feet. The vine loosened its grip and Tess jammed her fingers under it and tried to yank it away as Ian kept stabbing it and yelling, *"We're over here, I need fire!"*

Then he severed the vine and Tess jerked her arms upward and the vine slipped free of her legs and crumbled in her hands. She lurched clumsily to her feet and Ian grabbed her around the waist, steadying her. "Can you walk, Slim?"

"Yes. Yes."

The monkeys still swung, screeching, through the jungle, and Tess heard other animal sounds now, a cacophony of frogs, toads, insects. She and Ian ran toward a torchlight headed their way and Tess saw her mother, flanked by Wayra and Ricardo. Lauren swung a crude torch from side to side above the ground in front of them, exposing the vines that whipped away from the flames. Fire, Tess thought. The vines were terrified of fire, just like *brujos.*

"We burned a way through this shit." The monkeys' screeches were so loud Lauren had to shout to be heard. "But we've got to move fast. The vines grow back together in minutes."

"They're sentient." Tess swept her bag off the ground, slung it over her shoulder, and fell into line behind her mother, Wayra, Ricardo, with Ian bringing up the rear.

"It's all sentient," Ricardo said. "We're moving through Esperanza's memories. Tell her, shifter. You know it as well as I do."

"Her memories?" Lauren exclaimed.

"More like a goddamn nightmare," Ian said.

"I think Ricardo's right," Wayra said. "The city seems to be . . . reliving her own history. When Esperanza was nonphysical, she could be anything she wanted to be—a jungle, mountains, an island, cold, hot, and everything in between."

Shit. Tess moved faster.

2.

Charlie reached the engine compartment first, Sanchez covering his back, the others behind him. The door was locked but it was also flimsy, and when he threw his young virtual body against it, all that mass and muscle, the door sprang inward.

The engineer, standing at the console, glanced around and smiled and motioned them to come in. She was a diminutive woman with black hair so long and thick and gorgeous it invited fingers to comb through it, hands to caress it. The console she played like a piano looked like something from a science fiction movie, all lights and holograms rendered in 3-D. She got to her feet and came toward them. Her jeans had patches at the knees, the shirt she wore matched the pale blue of her eyes, she was barefoot.

Jessie barked at her, but when she held out her hand, the dog went over to her, sniffed her hand, then stretched out her front legs, arched her back, and dropped to the floor.

"So good to see you all," she said.

Charlie grasped her extended hand. The skin felt smooth and cool. "Who're you, exactly?"

"Oh." She gave a small, embarrassed laugh, lifted her arms quickly, and became Kali, the Amazon parrot who had been his constant companion until she had dived into the whiteness that covered El Bosque. An instant later, she was the woman again.

"A shifter?" Newton exclaimed.

"Not at all, Newt. I'm the fourteenth council member, the quintessence of Esperanza. Kali, at your service." She bowed deeply, mocking him, mocking the council. When she straightened, she fixed her hands to her narrow hips, a little teapot. "Did you really think this experiment would proceed without scrutiny? Without safeguards? That you chasers would be given everything without offering something in return? As it is, the impact of the events set in motion by the corrupt members of your council can't be undone. So I'm trying to find ways around it."

"What . . . are you doing here now?" Karina asked. "Why didn't you show up before?"

"I was always around, Karina. I was in the posada for decades, where you all perceived me as an interesting parrot ghost. I lived in the trees around the city, I flew freely through restaurants, cafés, an intriguing anomaly for tourists and residents. Even the *brujos* could see me. They tried to manipulate and control me just as the chasers did and quickly discovered it wasn't as easy or simple as they had hoped. Other trains are already picking up those individuals throughout the city who have chosen to stay behind when Esperanza is removed from the physical world. The people from El Bosque we'll be picking up will have the same choice, as will all of you."

"Even *brujos* will have a choice?" Pedro asked.

"Certainly. They have been as much a part of this city as everyone else."

"They'll fight you on it," Karina said.

"We'll see."

With that, Kali slipped into the engineer's chair, her fingers playing those intricate keys, and Charlie and Newton just stood there, understanding they—the chaser council—no longer controlled Esperanza's destiny and probably never had.

"Hold on, just hold on," Newton burst out. "The council has served Esperanza faithfully for a millennium."

"Really, Newt?"

Kali flicked her hand into the air and holographic images appeared of Newton and Maria, colluding, scheming, fixing votes, fucking. Even Maria's choices for a future life appeared, images of Newton and Maria as peasants in some repressive regime where she was stoned to death for adultery and he, a meteorologist, was executed for prognosticating about the weather.

Newton watched in horror, then burst into tears and ran from the engine compartment like a two-year-old. Charlie leaned forward, his mouth against Kali's cheek. "That was cruel and unnecessary."

"Let's see how you measure up, Charlie."

Another flick of her hand created holographic images from Charlie's life, his snafus in court, his personal failings. He relived the time when he had gone out for drinks with a female prosecutor to whom he was attracted and got her to drop charges against his client. He hadn't slept with her, he was married then, he loved his wife and Lauren was pregnant with Tess. But it had come much too close for comfort.

The display pissed him off and Charlie jammed his hands under Kali's arms, lifted her up, this little thing that weighed practically nothing at all, and hurled her out of the chair. Leo caught her before she slammed into the wall and quickly set her down on the compartment floor. "Jesus, Charlie, what the fuck's *wrong* with you?" Leo shouted.

"She . . ."—he stabbed his hand at the brunette, whoever the hell she was—"is one of *them,* Leo. Just as corrupt as Maria and her gang. Don't you see? It's their final extravaganza. They create the black sludge that swallows bits of the city. They create the blinding whiteness that covers the disappeared area. They create total chaos. Then they provide the solution. All hail the corrupt members of the council."

Kali got to her feet and pointed at the console. The train started to slow down. "You were always a wild card, Charlie. A gringo, through and through. But you had support from some of the council members, so I thought, *Hey, why not? It's an experiment, right?* Your problem is that you never fully left your life as Charlie Livingston, Tess's father, Lauren's husband, Maddie's grandfather. And because you were so young compared to the rest of the council, you were an anomaly, the white crow."

"None of what you just said convinces me you're anything but part of Maria's group," Charlie spat. "Or just another hungry ghost."

"And it's not my place to convince you otherwise." She looked at Leo. "Thanks for catching me." Then she hurled her left hand into the air, and said, "I'm curious about this, Charlie."

The scenes flashed by: Charlie in the posada where Tess and Ian had stayed as transitionals, and Kali the parrot greeting him hello as he tossed her peanuts; Charlie and Kali the night he'd gone to Wayra's home, their obvious camaraderie; Charlie and Kali at that first council meeting at the Última Café. The prosaic scenes suggested that Charlie had known she wasn't a hungry ghost or a corrupt council member and made him look like a liar or a fool.

Or both.

"So this is, what, a life review?" Illary asked.

"Up until Newton's outburst and Charlie's tantrum, it was supposed to be a rescue mission."

"We're wasting time," Sanchez said. "Let's get to El Bosque."

The others nodded and Kali pointed at the console again and the train picked up speed once more. It charged along the tracks, now covered in sand that sparkled in the moonlight. To either side of them, heaps of sand, dunes of sand, lay everywhere, a glinting blanket that lay across roads, drifted up against the sides of buildings, stranded cars. Here and there, Charlie saw people emerging from wherever they had hidden during the storm's fury.

"What about them?" Pedro asked, motioning at the people outside.

"They'll be picked up by one of the other trains," Kali said. "All of you should go back into the first car. It's going to get rough and wild."

Charlie lingered as the others hurried out of the engine compartment. "I apologize for throwing you," he said. "But not for my suspicions."

"Your suspicions are healthy, Charlie. And just so you know I'm not the monster you're thinking I am, the conductor didn't die. Esteban is sitting back there in the first car, enjoying Sanchez's dog. He has been with me too long to be allowed to die beneath the wheels of the train he has ridden faithfully for decades."

Charlie leaned back and peered into the first car. Sure enough, Esteban the conductor was sitting beside Jessie, his arm thrown across her back as he talked with Maddie and Sanchez.

"But his blood spattered my face and clothes."

"Illusion, just as Esteban said."

He looked down at his clothes and watched the bloodstains fading away. "What will happen to Esteban when Esperanza is removed?"

"I suspect he'll reincarnate."

"And what will happen to chasers who choose to stay behind in whatever replaces the city, Kali?"

"You mean, what will happen to you and Karina?"

Yes, he supposed that was exactly what he was asking. He nodded.

"You've already gotten a taste of that. Communication between the living and the dead won't be possible anymore. The living won't see the dead. You won't be able to assume virtual forms. There won't be any council, no *brujos*. But you'll still have all the splendor of the afterlife at your disposal."

Charlie tried to envision it but couldn't. "What will happen to you?"

"I've spent most of my afterlife period as a parrot and find I'm very comfortable in that world. Perhaps I'll reincarnate as a parrot in the Amazon. I haven't decided yet. It depends on Ricardo, on what he does."

"Why?"

"Because if the consciousness of one *brujo* can evolve, then there's hope. It's what I recently said to Lauren."

Before Charlie had a chance to ask her about that remark, she suddenly leaned forward, peering intently ahead. "What the hell. Do you see *that*, Charlie?"

Just ahead, a jungle of tremendous trees consumed the track and spread to either side of it so fast that within seconds, only the tips of the surrounding mountains were visible in the moonlight. "If you're the essence of Esperanza, then you're doing this, right? You're creating the jungle?"

"My consciousness is creating it but not from the part of me that is conscious. Do you understand what I'm saying? It's like when you and Karina created your beautiful home, Charlie, with that jungle in your backyard. Everything that chasers and *brujos* create here in Esperanza is created from the raw materials of my memories, my consciousness, and your own."

"Then if we created the jungle, we can get through it," Charlie said, and desperately wanted it to be true.

"I hope so. Better buckle up, Charlie."

I hope so? That was the best she could do?

Charlie quickly ducked into the first car with the others. Esteban, the conductor, nodded at Charlie and touched two fingers to his temple, as if tipping his hat. "Amigo, thanks for trying to pull me onboard."

"Thank you for helping us out."

Esteban opened his arms, an odd smile reshaping his mouth. "And here we are."

The train picked up speed and Newton pressed his face up to the window. "Jungle? Did you see that jungle out there? What's this crazy bitch doing now?" he demanded.

Jessie started howling and crawled under Sanchez's seat.

The priest blessed himself.

Leo knuckled his eyes.

Maddie reached for Sanchez's hand.

Sanchez raised her hand to his mouth and kissed the back of it.

Illary pressed her hands to her thighs.

Karina bit at her lower lip and Charlie threaded his fingers through hers.

Then the ghost train, Esperanza 14, charged into the jungle, into a tunnel of glistening green.

Twenty
The City's Memories

1.

The moon sped across the sky, night collapsed into dawn, the sun punched a hole in the sky and waves of heat shimmered in the air. Wayra's internal clock screamed it was all wrong, that night and day were too short or too long, that the position of the rising sun was no more accurate than the moon's position had been. Even though he understood they were traipsing through Esperanza's memories of her own history, he didn't have any idea what it meant for him, for any of them. He longed to find Illary, to return to their home in the foothills of Mariposa, to resume their lives. But he knew the last part wasn't going to happen, not now, not ever.

Reality had been turned inside out like a dirty sock.

The trees grew more profuse but didn't provide any relief from the heat. Instead, the canopy trapped the heat and humidity inside of it and turned the jungle into a sweat lodge. His perspiration-soaked clothes clung to him, sweat dripped into his eyes. Monkeys kept screeching and swinging through the trees, insects swarmed and chirred, and beetles the size of his hand scurried across the ground, up the trunks, and into the branches.

He had no idea how far they had traveled or how long. When they had first left the church, the depot had lain a mile or two north. The screaming muscles in his legs, his fatigue, told him they had gone fifteen or twenty miles or even farther. As the geography changed, so did distance, time, space.

Even though they tried to stick together, Tess had trouble keeping up and they finally stopped to rest in an area that looked as if a machete had been taken to the abundant growth. Remnants of a campfire were evident within a circle of stones, the ashes cold, physical evidence that they weren't alone in the jungle, that other groups of refugees were also headed for the depot. He didn't find any comfort in the thought. Suppose the other groups were hostile?

Wayra sank to the ground and dug his last bottle of water from his pack. The others did the same. No one spoke. He knew they were all thinking the same thing. What would happen when they ran out of water, when the geography shifted again?

He dropped his head back and peered upward and glimpsed the sun directly overhead now. High noon. Night to dawn to high noon in— what? Minutes? An hour?

Ricardo, seated beside him, suddenly sniffed the air and whispered, "People. Close."

Wayra cocked his head, listening. He sensed them before he heard or saw them, small groups converging, their collective bewilderment and terror infusing the air he breathed. A terrible urgency seized him. He glanced around at his group—Lauren with her legs drawn up against her chest, her forehead resting on her knees; Tess and Ian sitting back to back, propping each other up, her face pink and sweaty, her belly larger than it should be. Never mind that she now looked three months pregnant, an impossibility. The facts were simple: they wouldn't survive another attack and might not even survive another abrupt shift in the environment.

"There are *brujos* among them," Ricardo said. "And they're stuck, like me, in their virtual forms."

"So they don't present any threat to us."

"How could they?" He wiped his massive arm across his sweating forehead. "They can't seize anyone. They're as confused as the living."

Here and there through the trees, Wayra could see them now, bedraggled groups, loners, families, couples. Then a man broke away from a small group and loped toward them, waving his arms. "Wayra! Ian!"

"Javier," Ian shouted, and he and Wayra hurried forward.

In the blade of midday light that sliced through the trees, Javier looked as though he had been dragged through mud. His baseball cap, jeans, and shirt were caked with dirt, bits of gravel and earth clung to his hairline and unshaven jaw, his hair probably hadn't seen a comb for weeks.

Yet, in real time, Wayra knew Javier had been swallowed by the black tide at the Taquina on December 14. Three days later, when Wayra had gotten into the disappeared El Bosque, with Ricardo hitching a ride, he had spoken to an amnesic Javier. Wayra didn't have any idea how much time had elapsed since then. Hours, days, weeks? But when Javier flung his arms around Wayra and Ian, the lapsed time no longer mattered.

A visit to Javier's bakery had been a part of Wayra's daily life, of his rituals with Illary and, sometimes, with Diego and his shifter family, the humans he had turned on Cedar Key. He hoped they were still in Quito with Sanchez's father. He hoped they weren't en route back to Esperanza because he didn't have any idea what—if anything—they would find. He doubted Javier's bakery would be there.

The incredible coffee and baked goods, the lively conversation, the sense of belonging to a community: Javier represented all that. And Wayra suddenly felt that if they could hold on to these memories of how they fit into each other's lives, then regardless of what happened here in Esperanza, there would always be some similar or parallel bakery in whatever this place was becoming.

"*Dios mío,*" Javier murmured breathlessly. "It is so good to see you both." His huge dark eyes brimmed with emotions—terror and love, confusion and acceptance, panic and resignation, doubt and faith, so many stark contrasts. "I . . . I . . ." Then his head dropped, chin nearly touching his chest, and he started sobbing.

"Hey, amigo." Wayra slung an arm around the other man's shoulders. "It's okay. You're with friends now." He urged him forward toward Tess, Ricardo, and Lauren.

"It's a miracle, Javier," said Ian. "The last time I saw you, the black sludge was swallowing you."

"Now we're . . . in a jungle. How'd . . . we get into a *fucking jungle*?"

"The city is awake and conscious," Wayra replied.

Javier shook his head, a small, desperate shake. "I . . . I don't know what that means. I was sitting in my house in El Bosque and suddenly . . . suddenly these memories crashed into me and I ran . . . out into my front yard and saw the moon. Saw it for the first time since I don't know when. And . . . and then I ran."

Ian urged him to sit down and handed Javier his bottle of water. He gulped down what was left, wiped his arm across his mouth, and looked at each of them as if really seeing them for the first time since he'd joined them. "Tess? You're . . . pregnant? But how, I mean, *Dios mío*, was El Bosque locked in that twilight for months?"

"I think my pregnancy was fast-tracked because I got trapped in El Bosque, too. I figure I'm about three months along now."

Javier's eyes widened with a sudden comprehension. "It makes sense. The spinning clocks, the elevated EM readings, the weirdness. Time is accelerating, right? That's how it feels to me, everything flitting past like a dream, yeah, yeah, I get it." He paused, pressed the heels of his hands against his eyes. "Wow. Fuck." Javier took several deep breaths, his hands dropped to his thighs. "This is it, isn't it, Wayra, the choice we used to talk about in the bakery?"

"I think so. Why did you feel you should go to the depot?"

Javier rolled the bottle of water across the back of his neck. "After my memories started returning, when I ran out into the road and saw all these panicked people, I just *knew* I was supposed to go to the depot. Others knew it, too. There are dozens of small groups, probably more than a hundred people headed to the depot."

"Then let's get going." Ian grasped Tess's hand, pulling her to her feet. "It shouldn't be much farther."

They set their pace to Tess's and moved through the steaming heat. The jungle began to thin, and although Wayra could still hear the monkeys screeching, the sounds remained distant, like background noises in a dream. Towering thunderheads darkened the sky and crackled with luminous blue lightning. Thunder rumbled menacingly and echoed so loudly through the jungle that it was as if its source were the jungle itself. Then the lightning leaped from the clouds and tore across the sky, unzipping it, and torrential rains poured out.

A fierce and violent wind howled through the trees, hurling the lashing rain into their faces, making it almost impossible to see, much less move. They made their way to where the canopy was thickest. But rain streamed down through the branches and leaves, and water rose so quickly around them that within minutes, it was two feet high, washing around Wayra's knees.

"We need to get to higher ground," Wayra shouted.

His hands created a shield above his eyes so that he could keep the rain out of them long enough to spot a better location. But the rain fell too furiously for him to see farther than six inches in front of him. The river, a rushing tide of fallen vegetation, rose so swiftly that the dozens of people around them surged forward, trying to outrun it. Some were trampled, others were swept away, their screams and shouts swallowed by the pounding rain, the shriek of the wind.

Ricardo caught up to Wayra and gestured wildly to the right, where the ground appeared to slope upward. They linked arms and moved rapidly through the trees, a conga line that grew longer as others joined them.

The ground rose steadily and steeply, the rain burst erratically, like hiccups, the wind gusted and shrieked through the trees. Then the jungle began to fall away behind them and tall, slender pines rose on either side of them, bending like straws in the wet wind. The pines and tremendous boulders defined the boundaries of the path they followed, a soggy, unpaved road that climbed into high mountains.

Herds of sheep interspersed with goats emerged from the trees on Wayra's left, all of them bleating and scared, and scampered across the road, the little bells around their necks singing. When the road started to even out, the conga line broke apart and people wandered over to the trees to rest and find shelter from the rain and wind. Wayra hurried to one of the boulders and climbed on top of it, hoping he would be able to see something familiar, to get his bearings. But when he looked out, his heart seized up. The only thing he saw was a vast plateau of water that rain and wind whipped into a churning froth. The jungle was gone, El Bosque was gone, Esperanza as he knew it was certainly gone.

Wayra felt as if some unimaginable weight had fallen from his shoulders. He hadn't known that he'd carried that weight until just now and the sensation of its absence felt strange and unnatural to him.

If the endless water was another one of the city's memories, was it an early memory? Somewhere back at the edge of time? Perhaps it paralleled the sinking of Atlantis or of Lemuria. Maybe it went back even farther than that. And what would happen when this memory finished playing out? Back to the Big Bang? Would they all be reduced to cosmic dust?

He didn't see any point in venturing farther. For the first time since that black tide had swallowed part of the Café Taquina, Wayra despaired that any of them would survive to see whatever Esperanza was becoming. But maybe that was the plan, the bigger plan. Then again, maybe there had never been any goddamn plan and it was all just random chaos.

He made his way back to the others. He didn't see Ricardo. Javier was talking to a group of men and women and children, Ian and Lauren were sitting under the pines and Tess was stretched out nearby, her pack under her head.

Ian stood, his dripping clothes clinging to his body like a wet suit, and hurried over to Wayra. "Any idea where we are?"

"No. We have two choices. Stay here and hope the river goes down or keep moving to see where this road leads. But I think the depot is gone and that whoever spoke to Lauren during her NDE was some trickster ghost, whose intent was to mislead us."

Ian emanated a quiet despair. He raked his fingers back through his wet, dark hair, glanced up the road, then back at Tess and the others. "I say we keep moving until we can't climb any higher. Ricardo went on ahead to find out what's what. Let's see what Lauren and Tess want to do."

They hurried over to the women. Considering that Lauren had been dead back in the church, Wayra thought she looked remarkably healthy right now. "What's the plan?" Lauren asked.

"That depends on what you two want to do," Wayra replied, and explained.

"Move on," Tess and Lauren said simultaneously.

"All right. I'll talk to Javier and find Ricardo."

Just then, Ricardo raced down the road, arms tucked in at his sides, his long legs eating up the distance between them. *"It's there!"* he hollered. *"The depot is just up that road!"*

His voice boomed through the drizzle and galvanized the isolated groups here on the road with them. Maybe forty people, Wayra figured. But in the jungle, there had been more than a hundred. Had the others been swept into the river? Had they taken an alternate route? A haze of exhaustion made it difficult to think, to connect any dots.

Suddenly, they were all on the move again, Ricardo leading the way, carrying a young boy. The road ascended steadily, the rain fell in fits and starts, and as they neared the summit, the sun struggled to show itself.

It sat low in the sky, its position all wrong. But it didn't matter, Wayra thought. The sun gave off enough light for him—for all of them—to see the El Bosque train station half a mile ahead. It was separated from them by a chasm fifty feet wide and at least three hundred feet deep, the two sides connected by some ridiculous, rickety suspension bridge made of rotting wood, rope, and wire, something out of an Indiana Jones movie. Other buildings were around it, but from this distance, Wayra couldn't tell what they were and couldn't recall what had been in the vicinity of the depot when El Bosque was normal.

Right then, Wayra understood it had all been a test. Everything that had happened since the black sludge had swallowed parts of the café had demanded that each of them make a choice: you could leave with Esperanza when it was removed from the physical world, or you could stay behind in whatever would replace it.

Their decisions weren't necessarily fully conscious; Wayra knew that psychological forces were at work here, something unseen, hidden. The power each person had disowned throughout the course of his or her life now bobbed to the surface. You could run from it and leave with Esperanza to the nonphysical, or you could stay behind and confront it.

Do I really want to cross that awful bridge? And if I get to the other side what will I find? Would Illary be there? Would any aspect of his life, as he had known it for the last thousand years, be waiting for him?

2.

Ian eyed the flimsy suspension bridge. In the reluctant light, it didn't look as though it could sustain the weight of an army of ants much less that of forty-plus individuals.

He knew he could make it across, he had no fear of heights, and felt it was important to have someone on the other side as people attempted the crossing. A cheerleader on the far side of nothingness. Yeah, he could do this.

"I'm going across so someone will be on the other side to help people off." He hugged Tess quickly, slung his pack over his right shoulder, and moved to the mouth of the bridge.

The setting sun hurt his eyes, but when he shielded them, the entire bridge spread out before him, flaws glaringly apparent. It wasn't more than a foot and a half wide, the old wooden planks were unevenly spaced, slick from the rain, the ropes looked weathered and bleached from the sun, the wires were rusted. Not exactly a sight that inspired confidence, he thought, particularly with the wind gusting through the chasm. In fact, the wind might be a bigger problem than the bridge itself.

He gripped the ropes on either side and tested the first plank with his right foot. It creaked, but didn't fall apart. He moved forward like a toddler learning to walk. Five steps, eight, ten, fifteen. The bridge swung and swayed over the deep abyss below, a kind of Grand Canyon chasm, something so huge and incomprehensible that when he glanced down, he felt dizzy, nauseated not only by the height, but by the rushing, muddy river far below.

His left foot slipped and he went down, straddling the bridge like some awkward horseback rider. The gusts buffeted him and for long, terrible moments he couldn't rise, couldn't wrench his eyes away from the raging river in the abyss below him. The bridge swung and creaked, his hands tightened on the wet rope, and he forced himself to look away from the abyss, to focus on the depot on the other side.

Slowly, he brought his left leg onto the bridge, bent it so his shoe was fixed firmly against the surface, and brought his right leg back onto the bridge. He pulled himself up and stood there, hunched over like a cripple, gripping the ropes. Because he was so tall, he couldn't maintain a tight grip on the ropes unless he was hunched over. It also made him less vulnerable to the wind.

He moved forward, his eyes darting from the depot to the surface of the bridge, the abyss visible between the planks. He blocked it out and kept moving forward, one step at a time. Halfway across the bridge, he paused and glanced back at the men and women and children who lined the edge of the canyon, preparing themselves for the crossing. Tess stood next to her mother, fists at her mouth as she watched him. *We've made it this far, Slim. We'll make it the rest of the way.* Then he turned and fixed his gaze on the depot again.

In the strange light, it looked like a house in a fairy tale, its tin roof a chocolate brown, its many windows sporting bright red aluminum shutters on either side of them, the nearby pines bending in the wind like acrobats. He didn't see anyone waiting on the platform and not a train was in sight. A red caboose sat alone on a side track. The parking lot looked to be filled with debris but he couldn't tell if it was the result of receding waters or something else. The buildings around the depot appeared to be fading, but he hoped that was a trick of the light.

When he had about twenty-five feet to go, the bridge suddenly shook and Ian dropped to his knees and looked back. A fight had broken out as several men tried to get onto the bridge at the same time and the others attempted to hold them back. He didn't dare release the ropes to move forward on his hands and knees and the bridge shook too violently for him to risk standing up. So he gripped the ropes more tightly and waddled forward, one foot, the other foot, left, right, left, right.

The bridge swung fiercely to the right, nearly hurling Ian over the side, and he twisted his head around. The two men, both on the bridge now, were locked together like mismatched lovers, punching each other, people shouting and screaming at them. Then one man fell back against the rope and toppled over the side, plunging into the chasm. His shrieks echoed hideously.

Jesus, get across, fast.

Ian stood clumsily, struggling to balance his weight against the other man's. Terrified that the bridge would break and Tess and the others would be stranded on the far side of the chasm, unable to get to the depot, he moved forward as quickly as he could without losing his balance.

Ten feet.

Eight.

The bridge shook and swayed as the man behind him started running, shouting at him in Spanish, *"Get out of my way, gringo, get out of my way!"*

"Stay back or we'll both get knocked off the bridge!" Ian yelled.

But the man barreled into him and Ian pitched forward, arms shooting out to break his fall. He slammed into the bridge and the impact flung the other man over the side. The strap of Ian's pack had slipped off his shoulder, down his arm to his wrist, and the weight of it pulled him toward the edge. He lifted his hand and shoved the pack over the side and clung to the planks in front of him as the bridge shook and swung.

Don't look down, don't look down, don't . . .

His heart slammed against his ribs, blood roared in his ears, his fingers tightened over the lip of the plank. *Pull yourself forward, do it or die.*

Ian moved the fingers of his right hand toward the next plank of wood, wedged his fingers into the space between it and the next plank, gripped it, and used his feet as leverage to pull himself forward. When the bridge stopped shaking, he reached up with his left hand, grabbed on to the rope, and pulled himself up enough so that he could rock back onto his heels and reach for the rope on his right.

The wind continued to whip through the chasm, but it wasn't as powerful as it had been earlier, and he was able to cross the remaining few feet to the other side of the canyon. He sank to his knees, and gestured wildly at Wayra, hoping to make him understand that two people could cross at once if their movements were in synch, if neither of them panicked. But the deaths of the two men had apparently convinced everyone on the other side that civility came first, so that when an Ecuadorian couple started across, no one pushed or yelled or tried to butt ahead of them.

The woman froze up before she reached the other side, and Ian kept talking to her, urging her forward, but she refused to budge. Her companion finally caught up to her, slipped an arm around her waist and the two made it to the other side. The woman promptly dropped to her knees, sobbing with relief, and kissed the ground.

A woman and a teenage girl came across next and it went without a hitch. As Javier started across with the young boy Ricardo had been carrying, Ian realized the sky was changing again. The luminous blue lightning that had preceded the torrential downpour in the jungle now flickered and crackled through the waning light, but only in one part of the sky. Did it mean the topography was about to shift again? He felt a gnawing urgency to hurry things up.

Javier and the kid made it across safely. "You scared us, Ian."

"Scared myself. Where's the boy's family?"

"Gone. Listen, Wayra and Ricardo are having a hell of a time over there with some of the men who don't want them selecting who goes across the bridge next. They won't fuck with Ricardo, he's bigger than all of them, but—"

"I know. We need to speed things up. The sky's doing weird shit."

"Yeah, everything's about to change again." Javier turned toward the small group huddled together behind him and Ian and gestured toward the depot. *"Corren por allá."*

The group took off across the rocky terrain. "Go with them, Javier," said Ian.

"You sure, amigo?"

"Go."

Javier spun around and tore after the group.

On the other side of the canyon, Wayra motioned Lauren and Tess forward, but men and women in the other group charged past them, knocking Lauren down, and ran onto the bridge.

"No," Ian yelled, waving his arms. "It's going to break, there're too many of you, it's too dangerous!"

They stampeded forward and the bridge swung wildly, throwing them from one side to the other. A man and woman were knocked off their feet and the woman tumbled over the side, her shrieks echoing. The man rolled off in the opposite direction and clung to the edge of the bridge, pedaling air. His weight pulled down the right side of the bridge so that the remaining four people, three men and a woman, were forced to hold on to whatever they could grab on the left side to keep from sliding away.

They cried and screamed and pleaded for help. But they were in the middle of the bridge, which now sagged with their weight, and were too far away from either side of the canyon for Ian or anyone else to reach them. He watched in horror as the man clinging to the right side of the bridge dropped and the sudden release of his weight caused the bridge to flip over, hurling the other three into the raging river below.

"Shit, fuck."

Ian flattened out against the ground and grabbed on to the ropes closest to him and struggled to flip the bridge over again, so it could be used. On the other side of the chasm, Wayra and Ricardo were trying to do the same thing. The light kept ebbing, but the lightning got brighter, more frequent, and cast a strange pall over everything. Then the wind rose and a gust seized the bridge, shook it violently, and flipped it over.

Ian steadied it as best he could and Wayra and Ricardo did the same on their side. Tess stepped onto the bridge and, a breath later, so did Lauren.

Ian rocked back onto his heels, rubbing his palms hard and fast against his drenched jeans, and whispered, "Please, please, please."

He didn't know if his words were a prayer, a supplication, or a plea bargain. *If you get them across safely, I will . . .*

3.

Lauren held tightly to the ropes on either side of her. She tried to focus on where she stepped and not on the flashes of lightning that spilled an exquisite blue over the canyon, the bridge, her daughter, and rendered everything in such excruciating detail. She failed completely.

The lightning fascinated her, centered as it was in just one spot in the sky, a spot that moved about frequently, as though the lightning were seeking true north or its own source or something else altogether. When she'd first seen it in the jungle, she had marveled at its beauty—the sharpness, clarity, luminosity—and its color, an indescribable shade of blue she'd never seen before. Now she understood it to be more than a thing of beauty; it was a sign, a signal, and it seared its way into her consciousness and enabled her to see things more clearly.

And what she saw was that Tess now looked like she was three or four months pregnant. Never mind that Tess had not been pregnant this fall, when she and Lauren had sat on the balcony of a local café and talked about Tess's desire for kids. And how much time had elapsed since then? Two or three months?

And yet, Lauren wasn't sure. Her watch and its digital calendar hadn't worked since 9:28 had begun appearing all over Esperanza.

Even now, the hands simply spun, and the date showed zeros, just ze-ros. Her internal sense of time had vanished when she and Ian had climbed on board *Further* with Kesey, Garcia, and McKenna. But if, in real time—real time as it used to be—no more than a week had passed since the Café Taquina had been swallowed by a tide of black sludge, then Tess's pregnancy was an example of how deeply the impossible had become their norm.

Leo had been seized by a *brujo,* a giant white crow had rescued him. She had taken Segunda Vista and ridden on *Further* with the Merry Pranksters, all of whom were dead; she had penetrated the whiteness that covered El Bosque, died and conversed with the soul of Esperanza. Now here she was, moving across a shitty bridge that traversed a can-yon three hundred feet deep and on the other side of it lay a train depot where the soul of the city had told her to go. Uh-huh. She could lose her nursing license for this.

She suspected she already had lost her mind.

Gusts of wind whipped across the bridge, bile flooded the back of her throat, but she kept moving, right hand, left foot, right foot, left hand, forward, always forward. Tess moved slowly but steadily an arm's length in front of her.

She couldn't say for sure what Tess weighed now, but their combined weight had to be less than three hundred pounds. But that might be fifty or a hundred more than what the middle of the bridge could sus-tain at this point. She paused, allowing Tess to get a little farther ahead of her, and noticed the lightning had moved to a spot about a hundred feet above the train depot.

It burned like some biblical star, she thought, a sign, a signal. But of what? And as she watched it, she noticed that the buildings on either side of the depot simply faded away. And what were they going to do if the depot suddenly vanished, too?

Tess's foot slipped, she went down clumsily on one knee, the bridge shook, and Lauren's heart slammed into double time.

"I'm okay, Mom," she called. "I'm fine."

"Can you get up?"

"Sure. But talk to me, okay? Distract me."

Lauren moved a little closer to her daughter. "I'm right behind you."

"When did Leo give you an engagement ring?"

"The night of the black sludge."

"How come you didn't mention it to me?"

Lauren slogged through her memories. "Because I didn't see you till the next day, at the café, when Diego was seized. Do you remember that?"

"Vividly. Ian and I made love in the shower. I felt fat and unattractive. That's when I did the pregnancy test. When . . . what . . . date was that? How much time has passed?"

Lauren wished she had answers, but she didn't. "I don't know. Keep moving. Just keep moving."

They moved against the wind now. Lauren desperately yearned to see Leo again, to hold him in her arms. She longed to feel the tangible reality he had provided for her since they had met more than four years ago, when she'd gone to the hospital for an interview as an ER nurse and he had hired her to work in OB, as his assistant.

You in that depot, Leo? Please be there.

"It's not much farther," Ian shouted. "A dozen feet, if that."

Tess waddled forward and Ian reached out, caught her hands and pulled her into his arms. Now the traveling spot of blue lightning looked as if it were expanding, spreading like fire through the sky directly over the depot, with streaks of crackling blue arcing toward the canyon, toward them. Lauren felt the bridge behind her trembling as others started crossing it. She hurried as quickly as she dared, her feet slipping and sliding over the damp planks, her heart beating frantically in her throat.

The rope she gripped on her right, her handrail, suddenly snapped. Lauren threw herself the last few feet to safety and landed hard on her side. Air rushed from her lungs, she rolled onto her hands and knees, gasping for breath, and saw how the terrain on the other side was now shifting again.

"Hurry," Ian shouted. "Cross now, all of you."

Lauren saw how the surface of the rocks on the other side of the chasm now seemed to be ebbing and flowing, like water or light. Then the arc of lightning touched down and holes exploded open in the rock and fissures and sped outward from the center of these holes like threads in a spiderweb. The fissures traveled down the sides of the canyon wall and even from where she was, she could see them widening into cracks.

Lauren got shakily to her feet, terrified that the bridge wouldn't hold long enough for Wayra, Ricardo, and the remaining two men and two women to make it to this side of the chasm. Planks in the middle of the bridge broke apart and one man fell through the gaping hole and vanished into the river below.

More planks gave way, another piece of rope snapped, and Wayra, in the lead, leaped the remaining distance and landed dangerously close to the precipice, arms pinwheeling for balance. Lauren and Ian grabbed the back of his shirt and pulled him away from the edge. He lay on the ground, breathing hard, the fingers of his hand clenched against the ground, his paw jerking. Lauren thought he was having a heart attack or a seizure.

He finally raised his head and pushed to his feet. "Get out of here, all of you. What's happening to the ground over there is about to happen on this side, too. I'll stay till the others are across."

"No way," Ian said. "We're not separating again."

"The bridge is coming apart," one of the women sobbed. "Help us, the bridge . . ."

Wayra stretched out on his stomach and extended his long arms toward the woman. Lauren, Tess, and Ian held his legs so that he didn't get jerked over the side when the woman clasped on to his hand and paw. He pulled her to safety, then thrust out his arms again, shouting at Ricardo and the two others to move faster, faster.

A deafening rumble burst from the canyon, the ground shook, a hole burst open eight feet to Lauren's right and a geyser of stones shot out of it. Fissures appeared, speeding every which way. Another hole opened up behind them and a pine tree, fully formed, burst upward. Off to their right, a ceiba tree exploded skyward from the ground.

The man and woman ahead of Ricardo crawled off the bridge. And just when Lauren thought Ricardo would reach them, the bridge tore loose of its moorings on the far side of the chasm and swung out over the river, Ricardo clinging to it.

It swung toward their side of the canyon and Ricardo had the presence of mind to extend his right leg so that his foot struck the wall first, saving him from slamming full force into the wall. The bridge swayed in the wind and Ricardo climbed fast, like a monkey on a jungle gym, hand over hand, right foot, left foot. They struggled to hold the bridge steady and Wayra kept shouting, "You're almost there, Ricardo. Keep climbing."

But the old rope snapped and the bridge tore out of the rock and fell toward the river.

Ricardo flashed a thumbs-up, then hurled himself back, off the falling bridge, arms flung out at his sides, and vanished beneath the water.

Twenty-one
The Depot

1.

Wayra stared in disbelief. The last vestige of Dominica and his ancient past had been swept away. Ricardo, a dead man stuck in his virtual body, had drowned. His last connection to Dominica and the much earlier parts of his existence had just saved the lives of everyone on their side of the chasm. Sorrow overwhelmed him. He dropped his head back and howled, a sound summoned from the emotional depths of who he had been and would never be again. The howl resounded across the rapidly shifting terrain and even to Wayra, it seemed primitive, strange. He hoped that Ricardo could somehow hear it and would understand it was Wayra's tribute to him, a *brujo* who had evolved beyond evil.

Ian clasped Wayra's shoulder. "C'mon, let's *move.*"

They ran, dashing between and around trees that kept shooting up from the rocky surface. The ground shook, lightning flashed and crackled and riddled the entire dome of the sky. Eerie shadows swam across the ground, the air glowed a neon blue.

He couldn't see the depot anymore; the tremendous trees blocked his line of sight. But he worried that it might not be there any longer, that it had faded like the other buildings or had been swallowed up by an opening in the ground. *What then? What the fuck would they do then?*

Trees continued to burst upward from the ground, but not as quickly as before. The temperature started dropping, ten, fifteen, twenty degrees within a matter of moments. All of them had stripped off layers of clothes in the jungle and no longer had anything with which to cover themselves. Wayra could now see his breath. The chill bit through his skin, seeped into his bones.

Through the trees, he caught sight of the depot, now a lone building on top of a hill, bathed in blue light, pines to either side of it. Flickering candles lit the window, silhouettes moved around inside. A door in the depot suddenly flew open and Javier raced down the hill, as if he'd been on the lookout for them, and he carried a bundle of blankets. "Amigos, I thought . . . something had happened to you." He quickly passed out the blankets, then looked around, frowning. "Where's Ricardo?"

Wayra shook his head.

"*Carajo.*" Javier quickly made the sign of the cross. "He became good, Wayra. I never thought I would be able to say such a thing about a *brujo,* but it's true. We wouldn't have made it across the bridge if it weren't for him."

"I know. How many are in the depot?"

"A hundred and seven. With you four, a hundred and eleven."

"My God," Lauren breathed. "That number again."

"How'd they all get there?" Tess asked.

"Different ways. Cars, buses, bicycles, scooters, on foot. But they say that all the vehicles dissolved a long time ago, just like the rest of the buildings did right after I got into the depot."

The earth shook, booms exploded behind them, and they broke into a run. Around and behind them, the terrain shifted wildly, sheets of rock peeled away, trees shot upward, and geysers erupted, spewing stones, vegetation, water. Giant boulders cracked open like walnuts then blew outward in every direction, all of it illuminated by the neon-blue light.

Just before they reached the depot door, a wind kicked up and it started to snow.

2.

Charlie stared out the windows, watching the jungle as it blurred past, the train hurtling through light and dark at an alarming speed. Nothing he saw looked familiar. Now and then, through the trees, he caught sight of an unnatural lightning crackling across the sky. It was a neon blue that seemed to move from one location in the sky to another, without any apparent pattern. Karina sat mutely beside him, gripping his hand, her eyes darting from the window to the faces of the people who shared the first car.

The door between the first and second cars suddenly opened, a fierce, damp wind blew through, and Victor swept in with Franco and Liana. Newton leaped up and threw out his arms and shouted, *"You're here, the collective voice of sanity has arrived!"*

"This is the ghost train," Liana burst out. "I don't understand. I—"

Franco caught Newton's arms and shoved him back into his seat. "How the hell did we end up in here? Who's in charge?" he demanded.

"Calm down," Victor told him. "Just calm down, Franco."

"Don't tell me what to do!" Franco bellowed.

Charlie got up, his confusion about how they'd gotten here secondary to his concern that they apparently didn't have any idea what was going on. "Sit down, all of you," Charlie said. "We're headed—"

"You're behind this, Charlie." Franco faced him, eyes filled with fury. "*You.* I knew it, I fucking knew it. You've been nothing but trouble right from the start."

Sanchez, now on his feet, snapped, "Hey, sit down and stop yelling. Things are weird enough right now, okay?"

Franco pointed at Sanchez, his finger just inches from Sanchez's nose. "I know who you are."

"Get your goddamn hand outta my face." Sanchez pushed Franco's hand away, then suddenly exclaimed, "You traitor. You knew what would happen when Tess went to El Bosque and set off this whole chain of events. You were working with Maria all along. You never wanted Esperanza to be replaced by something else. It was all lies."

In that brief touch, Charlie thought, Sanchez had discovered the truth about Franco. It suddenly all made sense. But before he could say anything, Franco grabbed Sanchez by the front of his jacket and Jessie leaped at him, snarling savagely, and knocked him back. Her teeth tore into his arm and Franco kicked at her and beat his fist against her head and screamed, *"Get it off me, get it off!"*

Sanchez grabbed Jessie's collar, trying to pull her back, but she clung tenaciously to Franco's arm, blood pouring from it. Charlie sensed that Franco was armed—a gun or knife, he couldn't tell which—and hurled himself at the other chaser, tackling him. They slammed to the floor of the car, Charlie on top of Franco, pinning him down, trapping him there, their faces just inches apart.

"I knew that vote was too easy, you bastard," Charlie hissed.

"You're such a goddamn nuisance."

One of Franco's arms jerked free and he sank a knife into Charlie's stomach, the blade twisting cruelly through his intestines. Charlie slammed the heel of his hand into Franco's nose and felt the bones snapping, then punched him in the mouth, breaking all those pretty teeth to bits. Franco started choking on his broken teeth and Charlie rolled off him, his hand pressed against the wound in his stomach. Blood—real blood, red blood, human blood—seeped through his fingers.

How could he be bleeding? Hurting? Dying? He lifted his hands off his stomach and turned them this way and that, studying the blood. *Was it real?* It looked and smelled real.

The bedlam around him was certainly real: everyone shouting, Maddie and Karina beside him as Leo, Sanchez, and Pedro lifted him onto a row of empty seats. He heard Victor banging on the door of the engine compartment, shouting for help, heard Leo barking instructions, Pedro praying, Newton freaking out, Victor fretting over him like a protective parent, Franco groaning, Illary whispering to him as she clutched his hand.

And then Leo tore open Charlie's shirt, exposing the stab wound. His hearing faded in and out, his vision blinked off and on. He started dissolving, felt his essence coming apart, molecules and atoms drifting like boats that had broken free of their moorings. He abruptly found himself in two places at once—lying in a row of seats in Esperanza 14, bleeding profusely from the stomach, and floating through falling snow.

He fell out of the snow and into a kind of dream, a current of the past. He was Charlie before Franco had stabbed him, Charlie in the throes of his deal with Leo to find Lauren a job, Charlie embroiled in the lives of the people he loved, Charlie, ex-attorney, ex-father, ex-husband, ex-mentor, ex-everything. In yet another current of the past, he was at the council meeting, surprised that Franco objected to the council's plan to remove Esperanza from the physical world. As Franco demanded that people be given a choice and that Esperanza be replaced with something else, Charlie saw the smug glint in Maria's eyes as her gaze fixed on Franco and heard the voice of her dark, twisted heart. *He's in my pocket, too.*

Traitor.

The current shifted. He stood in front of the home where Maria lived, the last place where he had seen Franco and confronted him about following Tess to El Bosque. The house had faded to a translucency the color of pearls, the grounds looked washed out, bleached, the beds of flowers had wilted. Charlie walked through the translucent wall and found an infant swaddled in blankets on the floor of what had once been the living room. The baby kicked her little legs and her wide blue eyes impaled him. *She's in hiding,* the infant said.

Where?

I don't know.

Nice try, Maria.

She threw back her pudgy little arms and laughed hysterically. *You're dying, Charlie.*

I'm already dead.

Then why're you bleeding from a stab wound?

All the rules have gone south.

Which means you're dying.

She kept laughing and it enraged Charlie. He scooped her up, his fingers clutching at the back of the pale pink shirt she wore. *If I can die, so can you.* The baby wailed and cried, her face scrunching up, her tiny mouth falling open. He started to hurl her against the translucent wall, then thought of how Franco had stabbed him and twisted the knife so deeply inside him it had felt as if the blade might come out through his back.

He quickly set Maria back on the blankets. *As much as I'd like to smash your head against that wall, I'm not killing you. That would set me up for a really shitty next life.*

Maria kicked her stumpy, dimpled legs, pounded her baby fists against the air and her face turned apple red. *Kill me, kill me,* she sobbed. *Otherwise I'll just be left here until the transition is complete.*

And then what happens?

I'll be . . . banished into another life, one I don't choose.

How fitting. *Who turned you into an infant?*

Kali, this woman named Kali. She claims she's the fourteenth—

She is.

That's a lie, there was never a fourteenth council member, it's all just lies. Get Newton over here, he'll listen to me, he'll—

I'll send Franco. He's as corrupt as you are.

With that, Charlie backpedaled through the wall, the infant's wails pursuing him. *You can't do this to me, Charlie.*

He felt the train slowing down. Or was this sensation part of yet another dream? He didn't know, couldn't tell. He struggled to raise his head, but Kali ran her hand over his forehead and spoke softly: "It's okay, Charlie, really, it is."

What was okay? That he was wounded, dying, bleeding all over the train?

"I had to know whom I could trust."

He felt a sharp prick in his arm and Leo said, "It's morphine, Charlie. It'll help with the pain and I'll be able to . . . to stitch you up."

Charlie detected the hitch in Leo's voice and knew he was lying, that there would be no stitching up because he was bleeding internally, his intestines were the consistency of chopped liver, and he was, just as Maria said, dying. The morphine was simply intended to make him comfortable. Or maybe Leo had given him an overdose so that he could die peacefully.

"Stay with me," Karina whispered. "Stay with me, Charlie."

The morphine ran through his blood now and a blissful silence held him, rocked him, caressed him. He felt his senses shutting down, turning off, one by one.

3.

Tess nearly gagged when they entered the depot. It smelled of piss and body odor, fear and uncertainty. People stood around in small groups, families or their equivalent, and dozens of candles illuminated the interior and cast faces into odd reliefs of light and shadow. In a corner, a man played a harmonica, the notes hauntingly sad.

Javier led them over to some chairs along the wall and suddenly a small boy leaped up and ran over to Tess and threw his arms around her. "Señora, señora. You saved me, thank you."

What the hell? It was Hugo, the kid from the Mercado del León. "I was glad I could do it, Hugo. How did you get here?" Tess asked as he took her hand.

"With my mommy."

"Where is she?"

Hugo pointed at a diminutive Ecuadorian woman hugging Wayra and Ian hello. Tess recognized her from the market, and as she and Hugo approached her, her eyes widened. *"Dios mío,"* she said softly, and brought her hands to the sides of Tess's face. "Thank you for saving my son."

"Tess, this is Quintana," said Wayra.

"The pleasure is all mine," Tess said. "How . . . did you two end up here?"

"I was just explaining that to Wayra and Ian. After El Bosque disappeared, we stayed at Wayra and Illary's, and I . . . woke in the middle of the night and . . . and suddenly knew we were supposed to be here. But we couldn't get in until the whiteness broke apart. We came by car. But all the vehicles started disappearing when the jungle sprang up." She paused. "Forgive me. May I speak to your baby?"

"Uh, sure. Of course." Tess glanced at Ian, who mouthed, *Shaman.*

Quintana brought her hands to Tess's belly and shut her eyes. After a few moments, she said, "Twins. They will usher us into what lies ahead. So it is written."

"Written where?"

"In the *Book of Hope.*"

"I've never heard of this book."

"It's a sacred book among the Quechuas. Your and Ian's arrival as the first transitionals in five hundred years is written there. Dominica's defeat was written in the book. Your niece's possession by Dominica . . ."

"So all these events were *destined*?"

"No. There were many possibilities."

"Are you familiar with this book, Wayra?" Tess asked.

"I've heard of it, but I've never seen it."

Lauren, who had been standing with Tess and Hugo, said, "By now, it's probably gone. Along with the rest of Esperanza."

Quintana moved her hands away from Tess's stomach and shook her head. "No. It's not just a physical book. Over the millennia, the Quechuas and other guardians of the planet have made sure that the predictions are recorded in sacred sites around the world."

"What do these predictions say about what's happening now?" Ian asked.

"The predictions say the transition will not be easy. Many will choose to leave with Esperanza. There will be trains that will carry a hundred and eleven passengers each to whatever replaces the city. A lot seems to ride on what a certain *brujo* does."

If that *brujo* was Ricardo, Tess thought, then the end result had to be somewhat positive, right? Like, well, she would have her twins, she and Ian would live happily ever after.

Tess glanced toward the picture window at the front of the depot, the platform out there, the tracks just beyond it, all of it illuminated by the fading blue light. Wind gusts blew the falling snow at an angle, yet the wind didn't make a sound. If she just watched the falling snow and listened to the silence and didn't think about anything else, about everything that had led to these moments, then the scene was actually peaceful.

"How did you know to come here?" Quintana asked.

Tess slipped her arm around Lauren's shoulders. "My mother died and spoke to the spirit of Esperanza, who told her that if we chose to stay behind, we should go to the depot."

It sounded absurd when she said it aloud. *Yeah, lock us up.*

"But . . . that is what shamans do," Quintana exclaimed. "The fact that you are here, Lauren, walking around, functional, means that you now have the gift of second sight."

"I'm a nurse," Lauren said. "That's all I am."

A whistle pierced the silence, and they all heard it, all one hundred and eleven people inside the depot. The squeal of brakes brought them, en masse, to the picture window and minutes later, Esperanza 14 coasted into the station.

People crowded through the depot's front door and spilled out onto the platform. Fourteen cars total, Tess counted them, and the doors whispered open simultaneously. A conductor hopped down from the second car and made his announcement in three languages—Quechua, Spanish, English. "All aboard, please don't push. There's plenty of room for everyone and we aren't pulling out until all of you are on the train."

Tess groped for Ian's hand on her right, her mother's hand on the left, and behind them were Quintana, Hugo, Wayra, and Javier. The door to the first car slid open and there wasn't enough light for Tess to see the woman's face. But she recognized that wild hair and that stance, arms thrown open, hands pressed against the sides of the door, as if her presence alone were powerful enough to keep the door open. Maddie.

"Tesso," Maddie shouted. "You out there?"

Behind her, another figure appeared, a woman wearing some sort of strange headdress. She brought her hands to the sides of her mouth and called for Wayra. Tess realized that what she mistook for a head-dress was Illary's equivalent to Wayra's paw, an incomplete shift. Then Tess saw Leo, Sanchez, the priest, and she and her group surged forward, toward the enchanted train, the ghost train, Esperanza 14.

Twenty-two
The Voice of Esperanza

1.

Lauren stumbled into Leo's open arms and they fell back into the car, his arms clasped so tightly around her she didn't want him to ever let go. His fingers combed through her hair, his breath exploded against the side of her neck, his mouth sought hers.

"I—" they stammered simultaneously, and then laughed hysterically, laughed through their panic and uncertainty, laughed because the alternative was to break down completely and sob with terror. They fell back against the seats, both of them talking at once.

"They—"

"We—"

"How—"

"Where—"

"When—"

He touched two fingers to her mouth. "Prankster, Charlie got stabbed. I gave him the last of the morphine and did what I could for him, but he . . . didn't make it."

He spoke so softly, with such pain, that it took a moment for the words to sink in. "Charlie stabbed? By who? How can he die again?" But of course she knew the answer to that one. The realm of the impossible was now their reality.

"He's back here," Leo said, and led her to the rear of the car, where Tess and Ian, Maddie and Sanchez and Karina already were.

Charlie lay across three seats, a leather jacket covering his chest, his face so strangely peaceful he didn't resemble the Charlie she had known or even the chaser who had appeared to her during her time in

Esperanza. Lauren leaned over and brushed her mouth across Charlie's cool cheek. "Thank you," she whispered. "For everything."

As she rose, her eyes met Karina's. The chaser looked devastated, tears coursed down her face. Lauren gave her arm a quick squeeze. "I'm glad you two found each other."

"Found and lost way too quickly," she said softly.

Lauren didn't know what to say to that. She looked at the three chasers who stood closely together, guarding a fourth chaser who was tied to one of the seats, blood oozing from his swollen nose, bruises like dark smudges beneath his eyes. "Chaser council?" she asked.

"Yes, ma'am. I'm Newton. That's Liana and Victor."

"Who's he?" She gestured at the man who was tied up and bleeding. "Franco."

"Why did you stab Charlie?" she asked, staring at Franco.

He just grinned at her, a grotesque rictus of broken teeth and blood. "'Cause h'deserved it," he muttered.

"Oh, Franco, Franco," said a soft-spoken woman who came up the aisle.

Lauren was shocked to see the woman who had spoken to her when she was dead. "*You,*" she burst out. "You're the engineer?"

"So good to see you again, Lauren." She turned her attention back to Franco. "I'm afraid you're going to have to join Maria in the afterlife version of the deep freeze until conditions are right for your rebirth."

"Who're y'o?"

"The voice of Esperanza," Lauren said.

"Kali," the woman said.

Franco snickered. "S're, s'ure, and I'm—"

Kali flicked her arm toward Franco and his body shrank until he was a wailing infant swaddled in blankets. Then he simply faded away, and as she moved her hand through the air an image appeared of a fading structure somewhere, its yard overgrown with weeds.

"That's Maria's place," Newton exclaimed.

"*Was* Maria's place," Kali corrected. "Now it's a nursery."

There, through the translucent wall, Lauren could see two wailing infants on blankets, beating their little feet and fists against the air. Even as they stood there staring at this strange sight, four more wailing infants appeared. "José, Simon, Rita, and Alan," explained Kali. "Those chasers were the most corrupt."

Victor, Newton, and Liana moved away from her. "You can't . . ." Newton stammered. "You can't just . . ."

"Don't worry," Kali told him. "You're not going to the nursery. That's reserved for them." She motioned toward the wailing infants. "For all of you, though, it's time you returned to the afterlife and made your own decisions about your next lives."

Victor held up his hands, patting the air. "I helped Wayra and Charlie rescue Maddie. I was always on the right side of decisions for Esperanza."

"This isn't a punishment, Victor. I'm simply releasing all of you from any commitment to Esperanza, that's all." Then she blew three kisses at the chasers and they faded away.

"Release me, too," Karina said quietly.

Kali leaned toward Karina, whispered something, and Karina drew back, her eyes wide with wonderment. "Really?"

"I believe so."

Kali drew the back of her hand over Karina's cheek and she faded slowly away.

Jesus. Lauren groped for Leo's hand and he slipped his arm around her, holding her tightly against him as Kali touched Charlie's forehead. Her caress lingered lovingly, Lauren thought, then Charlie's body simply dissolved.

Lauren and Tess stood there for a moment, staring at the spot where he had lain. Then Tess flung one arm around Ian and her other arm around Lauren and Leo, and drew Maddie and Sanchez and Wayra and Illary into the circle, too, hugging them all. "We'll remember," she whispered. "We'll remember because we must."

"Kali," called the conductor. "Everyone's aboard. And the river is rising fast."

"Get us out of here, Esteban."

The conductor slipped into the engine compartment and shut the door. Moments later, the train started moving and they all took seats. Through the windows, Lauren watched as the train pulled away from the depot, its snow-covered roof briefly visible in the crackling blue lightning. Just beyond it, a rising river moved steadily toward the tracks. The train's whistle blew twice, paused, then blew three times and sped through the neon-blue light.

Kali came back up the aisle and touched each of them on the head or shoulder. Lauren didn't have any idea what, if anything, the touch meant, but the spot on her head that Kali had touched tingled with a comforting warmth.

When she reached Wayra and Illary, she said, "What is your preference? Animal or human?"

"Human," they said simultaneously.

She drew her hands back over Illary's feathers and they fell away and her lustrous hair appeared. Wayra held up his paw and Kali kissed it. As the fur vanished, it was replaced by skin, fingers, nails, knuckles, a perfect hand and forearm. Then she leaned forward, hugged him, and said something in Quechua that Lauren didn't understand. She pressed her hands together, bowed her head slightly. "Namaste, Wayra. May you remember what you need to know."

Kali now stood at the front of the car, flipped a switch on the wall, and when she spoke, her voice boomed through the train, back through all fourteen cars.

"In the days ahead, I hope that all of you who have chosen to stay behind can form a strong community based on mutual trust and cooperation. Thanks to Ricardo, one *brujo* who evolved into goodness, I'm adjusting my original intentions, but your lives will still be quite different than before.

"Communication between the living and the dead, the existence of chasers and *brujos,* and the profound healing properties of Esperanza will be relegated to the realm of legend and myth. Evil will always exist in the world, but never again will it gain the foothold that it did in Esperanza. It is my deepest hope that you will take what you have learned from the magnificence of Esperanza and use it for the benefit of the greater whole. You can leave the city, but unless you hold on to Memory, you won't be able to return."

What does that mean? Lauren wondered.

Then Kali raised her arms so that they covered her face, bowed her head, and faded away.

The train raced through the crackling blue light, through darkness and sunlight, water and snow and jungle. Then there was only blackness, a blackness so deep and profound that Lauren couldn't even see the sky. And suddenly, she couldn't pull air into her lungs, couldn't breathe. Her fingers turned to claws against her seat. Her peripheral vision shut down. She squeezed Leo's hand twice. *Love you bigger than Google.* He squeezed back once: *Ditto.*

Lauren sank into the blackness.

2.

The contraction drove Tess forward, screaming. Leo, ever calm, said, "Good, good, c'mon, one more push, Tess. The first one's crowning."

Her mother and Ian gripped her hands, and she gave one great heaving push and felt the baby slide out. "A boy, it's a boy," her mother squealed with excitement, and Leo cut the umbilical cord and Lauren whisked her grandson away.

Tess thought she passed out after that, but perhaps she only dozed and went away into Demerol land again. Suddenly, she heard Leo, the cheerleader positioned between her legs—forget he was her stepfather, forget all that—urging her to push again. "C'mon, one more push, Tess, you can do it. His sister's coming."

As Tess pushed, her eyes fixed on the ceiling of the delivery room in the Esperanza Hospital. She had no idea how she'd gotten here, when she had arrived, what the date was, what time it was. She felt as if *she* were the newborn, clueless and unaware.

So she pushed and pushed and her daughter popped out into the world and Lauren took her away, too. Then Lauren brought them both back, a boy and a girl, five pounds five ounces and five pounds six ounces respectively, and set them in the crooks of Tess's arms. She felt the flickering reminder of a memory, of being on a train, in a jungle, crossing a terrible rope bridge. Had to be the Demerol injection her mother had given her.

"The times," Tess said. "I need their times of birth. Maddie said that's important."

"Eleven–oh-one for your son," Lauren said. "And let's call it eleven-eleven for your daughter."

Eleven-oh-one, eleven-eleven. As soon as those words were out of her mother's mouth, Tess felt something profound shifting inside of her, something she knew she should remember, but which refused to surface.

She saw the look that her mother and Leo exchanged, though, and wondered what it meant.

3.

Wayra and Sanchez bounced along in the old pickup, headed out of old town Esperanza. Wayra had the sensation, as he often did these days, that something was missing in the city or markedly different about it, or both. But he couldn't pinpoint it. The railroad tracks where a slow-moving trolley now moved seemed all wrong to him, but he didn't know why. He kept seeing the city covered in white sand, but didn't know why. When he looked at certain landmarks—Parque del Cielo, La Pincoya, the Posada de Esperanza—he felt that he wasn't remembering the truth. Weird. He didn't know what it meant.

Once they were in the countryside, on an unpaved road, Sanchez picked up speed, driving so fast that the tires kicked up dust that settled on the windshield and drifted through the windows. A CD blasted from the player—Esperanza Spalding singing "I Know You Know."

Wayra lowered the volume. "And that's the thing, Sanchez. I *know* that I know. I just can't pull it out, identify it."

"We all know that we know."

"Do Tess and Ian know?"

"I don't think so. They're too busy with the twins and their online magazine, I guess. What about Pedro?"

"Pedro is too sick these days to talk about what he does or doesn't remember."

"You, me, Maddie, Illary, we're the only ones who have had the dream, Wayra. How can four people dream the same dream? And not just once, but repeatedly for more than two years?"

The dream always took place on a train. "What about Lauren and Leo?" Wayra asked. "Have you talked to them about it?"

"Maddie has. They're already at the house. They're going to join us for this excursion."

"Then we need to get Tess and Ian to the house as well."

"They left for Punta yesterday, drove down with the twins for a long weekend. There's a great place down there where the kids can swim in a lake . . ."

Wayra didn't hear the rest of what Sanchez said. He suddenly had a very bad feeling about Tess and Ian leaving Esperanza and felt a kind of desperate urgency to call them. But why? What the hell would he say to them? "It worries me, that they left."

Sanchez nodded. "Me, too. But I don't have any idea why. Maddie and I were talking the other night about how we haven't left Esperanza since we got here in 2009, more than five years ago."

"Illary and I haven't left, either."

The two men looked at each other. "So . . . is that random or is it important?" Sanchez asked.

"I don't know. What about Leo and Lauren? Have they left at all?"

"No."

A pattern. But what did it mean?

"Maddie says the Segunda Vista will fill us in on everything we need to know. Apparently the shamans she's been working with call Segunda Vista the DNA of Esperanza, but claim the distillation has to be just right. She thinks she's got the perfect essence this time."

Sanchez turned abruptly onto a narrow dirt road that ran between fields of Segunda Vista, a blanket of green crowned with delicate flowers that looked as if they'd been spattered with paint by some mischievous abstract artists. Blues, violets, reds and pinks, yellows and gold, a rainbow spectrum of colors. A light breeze rippled across the fields so the flowers seemed to sway and dance.

"Why does Maddie think we can enter the dream by taking Segunda Vista?" Wayra asked.

"The Quechuas do it all the time, in a ceremony called Memory."

Sanchez pulled into the driveway of the bed-and-breakfast he and Maddie owned, and parked in between Leo's VW and Illary's smart car. The four of them were sitting on the front steps, a small cooler at their feet, Jessie snoozing nearby in a pool of warm light. As Wayra got out, he noticed a blue and green feather on the ground and picked it up. In the light, the colors shimmered.

"Look at this beauty," he said, showing it to Sanchez.

"Gorgeous. It looks like a parrot feather." Sanchez elbowed him and smiled. "Powerful medicine, Wayra. That's what a shaman would say."

Wayra tucked the feather in his hair.

"Hey, mi amor," Illary called. "What took you guys so long?"

"We had to stop for gas," Wayra replied, and hugged her hello. In the light, the hawk tattoo that ran from her shoulder and up her neck seemed to move. She couldn't recall when or where she'd gotten the tattoo. Always, they experienced these gaps in their memories.

She plucked the feather from his hair and ran her fingers over it. "Awesome. Where'd you find this?"

"In the driveway."

She slipped it back in his hair. "A good omen, Wayra."

"Are we ready for this, people?" Lauren asked, and flipped open the lid of a small cooler.

"I'm as ready as I'll ever be," Leo said, and reached into the cooler and brought out one tiny glass canister after another and passed them around.

"Drink up," Maddie said. "We'll be deep in Memory when we reach the field. Then we'll drink a bit more and swim inside of Memory."

"*Salud,*" Leo said, and clicked his canister against Lauren's and drank it down.

Wayra and Illary, and Maddie and Sanchez did the same. It tasted strange—not unpleasant, just strange. Thick, like nectar, it was an avocado green, held the sweetness of a mango, the tartness of a fresh radish, and some other quality Wayra couldn't identify.

"Hey, Maddie," Wayra said as they started toward the fields, Jessie trotting alongside them. "I heard this stuff was taken as flakes."

She flashed him a quick smile and hooked her arm through her husband's. "It depends on what you're using it for. This shit will knock your socks off, Wayra. That's the only way into Memory."

Within minutes, they reached the field of Segunda Vista behind the house, and each of them dropped to the ground, gathered in a small, tight circle, and held hands. Suddenly, Wayra felt as if the top of his skull and the center of his chest blew open simultaneously and then a great, rushing warmth flowed down through his head and into his heart and visions swept across his eyes.

"It's Memory," he whispered.

And Memory streamed through him, vivid, bright, utterly clear. He saw himself as he had once been, a shape shifter whose destiny had been tethered to Esperanza. He saw it all, the strange and magnificent canvas of his life before the city's magic had been stripped away, before Kali and those moments on the ghost train. He saw himself turning three humans on Cedar Key, to save their lives, and wondered what had happened to them. He saw himself discovering that the hawk one of those humans had nurtured back to health was Illary, a shape shifter more ancient than he was. He saw Dominica and her *brujos* and the chasers and heard Kali's final words on that train: "*You can leave the city, but unless you hold on to Memory, you won't be able to return.*"

It was all there, the horror and tragedy, the magnificence and splendor of a city called Hope. And he understood why none of them had left and why Tess and Ian should not have left. Then he wept for all he had lost and for the memories that Segunda Vista had now returned to him.

4.

During the three-hour trip from Punta to Esperanza, the twins fussed and fought over their toys, their snacks. They wanted the windows down, then up, then down again, and they made so much racket Ian could barely think. He kept struggling with a vague memory of being on this road in an unusual bus with Father Jacinto and Wayra, but couldn't remember ever having made such a trip.

In fact, their long weekend to Punta was the first time they'd left Esperanza in years. "You two want to watch *Finding Nemo*?" Ian asked, eyeing the kids in the rearview mirror.

"*Nemo*," squealed Charlie, clapping his hands. Named after Tess's father, he had her blond hair and blue eyes. Rina had Ian's dark hair and eyes. "Rina and me love Nemo."

"Charlie loves Nemo more than me," Rina said. "Can't we watch *The Little Mermaid*, Daddy?"

"We don't have *The Little Mermaid* with us," Tess told her, and popped a disk into the player.

"Are we there yet?" Rina asked.

"Not too long now," Ian said.

"Just up the road from Dorado and the Río Palo," Tess said.

Up the road by a steep six thousand feet, Ian thought. Even though the SUV had four-wheel drive, he wasn't surprised when the engine strained.

"Tess, I have this weird feeling about being on this road in an odd bus with Father Jacinto and Wayra. We never went to Punta with them, did we?"

"I don't think so. But I have this kind of half memory about being on an unusual bus on this road with you and my mom and Maddie."

"That kind of bus?" He pointed at the bright blue tourist bus in front of them. Red hummingbirds had been painted on the sides and back and they were so beautifully detailed the bus looked like a work of art. Across the bumper were the words DORADO EXPRESS.

"The Dorado Express? I've never heard of that bus line," Tess said. "And no, the bus I'm sort of remembering looked much different. The roof rack was piled with all kinds of stuff and it was really filthy. I think it was called Dorado thirteen. Can you pass it?"

"Not on this curve."

"Mommy," Charlie said. "Are we lost? The road looks different."

"You've never been on this road, Charlie," said Ian.

"Have, too. I waited near the Río Palo for Mommy."

"That was way before," Rina said with a laugh. "When we were chasers."

"You waited by the Río Palo for *me*?" Tess teased. "But why, Charlie?"

"I think you were angry with me."

Ian glanced at Tess, who looked as mystified as he was. That happened frequently, the twins jabbering away about stuff that made no sense to him or Tess. But Tess turned in her seat and played along. "I'm not angry with my Charlie or Rina."

"Wrong road," Charlie said again. "Wrong road."

Then the road came out of the curve and Ian darted out to the left and sped past the bus. He shifted into fourth gear for the last five hundred feet to the top of the plateau and began to notice changes around them—how overgrown the trees and brush were on either side, the roadside crosses decorated with flowers, marking the spot where someone had died in a car crash, and then the weathered signs with the number of kilometers to Esperanza.

At the top of the plateau, Ian turned into the rest area and slammed so abruptly on the brakes that the SUV shuddered and died. He punched the seat belt release button, leaped out, and ran over to the railing, where a sign was posted in Spanish, English, and Quechua:

> Welcome to the Esperanza Ruin. Excavation at this archaeological site is ongoing. Please stay on the designated paths. You will find brochures about this excavation at the entrance. Smoking is not allowed.

"What the fuck . . ."

"Ian," Tess shouted, running toward him with Rina in her arms and Charlie stumbling alongside her. "Where . . . how . . ."

"*Noooooooooo,*" Charlie shrieked and tore toward the entrance of the site as fast as his little legs would carry him.

Rina wailed and kicked and flung herself from side to side until she escaped her mother's arms, and tore after Charlie, screaming, "Charlie, Charlie, where'd it go?"

Ian and Tess raced after them, through the entrance, down the steps, and off the designated path. Ian couldn't process what his eyes told him, that Esperanza, which they had left only four days ago, was now an archaeological ruin. Confusion and horror rolled through him in powerful, almost crippling waves that drove him forward, faster, faster. Tess, now sobbing, kept pace with him, and when they reached Charlie and Rina, they were both so winded they sank to the ground.

"Daddy!" Charlie cried, stabbing his finger at the ruin of what looked like an old hotel. "The Pincoya, this was the Pincoya. You and Wayra blew it up."

"Boom!" Rina shouted, throwing out her arms. "Boom, boom, fire everywhere. *Brujos* fleeing."

"Oh my God," he whispered.

Tess groped for his hand. "Bus depot."

"We were waiting for Esperanza thirteen, Tess."

"That's not what you called me then."

The nickname popped into his head. "Slim, I called you Slim. Bogie and Bacall."

"Clooney."

"The *Expat News*."

"Shape shifters."

"*Brujos,* chasers, the . . . ghost train."

"The city covered in sand . . ."

"Nine twenty-eight, eleven-eleven, Victor and Franco and—"

"And me," Charlie said, coming over to them, patting his chest, tears still coursing down his cheeks. "Me and Karina."

And right then, Ian understood who the twins actually were, Charlie and Karina, the chasers, and remembered all of it, remembered how he and the priest and Wayra had set off explosives in the abandoned Pincoya, which the *brujos* had been using as a portal. He remembered the black sludge sweeping across the Café Taquina and how he had tried to rescue Javier. He remembered taking Segunda Vista with Lauren, the wild ride on *Further* with Kesey, Garcia, McKenna, and piercing the whiteness that enclosed El Bosque. He remembered the strangeness and mystery of Esperanza in the time before. He remembered all of it— too late.

Everything inside of him collapsed, he could barely breathe.

"Excuse me, do you need help?"

Ian glanced around at a dark-haired man in a tourist guide uniform.

"Are either of you injured?" the guide asked.

"No, we're . . ." Ian got to his feet and helped Tess up. *"Javier?"*

The man frowned, then his face softened and he took Ian's hands in his own, fighting back tears. "Ian, Tess. *Dios mío.*" He threw his arms around them, hugging them tightly. *"Dios mío."* Then he stepped back from them and looked at Charlie and Rina. "The twins. In the jungle . . . you were several months pregnant, Tess. Do you remember?"

She swiped at her eyes, whispered, "Yes. All of it."

"There are others like us, people who left and remembered too late and couldn't get back. We're not alone."

"But . . . how can that happen?" Ian stammered.

"Shamans tell us that reality split somehow," Javier said, moving his hands outward, in opposite directions. "That Memory is key. All of us remembered too late. I don't understand a lot of what they're saying. But there are others."

"How many?" Tess asked.

"Over two hundred of us now. We have places in Dorado where you can live. There's plenty of work. The schools are great. I can take you there. Let me tell the other guide to go on without me. We need you." He loped off to the group of tourists.

Charlie took Tess's hand. "Mommy, it'll be okay. It's a new story."

"New story," Rina chimed, and clasped Charlie's hand. "Let's go to our new story."

Ian slipped his arm around Tess's shoulder. "Slim?"

"Clooney?"

They gazed out longingly over the ruin. "I'm game as long as I've got the three of you," Ian said.

"We'll make it work," Tess said.

Javier trotted back over to them. "Ready?"

"Yes, yes," chimed Charlie and Rina, and ran toward the car.

Ian glanced back just once. Afternoon light spilled across the ruin, a soft mountain light that varnished the ancient stones and crumbling paths so that for an instant, everything shimmered and shone. He thought he could see Esperanza as it had once been, the twisted streets, the old buildings, the parks, peaks, the old railroad tracks, even the Pincoya. For an instant, he could see the beauty and grandeur of a place called Hope.

Then a cloud drifted across the face of the sun, and a brisk breeze caused him to shiver. He turned and hurried to catch up with the others.